I0700139

Marked by the Crown

The Marked Series, Book 3

Jayme Hunt

This book is a work of fiction. Names, characters, places, and incidents are the product of the author's imagination or are used fictitiously. None are intended as a faithful representation of any one country or culture at any point in history.

Copyright @ 2024 by Jayme Hunt

Cover art designed by Miguel Firewolf (miguelfirewolf.artstation.com)

Editorial services provided by Eden Northover (edennorthoverfictioneditor.uk)

The scanning, uploading, and distribution of this book without permission is a theft of the author's intellectual property. No part of this book may be reproduced without the permission of the author except in brief quotations or a review or a blog. This author expressly prohibits any entity from using this publication for purposes of training AI technologies to generate text, including without limitation technologies that are capable of generating works in the same style or genre as this publication. Thank you for your support of the author's rights.

AI Pledge:

No part of this book was written using AI technology. All the words that make up this book — the good and the bad — are my own (with the help of editors, beta and ARC readers, and my mother... sorry mom).

ISBNs: 979-8-9874208-3-6 (pbk), 979-8-9874208-6-7 (ebook)

Contents

To everyone who loved fairytales as children, but unfortunately had to grow up.

Here's another Faerie smut treat for you.

Author's Note

Dear reader —

This book contains depictions of single-parent family dynamics, offensive adult language, death, violence, and explicit sexual scenes.

If any of this content is upsetting to you, please protect your well-being and do not continue.

CORRYN

In all the years Corryn had worked as a staff member in the palace, she counted herself lucky. Though Sairas was a cute little town, the grandeur of the palace couldn't be beaten. It boasted luxurious, oversized beds, sprawling gardens, and glimpses of royalty as they came and went. She was able to visit with her friends in the kitchen daily, sneaking morsels of the delicious food they prepared and washing it down with a large gulp of sparkling wine that never seemed in short supply. The most excitement she got was stealing kisses with her partner in shadowed corners and watching the antics of the young prince when he visited. That was fine by her. She enjoyed having a quiet life.

That was, until the young human girl had shown up. *Katherine.*

She'd breezed in with her strange questions and outfits, challenging attitude, and obvious secrets months ago. And, Corryn had to correct herself, Katherine wasn't fully human. She was half-Aes

Sídhe. Her father — who had also shown up out of the blue — was apparently from a powerful bloodline that had long been considered extinct. Katherine had moved into the palace without question, and though she'd never been anything but nice to Corryn, it was hard not to notice that everything seemed to go sideways from then on out.

As if overnight, dark Fae were invading the palace, royals and lower Fae alike were taking extended stays and sharing hushed conversations, and gossip amongst the staff grew. Most recently, armies had gathered from surrounding lands, summoned to Sairas without warning. Corryn found herself rushing from visitor to visitor, her alarm growing with each piece of information that made its way to her ears.

"The curfews were only the beginning. They're saying the dark Fae are taking over…"

"—heard the goddess of death herself was back. She's reuniting with her sisters, and then we're all next!"

"But aren't they all dead? How could that be possible?"

"She's a necromancer, of course! No one is safe from her powers…"

"I heard that golden-eyed girl has some sort of weapon meant to take her down. Went all the way to the Otherworld for it, she did."

"Pffft, get a load of that horse shit! The prince is just keeping her around 'cause she looks pretty. That's all."

Corryn tried her best to tune out the noise. She could only think of her partner, out there amongst the ranks the new commander, Larke, had brought with him. Their goodbyes had been quiet, her partner slipping out of bed and donning her soldier's uniform, giving her a kiss goodbye. Her voice hadn't wavered on her farewell, but the sign of her partner's fear had been in the wet tears Corryn felt as they brushed cheeks.

It told her all she needed to know. No matter which rumors were true, the truth was dangerous enough that there was a chance she'd never see her again.

Though the chaos before the armies left had been unsettling, the quiet that followed was somehow worse. The sun rose and set, an entire day passing with unnerving silence, as though even nature itself was holding its breath. The only visitors left mulling about were the soldiers from Brytham, and even they kept to themselves. An illness in their ranks, the staff said. They scoffed at the mismanagement by the duke's two sons, Aerrin and Thaddeus. Corryn gave the troops a wide berth as the next few days progressed.

It was because of the silence, then, that the whispers Corryn heard were so loud. She'd been rounding a corner, ready to take a fresh set of bedding to a downstairs room. Normally, she'd breeze past gossiping staff, but something about the tone of the hushed words pulled her up short.

"There is *no way* it was an accident," a deep male voice hissed, the statement echoing through the corridor.

Another male voice, slightly higher-pitched, countered the first one's claim. "But the queen and the duke always have guards around them!"

"And they did this morning, too. Didn't you hear that part? The guards outside were poisoned! They willingly drank something, the likes of which the physician had never seen before. That's how we know it wasn't an accident. The duke would have left the guards alone if he'd done it."

An accident? Guards poisoned? Corryn's hands wound around the sheets, even as they grew clammy. *Now what has happened? What did the duke do? Is the queen okay?*

"Why not take a knife to the guards, too? What does the poison have to do with anything?"

"Because if there had been a struggle, the queen and the duke would have known someone was coming. Whoever did this wanted those two to think they'd been let in, expected."

There was a hesitation, the second voice clearly unsure what to do with this information. "But if the queen and the duke would have expected this person... why did they kill the guards, too? Why not just sneak past?"

"Because they wanted it to look like the duke did it!" The deeper male voice rose, clearly irritated at having to explain himself. "Make it look like he took poison to the guards, a knife to the queen, then his own throat. If the guards let someone in, and then back out, then we would know who did it, of course!"

The bedding Corryn clutched to her chest fell to the ground in a soft heap. It was inevitable. They were talking about the queen and the duke, as though... as though both were *dead*. She shook her head, trying to dispel the information. *Impossible.*

"So you're saying it wasn't the duke? It was an inside job?"

The first voice didn't respond, leaving Corryn to wonder what physical response he offered up. A shrug, perhaps? Maybe a nod?

"Good gods... that would have to be someone incredibly close to the two. Certainly the guards wouldn't accept poison from just anyone, and I doubt any lower Fae would be let in to see those two without an appointment." There was a pause. Then: "And you're certain they're all dead?"

Again, the first male didn't respond verbally, but the second let out a soft curse, confirming the worst.

It was true. The queen and the duke had both been killed.

Though the palace had always felt so vast to her before, now, it grew impossibly small. The walls seemed to squeeze in on her. Though Corryn had never had much interaction with the queen, she'd been a figure nearly everyone revered. She'd been beautiful, powerful, enigmatic. Corryn had never considered the moment she'd be *gone* from this world.

And yet... here it was. And with her, the charming, ever-lively duke, Lachlan. One framed for murdering the other. Both gone.

Reeling, she stepped over the laundry and stumbled her way down the stone steps, searching for the nearest exit. What would happen now? Living and working here had been her dream. She'd never felt safer or happier than she did here. But... was she safe here anymore?

Her thoughts kept spiraling, the palace closing in on her, constricting her lungs. Clearly, word was spreading, and fast — people darted around her, crashing into her as they rushed to either get help or spread word; which it was, she didn't know. She didn't care. She sucked in air, desperate to fill her shrinking lungs. Her footsteps quickened as she saw the night skies nearing, the entrance to the palace flung wide open.

"Corryn!"

Her name rang out, snagging her attention despite the commotion around her. She tripped as she turned to face the voice, recognizing it as the prince's. Behind him stood what looked like a large majority of their forces, donned in purple and gold and wonderfully whole. *They're back! They're alive!*

She squinted, the tightness in her chest decompressing slightly as she caught sight of a familiar face, like a beacon even in the darkness. Relief coursed through her, and she struggled to organize her thoughts around the prince's following question. "What's happened?"

What's happened?

Corryn could scarcely believe the words as she forced out her response. "Th-the queen, and the duke. They have been — murdered."

She inhaled deeply, attempting to reorient herself now that the terrible truth was out. As her focus sharpened, however, so did the logic of what her words meant for the young, blonde Aes Sídhe who stood before her, his face shrouded in a look that was equal parts confusion and concern. The last direct descendent of the late queen.

He wasn't a prince at all, anymore. He was her *king*.

She dropped into a low curtsey. "Your Majesty."

With her head bowed, the racket around her grew clearer, and she heard the realization spread. The same two sentences erupted all around her as staff took note of who stood in the hall with them.

It was an eerie chant, one that embraced the solemn event that had transpired tonight, as well as respect for the new leader. The exclamation was all the more powerful with the way it echoed off the stone walls, as though the palace itself was solidifying the news.

"The queen is dead! Long live the king!"

Chapter One

C haos surrounded him, but it positively paled in comparison to the bedlam that erupted inside his head at those eight words.

"The queen is dead! Long live the king!"

The only thing that registered in his brain was Kate, who was staring at him, openmouthed. He blinked as he locked onto her features, using her appearance to ground him. Her silken, rich brown hair, still wind-blown from their ride home, her delicious, rosy lips, her wide amber eyes... the shock in those eyes threatened to crack his careful hold he had on his composure. He averted his gaze quickly, but the realization flooded through him regardless.

This means... this means...

"Finlay!" His cousin's voice broke through the inner turmoil. They turned to see Darrya, breaking free from a group of staff she'd been questioning. She hurried across the entrance to the palace, her posture rigid and her face inscrutable, clearly wary of gazes tracking her movement. Her deep brown eyes flashed as she glanced between the two of them, and without another word, she grabbed their wrists, dragging them away with her.

They wound through the palace, running into countless palace workers, each of which dropped into a bow or curtsey, their eyes wide. Finlay dipped his head each time in shocked acknowledgement, but remained silent until they reached Darrya's room.

Darrya tossed them in the room first and closed the door behind her. Kate and Finlay sat immediately, but she stood for a long moment, simply facing the closed door. Finally, she loosed a deep sigh and turned. "Well, this is a new kind of fucked."

A strangled laugh escaped Kate, but Finlay remained silent. Darrya eyed him with apprehension.

"I want to be sure you understand what this means, cousin," she ventured, her voice soft but firm. After a beat, Finlay nodded.

"Just so we're clear... we all have an idea of who is behind this, yes?" Kate put in, looking between the two of them. Darrya's lips tightened into a thin line, and she bobbed her head in confirmation. Finlay hadn't even gotten that far, hadn't attempted to uncover the why, but ... of course.

Aerrin and Thaddeus hadn't been a part of the battle. Neither had their soldiers. The lands had banded together before the battle, but once they had marched on Nemain, the vivid blue and orange denoting Brytham's soldiers had been noticeably absent from the sea of other colors.

This had to have been their plan from the start. Divide their alliances between Nemain and the queen, weaken the guard left at the palace, distract the armies — and then leverage it all for their own benefit. Now with Lachlan gone, Aerrin and Thad were free to lead all of Brytham, as well as step in as dukes of Daersill.

And with the queen gone as well, it left *him* as king of Muiranvia, patriarch of the Fae lands.

"Fuck!" he roared, causing Kate and Darrya to flinch. He stood, sending the chair skittering a few feet behind him as began pacing. They both knew better than anyone that he had never wanted to rule, had never paid as much attention as needed when it came to political dalliances. But the Byrne brothers knew this as well. Finlay could almost feel the mercenaries they'd hire to rise up against him and the people of Muiranvia. Maybe they already had.

"Are they still here?" he inquired.

Darrya didn't have to ask to know whom he referred to. "I assume so. Those sick bastards will want to see how this plays out."

"Get them."

"Finlay," Kate cautioned, but he shook his head.

"I won't do anything but have a chat. They've played this slowly and carefully." He gritted his teeth. "If I move against them, we'll be sure to have another war started by morning."

Darrya frowned, but grumbled in agreement and slipped out the door. Before the door could close following her departure, Patrick swept inside.

"There you two are. We have a problem," he said. His face was solemn, but his eyes were wide, his lips pressed into a thin line that betrayed an undercurrent of panic. Kate and Finlay exchanged a wary glance.

"Aside from the obvious?" Finlay asked, raising a brow.

"Unfortunately, yes. Your palace, its workers, and the town all see you as the new king. That much is obvious." He fixed Finlay with his golden gaze, and after a moment, Finlay glanced down, unable to bear the bluntness of his words.

"But," he continued, his eyes sliding to Kate. "After what happened on the battlefield, the armies — and in turn, their lands — are questioning whether or not the Egan bloodline is the rightful royal line, or if Katie is now the rightful ruler."

Now it was Kate's turn to shoot up from her seated position, shaking her head. "No. It was only meant to — to inspire the armies as we rode into battle. Nothing more. I don't want more."

Finlay bit back the fact that he didn't, either, opting to remain silent.

"That won't matter to them, Katie," Patrick replied, his expression sympathetic. "And it's already pitting them against one another."

Shit. Thaddeus and Aerrin would have a field day with this the moment they found out.

"We can't afford to have the lands split even further," Finlay ground out, running a hand through his hair in frustration.

Patrick slumped against the doorframe, a defeated look in his eyes. He examined them for a moment, and Finlay could only imagine what he saw before him: two young Aes Sídhe, fated to rule but wholly underprepared for the task. Their simple existences already causing a new uprising, when they hadn't even changed out of the bloodied clothing from the one they had just quelled.

Patrick straightened abruptly. "There is a way to unify them. To squash any question of civil dispute."

"How?" Kate questioned, confused.

Though he'd seemed excited just a moment before, his answer came slowly and with more than a hint of apprehension. "With marriage."

Finlay's gaze didn't waver from Kate's face. The second Patrick had spoken of a way to unify them, he knew where it was headed, and he wanted to absorb every reaction Kate had. He had no real idea of how marriage worked in the human realm, but he had a hunch it was something that she wouldn't take lightly, especially at her age. Hell, he still considered himself young for marriage.

Kate's brows knit together for a moment as she absorbed her father's words, her gaze going distant. Then, her lips parted slightly, and he witnessed the brief flash of terror flit across her face. Before she could speak, he announced, "No."

"No?" Patrick echoed, swiveling to face Finlay with a puzzled frown. He knew, then, as well as Finlay did, that royal Aes Sídhe rarely had a say in their marriages. Especially a prince — or, he corrected himself, a king. Finlay had expected to be married off well before his time to rule came and, honestly, if it was anyone else, Finlay would have merely rolled his eyes and accepted with minimal complaint. But Kate... Kate was so young, and their relationship was so fresh. Too fresh. To put her back against the wall — well, in *this* sense, at least — was something he didn't want to do.

"You'd force your own daughter into a marriage?" he countered, exchanging a glance with Kate. The look she shot back was one of relief.

"Well, not a full *marriage,*" Patrick said, as though they were vapid. "An engagement should be enough to placate the masses."

"Ah, yes. Just an engagement," Finlay scoffed, crossing his arms. "Look, I'm not opposed to the idea. Honestly, I see where you're coming from. But the point remains." He shifted to speak directly to Kate. She gazed back at him, her fist pressed against her lips, as though lost in thought. "I won't do that to you, little angel. We've known each other for less than a year. And if I'm not mistaken, you've hated me for at least half of that time."

He smiled at her as he said the words, just to show there was no animosity in them. Kate opened her mouth to respond, but was interrupted as Darrya opened the door, poking her face back in. It was slightly flushed, even as she kept it stoic – the only indication of her barely constrained temper.

"They're still here. They'll meet with you in the cabinet room in the west wing," she said, glancing between the three of them. "I'm going to grab Larke, and I'll meet you there."

Finlay nodded and made to move the room, but jolted as a soft, cold hand slid into his own warm one. "I'm coming with," Kate asserted, her gaze burning with a look that gave no room for discussion. He nodded, secretly thankful for her presence.

"But," she continued, "I think we need another important member there. Where would the queen have kept her hound?"

It took Finlay a moment to register her request, and then the image of the queen's large wolfhound popped into his head. "Adair?" he inquired. Why would she want to bring a dog along to a political meeting?

She nodded emphatically. "Kipp told me once that it can detect lies. That would certainly be useful to meet with the Byrne brothers."

Finlay blinked in surprise, and Patrick raised his brows at Kate's words. "So, her dog is a Cú Sídhe. A spiritual aid, like Shadow."

Kate nodded. "And I would assume that he now belongs to you," she added softly, squeezing Finlay's hand, and his heart squeezed alongside it. He didn't agree with much of what his great-grandmother had done, and they had never been what he would call close, but she had still loved him. Had been family. He didn't have much of that left in this world, but this dog was apparently still a part of it.

"All right," he agreed. "I assume he is in her bed chambers." He explained the directions quickly, and when Kate looked confused, he added, "Let me know if you find him. I still want to discuss some things with your father."

Kate hesitated for a moment, her gaze flicking between the two of them before she nodded and slipped away. The silence that grew in her absence had a physical weight, and both Finlay and Patrick shifted their feet, sensing it.

"So," Finlay began, a nervousness fluttering its way up his throat. Patrick rubbed his chin, then folded his arms across his chest, shooting Finlay a look that said, *get on with it.* "I need you to know, if Kate agrees to this, it's not just political, between her and me. I would have been ready to make this commitment without any pressure." He paused. "If I'm being honest, I was ready the first moment I laid eyes on her. I love your daughter. And it would still mean the world to me if I could get your blessing. Um, sir."

Patrick choked out a gruff laugh. "I don't think the king of Muiranvia needs to call me sir. Or ask me for my blessing." He tossed Finlay a sidelong smirk. "But... you have it, regardless. I know you love my daughter. And you'll protect her at all costs."

"I will," he promised, and they exchanged tentative smiles. By the time Kate returned with Adair in tow, the heaviness of the moment had lifted.

The hound greeted Finlay with a friendliness he'd never shown before, walking right up to him and shoving his tawny nose into Finlay's palm. The hound had never given Finlay as much as a sideways glance before, and now, as Finlay scratched behind his ears, he let out a soft whine and pressed further into Finlay's hand, gazing up at him. Finlay gazed back, wondering if there really was some truth in the dog belonging to him, as though he understood the queen had passed and already recognized Finlay as his new master. He felt the first real pang of sadness, then, allowing himself to realize what he'd lost tonight. With a deep exhale, he straightened, forcing himself to move past the moment for the time being.

They set off, and by the time they reached the cabinet room, Adair was strolling easily alongside Finlay's heels. Finlay was slightly unnerved, but he had to admit, the calm demeanor of the large, wiry beast was starting to rub off on him. It also didn't hurt to see Kate's reaction to his proximity. She'd already ruffled his silvery ears several times, and laughed when he gave her hand a sloppy kiss.

The tender moment faded quickly as they opened the door to the room, however, and saw the group waiting for them. Aerrin and Thaddeus stood rigid, ever the eerie picture of two similar physical features and yet, opposite expressions. Both boasted Lachlan's sapphire eyes, chiseled jaw structure and dimpled cheeks, but Aerrin wore his permanently defiant smirk, whereas Thad looked, as usual, disinterested and unamused. Aerrin had inherited Lachlan's bright red hair, but whereas it had matched Lachlan's warm personality, on Aerrin it just reminded Finlay of blood. Thad's was much darker, as if his shadowy personality had bled into it.

They also had a soldier with them, and he was busy training all of his attention on Larke, who stood protectively in front of Darrya. Though the soldier from Brytham was clearly well-trained, he was dwarfed by Larke's sheer presence. The commander hadn't had a chance to change out of his gear, either, and though some of the gold of his armor still gleamed brightly against his ebony complexion, it was mostly tarnished, slick with the dark blood of the Fae he'd cut down in battle. The sight of the brothers and the soldier, clean and unblemished, was almost laughable by comparison.

"Finlay. What a surprising way to meet with you," Aerrin began, then cocked his head at him. "Though the surprises never seem to cease. It would appear my brother and I are now dukes. And... should I be calling you Your Majesty?"

"I don't give a shit what you decide to call me," Finlay snapped.

Thad coughed behind Aerrin, almost as though concealing a surprised laugh, even as Aerrin glowered. Then Thad's eyes slid to Kate and widened with surprise.

"Lady... Lynn?" Thad asked, notes of incredulity and wariness in his tone. Finlay felt her sidle up closer to him, and instinctively reached his hand out to grab hers. She didn't respond, choosing instead to let the silence speak volumes.

"Looks like someone is working their way up through the royalty," Aerrin remarked, raking his eyes over Kate slowly before flicking them back to Finlay. "Is she as fun in bed as I'd expected?"

For a moment, Finlay saw red. He stepped forward, but was halted by Darrya's cool words. "She's not Lady Lynn. You have the pleasure of speaking with Katherine Doyle. Great granddaughter of Cú Chulainn, and slaughterer of Nemain, the goddess of death. I'd choose your words more carefully in front of a godslayer, if I were you."

She spoke the words with such authority, it made it seem as though the moniker had already run rampant through the masses. For all Finlay knew, it truly had. Regardless of the nickname, the truth of her words struck home, and a myriad of expressions flashed across the brothers' faces in a matter of moments. Thad's eventually landed on disbelief — easy enough to understand, seeing as he spent several hours with Kate without truly knowing her identity. Aerrin, however, looked furious.

"You're telling me we invited a rogue guest into our home for days, under false pretenses?" he hissed, fists clenching. "She's a threat to us all. She should be tried for treason!"

At Aerrin's tone, the soldier behind him moved a hand to the hilt of his sword. Larke reciprocated instantly, palming his own sword as he stepped in front of Kate. Everyone tensed, the energy in the room practically crackling with the surge in magic.

"If anyone should be tried for treason, Aerrin," Finlay growled between clenched teeth, "I believe your name would be first on the list. Care to explain why your soldiers didn't partake in the battle against Nemain and her dark Fae?"

"Several of our soldiers fell ill the night before." Aerrin waved his hand dismissively and glanced at Thad, who returned his look with a tight-lipped one of his own. "It looked like something highly contagious. We didn't want to compromise the rest of your forces."

A low snarl had everyone looking down at Adair. His hackles were raised, lips peeled back to bare sharp canines, his icy gaze fixed on Aerrin. For the first time, the new duke looked slightly uneasy as he sized up the angry hound.

"If you're going to lie to me, Aerrin," Finlay said quietly, "at least have the decency to look me in the eyes."

Aerrin lifted his chin, eyes narrowed but unflinching as he met Finlay's gaze. Thad leaned over to murmur something in Aerrin's ear, and a muscle in Aerrin's jaw jumped, the only giveaway that he was put on edge. He smoothed the front of his coat and continued.

"As much fun as this back and forth is, we are not here to dethrone you. I have a feeling you're capable of that all on your own. Especially with the whispers we've heard. It seems your people are torn between you and ... Lady *Katherine* here."

Finlay bit the inside of his cheek in frustration. So, the news was spreading rapidly. He could only imagine the loyalty lines it had cleaved in their people already. He doubted they'd accept the two of them ruling as equals without some sort of formal alliance. Each side would still maintain adamant favoritism for one of them over the other, and he'd seen brawls in the streets over lesser issues.

He opened his mouth to respond, but Kate's words cut him off.

"Luckily, I don't foresee that being an issue — considering our engagement."

Finlay's eyes snapped to Kate's. While she stood stoically, there was no disguising the slight flush of pink to her cheeks, the wild gleam in her eyes. It was a last-minute decision, but she didn't seem inclined to take it back. His heart thrummed wildly as he took her in. Darrya shifted in his peripheral, a hand over her mouth in a casual attempt to hide what was clearly a smile.

"Your engagement?" Aerrin barked, staring at Kate. A piece of Finlay, deep and feral, flared with jealousy at the look. He dropped Kate's hand and wound his around her waist, tugging her flush against him. It was all he could do not to bare his teeth at the new duke.

"Yes," she replied coolly, her lips curling into a smirk as she kept her gaze locked on Finlay. Gods, he was going to devour that smile later.

Aerrin cleared his throat. "Well. In that case, we look forward to hearing that official announcement at the Last Honors Ceremony tomorrow."

Finlay remained silent, waiting to see if they would provide any more information. He could unleash all of his accusations on the brothers, but clearly, they were holding their actions — and motives — close to their chests. And with the lands already having banded together for one battle, with lives lost in the process and citizens now divided on leadership... they were at an impasse. Finally, he simply nodded. "Indeed. We shall speak again tomorrow."

Aerrin gave a knowing smirk and nodded back, then motioned to Thad and their soldier, who turned to exit the room. The others left quickly, but Aerrin paused at the door, glancing back one last time. He tapped his fingers on the doorframe, observing them for a long moment before he spoke. "Such exciting times. I can't wait to see what they have in store for us all."

Chapter Two

"Are you sure?" Finlay asked for at least the fourth time, eliciting a groan from me.

"Yes, Finlay! Now stop asking, before I change my mind."

He grinned at the snarky response, but it was short-lived as he glanced back down at the piece of parchment beneath him, doubt etching his features once more. He'd been working on the Last Honors address for the last two hours, scribbling and scratching out words as he went. While the Last Honors Ceremony was technically a ceremony to honor those who had fallen in battle, it was unfortunately convenient to combine it into a remembrance ceremony for the queen and the duke as well. It was only natural for Finlay to draft an address that encompassed both.

I offered to help, but he'd ushered me away, telling me he needed to get his thoughts down before I took a look and provided feedback on what to add or remove. "There are some things I'm expected to say," he'd explained, "and some things I know they'll need to hear. I just need to figure out how to get them out of here—" He'd tapped his head to illustrate the point. "—and onto the paper."

I smirked at the memory as I studied him now, sitting at the desk in his bedroom, looking no less frazzled than he'd been when he started. I'd tried to convince him to rest for a while, but he'd only conceded to a shower and change of clothes before beginning his work. His golden hair was thoroughly tousled, standing on points where he'd run his hands through it time and again as it had dried. His pale blue eyes were tinged with exhaustion, but still stunning as ever.

The sight tugged at my heart, reaffirming my decision. It was a scary leap, yes, but an exhilarating one as well; one that if I peeled back the layers protecting my heart, I knew I was sure of. Finlay hadn't hesitated, except to protect me when he saw my fear at the prospect. That was all the answer I'd needed, and when I heard Aerrin taunting his leadership, I knew without a doubt that it was the right choice. Truthfully, I'd never felt such overwhelming feelings for someone before — friendship, desire, protectiveness, love. All for him. And besides, my dad was right: it wasn't a formal marriage. We could remain engaged as long as we chose. I was absolutely certain this was the right path.

"Wren asked for a room at the palace," I said suddenly, biting back a grin.

Finlay raised his eyes from the paper to blink at me. "Oh?"

"She said it's been a bit... *loud* at Cas's place."

Finlay's lips twitched. "I can only imagine. At least someone is celebrating properly."

"Well, two someones."

Finlay snorted but smiled fondly, having also noticed how happy Kipp and Cas seemed as a pair. They'd finally admitted their feelings for each other on the battlefield, and their coming together had been... intense. I could only imagine how much catching up they had to do since that first passionate kiss – and how quickly that would have sent Wren scurrying out of the house. I chuckled to myself at the thought as Finlay pushed the paper across the desk. "Okay. What do you think?" he asked, leaning back.

I came over to inspect his speech, noting things I remembered from the queen's speech several months prior. The thought of her speech sent a confusing pang through my chest. Though she left plenty to be desired as a leader, her love for Finlay had been unmistakable. If she saw the way he was readying himself for leadership now, I imagined she would be proud. And Lachlan... poor Lachlan, who we learned had nearly been framed for their murders... he would have loved Finlay's addition to the ceremony. Finlay had included an announcement of our engagement, phrasing it as a unification that would provide hope, peace, and stability for our grieving lands. I swallowed a lump of emotion as I skimmed that part, praying we could live up to such powerful promises.

Finlay's gaze met mine as I finished reading, the question clear in his eyes. "How many times did you say "I" in your speech?" I asked, smoothing the paper back down on the desk.

He leaned back over the paper, brow furrowed as he reviewed it. "I didn't?"

"Exactly." I smiled. "It's perfect."

"No, little angel. That would be you. These are just words." He reached up to brush a stray strand of hair from my face, and warmth blossomed in my chest in response.

"Well, words have tremendous power. Don't forget that," I chided. "Is there anything else I need to do for the ceremony tomorrow?"

Finlay shook his head. "Darrya is handling the floral arrangements and the veils for the mirrors. Larke is handling the armies."

"And the whiskey and voitín?" I inquired.

Finlay's expression turned devilish. "Why? Are you hoping to take advantage of me again, like last time?"

My cheeks flushed furiously. "I did *not.*"

"I seem to remember otherwise."

My mind wandered briefly back to the moment, recalling the way I'd straddled him, reveling in the feeling of his soft fingertips trailing across the exposed skin of my back. My flush grew stronger, but I pushed the memory down. "Well, I seem to remember you telling me you'd find someone else to spend the night in bed with," I bit back, watching his reaction closely.

Instead of guilt or shame, however, his eyes sparked mischievously. He pushed back from the desk, and before I could react, he gathered me in his arms. I squealed as he carried me to the bed, dropping me on it.

He leaned over me, hands resting on either side of my head. "Is that a hint of jealousy I detect, little angel?"

"Never."

"Mmm. I'm going to call your bluff. Tell me, was I stuck in your head that night?"

He dipped his mouth down to my neck, and I thought back to that night; the way my hands had trailed down under the covers as I'd imagined him in a very similar position to the one he was in now. "No."

"Liar," he growled in my ear, nipping at it playfully.

I bit my lip. "Never. But I'll bet you spent a lot of time alone with your hand, thinking about me."

"We aren't talking about that. I want to hear how you touched yourself thinking about *me.*"

I sucked in a gasp at his words, but answered the challenge with one of my own, parting my legs wide and letting my hand slide down. "How about I just show you?"

At that, Finlay pulled back, surprise and hunger rippling across his face in unison. I smirked as I met his gaze tauntingly

Before we could make another move, though, a knock came at the door. We both looked at the door, then back at each other.

"Ignore it," he whispered, but even as he did, Darrya's voice sounded.

"Finlay! We need you to approve a few things before you go to bed."

He dropped his head and groaned, then made for the door with reluctance. "This isn't finished," he promised me with a wink, before opening the door and slipping out.

I smiled, desire curling its way pleasantly through my belly. But even as I rolled over, I felt the crushing weight of the exhaustion I'd been fighting. Truly, it was a wonder that Finlay and I had stayed awake as long as we had, feeding off the surge of adrenaline that came with our dual realization: the responsibility of the realm — and with it, the uncertainty of the future — was on our shoulders. This kept our bodies and minds racing with nervous energy, and it was hard to simply shut off such apprehension.

I willed my breathing to slow, listening to the sound of Darrya and Finlay exchanging soft, unintelligible words just beyond the door. Within a few minutes, I felt the anxious buzz drain slowly from my body, sinking closer to sleep. By the time Finlay reopened the door and settled in next to me in bed, my eyes were shut and heavy as lead. I snuggled into his embrace, and just a few breaths later, a deep sleep finally overcame me.

As I'd expected, Finlay's speech went over extremely well. Despite the chill that still hung in the air, winter chasing spring and nipping at its heels, the ceremony was held outside, simply due to the size of the crowd. All the armies remained from the other lands to mourn their fallen. I had no idea how they transported the dead from the battlefield so fast, but I supposed there were still parts of magic I couldn't wrap my head around.

Darrya had done an excellent job ensuring everything looked the part, with white lilies scouring the grounds and climbing up walls. We all wore black, aside from the soldiers who wore the colors and leathers of their lands. When they knelt to pay their respects, it was a simultaneous wave, as though a string had been pulled on each. It had been chillingly, achingly beautiful.

Finlay had made a point to clear up any questions regarding Lachlan's part in the queen's death — though pointing out that it was still an 'ongoing investigation' only seemed to steer concerns from one issue to another. There had also been a long moment of silence dedicated to the queen. As everyone raised their heads from the silent tribute, I cut a glance around, noting that nearly every eye in the crowd was glassy, either from respect for their fallen leaders or a personal lost loved one. When I met Darrya's gaze, I had to quickly avert my own, fighting not to share in the tears she shed. Finlay and I still had important parts to play in the ceremony; I couldn't afford to break down. Not yet.

"Until we meet again," everyone repeated as Finlay concluded his speech. There was no magic in the words, and yet, they echoed like an enchantment, binding everyone's grief together. I thought back to my own loved ones, fallen before the final battle even took place, and sent a small prayer of my own their way. Still, I didn't allow myself to linger on the thought of Blaise, or my mother, or the many others we were mourning today. *Not yet.*

As the whiskey and voitín made its way around, Finlay grabbed a small shot glass and motioned for me to join him, an unreadable emotion rippling across his face. I hesitated for a moment, then nodded, grabbing one of my own and making my way to where he stood on a raised platform. The many faces I'd scrutinized earlier — familiar and not, in various states of mourning and celebration — peered up at us. My heart hammered against my chest.

It was time.

I reached his side, and Finlay cleared his throat, flicking the enchanted ring on his finger. Then, he reached the ring up to rest against his neck. When he spoke, it rang out for the entire crowd to hear.

"As we engage in this last party to honor those who gave their lives, we have one more reason to celebrate. As some of you may know, this lovely lady standing beside me is Katherine Doyle. She is the one who was able to reunite the talismans and lead us successfully into battle. It was she who was able to slaughter the goddess of death, Nemain, with the sword of Nuada. And as of last night, she agreed to take my hand in marriage."

Some gasps and murmurs erupted from the crowd, questions already flying from person to person. I glanced at Finlay nervously as he offered me the ring, which I slipped on my already sweating hand, raising it tentatively to my neck. Gods, how was I supposed to follow after him?

"Even as we mourn those who are no longer with us to witness it, we hope this union can provide answers as to how we move forward, stronger and more unified than before. Together, we will fight for peace, stability, and unity, and we look forward to sharing that bright future with each and every one of you."

With that, I lifted my shot glass, seeing Finlay doing the same. It took a heartbeat for the crowd to repeat the gesture – a terrifying, long heartbeat – but slowly, each one of them lifted theirs as well. A sigh of relief whooshed out of my lips, and I offered a small smile before gulping down the burning liquid. Before I could continue analyzing the crowd, Finlay's lips crushed against mine, the spice of the liquor mingling between our mouths. A few cheers came from the crowd this time, and I slowly relaxed into him, enjoying the strength and stability of his body against mine. The prince – no, the *king*. And my fiancé.

We could do this. We could actually do this.

CHAPTER THREE

Giggles bubbled up from my throat, unbidden, as I twirled and danced with the crowd. The dancing wasn't as strict as it had been at the solstice, but it was more collaborative than at Lughnasadh, where we'd all been twirling separately. We remained outside, milling about the garden, and I wondered if the closeness of the dancing had to do with the sheer size of the crowd or the stark chill that still hung in the air, threatening to bite at anyone who wandered too far from the warm bodies. I held Kipp's hand in my left and Darrya's in my right as we bounded in a circle to the music, the sun beginning its slow descent toward dusk.

It was hard to tell if the grin I wore was due to the copious substances I'd ingested, or from the company surrounding me. My eyes trailed over Finlay, my father, Wren, Larke, and Cas, all making up various other circles around us. I knew we were doing this to celebrate the lives of those lost. But along the way, I realized, it was also to bring us closer to those who remained with us. There was a distinct comfort in that.

We dropped hands as the music slowed, and I spun away, only to be picked up in someone else's arms. When I looked up, it was into familiar blue eyes — but not Finlay's. Aerrin's. All humor fell from my face. I glanced away, muscles poised for retreat, even as I forced myself to stay put.

"Congratulations on your engagement, Lady Katherine," he said as he lifted his palm up, initiating the dance. After a moment's hesitation, I mirrored him, and we turned together, eyes locked. "And I must congratulate you on your excellent duplicity. There is certainly more to you than meets the eye." He licked his lips, even as his face remained serious. "Though what meets the eye is pleasant enough."

My eyes narrowed as we switched course. "For someone so intent on wreaking havoc while we restore peace, you sure do seem to have a bone to pick with me personally."

"It's quite simple, really. I don't like being lied to."

"Then that makes two of us."

Aerrin went silent for a moment, and I felt his body stiffen as we continued our dance. I took the moment to inspect a piece of fuzz stuck to the fabric of his jacket, feigning indifference. "What if I made you a promise?" he finally asked.

I lifted a brow in response, waiting for him to continue. The song came to a stop, and we separated. He bowed. "No more lies between us."

I curtseyed in response, remaining in the position as I considered his words. He had everything he wanted in this moment: no solid proof of his involvement in the palace deaths, his soldiers unscathed from battle. He had to know stoking my anger would only cause more trouble for him. Did he want a chase? Was he toying with me?

Finally, I rose, meeting his solemn gaze. "I've got my eye on you," I hissed.

Aerrin broke his stoic expression long enough to flash me a grin, stepping back. "I'd be devastated if you didn't."

I stood for a moment as people danced around me, considering. I didn't think he was still pursuing me out of desire. The new duke had plenty of ladies within his grasp, and with Finlay newly off the market, the number had surely doubled. It had to be to set me off-kilter, potentially ruin this new engagement with Finlay. Certainly, us separating would be an aid to whatever agenda he and his brother had.

As if on cue, I felt a heated presence behind me. Finlay's jaw was clenched, and his gaze was icy as he stared Aerrin down, who simply dipped his head to the king as he returned to the dancing.

"Don't," I groaned, and he glanced down at me in surprise. "I have a feeling he just wants to cause some public conflict. What better time than right after we announce our engagement, right?"

A muscle in Finlay's jaw twitched as he considered. "Fine. But then I think we need to get out of here. I can't take him chasing after you like a piece of meat for a second longer."

I grabbed his hand in mine, feeling the heat of his anger in it, making it just a touch above comfortable. My gaze skirted the crowd, noting the revelers who glanced in awe at us as they walked and twirled past. "Are you allowed to just leave?" I asked.

He gave me a lopsided grin as he looked down at me. "Oh, little angel. I'm the king. I can do whatever I want."

My heart fluttered a little with desire at the words and the rough, bemused tone he used. I realized with a start that we'd never finished what we started earlier.

"And what does the king want to do?" I whispered, teasing, and watched as his grin turned a little darker, a little more wicked.

"Hmmm... what do *you* want to do?" He tugged me closer so that he could wrap his other hand around my waist. I feigned contemplation, enjoying the pleasant feeling of him close to me, while also giving in a bit to the lightheadedness I felt. Suddenly, the dancers and passing waitstaff were forgotten.

"I want to play a game."

"Oh, then we can play a game. But if we do, it's going to be dirty." My thighs clenched tighter at his words, and he smiled as though he knew exactly what he was doing to me. He brushed the hair back behind my ear, leaning in to whisper in it. "I'll count to twenty, and you hide. If I find you in ten minutes, it's my way. If I don't, it's yours."

With that, he spun me around, giving me a gentle shove toward the palace stairs. When I glanced back over my shoulder, he winked.

"One..."

I laughed and ran, grinning like an idiot as I passed Darrya, conversing with Cas at the edge of the garden. She gave me a quizzical look, but I didn't stop to explain. Twenty seconds, after all.

I counted mentally, darting into a storeroom as I hit eleven seconds. I tried to quiet my breathing as I backed against the shelves, lined with an abundance of potatoes, onions, and other goods. My heart thrummed with anticipation, and I wavered back and forth on wanting to get caught and wanting to win as each pair of footsteps strode past.

After a few minutes, my grin faded, and I began to feel a bit silly for requesting the game. Had I completely ruined the night?

Just as the thought crossed my mind, a pair of footsteps stopped right in front of the door, and moments later, it flew open.

Finlay grinned down at me, teeth gleaming. "Gotcha."

"How did you know?" I squeaked.

He slid into the storeroom, closing the door behind him, and I felt the warm brush of his energy tapping against mine in answer. "Your magical signature is like a beacon. Completely unique, and utterly irresistible to me. If you're within a half-mile of me and my magic, I think I'd be able to pick you out from a crowd."

My lips quirked into an amused smile. "That's kind of hot."

"Oh, little angel. You have no idea how hot." He closed the small space between us, pressing me against the wall, his lips finding mine. I returned the kiss happily, greedily, as he ran his hands down my hips to my backside, lifting me so that he stood between my legs.

"Tell me what you want me to do with you. Or to you," he whispered against my collarbone as he trailed kisses down to the curve of my breasts, and back up. "Don't leave a single detail out."

A whimper built in my throat at his words, but I managed to choke out, "But — you won?"

He chuckled against my bare flesh, the breath warming my skin. "I'm well aware."

A brazen confidence overtook me then, spurred on by him and his words. Always giving. I wanted to make damn sure he knew he won. I sank my legs to the ground and pushed him back, gently but firmly. Confusion flitted across his face as he stepped back willingly, allowing the space to grow between us until his back hit the door.

"Did I—" he began to question, but I made a shushing sound, dropping to my knees before him. His brows furrowed at first, then rose as my hands trailed up his legs, reaching the belt of his black leather pants. As I unbuckled them, tugging down, he sucked in a breath of air, and I glanced up to see his expression. His lips were slightly parted, eyes darkened with desire.

A moment of hesitation overtook me as I realized what I was doing. He had far more experience than I did. Was I just going to make a fool of myself?

As if he saw the hesitation there, his gaze suddenly softened, and he touched my shoulders lightly. "You don't need to—"

His words cut off into a guttural hiss as I took him in my mouth, forcing him to stop his train of thought as well as my own. I started experimentally, licking from base to tip, and then smiled around him as I felt him shudder. Growing bolder, I closed my eyes and took him deeper, cheeks hollowing as I sucked.

He groaned, his fingers moving up from my shoulders to fist in my hair, still gentle, but clearly on the brink of losing control. That feeling of control... it felt fucking amazing. I took him in deeper, swirling my tongue around him, and looked up at him through blurry eyes. His entire body was tense, head thrown back, and as I watched, he moved one hand to the wall, stabilizing himself.

"Fuck, Kate," he moaned, and I increased my movements, compelled by his sounds, until finally, he shuddered once more.

I removed my mouth only after he finished, wiping it and gazing at him. His expression was unreadable, his eyes closed as he breathed deeply. My stomach curled with fear once more, and I stood, backing away.

"I — I'm sorry if that didn't compare to what you're used to, I'm not very..." I trailed off, but his eyes flashed open, and he straightened instantly, grabbing my face in his hands.

"Believe me when I say this," he rasped, his gaze burning fiercely into mine, as if making sure I didn't miss a single word. "Nothing and no one will ever compare to you, little angel. Somehow, I've won. And you're the best prize I could ever ask for."

Chapter Four

If Kate thought she was leaving the bedroom after that, she had another thing coming. It had taken all of his restraint to return to the ceremony and say his respectful goodbyes, all the while counting the seconds until he could get back to their bedroom that night.

But now they were here, and while he wanted to return the favor, time and again, he'd seen something new from her in that storeroom. Her look of apprehension and the way she'd blurted out an *apology* of all things — that told him she perhaps needed a different type of nurturing. So, as he slowly removed her shirt, he refrained from putting his lips to her bare skin, and instead patted the bed, encouraging her to lie face down.

She paused for a moment, fixing him with a quizzical look, and he gave her a soft smile. "Trust me."

When she obliged, he shifted to straddle her from above, shrugging his jacket off and allowing his hands to warm. When he touched her shoulders, she tensed, and he frowned, taking a few moments to run his palms lightly across her bare back. Finally, she relaxed somewhat, and he began working on her back in earnest.

"I feel like if we're getting married, I should probably know you better than I do right now," he began lightly. "Starting with... why you apologized to me after absolutely blowing my fucking mind. Among other things."

Her laugh was brief, more of a courtesy than anything else, and then she went silent. He chewed on his lip, his hands grazing down the slope of her back as he contemplated his next move. Before he could ask another question, however, she began answering.

"I... didn't have a great time, in the human realm. Especially with relationships."

Finlay said nothing, instead letting her divulge the information at her own pace. His hands began working deeper, exploring the muscles along her shoulders as he imagined a younger Kate, working her way through the human realm. It was hard to imagine her without her confidence, her magic, without that spark of light that made her, well... *her*.

"For a while I wanted so desperately to fit in," she continued, her voice soft. "I tried, I really tried to make an effort. But it always felt like pulling teeth. It was so hard... and deep down, I think I knew it shouldn't take so much effort, trying to find a group of people who I liked, and who liked me. That's not the way it should be."

She sucked in a quick breath, and he wasn't sure if it was from his hands, which had just found a knot under her shoulder blade, or from her story. Regardless, she continued.

"I always got some attention for looking a bit unique, but nothing serious, until I was seventeen. Then, this guy showed a real interest in me. We talked, all the time, for weeks. I gave... I gave everything to him." Her voice cracked on the last sentence, and Finlay's hands stilled.

"What happened?" he asked quietly, even as he felt a protective rage settle over him.

"We slipped away at a party, and... it was over so quickly." The words escaped on a soft breath, as though she had to rush to get them out. "Afterwards, he said *nothing*. He didn't look me in the eye or anything, he just started chuckling. I was confused, wondering if I did something wrong, if that was what everyone had always talked about. And then... everyone burst in. All of his friends. All recording with their phones, which are—"

"I know what they are," he interrupted, speaking through gritted teeth. She took a long moment before continuing.

"He didn't try to stop them, just laughed harder, like he was in on it. I yelled at them to get out, and when they finally did, I got up and left. He stopped talking to me after that. And nobody ever said anything to me about it. But somehow, the wondering made it worse." She paused, taking a shaky breath. "I wondered... is that the only reason he paid attention to me? Was he in on it? Were they sharing it, laughing with one another?"

He knew without a doubt that the answer to many of those questions was probably yes. And she was smart enough to know that, too, even if she didn't voice it. The thought of the image of her, naked and vulnerable, for the world to see — for a minute, Finlay saw red. He lifted his hands from her for a moment, praying his anger hadn't channeled into heat.

"After that, I stopped caring. I'd already lost my dad, and I couldn't relate to my mom. I stopped wanting to fit in, to be liked." She went silent for a long heartbeat. "I couldn't even begin to imagine being loved."

He felt her shudder beneath him as she took a deep breath, and he opened his mouth, wondering what to say. All that came out was: "He should pay for what he did."

She twisted slightly, attempting to face him. Though tears rimmed her eyelids, they hadn't yet spilled. She frowned in confusion. "Because he had me, once?"

"Because he *hurt you,*" Finlay growled in reply. He surprised even himself with the violence in his tone. It wasn't jealousy that elicited the murderous emotion from him — though he had that in spades. It was the way this person had left her humiliated, ashamed, and unloved. Three things he never wanted her to feel.

Kate was silent for a long moment, as if digesting that reaction alongside him, before she continued.

"All of this is a long way to say… it's still hard, sometimes, to imagine being good enough for someone to love. Especially for someone who had an easy time with relationships. Someone as… experienced as you."

It was all he could do not to choke out a startled laugh. For all of her strength and fire, she still managed to catch him off guard, reminding him she had vulnerabilities, just like him. He loved her that much more for it.

"I've had many dalliances, little angel. But none have captured my heart the way you have. Before you even paid me any attention, I found myself wanting to be better for you. I'd been so busy trying to forget the way I could be without hiding behind a mask. Maybe..." he hesitated, running a hand nervously through his hair. "I never really knew what I was like without it, at all. Not before you."

Her response was immediate, paired with a teary but genuine smile. "Well, who you are without the mask — I love it."

"And I love you," he replied, smiling as he returned his hands to her bare skin. She squirmed slightly underneath him as he felt a particularly tight knot begin to unravel, slipping under his thumb.

"Where did you learn to do this?"

"From a land further south, Dahín. An island, really. They have a unique take on things. They don't enjoy using magic; instead, they prefer to tackle things using more holistic means."

"And they showed you this?"

"I wanted to learn."

She was silent for a long moment. "You keep doing that."

"Doing what?"

"Surprising me."

"Is that a bad thing?" he asked with a laugh, and watched as she shook her head.

"No, not at all! I love hearing that there are so many differences in this realm. And it's refreshing to know you love exploring what makes each land unique, too."

Finally, he heard the full smile back in her voice, and this time, when she twisted under his embrace, he shifted to allow her up. She trailed her fingers across his remaining undershirt before moving to unlace it. He allowed her to take her time, watching intently. When she skirted her hands under his shirt, though, lifting it over his head, his patience snapped.

Unable to show any more restraint, he tugged Kate against him, relishing the feel of bare skin on bare skin. They fell backwards, Kate landing on top of Finlay with a laugh — this one genuine. He trailed his hands up her sides, dancing along her curves, relishing the idea of consummating their engagement.

His *fiancée.* He curled a hand behind the nape of her neck and tugged her to him.

Just as their lips came together, however, an insistent knocking came at the door, followed by his name being called. Darrya. Again.

Finlay groaned. "Not now, cousin!"

A pause. Then: "It's kind of urgent."

The shift in her tone had both Kate and Finlay jolting up, exchanging a look of alarm. A quick shuffle, an exchange of garments, and they were pulling their clothes back on as they stumbled for the door.

When they opened it, they were surprised to see Larke standing at her side, the expressions on both of their faces stopping them in their tracks. Larke had a dark look Finlay had never seen on him before, one of pure wrath. Darrya's own features were entirely blank, save for the pallor of her skin. Somehow, that devoid expression frightened Finlay even more.

"Aerrin and Thad left a... parting gift," she choked out, handing Finlay a long sheet of paper.

Before he could look down to read it, Larke supplied the information, his voice hoarse with emotion. "Apparently, with Lachlan gone, Aerrin and Thad took the liberty to reinstate Darrya and Aerrin's engagement."

"And not just that," Darrya added weakly. "They still had old paperwork from the queen and Lachlan... so they already performed it by proxy."

Finlay crumpled the paper in his fists, hands trembling with fury and terror as realization dawned on him.

"Wait — what are you saying?" Kate asked, glancing between Finlay and Darrya with wide eyes.

The paper turned to cinders in Finlay's hands. "She's saying she and Aerrin are married."

CHAPTER FIVE

T had swirled his drink impatiently as he watched a lithe, brown-haired girl throw back a shot of whiskey and wink at the bartender. The bartender grinned back as he moved on to the next customer, and the young woman wiped her mouth, turning around to lean against the table and assess the crowd in the pub. To any unsuspecting customer, the young woman, Briar, would look downright alcoholic, not even blinking as she pounded drink after drink. Little did they know, Thad had a running agreement with the barkeep here — and in all the pubs in Brytham's capital city, Reviere — that anytime she and her crew ordered a whiskey, neat, they were actually asking for oversteeped tea. A quick sleight of hand, a gulp of bitter, lukewarm tea later, and Briar looked thoroughly like a young woman on the brink of hitting that alcoholic stupor. She was playing the part of the Hounds' mantra perfectly.

Think like a predator, act like prey.

Other than Kuiper, Briar was the cleverest Hound, despite her young age of nineteen. The Hounds were a rogue group in the city, meant to hunt down fugitives and exact justice when the regular law wouldn't or couldn't. Though Reviere, as the capital city in Brytham, had technically belonged to Lachlan and his appointed governance for centuries, the Hounds belonged solely to Aerrin and Thad.

And Thad had hand-picked Briar himself.

It was no accident that whispers made their way through the children's homes in Brytham, trailing through the ears of the oldest kids. Once they hit the age of fourteen, the likelihood of adoption was slim, and they had to begin looking for employment regardless. What better job could there be for kids who had been forgotten than with a group whose main purpose was to live in the shadows?

Briar had been just shy of seventeen, coming to Reviere from some city in the countryside — the children's home in Varyn, perhaps. She'd been roaming the streets as a rogue and a thief, but she'd eventually caught his eye for her talents. As far as Briar knew, she'd never met Thad. She'd been recruited on his behalf, and Kuiper had seen to it that she proved herself. As it turned out, her fists were her preference over words, so the brutal physicality of training was no barrier for her. Thad was happy he'd chosen correctly with her enlistment.

Thad watched out of the corner of his eye as an older gentleman gazed at the woman, a hungry look gleaming in his eyes.

Bingo. So, this was her victim.

While the Hounds' headhunting toed a fine line of legality, the local barkeep had a mutually beneficial agreement with them. Oftentimes, the Fae the Hounds were brought in to dispose of had run up an impossibly high tab, unable to pay it back but incapable of staying away from the bottle. This particular older gentleman was one of those, and he'd already drunk enough to make him a bit brazen. Tiny flames sparked at the end of his fingertips, telling Thad he'd already lost some control. A few more drinks, and this old Fae would surely be kicked out for the damages he would incur.

Briar made a show of glancing slowly around the room, feigning delighted surprise as the gentleman's eyes met hers. She winked, tilting her head slightly. His eyes widened, lips parting slightly in shock at her bold gesture, and Thad grimaced at the expression. The man was far older than Briar, with most of his teeth missing and what was left of his hair clearly unwashed. Surely if he'd been sober, he'd be questioning the young woman's willingness to dally with him. Luckily, sobriety seemed to be on her side tonight.

As they stepped into the alley, Thad followed a few beats behind, slipping into the shadows. It was already dark enough that he didn't require much cover, well past the time most casual drinkers left the bar. He took a quiet inhale of the fresh, salty air, glad he could easily observe the interaction unnoticed.

Briar shrugged off one side of her shawl, exposing her entire shoulder and a sizable tease of one breast, only just covered by the scrap of a chemise. "My place okay?" she purred, watching the old Fae's gaze remain locked on the bare flesh. He simply nodded, and she backed up, letting her shawl drop lower as she walked. One street over... then two. Thad followed, wondering how far the chase would go, with the intoxicated Fae believing himself the predator and Briar the prey.

Two streets were all Briar needed.

She paused and turned, giving him a knowing grin. He took in the look greedily, all patience snapped, and lunged for her — only to be met with her fist, connecting with his throat. She followed it quickly with a punch, aimed right between his eyebrow and his hairline.

He stumbled back, but his reflexes were just fast enough to raise one hand against her fist, and Thad caught sight of flames just as Briar cried out, yanking her hand back. Thad raised a brow, wondering if he would have to intervene.

But Briar adjusted, leveling a strong kick to the groin, and when he doubled over, she caught his chin with her knee. Thad heard the clack of his remaining teeth, and he dropped instantly. She took his pulse for a few long seconds, ensuring he was unconscious, and then adjusted her stance, crouching to loop his arms around hers. Then she began to haul him away, presumably to the Hounds' Den several streets over — centrally located to the seedy underbelly of Reviere. Most wouldn't glance twice at the sight as Briar made her journey there. Thad smiled at her success and waited a few moments in silence.

Just as he expected, Kuiper materialized from the nearby shadows. Thad glanced his way, assessing him as he drew closer. The leader of the Hounds truly looked like one of the shadows. His long, inky hair was constantly pulled back in a bun, and his trimmed beard contributed to him blending in with the darkness. As expected, he wore all black, from his loose jacket to his trousers and leather boots.

"So," Kuiper said, voice low and raspy. "Is she the right choice?"

Thad brushed a thumb over the paper in his pocket and nodded. "I want you both on the assignment."

Kuiper ducked his head in acknowledgement. Though Kuiper was only perhaps forty, he'd been a founding member of the Hounds two decades ago, and Thad trusted him with his life.

"It'll be difficult, but I need the best of the best. So, it's you and the kid."

Thad glanced sidelong at Kuiper, catching a momentary flicker of curiosity before the man rearranged his face into careful disinterest. Thad then looked around carefully, listening for any eavesdroppers. There were distant conversations, probably back at the bar they'd left, but none close by. Most citizens were likely tucked away for the night, fast asleep in their homes far above the sordid streets he and Kuiper currently preoccupied. All he heard was the low sound of water lapping against a canal and the rumble of thunder above, indicating a looming rainfall. Still, he leaned in to whisper in Kuiper's ear as he continued.

"Two targets this time, both very high-profile. We only have a short window where they'll be in Reviere, so you'll both be working on this one, starting tomorrow."

"Capture or kill?" Kuiper asked.

Thad paused, considering his answer. "Ideally capture both. But it will be difficult. Keep her alive at all costs, but for him... kill is not out of the question."

With that, he pulled the paper out of his pocket, taking a brief moment to look down at the portraits before passing it discreetly to Kuiper. The image remained marked on the back of his eyes as he walked briskly away into the night.

The image of the king and future queen of Muiranvia staring back at him.

CHAPTER SIX

Things happened in rapid succession after discovering the marriage announcement. Finlay began packing a bag of essentials, motioning for me to do the same. There wasn't much of a plan, except to try to talk some sense into Aerrin and Thad, and potentially get our hands on the by-proxy marriage arrangement to burn — or the dissolution of their engagement that Lachlan had ordered, though we all had a sinking suspicion that it was long gone.

Darrya, for all the open emotion she usually displayed, kept it carefully guarded since the news broke. She kept herself busy, distant, running to gather things we may need in our departure to Brytham, but she was paler than usual, a deep crease set between her brows. I wanted to ask her how she was feeling, if she wanted to talk about it, but every time I opened my mouth, the words died in my throat. She was clearly avoiding the topic, and I didn't want to pry, potentially pulling some emotions too big and painful for her to unpack yet. Hell, I wasn't sure how I felt about the potential of marriage with someone I knew I loved. My pulse still spiked at the idea that my future was irrevocably bound to someone else I'd only known for a short while. Aerrin was the source of some of her worst memories, and though I couldn't begin to fully comprehend what it meant for her, I did know I wanted to throttle him on her behalf. For this, and everything else.

Clearly, I wasn't the only one.

"I don't understand," Larke complained as he passed Finlay weapons to load in a chest. Darrya and I sat on the bed, folding handfuls of clothing to place in a separate trunk — though I snuck a few blades in, wrapped in leather pants. "We suspect they're behind the murder of Lachlan and the queen. Why aren't we marching on Reviere with our armies? They're already amassed."

Darrya rose from the bed and settled next to him on the floor. She placed a reassuring hand on his shoulder and exchanged a look with Finlay. "This isn't the fight we asked them here for, Larke. We've lost so many already — the queen, the duke, our combined armies. You know better than anyone."

"Not to mention, the two were very careful about covering their tracks," Finlay added. "We'd be instigating another war with what the people view as no justification. We would lose the faith that's already feebly placed between Kate and myself."

Larke grumbled, and despite his eventual agreement, he still suggested gathering a handful of his best soldiers for the planned trip. Finlay looked ready to argue, but I stopped him with a shake of my head. It wasn't about protecting us — though he would, without hesitation. This was personal. He needed our plan to succeed for Darrya.

Larke was quick to fire off options for our next steps, still holding onto his kernel of vengeance. "The brothers set sail with the rest of the Brytham army right after the ceremony. They only have a few hours on us. We could still catch up to them in the open waters."

Finlay stopped his packing and straightened. "And do what, exactly?"

Larke's mouth opened and closed, and Finlay hummed. "That would be Aerrin's ideal scenario. We storm their ship, giving him reason to retaliate. And we'd be landing smack in the middle of their entire army, with only a handful of us to face off against them."

I clenched and unclenched my fists, feeling the crescents of my nails push into my palms. Less than a few days, and Aerrin and his brother were already proving to be a different kind of foe than Nemain. She had been tricky, sure, but at least we'd all had a common enemy, one we could use blatant force against. By striking directly against Aerrin and Thad, we would be opening the doors to a civil war between lands. Perhaps that was their aim; if they could justify a civil war, they would have grounds to come for us and claim the crown for their own. They were leveraging that to their advantage, and they knew the political dances just as well as Finlay and Darrya — far better than I did, to be sure.

"Should I come with?" Darrya asked. A bit of color had returned to her face, having realized we had a plan to work our way out of this.

"No. Go to Leven," Finlay said gently. "Be with our family. If you come with us, I worry..." he trailed off, but the words hung in the air as though he'd voiced them. *If she came, she might be forced to stay at Aerrin's side.* I ground my teeth so hard I feared they might crack.

"When I marry — truly marry — I'm marrying a man. Not this petty child," she spat. Larke moved closer to her side, and I swore his chest puffed out proudly on her behalf. That, paired with the heat in her words, made me smile. Though Aerrin was likely trying to break her spirit by putting her in this position, he hadn't been allowed around her enough to know who he was dealing with. He thought he'd be getting someone tame, mild, broken. Little did he know what a warrior Darrya had grown up to be. Part of me wanted to take her with and have her square off with him, just to see what would be left when she was done with him.

Finlay latched the weapons chest and stood, exhaling deeply. It was the only sign since he'd burned the marriage announcement in his hands that he was truly rattled. "Larke, can you get word to Captain Hogan to get one of the royal ships ready? We'll use some dust and be on the coast in an hour."

Larke nodded at the order and I turned to Finlay, cocking my head curiously. "We're not using Faerie dust to get straight to Brytham?"

"No," he replied, shouldering the bag as we all exited the room. "Even though the capital, Reviere, is right on the edge of the water, it's too far to travel by dust from here. It's not like Leven, where it's just a small channel separating Muiranvia and Daersill. There's a whole ocean between the lands, and one miscalculation could land us right in the water."

Unease curled in my gut at the image of landing unexpectedly in the vast, open water. "Oh."

"Oh, indeed." Finlay offered a small smile of amusement, and then his eyes traveled back to Darrya. Though some of the color had returned to her face, that worried crease remained, betraying her nerves. In two large strides, he met her in a crushing embrace. "We'll get this sorted out, cousin. I promise you that."

Their embrace tugged at my heart, the protectiveness and love between them apparent. He'd saved her from Aerrin once before, all those years ago. In return, Darrya had stood resolutely by Finlay as he'd worked to escape his memories by chasing them away with drugs and alcohol. She'd been there to help me with Nemain, too, without so much as a question. Now it was our turn to defend her once more.

Would there ever come a day when one of us wasn't in need of saving?

They stepped back, and I came to hug her as well, tightly but briefly. "Be safe," I whispered.

"You too, Katie," she replied, glancing over at Finlay. "And keep him safe, too."

I nodded, pulling back and returning to Finlay's side. Larke met Darrya's gaze but said nothing. Instead, his eyes softened and he dipped his head. She eyed him for a long moment, and then closed the gap between them, grabbing at the front of his fighting leathers. Surprise alone allowed her to pull his large frame toward her, and when their bodies connected, she stood on her tiptoes, pressing her lips against his.

A soft groan escaped Larke, and he instantly wound his hands around her waist, tugging her closer to him as he took what she offered. The moment was gentle but heated, clear to anyone who witnessed it that it had been a long time coming. I averted my eyes to give them some privacy, but grinned to myself. They deserved this moment of happiness.

A soft snicker escaped Finlay, and when I looked up at him, he met my eyes and winked. My heart fluttered at the sight of his dimples and pale blue gaze, and then sank as I glanced back at Darrya and Larke. Their own moments with each other were only just beginning, and already, far too fleeting. I slipped my hand into Finlay's, giving it a small squeeze. He squeezed back, shooting a comforting warmth down to where our palms connected.

When Darrya pulled back and faced us once more, her eyes glistened with unshed tears. She offered a final smile to all of us, and with a flash of blonde hair, she turned and strode the opposite way down the hallway. We all stood still for several heartbeats, digesting what had just transpired and building up to what came next.

Larke moved first, clearing his throat before continuing down the hall in the direction of the courtyard. As we walked, the tenderness I'd felt soured to anger, roiling inside me at the unfairness of it all.

"Fucking hell. What is Aerrin playing at? I just want to... to grab him by the balls and *twist,*" I seethed as we walked, gesturing violently. Larke made a point to move a few steps further to the side as we walked, giving me a wide berth. Finlay raised a brow and eyed me with trepidation.

"I'd prefer if you didn't handle anyone's netherregions aside from mine, little angel," he replied, his tone light. My response was a mixture of a huff and a growl, and he laughed.

"Let's go make sure your dad knows what's happening and where we're going," he said, then paused. His eyes raked over me, a mischievous glint in them. "But stay angry. It looks beautiful on you."

"I feel like I'm always losing you, just as I get you back again," my dad murmured, and I hugged him tighter, closing my eyes.

"I know," I choked out, fighting against the lump rising in my throat, hard and painful. There was a stinging sensation behind my eyelids, and I wondered if tears would fall, if they were open. We'd come a long way since I'd gone from believing him dead, only to realize he had left my mother and me while I was young. It had been to save us, I now knew, but it had been a complicated path to reconciliation. More unfortunate was that it took losing my mother this past winter to bring us closer than ever. Perhaps someday, we'd be able to act like a normal family again... but my family also included Darrya, and I owed it to her to do everything in my newfound power, both politically and magically, to secure her freedom.

After a few moments, my dad loosened his hold on me, and I could feel the reluctance in his posture as I stepped back. He held up a finger and disappeared into his room for a moment. When he returned, he held out an old leatherbound book.

A dictionary. I raised a quizzical brow.

"You'll have a few days on that ship. I know you, and you'll be bored out at sea. This way, you can keep practicing your Ogham letters," he explained.

I glanced down at the book once more, and when I looked back up, his expression was strained. Though he still looked young — almost too young to be my father, thanks to our slow aging — I could see the worry lines etched into his face, deepened from the past few months.

"It's just a quick political visit. I'll be back soon," I promised, my voice barely more than a whisper.

He smiled, though it didn't quite reach his eyes. "I know, kiddo." After a pause, he added, "I love you."

This time, the prick I felt in my eyes was most certainly real. "I love you too, dad."

CHAPTER SEVEN

"Where are we?" I asked, confusion muddling my brain as I looked around. There wasn't a speck of water in sight; rather, the terrain looked absolutely barren. We were in a broad clearing with a town a short distance away, but even the grass was withered to a dusty tan. Sairas teemed with life, its houses covered in flowers and greenery, boasting a certain charm, but the houses in this town looked... bland, weather-worn, as though they were fighting a constant battle with the elements and on the brink of losing.

"There is still a bit of time before the ship will be ready," Finlay explained. He shook the remaining Faerie dust from his hand into the leather pouch he held and extended it to me. "I had an important errand to run before we set off, and I figured it was one you would want to join me on."

I took the pouch tentatively, and he took off, clearly knowing exactly where we were going. I took in the surrounding structures, noting flashes of distrustful eyes in a few windows. As we walked, a few children ran by, shrieking as they kicked around a ball. They were thin in a way that told of more than overzealous exercise, and their clothing was ragged, ripped in several places, and dirty to the point that it had clearly accumulated over several wears, rather than just from a few tumbles during their current game.

The group of children stopped short when they saw us, tilting their heads curiously. I ran a hand over the Whisperer, ensuring it was still masked in its scabbard, the glow hidden to disguise it as any basic sword, rather than the legendary reunification of ancient talismans. Then, two things struck me at once, the first being that even in our relaxed traveling wardrobe, we were dressed far above the clothing they wore, and likely any wardrobe in the surrounding area. The second was that we were far enough removed from Sairas that our presence — mainly Finlay's, who'd had ages for his face to spread across the lands — was still unrecognizable. News clearly didn't spread here the way it would in larger cities. We were nobility to them, which was surely curious, but they didn't have a clue *who*. A cautious smile spread across my face at the surprising relief of that fact.

I reached for my pocket before stopping short, realizing I still didn't quite understand what was acceptable here. I caught Finlay's gaze, the question in my eyes apparent, and he smiled gently in response. He reached for his own pocket, pulling out a handful of coins. The children perked up, racing forward, and he dropped a few coins into their hands, one by one.

"Don't spend it all in one place," he murmured as he went, a serious expression on his face.

A chorus of "thank you" resounded from them, and they flashed giddy, toothy smiles up at us. I felt the infectious joy reach me as well, grinning in return. As quickly as they'd come, they sprinted off, whooping in excitement.

"I didn't want to give them enough that they'd find trouble in the market if word got around," he said to me, softly, as though he felt he needed to explain. I grabbed his hand and squeezed it in reassurance.

"Where are we?" I asked instead, my tone hushed.

"Leyterras."

Leyterras. The name struck a chord, and I dug in my mind to recall where I'd heard that before. *Blaise,* I realized. It was where he'd grown up, alongside Soren and Larke. Though... he'd been in the worst part of the city. I wondered if the worst part was what we'd already seen, or if there was more in store. I pulled up short, my feet frozen between two paths. One would drag me deeper into this world I'd only scratched the surface of with Blaise. It would press into that wound between my ribs that was still raw. The other path would drag me away from here, back to safety. But that path would leave me with questions I'd never get answers to.

Finlay tilted his head at me, waiting. I decided to state the most obvious fact on my mind. "I... I didn't realize that there were the same kind of issues here. As in the human realm, I mean," I ventured, the words sounding feeble even as they left my mouth. It was ridiculous, I realized, to have held this realm to such a higher standard. There was still discrimination, violence, and dirty politics here, all of which I'd already witnessed. Of course, there would be serious wealth discrepancies as well.

"It's not acceptable by any means, but from what I've gleaned, there is a large barrier to change with much of the population." There was a frustrated undercurrent to Finlay's response.

"Let me guess," I ventured, "from those who live nowhere near this?" I gestured broadly with my free hand, and he nodded. "In that case, then, this realm is exactly like the human realm."

Finlay fixed me with his lopsided grin and tugged me forward. "Well, little angel, I hope you keep that fighting spirit. Because we just came into a lot of power to help change that."

For the first time, I felt a mixture of terror and joy at the responsibility that loomed ahead of us. It was reassuring, knowing Finlay and I shared the same ideals, and our new status opened doors I couldn't previously fathom. The problem was, that meant we had to figure out how to enact meaningful change. Could we really do such a thing? My stomach flip-flopped.

Finlay came to a halt in front of a small, inconspicuous home, tucked on a back street. The only sign of habitation was a new layer of paint that was clearly in process, covering half the home. The windows were boarded and the pale yellow paint on the side that wasn't refreshed was peeling away. I cast him a curious glance, and he simply grabbed my hand again, tugging me up the front porch.

He knocked, and after a moment, the door creaked open, groaning on its hinges. A young woman answered, strikingly beautiful with her dark hair and hazel eyes, which widened in surprise.

"Prince Egan," she whispered, and dipped into a light curtsey. I blinked, surprised that she recognized the prince. Clearly, they'd met in the past, but she had not yet received the news that the queen was gone.

Finlay bowed his head in response, and then turned to me. "Sera. I've come to see how things are faring. And to introduce you to... Katherine."

I jerked in surprise, both at his use of my full name and the fact that he didn't feel compelled to pair it with my relation to him. A small surge of jealousy flared alongside my confusion. Though I lacked understanding of the situation, this woman's countenance was rife with it. There it was, written like tragic poetry across her face. Understanding and... rage.

"Katherine," she hissed. I stepped back in alarm from the venom in her tone. "You're the reason my brother is dead."

I was fairly certain the only thing keeping Blaise's sister from crossing the threshold to strangle me was Finlay's presence. As if he knew this as well, he took a deliberate step in front of me.

"As I've told you, Sera — Blaise sacrificed himself to ensure Katherine could lead our troops to the final battle against Nemain," Finlay said, his tone quiet but commanding. "A battle that proved successful, I might add. Though a lot of people died for our freedom. Including Kate's mother. And my great-grandmother."

This seemed to give Sera pause. She opened her mouth to answer, but a low, rasping voice behind her spoke before she could get the words out.

"The queen is dead?"

An older woman appeared from the shadows. From the expression Sera wore as she looked back, I realized, this was likely Blaise's mother. She was beautiful, with a soft face and hair that shone a mostly ashy color, spreading from her roots to gain gracefully on the rest of her dark hair. Her jaw was square and her nose slightly upturned, two features she'd bestowed upon her handsome son. She moved slowly, with deliberate steps. I'd seen those movements before, and realized with a start — Blaise's mother was blind.

"Yes, ma'am," Finlay answered, and my heart squeezed in on itself at the deference in his tone. Everyone here had now realized they were speaking with the king and yet, he still gave her the respect she deserved.

"Long live the king," Blaise's mother murmured, and after a belated moment, Sera echoed the sentiment.

"Did I hear you brought Katherine with you?" Blaise's mom asked. When Finlay replied with a yes, she stretched out her hands. "Come here, child."

I paused, taking a moment to dissect her voice. I heard no malice in her tone; rather, a wise gentleness that had my feet moving forward of their own volition. As I strode forward, I could feel Sera's eyes boring into the back of my skull. I had the uncanny sense that if she could, she would be willing my head to explode.

I tried to ignore it, focusing on the feel of Blaise's mom's rough, calloused hands as I placed mine in hers. She held them tightly for a moment before dropping them to reach up, tentatively, to explore my face. I stood still, allowing her to trail them over my face, absorbing my features as she went. I tried to imagine her with Blaise, holding his hands in her tender grasp as he spoke to her of his adventures as commander. I closed my eyes as the grief washed over me, more potent than it had been in weeks. Finally, his mother lowered her hands to grasp mine once more and spoke.

"One of his biggest fears was abandoning us," she said, her voice trembling slightly. "But more than that, he was afraid of the life he would leave us with if he didn't do his job."

"He — he was too good for this world," I whispered, wincing as my voice broke on the words. Instead of commenting on it, her expression turned into a sad smile.

"He loved you, you know. And he wanted the world for you." She paused, giving my hands a gentle squeeze. "Don't let that be in vain."

The breath hissed out from between my teeth as I exhaled shakily. She dropped my hands and stepped back, and after a heartbeat, Finlay spoke again.

"With my new position, I want to assure you, the monthly stipend will not be going away; rather, I intend to increase it. And extend accommodations in Sairas, if that's something that interests you."

His voice was confident, but tight with a layer of emotion that I was certain only I could identify. I wanted to turn to see his expression, but I kept my eyes glued to Blaise's family, drinking in this part of his life I'd never known.

Sera and her mother shook their heads at the offer, nearly in unison, and her mother spoke once more. "Thank you. Truly. But we have found a good existence in this new dynamic." Sera sidled over to her mom while she spoke and clutched her hand. "This is our home. We have each other, and in that, we have everything we need. We're happy."

A faint smile danced across my lips at their bond, even as it made my ache grow at the memory of my own mother.

Finlay dipped his head in acknowledgment. "That makes sense, and I am happy to hear it. In that case, though, I unfortunately have to cut this meeting a bit short. Katherine and I are needed elsewhere."

They nodded. "We understand."

Finlay bid them farewell, and in a last-minute decision, I threw my arms around Blaise's mom. She stiffened at first, and then wrapped her arms around me in response.

"I'm so glad to have met you," I whispered.

She hugged me closer. "Likewise, child. Don't be a stranger."

As we walked back out of town, Finlay allowed me time to silently digest the meeting. Emotions curled their way through my stomach, the pleasant and painful crashing together in my very core.

"He would have wanted you to meet them," Finlay murmured as we drew to a stop, his pale eyes downcast. His words, paired with the ones Blaise's mother left me with, turned the emotions roiling through me to ice. I wrapped my hands around my stomach, squeezing against the pain of them. *What would he think of me now?* I wondered. Would he be happy I was visiting his family? Knowing they were taken care of? It was hard not to imagine how much happier they would be having him back in their lives, rather than the visit from two royals, shoving everything they lost and all the things they likely never had in their faces. While the image of his mother embracing me warmed my soul, his sister's words instantly curdled the feeling.

"Kate?"

I tilted my head up to Finlay, attempting a faint smile in response "Thank you for this. I'm really glad I got the chance. Even if it hurts."

Finlay raised his brows in question.

"It's hard not to see the truth in Sera's words." I swallowed. "I am the reason her brother is... dead."

I forced the last word out, and Finlay reached out, cupping my chin in his palm. He tilted my head up to meet his gaze. Even through the tears that began to swim in my eyes, I noted the concern and anguish in his own expression.

"And you don't think I blame myself for not being able to stop what happened with your mother?" he asked. "You don't think Kipp and Cas blame themselves for Wren being injured? You don't think Darrya wishes Lachlan were still alive? You don't think Larke takes every death of every other soldier out there personally?"

I winced with every question he asked, stepping away. On a logical level, I understood what he was saying, but it only compounded the senselessness of our losses, and the anger at how many directly affected my friends and family. As my hand slipped from his, the loss of his contact snapped the last tether on my emotions, and the tears spilled over, streaming down my cheeks. I skimmed my fingers over the Whisperer at my waist before clutching the pouch of Faerie dust.

"There's a difference, though, Finlay," I rasped out, the words nearly catching in my throat. I shoved the pouch back at him and put another large step of space between us. His brow furrowed, and I opened my fist, exposing the handful of dust I'd dumped out into my palm. He opened his mouth to question it, but I cut him off. "We couldn't do anything about it, then. But now, maybe I can."

I threw the dust over my head and allowed it to whisk me away.

CHAPTER EIGHT

I landed precisely where I'd hoped to, and as I took in my surroundings, I felt my roiling emotions center into a point of clarity. I stalked forward, taking in the gorge that stretched above and around me with a tingling sense of familiarity. I'd been here once before, but not as myself, so when the twin gates appeared, stretching high to either side of me, it felt like returning to a dream. I examined the figures depicted on them for a long moment before turning my gaze to the statue directly ahead.

Arawn.

His statue alone was intimidating — head covered by the large stag skull, long antler points stretching out at various angles to form a grotesque crown. He sat, clutching a sword, with a long fur cape draped over his shoulders. But the hounds at his feet – three, as large as Kipp in his wolf form — were even more intimidating. He was the true god of death, the ruler of Annwn, the Otherworld, and these were the nightmare hounds that did his bidding.

Shoving the prickle of fear aside at the sight of them, I strode forward and unsheathed the Whisperer. Its glow was brighter than before, surpassing the soft hue left from the original sword of Nuada. Mimicking Arawn's stance, I grasped the hilt with both hands and placed the tip on the ground. I knelt, offering myself and the combined talismans to him.

And I waited.

Slowly, a rumbling began, echoing off the slabs of taupe rock that stretched toward the skies, sending granules of dirt skittering below my feet. A few loud cracks resounded, and I glanced up to see Arawn's statue begin moving. The movement began at his hands, with pebbles cracking off his fingertips, allowing them to twitch. Rock tumbled from his torso next, and finally, his legs. Once every solid fragment had cracked and fallen to his feet, the god began to blink, looking down at himself. He then stood slowly, brushing stone and debris off his arms. His hounds followed suit, shaking rubble from their coats before fixing me with their otherworldly stares, their eyes burning like live coals.

The hounds moved like wraiths, circling me, their bodies not entirely solid. Though I knew I had nothing to fear from them, their sheer preternatural presence made my pulse spike. Arawn flicked a hand, and I saw one pair of gleaming eyes disappear, though I couldn't be sure where it went. The hairs on the nape of my neck prickled at the thought that the hound might be disappearing to read my memories and pass judgment along to Arawn, as they were intended to do. Suddenly, my appearance here felt slightly foolish. What if Arawn decided he didn't want me to leave? I glanced briefly at the gate to my right, where the figures had their gazes fixed downward. I shuddered at the thought of going back to hell.

"Katherine," Arawn spoke, causing me to snap my eyes back to him. "Child of Cú Chulainn. I wondered when you'd be making a visit." I opened my mouth to answer, questioning his choice of words, but he held up a hand, stopping me. "I make a habit of keeping track of lost souls. And you, child... you are as lost as they come."

I absorbed this answer and watched as his eyes slid to the Whisperer. It seemed to pulse even brighter under his gaze. "I must congratulate you, however, on your victory against my sister. Nemain has spent countless centuries disrupting the order of things. My duties here have not allowed me to leave my post, but to see her claim herself as the goddess of death, abusing such powers, exacting her own twisted, selfish justices..." He shook his head. "It has brought me immeasurable pain to witness the souls she brought here before their time. I owe you a debt for ending it all."

The breath caught in my throat. A debt, owed, from the god of death? Perhaps there was a way, after all.

"I... if you truly owe me a debt, grant me this." I bowed my head, feeling the breath in my throat tighten further as an emotional lump formed. The intensity of his gaze weighed me down, making it difficult to phrase my request clearly. "I need to fix this. Tell me how to make this work. Tell me how to bring them back."

I lifted my eyes but remained kneeling, pleading with my stature and my expression. Arawn tilted his head and glanced at his remaining two hounds, who came back to sit at his feet. Finally, he looked back at me, expression filled with gentle understanding.

Understanding, and pity.

My heart plummeted.

"This, child..." he trailed off for a moment. "This, I cannot do."

The words landed like an anvil on my already sinking heart. He knew, without asking, exactly whom I was referring to. My mom, Blaise, Lachlan, the soldiers lost to Nemain's bloody battle... with his words, he took that final chance from me. From *them.*

He took in my expression and closed the gap between us with two large strides, placing a hand on my shoulder. It was surprisingly warm and tender, though it radiated the strength only a god's touch could.

"But Nemain told me—" I choked on the words as they ran through my head once more. *Bring back the dead.* "She told me it was possible. Once the talismans were activated. To bring them back," I finished.

Arawn lifted his hand from my shoulder and knelt beside me. He removed his skull and observed me for a long moment. I met his gaze, studying him back. Beneath the mask, he looked... surprisingly normal. His face had all human features, though they were stunningly beautiful, and clearly ageless — etched with just enough lines to show wisdom, but still youthful. His irises were so dark they were nearly black, and gleamed against the light shining down from the gray skies. His dark hair was pushed back out of the way of his face, which was shapely and masculine, but non-threatening as he smiled sadly at me. "Perhaps. Perhaps there is a way. But I've known my sister for quite some time. She could have meant what she said, or she could have told you what you wanted to hear. She could have even believed it herself, but not known for certain."

I gazed at the sword, skepticism washing over me. Arawn continued. "I imagine if she believed you could bring back the dead, her goal was to come here and kill me, taking my place. She would have had you turn the sword against me, and then test the theory of reincarnation herself. Starting with her sisters, and perhaps bringing your loved ones back as a reward. Perhaps not. I suppose we will never know, now."

"Didn't she come here?" I asked. "Wouldn't you have seen her memories and known the truth?"

He shook his head and stood. "I have ferried infinite souls between the two gates. From every realm, human, Fae, and god alike, they all come to me in the end for their judgment. But Nemain? She did not. What this sword *might* do—" he motioned at the Whisperer. "—is uncertain. But I do know it can cause certain death. At least for a goddess like Nemain."

"So whatever I did gave her a permanent death. No afterlife." I rose to my feet as well and lifted the sword, staring at it.

"Indeed," he agreed. "And before you ask the favor of attempted reincarnation, I must decline from a moral standpoint. My job here is to exact justice. To play with life and death this way would make you no better than Nemain herself." I took a step back, his words hitting me like a physical blow. I recognized the truth in what he said, but that didn't stop it from hurting. "Not only would this upset the order of things, but to attempt it with such unpredictable outcomes... would you be willing to risk the potential of permanent death, with no afterlife, on the scrap of possibility that they could come back?"

He narrowed his eyes at me, and I winced at the scrutiny, shaking my head. He pursed his lips, pausing for a moment to ensure I was serious, then nodded in approval. "Neither would I, child. Especially seeing as all of these loved ones are currently at peace."

My eyes went wide, and he offered me another smile, this one full of warmth. "Yes, child. They are at peace."

I swayed on my feet. The information brought back all the emotions that had been toiling in me from the moment I left Leyterras to the moment I dropped to the ground to appeal for Arawn to help me bring them back. I couldn't bring them back — not without becoming the very evil I had just destroyed, and not without risk of sending those I loved to the abyss. I couldn't bring them back...

But.

They were safe, and presumably happy, and at peace.

My vision blurred with tears, but I still made out the motion as Arawn gestured behind me. "I believe there is someone waiting for you."

I turned, wiping tears from my eyes as I heard the familiar voice.

"Little angel."

Before I could make a move, I was wrapped up in Finlay's arms, and the feeling — his warmth, his scent, his solidity — clashed with my other emotions so intensely that I collapsed. He followed me to the ground, still holding me, allowing me to cry against his chest. The tears flowed freely, and I buried myself further into his embrace. He kissed the top of my head, and I felt his jaw move softly against my hair as he spoke to Arawn. "Thank you for getting me."

"I did nothing. I simply sent my hound for you. You — correctly — inferred the rest."

Finlay's arms tightened around me almost imperceptibly. "Yeah, I don't know why they love me so much. I just got a new dog. I don't need another."

A low, short chuckle. "I shall be sure not to send them to fetch you again unless it's absolutely necessary."

I felt Finlay's magic tap against mine, and I allowed him in without hesitation. Our energies swirled and combined, and the heat of his power warmed me, while the electric hum of mine answered happily. I melted into him, body and soul, and closed my eyes. Eventually, I took a deep breath, willing myself to calm down.

When I could finally look up at him again, he was gazing at me, pale eyes gleaming with concern. He shifted, moving his arms so that he could cradle my face in his palms.

"You scared me, little angel. I thought you went to the ship, but nobody had seen you. And then the nightmare hound showed up... gods, the soldiers nearly pissed themselves." He brushed the hair back from my face, studying me. "What happened?"

I glanced back at Arawn, and he cleared his throat. "The child wished to see if I could assist in bringing back the dead. The talismans may have allowed such powers."

Finlay's eyes widened, and he gaped at me. I shook my head. "We didn't. He won't... I won't." My voice cracked slightly. "There's no guarantee it won't make things worse rather than better. And I don't want to be like *her.*"

Finlay studied me carefully. "I am so, so sorry I took you to Leyterras. It wasn't fair of me to spring that on you."

"No, I'm happy you did. I just... there has been so much death." I exhale a painful breath. "And I know now, I know they're at peace, but it doesn't make it any easier. And seeing all the love Blaise left behind, knowing he left it so that I could keep living—"

"Kate." Finlay cut me off, fixing me with a serious expression. "I miss them all, too. And we could go in circles all day, but the truth of it is, Blaise is the only one of them who knew his fate from the very beginning. And yet, he still chose it. And he would choose it again, and again, knowing the outcome. I doubt he meant for you to spend this time wishing for different outcomes, because it's exactly what he'd hoped for. His family is taken care of, and you..."

He paused. "Well, I am trying my best every day to fulfill that wish. But I might need some help from you, little angel. You have people here, waiting for you to look forward instead of back. Everyone is rooting for you. Everyone loves you and wants you to be happy. But you need to allow yourself to be happy as well."

His words brought back something Kipp said a long time ago. *While humans look forward, we look back, and none of us realize we are right in the middle of what we should be enjoying.* I thought of him, finally happy with Cas, and of Wren, and of my father. I thought of everyone I now knew was at peace.

And when I looked at Finlay, with the gentle, hopeful expression on his face, a single tear made its way over my cheek as I offered him a small but genuine smile. He wiped it away with his thumb, and I shivered.

"As long as I still have this, I think I can be."

CHAPTER NINE

Finlay stood at the helm of the boat, studying the expanse of ocean that stretched out endlessly in front of them. His thoughts drifted to the fact that Aerrin and Thad both possessed the signature element of water, thanks to their bloodline tracing back to the powerful god of the sea, Manannán. Though Finlay's power with fire was stronger than theirs with water, waves would always dampen flames, and they were in the domain of water gods. His fingers twitched restlessly, the spark he brought to them jumping nervously at the prospect of so much water beneath him for so long.

I wish Larke was here, he thought, recalling the stories of how the commander had channeled the storm in their battle with Nemain to do his bidding. Even though he knew they had talented Fae on board whose signature elements were water, they weren't as strong or as well-versed in magic as Larke. He would have felt more comfortable with the commander alongside him. *No,* he reminded himself. *He's better off at Darrya's side.*

When the time came to depart for Brytham, Larke had decided to stay behind. He'd had many reasons, including needing to keep the peace with everyone confused by the shift in leadership, and ill at ease from the way it espoused. Larke's reasons were valid, but Finlay guessed the strongest reason was the one he left out: the one at his side, holding his hand firmly as the rest of the group departed the palace. Finlay had never seen Darrya so happy with a partner. A bitter taste of anger filled his mouth as he recalled why they were leaving the pair, and he rubbed a hand over his face as he tried to dismiss it. They were on their way to do what they could so she could keep that happiness. But what were Aerrin and Thad playing at? What was the end game here? Finlay had a feeling this was nothing more than a distraction, toying them along, reeling them in.

Kipp appeared beside him, and he glanced down as something cold bumped against his wrist. Two glasses of amber liquid were clasped in Kipp's hands, filled generously. "Figured you could use one as well," he muttered.

Finlay nodded, taking one. "Thanks." He took a long, slow sip and turned to face back inside the boat, observing. Wren and Cas were talking with Kate across the deck, with Cas gesturing wildly as he explained something or another. Each had a specific purpose on this trip, posing as different members of their royal entourage, but that had been after a lot of argument back and forth at the palace that they would *under no circumstances* be left behind. Kipp had started the train, followed by Cas, who was followed by Wren. Stubborn assholes, the lot of them. Finlay loved them for it.

"It feels like we just got our happiness back, only to have it ripped away again," Finlay observed. "There's something bigger afoot here. I can feel it, and I don't like where it's headed."

"It definitely feels that way," Kipp agreed, his expression turning soft. He glanced back at their group of friends and, after a pause, he added, "It's not all ripped away, though."

Finlay raised a brow at him, and Kipp motioned out to Kate and the others, just in time for Finlay to see Kate toss her head back and laugh at something Wren had said. After all the heartbreak they'd endured lately, the sight of Kate laughing was like a salve on Finlay's heart. Cas laughed alongside her, resting his head against Wren's shoulder, who leaned into Cas in return, the picture of sibling affection. It was only a brief moment, but it served to remind Finlay what they all still had, and he hummed in agreement. "I see what you mean."

"It's because we don't want it ripped away that we're out here, fighting for it. For everyone we care for. It's a sad day when we no longer have that." Kipp's voice grew soft. "Even when I was a realm away, I still knew what was waiting for me at home. What I had to fight for." He took a long sip of his drink and continued. "And you have that, with your cousin. With your friends. And with your fiancée, now."

Finlay extended his glass. "Then here's to things worth fighting for."

Kipp clinked glasses with him, nodding. "Indeed."

They took a sip together and watched as Kate, Wren, and Cas made their way across the deck to join them. The day was sunny and the sea was calm, with a light breeze to cut the heat of the day and drag the salty air across their noses.

"Whatcha two celebrating?" Kate asked.

"You, in fact." Finlay smirked, and reveled in the surprise that flickered across Kate's face.

"Well, I'm always down to celebrate that," Cas said, and motioned to the glasses. "Where can we find our mini celebrations?"

Kipp gulped down the remainder of his glass and chuckled. "In my secret stash. But I suppose I can share. I'll be back in a few."

He left, shaking his head as his exit was followed by cheers from the group, including one "Kipp for king!" holler from Cas — who was promptly smacked by Kate.

"Ow!" Cas rubbed his arm, tossing a playful glare at Kate, and Wren simply rolled her eyes. Finlay smirked and took another sip of his drink as Kipp reappeared, more full glasses in his hands.

"So, I know it's still new," Kate began, smiling. "But how are things going with you two?"

"Well, we definitely haven't reached the point of engagement, like some people here," Kipp replied with a teasing grin. "But it's certainly a relief to get everything off our chests after such a long time coming."

Cas hummed in agreement. "Just imagine," he began, "all the time we spent simply talking when we could have been–"

An even louder smack and "oomph!" followed, the blow delivered this time by Kipp. Finlay choked on his drink, laughing, and his gaze meandered to Kate. Her eyes shone devilishly as she laughed alongside him, and the energy that sparked between them was tangible, promising what would come later that night.

From there, they settled into comfortable conversation. They avoided any topics revolving around where they were headed and why. Instead, they found themselves swapping stories, laughing over 'remember-when's' and generally catching up as they would anywhere else. At one point during a particularly funny story Wren was sharing about Cas — involving an attempt at running, following a long night of drinking, before his healing powers had fully set in, and nary a bathroom in sight — Kate was draped over Kipp, laughing and wiping away tears. Finlay caught Kipp's eye once more, who gave him a knowing smile, and Finlay was again struck with that sense of warmth, still somewhat strange to him but already wrapping him in its comforting embrace.

This is what it's like to have friends we can call family. This is what we will always fight for.

The gentle rocking of the boat threatened to lull Finlay into a deep sleep, one he hadn't truly had since before their final battle with Nemain. As he set down his bag on the bed in their private quarters and met Kate's eyes, however, he knew there was a lot to discuss that took precedence over sleep.

She gazed back, those amber-colored eyes assessing him in that uncanny way of hers. Her hands went up to her hair, tugging at the ends, which he'd come to learn as a tell that she was nervous. As if reading his mind, she asked softly, "How are you? Really?"

He sat down on the bed and ran his hands through his own hair. "I don't know. Ever since we got back to the palace, I've been so focused on getting justice for my great-grandmother and Lachlan, and now this with Darrya... I know they're connected, and I know Aerrin and Thad are behind it. We just have to prove it." Kate let out a soft sound of affirmation. "I know I should be grieving and preparing, but I feel like none of us have even had a moment to absorb everything that's happened. In a way, that's been my saving grace. If I think about it too long, the responsibilities, the weight of it all..." He let out a quick, harsh breath. "It might crush me."

Kate padded over to him on light feet, and when she sat down, she took his hand, turning the palm to face up. She traced the lines there lightly for a moment before speaking. "You never wanted to be king."

Finlay considered for a moment. "No. I never did, growing up. I was always worried I couldn't compare, especially without my parents to see what they would have done. But you... you changed something in me, along the way. I want to be a better man for you. And that includes being a better ruler than my great-grandmother ever was." He looked at her for a long moment. "With you, the weight isn't from fear of failure, as it was before. It's a hopeful weight — one that bears purpose, and the promise of change."

Her smile was one of wonder and awe, his favorite smile. As if everything he said constantly surprised her. He only hoped he could continue surprising her for the rest of their lives.

"We're stronger together," she confirmed, leaning against his shoulder.

He reached over, combing his fingers through her hair. "And you? I know we've already discussed plenty, but... how are you feeling, with your new powers?"

Kate stiffened slightly, the only sign that it had indeed been weighing on her over the past few days. Since they'd returned to the palace, she hadn't so much as brought up the new magic he'd never witnessed before. It'd been the turning point of their battle with Nemain; the magic that had lit up the sword of Nuada before its final strike, and caused a storm so strong it turned the tides against the remaining dark Fae.

The sword in question rested against the wall of their quarters. It still glowed, but Kate hadn't made any attempt to imbue it with her power once more. She had been transfixed by the magic on their way home, allowing it to dance across her fingertips. The joy on her face had been one of his favorites, but it appeared she had bottled it up, holding it close to her chest since that day.

"I can't afford to give anyone any reason to distrust me," she admitted. "And a power that no one can understand, including me, is a great reason."

He nodded in understanding. "Can I... can I see it?"

After a heartbeat, Kate removed her hand from his, turning her palm upward. Her eyes darkened with focus for several long moments before lighting with a soft glow. It wasn't as obvious as when she'd exerted herself on the battlefield, but it was still there — the change of her eyes, from a burnt honey color to pure gold, flickering with the energy she expelled.

A spark crossed her palm, starting near her wrist and dancing up to her fingertips. Then more joined, traveling in a criss-cross pattern across her hand, until a solid ball of lightning remained steadily in her fist. A nervous, triumphant smile spread across her face as she gazed down at what she'd created.

Finlay ran his hand in an arched pattern over hers, feeling his hair stand on end at the proximity to the electric current. "You know," he began, wheels turning, "Lugh was considered a god of sun and light, but also a god of storms. It stands to reason that this could still be a power from him."

She considered what this meant. Was she the only one with this gift, or were there others, from other bloodlines? What could she do with this gift — this *weapon?*

"But we worship him as a harvest god for a reason," she pondered aloud. "Our lineage from him was earth magic. Just look at my dad."

"He wasn't just a god of the harvest. He was a powerful warrior, a god of justice. He helped save the Tuatha dé Danann from the unfair reign of Balor. If I had to guess, his bloodline produces warriors who can exact justice at times they're needed. Like Cú Chulainn. And you."

Kate turned her hand over, allowing the lightning to travel over the back of her hand and down her arm. Had Lugh really given her this magic? "Do you think Cú Chulainn had this power, too?"

"Possibly. Maybe that was another reason Nemain was hunting your bloodline. Even though she defeated your great-grandfather, she knew that eventually, another heir would come to rise who had that power, the one that activated the talismans. The only thing that could stop her."

She bit her lip, extinguishing the current that had raced up her arm. "Damn you for making so much sense."

He chuckled, and she joined him with a soft laugh. He felt a slight rush course through him as he realized how genuine the sound was. A minute later, though, she fixed him with a somber stare, reminding him of the task at hand. "So, what are we going to do when we arrive? What's our plan?"

He sighed, shifting on the bed. "I'm not sure, little angel. I suspect we'll have to do a lot of lying, schmoozing, and snooping to find the ammunition we need."

She groaned, pulling at her hair once more. "We're dangerously low on moves."

"Then I suppose we play the only hands we have left."

Chapter Ten

"Get out of your head and into your body." The order carried down the hall as Thad wound through the underground corridors that made up the Den. He paused and cocked his head, recognizing the voice as Briar's, and followed the sound of it.

When he turned the corner to a large room carved out in stone, he decided not to interrupt; instead, he leaned silently against the doorway and observed a young blond boy as he twisted and struck forward with a fist, sending a hanging bag of straw back a few inches. The boy — Brooks, if Thad remembered the young recruit's name correctly — tripped and stumbled, causing Briar to sigh.

"Use your hips to drive up!" she barked, grabbing the straw bag to steady it. The boy adjusted his position, his face pinching as he focused. When he struck this time, it was with renewed vigor.

It always surprised Thad to see children so young with so much to take out on the world. This boy couldn't be any older than fourteen. That being said, one didn't find themselves as part of the Hounds if they spent their formative years in an affluent household with loving parents. Which wasn't to say, he reminded himself, that those things exclusively meant a happy childhood.

Thad's mind wandered to his own younger years, and the time spent with countless other young children of the royal courts. His magic had come to him embarrassingly late, and no matter how much he called out to the elements, none answered. So for many years instead, he'd resorted to learning through books and fists.

Every few months, when they took trips to the human realm, the other children would scramble to wreak havoc with the scraps of magic they had left, leaving him to stand there, quietly observing the way human life carried on without feeling the absence of magic. And while the others begged their parents to teach them enchantments so that they could pull pranks or pilfer things to bring back to their realm, Thad was busy marveling at what humans achieved with only their bare hands and open minds.

When they crossed realms once more, the others cried out with joy to feel the return of their magic. But even years after all of his magic fully flourished, Thad only felt a surprising emptiness, one that wasn't filled by his magic flooding his system once more. It was strange, he mused, how something that gave others here so much privilege gave him nothing but nightmares.

Heavy breathing brought him back to the moment, and he eyed the boy and Briar in front of him.

"Come here," Briar said, ushering him forward. Brooks wiped beads of sweat from his brow and approached, bending at the knees and mimicking her shoulder-width stance. On her first swing, he ducked, and Thad watched as he twisted his foot, clearly intending to come back with an uppercut. In the process of ducking, however, he'd left both hands raised above his head, and Briar capitalized on the error with a swift punch to his gut, now left wide open for the shot.

He doubled over with a short gasp. Thad noted with interest how Briar could have returned an uppercut of her own, but she merely tsked, lowering her fists. "Keep your hands close to your chin, kid, or else you leave your entire body exposed when you duck."

Unable to resist, Thad stepped fully into the room, offering a slow clap. Brooks whirled and looked up, his eyes going wide. It dragged Briar's attention away from her trainee, and she turned to him, immediately averting her gaze.

"Lord Byrne," she said, dropping into a brief bow. "I hadn't realized you'd arrive so soon." She certainly sounded surprised. His interactions with the Hounds were normally private, always ensuring their dirty work could never be traced back to him. Kuiper was the liaison between the Hounds and Thad or Aerrin, taking their requests and doling them out to the group. Briar had never associated with Thad or his brother directly, only seen them in passing within the Den.

"I had some spare time and figured I would use it to check in on my investments," he replied, his gaze tracking the rest of the room for Kuiper. He saw only various instruments used to train the Hounds in strength and agility, crafted from wood and stone, as well as a wall of weaponry. "Where is your leader?"

"I'm not entirely sure. He should be back by now." Briar turned and motioned to Brooks, who took the cue to leave. Once he left, she stalked over to the corner of the room, where she picked up her jacket and her weapon, a chakram. "You're welcome to wait here. I plan to do the same."

Thad nodded but remained standing. Finally, Briar shrugged and sat in a chair across the room, spinning her chakram patiently with both index fingers. The two blades twirled faster and slower, rising and falling in a circular motion. Eventually, Briar sighed and lowered them, reattaching the two blades to one another to complete the full circle. She caught his eye and cocked her head. He averted his gaze, attempting not to show more curiosity than the weapon warranted.

It was, however, a work of art: gold-plated on the inside, while the outer blade portion remained razor-sharp, rarely requiring upkeep. The round weapon served as a great multipurpose blade, good for both throwing and close combat, as it could be used as one large circle or two independent crescent blades.

It was not an item easily found in this realm, so Kuiper had to bring the request to Thad, asking him to acquire the weapon for Briar's eighteenth birthday. Though the normally gruff man would never admit it, it spoke volumes to how attentive he was to his trainee's strengths and weaknesses. While she was quick and strong, great at hand-to-hand combat, she was short, meaning a normal sword would not have the same reach as her opponents. According to Kuiper, she also had relatively terrible aim, so a bow was out of the question. This, though — she didn't need to have stellar aim for it to inflict damage. It just needed to hit. Anywhere it made contact, its sharp, full outer blade would do its job.

Thad heard muffled conversation in the hallway, alerting him to Kuiper's presence. A soft murmur, then a high-pitched feminine giggle and a distinct smack. Briar rolled her eyes and flopped back against the back of the chair as he entered the room, dragging her chakram back out.

Kuiper slowed his pace, gaze flicking between her and Thad. "Can you put your toy away?" he asked, eying her weapon.

She belted the round weapon to her side, giving a pointed look to the door he'd just come through. "Funny, I was about to make the same request."

Thad held back a chuckle, instead clearing his throat. Kuiper gave Briar one last look and strode to Thad, where he ducked his head and crossed his arms behind his back, waiting.

"Have you both had a chance to review the assignment?" Thad asked, and they nodded in tandem. He could tell they had questions burning in the back of their throats, but they wouldn't dare voice them, especially not to Thad directly.

It wasn't on them to ask questions. They followed orders.

"We expect them to arrive tonight, and we aren't sure how long they will stay. You may have a week, or you may have only a day or two. We will try to keep them here as long as possible, but regardless, I'd ensure your plans are made on an expedited schedule. I'll try my best to get you more information tomorrow."

"We'll work on a two-day schedule, if possible." Kuiper replied. "One day to stake, one to strike."

Thad hummed in approval. "Remember. These won't be like your other targets. They have power and wits incomparable to others." He mulled over the stories circulating about Katherine; the way she'd harnessed the skies themselves and used their power to drive home into Nemain. They were already calling her a godslayer. If she found out what they were doing... he suppressed a shiver and refocused himself.

"I've heard the new king has the strongest fire magic his lineage has ever seen," Kuiper said, his face drawn. Thad knew what he was thinking; even with their tricks and physical strength, they often had to rely on the element of surprise when it came to the stronger magic wielders within the city... and drunkards with unpaid tabs didn't hold a candle to the new king, even with his known penchant for liquor.

Thad reached into his jacket pocket, retrieving a small leather pouch. "That brings us to the second reason I stopped by." He undid the knot at the top and emptied out what looked like Faerie dust into his palm, except it was a pale silver, shimmering as though extracted from the stars themselves.

Briar strode forward, her face falling into awe. "It's beautiful," she whispered, reaching a hand out. Before she could touch it, however, Thad pulled his hand back.

"Beautiful, but dangerous." He pocketed the dust, careful to wipe any remaining particles from his open palm. "We call it *buair*. If ingested, it removes your access to magic temporarily, while keeping you awake. It's concentrated, potent stuff — it can last minutes to hours, depending on how much is ingested."

Kuiper and Briar gaped at him as he continued. "The queen had some physical objects left from ages past, suffused with an unknown enchantment that had the same effect. But we all wanted something that could be used at a distance, with the element of surprise. The queen was working with a goddess with the power to remove magic for quite some time, attempting to perfect the union of such power with existing enchantments."

The queen had wanted such a thing to ensure the delineation between royals and the lower Fae remained steadfast, but he didn't voice that part aloud. In his opinion, it wasn't the bloodline that dealt the power. The Hounds were proof enough of that, cutting down rich and poor alike. "We made a breakthrough a few weeks ago, but before we could relay the information to her, she..." He cleared his throat, trailing off. Briar and Kuiper both nodded in understanding.

"Anyways, we had a Ban Sídhe who owed us a sizable favor. She's... gone now, but we were able to generate quite a bit of dust imbued with her magic and the enchantment. We're working on different, more permanent variations, and securing more Ban Sídhe to continue the process."

Thaddeus put the pouch in Kuiper's hands, who held it gingerly. "For now, you both can use this. But be careful and use it sparingly. Blow it directly into their faces. It should incapacitate their magic, allowing you to do the rest."

Kuiper nodded and, with that, Thad gave him a clap on the shoulder and left, his mind racing with everything he had — and hadn't — disclosed. This dust could change the game, not just for them and their line of work, but for everyone. He would be the first to admit he saw magic as more of a burden than anything, but even he couldn't help but wonder if this was too dangerous a thing to bring into their world.

Chapter Eleven

Our sleep on the ship, though restless, was still better than we'd had in a week, easily. We were a tangle of limbs, escaping the chill in the air beneath the covers and with more than a little aid of Finlay's fire magic.

Early in the morning, a soft knock came at our door, rousing Finlay from his sleep. He gave me a groggy kiss and slipped away. I tried for several long minutes to chase down the tendrils of sleep, command myself back into their enticing embrace. However, something nagged at me, unrelenting until I rose. I draped a warm, wool tartan blanket over my shoulders and stepped out of the room, making my way to the deck.

I stood for several long moments in silence, letting the cool breeze redden my cheeks and fill my nose with the scent of saltwater. The deck was empty, telling me Finlay had likely been summoned to the opposite side of the ship, and the water was illuminated by the faintest strip of orange, indicating the beginnings of dawn. The waves rose and fell in a consistent, peaceful rhythm.

Until they didn't.

I stood straighter as a wave remained high after cresting, eyes pinned on the unusual movement. It was high enough to knock the ship, but it didn't roll forward; instead, the water collapsed straight back down into the ocean. As the water fell away, a dark shape emerged from the abyss, rising above the swell of the ocean and far above the deck of the ship. I gasped and stumbled back, taking in the impressive sight.

It was a scaled creature, shimmering a navy blue only slightly lighter than the water itself. It was long and rounded like a spire, except where its head stood tall above the rest of its body. There, a set of slitted, serpentlike glowing eyes stared down at me where I stood at the edge of the ship.

Any other person may have cowed at the sheer size of the beast and the clear threat it exuded. But I recognized those eyes immediately.

"Grom!" I exclaimed, gripping the railing with nervous excitement. "How are you here?"

The beithir lowered its head to see me clearly, its two horns coming into view as its neck-frill extended, ruffling as it assessed me. A sound rumbled deep in its chest in a way that could appear fearsome, but was clearly a sound of pleasant recognition. I couldn't help but grin.

Katherine. You remember me.

It spoke directly into my mind, like it had during our first meeting. Its voice was exactly how I remembered it, deep and grating, like stone grinding on stone. It held a slight tone of surprise, which made my lips curl further in amusement.

"Of course I do. I don't make a habit of meeting many ancient Celtic beasts." Grom rumbled again, the sound deep in his chest, and I tilted my head curiously. "How did you find me, though?"

Like calls to like. When I sensed your presence in my waters, I had to venture out to find you.

Right — though Grom resembled a dragon in some ways, he had no wings; rather, he made his home in the deep blue abyss. The last time we'd crossed paths, it had been in a cave carved out by water, where he had been guarding Dagda's cauldron. Memories surged in my mind, and I recalled the last conversation we had.

"You once said I was similar to you," I began, the pieces falling together in my mind as I took in his eyes, glowing like golden embers against the dark backdrop. I twisted my hands, allowing the cap I had learned to keep on my new powers to release. The air around us crackled, and within an instant, lightning danced across my palms, darting from one hand to the other.

Grom arched his head higher, nostrils flaring as he took in my magic. *And that you are, descendent of Cú Chulainn. Our magic is the rarest — far rarer than the main elements; rarer still than healing. I am glad to see it remains strong in your bloodline.*

"Our magic?" I echoed, turning his words over in my head. The way he spoke told me Finlay's hunch may very well be correct – Cú Chulainn had harnessed this power before me, and likely Lugh before him. But Grom spoke as though he had this power, too.

My lips parted in surprise as the air grew heavy with an electric surge far greater than my own. The current between my hands began to stretch out, as though it wished to split off toward Grom. When I followed the line it traveled, I saw a bright glow beginning under Grom's scales, peeking out like a light beneath a closed door. Clouds raced across the sky, darkening and growing heavy with the threat of rain.

Finally, Grom opened his mouth, and an orb of light encompassed his throat, shining bright against his scales with an almost white-gold hue. I squinted, readying myself to throw an arm over my face and lift an air shield, though I wasn't sure what it would do against such power. He didn't release it, however. Instead, he seemed to swallow it down, and though a light drizzle had begun, the crackle within the air subsided, the only trace of it having appeared in the first place lingering in the metallic taste left on my tongue.

Our magic is a rare form of energy. This energy is one most will never have the privilege of harnessing. Some run from storms as they brew, but we are made from them. We weather them, conquer them, and wield them. We are formed from the harshest conditions, you and I. And now, we are the storm.

A pleasant warmth spread through me as I took in his words, calming the turmoil that curled in the pit of my gut. I was forged from the tempest, and in turn, I became it. Exactly what I was meant to be.

Even as I mulled that over, though, I recalled something Grom had said when he'd mentioned our similarities during our first meeting. He'd said the phrase *they failed to mention we were similar*, as though he'd had a conversation about me with others before he and I had even met. Others who had, shortly after, captured me.

They had failed to mention we were similar. *They* meaning...

"You knew," I hissed, dousing my lightning abruptly. "You knew Nemain was planning a trap for us with Soren, Aerrin, and Thad. And you still let us walk right into it. Let *me* walk right into it."

Grom reared back as though I'd struck him, the black slits of his eyes narrowing slightly. A flash of cold fear coursed through me as I realized that it was likely a poor choice to go toe-to-toe with a storm dragon, and I took a step back. But he ended up only lowering his head, as though hanging it in defeat.

I am aware. And this is part of the reason I rushed to discover if it was truly you. I am glad to see that you escaped. You've come into your power and remained whole.

"Not entirely," I replied bitterly. My hand brushed over my collarbone, envisioning the raised, white scars that lay below my clothing, indicating the marred remains of the marks that had protected and controlled me over the past year. Grom's long whiskers trembled as his eyes followed the movement, as though sensing what lay beneath my fingers.

It is not an excuse, but our kind is very rare. I have family, family that the Byrne heirs captured long ago. Nemain knew this, and had promised to free them in exchange for my compliance in her deeds. I see now that my trust was misplaced. For that, I apologize.

I was silent for a long moment as I considered his words, bristling slightly at the mention of Aerrin and Thad. How was it that they seemed to have their hands in everything?

It would be easy to take the route of harboring blame, of wishing that the right thing was done from the beginning, all the time. But that wasn't the way life went. We start life with our canvas only in black and white. And then shades of gray begin to blend in, as we realize the different paths life can take, the effects each decision we make has on one another. Hell, I was just coming off my own desperate plea to Arawn to bring my family back, willing to sacrifice whatever was needed. I couldn't begrudge Grom's attempts at the same.

Everyone had something they could atone for, if they searched their decisions hard enough — including myself. Though I still believed I had done the right thing, leading our soldiers into battle to fight against Nemain, there were those out there who blamed me. I thought back to Blaise's sister, glaring daggers at me as she cursed me for ending his life, and bit my lip. For all intents and purposes, I was still here, and whole. Even as Grom apologized for the part he played in that journey.

I extended a hand, palm facing up in a sign of camaraderie, feeling a bit foolish even as I did so. "There is nothing to apologize for. Nemain is gone, and I'm happy to take over her promise, with no strings attached."

The beithir went still as he took in my words. *You would do this for me?*

"Absolutely." My voice was firm. "I have seen the injustice our kind likes to impart on those they don't understand. And as luck would have it, we are headed to Reviere to meet Lachlan's sons now. We have our own scores to settle with them."

Grom's nostrils flared as he let out a surprised breath. *I am forever grateful for your forgiveness, Katherine. If you are ever in need of me again, use our magic to summon me. I will come to your aid.*

With that, he pushed his nose gently against the palm of my hand, and I gasped at the electric connection. It was a jarring feeling; the sense of something so large and powerful resting beneath the palm of my hand. It was an act of trust — a promise I vowed to make good on. A pact between storms.

I dropped my hand only when I heard the sounds of the crew waking up; the crash of a pot on the ground and a few scattered curses. By the time I looked back, Grom was gone, again a silent figure beneath the surface of the sea.

CHAPTER TWELVE

"Once more, so we're clear: Cas is our court healer and temporary attendant, Kipp is a bodyguard, and Wren is my lady-in-waiting. This way we have someone we trust at our side at all times—" I gave Kipp an affectionate smile. "—and two people whose comings and goings won't seem suspicious, even though you'll be doing recon for us."

Everyone nodded in agreement, shifting impatiently. Though the trip across the ocean had only lasted a few days, clearly everyone was feeling cooped up and ready to be on dry land. "We'll try to be in and out as quickly as possible, but anything you can discover while we're here will be of vital importance," Finlay added. "We need you as our eyes and ears while we're in meetings."

I felt a twinge in my gut, reminding me that this was very likely more than just a quick political meeting. We were entering their domain, a new court of whispers and deceit that I'd never faced before. I glanced over at Finlay, who gave me a firm, comforting smile, though whether it was for my benefit or his own, I wasn't sure. Either way, as the land appeared, I felt my heart rate began to slow.

Reviere was a mountain of concrete, rising up in thick pillars of various heights, but all roughly the same tawny color. In the middle of the vast expanse of buildings perched one spire, twisting elegantly and taller than the rest. It was a deep blue, with smaller spires on either side, signaling it as the palace where the Byrne brothers resided. Whereas the castle Lachlan favored in Daersill had a soothing, warm atmosphere, as if the late duke strove to make it welcoming, this palace was imposing, its statement purely one of grandeur. It was beautiful, yes, but it certainly was not inviting.

Despite the height and modernity of the buildings, they were all surrounded by a maze of canals, the chosen pathways of the Revierans. As we grew closer, I began to see tiny beads of movement, people bustling on with their days across bridges and on or off of narrowboats. A handful of people stood at the edge of the mooring as we pulled up; none, I noticed, were the Byrne brothers.

"Welcome, Your Majesties." A small, polite Faerie greeted us — an Asrai, I presumed, from the way her hands moved as she spoke, guiding the current to moor us safely. Her hair was blonde and straight, dotted with braids that held a myriad of charms. She wore a simple blue tunic, but the belt that fastened it was sprinkled with small orange jewels. "We've been expecting you. Please, come."

I thanked her but didn't move until I was sure the rest of our crew was alongside me. We disembarked the large sea-faring boat only to step onto a smaller narrowboat, which took us along the canals toward the palace. I sat next to the Asrai, my mind racing with questions for the first Fae I'd met here in Reviere.

"May I ask your name?" I questioned.

"Maia, Your Majesty."

My mouth twitched at the term, but I refrained from correcting her. "Maia. And have you lived here long?"

"All my life, Your Majesty."

I bit back a groan of frustration. All of this 'your majesty' talk was already getting old. Finlay cast me a knowing smirk, and I looked away to avoid rolling my eyes at him. "And how do you find it?"

"I quite enjoy my life here. Though I do wish to see more of the world someday." She spoke easily, conversationally, and I realized that this was likely her only job — to ferry people to and from the palace. She flicked her wrists, sending a gentle wave behind the narrowboat to usher us along.

As we pulled up alongside the palace, I pulled a few coins out of my purse and handed them to her. "If you ever do decide to see more of the world, please be sure to visit Sairas. I'll make sure you're well taken care of."

Her face flushed as she gazed down at the coins, and when she glanced back up at me, her eyes shone. "I'll be sure to, Your Majesty," she answered breathlessly. I smiled and waved as we stepped off the boat, but was quickly pulled into a familiar embrace.

"You realize your tip was approximately seven boat rides' worth, yes?" Finlay murmured in my ear.

I let out a soft chuckle and leaned against his warm chest. "And?"

"And. Have I told you lately how much you delight me?"

"I assume you'll keep saying so until I bankrupt us."

He chuckled, his warm breath fanning across my cheek. "Then we'll all shack up in Cas's house. One big happy family."

"Ahem. I don't believe I approved that," Cas called out from beside us, and we separated with a laugh. The jovial attitude subsided, however, as we were ushered into the palace by a far colder attendant.

Whereas the palace in Sairas flaunted its opulence, bordering on gaudy, and Lachlan's castle in Daersill radiated warmth, this palace sat somewhere in between. It had touches of warmth that reminded me fondly of the old duke: the wooden accents in the hallways, the large windows that allowed light to spill inside, and the lit fireplaces that chased the bite of the cool, early spring air away. But upon every table sat ornate, gilded statues of various animals and figures — I assumed, famous gods and goddesses in the Byrne lineage — and portraits of Lachlan and his sons hung on nearly every wall. It was curious to see that even individual portraits of the late duke still remained — though, I supposed bitterly, they had to maintain some kind of semblance of grieving.

As we set our luggage down beside our bed, Finlay called out to the attendant just outside the bedchamber door. The attendant popped inside almost immediately. "Yes, Your Majesty?"

"When can we expect to meet with Lords Aerrin and Thaddeus?"

The attendant looked startled, which was, I noted with satisfaction, the first real emotion he'd shown since guiding us to our rooms. It took him a moment to respond. "I have no set time to give you, Your Majesty."

"Would you mind setting one, now that we're here?" Finlay clasped his hands together in front of him expectantly.

The attendant fidgeted, his face blanching slightly. "We were told to wait until the Lords came to us with a time, Your Majesty."

Finlay sighed. "Please relay to the Lords that we look forward to discussing matters promptly tomorrow. We look forward to having a set time before we break fast."

"Y-yes, Your Majesty," the attendant stammered, and slipped out of the room.

I turned to face Finlay with a smirk. "That was pretty hot. Though I think you made him piss his pants."

"I was very nice!" he retorted defensively, and I laughed, winding my arms around him.

"I didn't say you weren't. I think it's just who you are. You give off this... *aura.*"

"Do I, now?" He nuzzled into the side of my neck, pressing his warm lips against my throat. "I get the feeling you like my *aura.*"

I sighed. "I do. I like it a lot."

"Good." His hands wound their way down to my waist, tugging me closer to him. "I'd enjoy seeing where all this *liking* gets me."

"Close the door," I whispered, and he smirked, grazing his teeth against my skin.

"Why? Perhaps we should let the citizens know what their future queen sounds like when she's screaming out in the throes of pleasure."

I inhaled sharply, my breath stuttering at his words and the way his fingers trailed suggestively up my thigh. *"Finlay."*

With a groan of complaint, he removed the hand from my thigh and flicked it toward the door. A large gust of wind sent the door slamming, along with several decorative vases and figurines that went flying off the dresser, shattering across the floor. I gasped and pulled back, fixing him with an accusatory glare.

"What?" His face remained impassive. "The door closed, didn't it? Does the collateral damage matter?"

I closed my eyes and laughed. "Okay. Point taken."

"Good," he growled, shoving my dress up as he lowered to his knees, the urgency of his movements drawing a shaky gasp from me. He pulled my panties down in one swift movement, tossing them to the side. "Because I still plan on making you scream."

He ran his hands up my thighs, then pushed gently to guide me back to the bed. As soon as the backs of my knees connected with the bed, I lowered myself onto the sheets, and he spread my legs. I shivered, though not from the cold air — no. It was from the intensity of his gaze, those icy blue eyes that set my body on fire.

"Touch me," I whimpered, and watched as his soft smile turned into a devilish smirk.

He rubbed his face against the inside of my thigh, letting the soft stubble of his chin graze me. "Here, little angel?"

I let out a small sound of frustration, and he chuckled. "Oh, no. You mean *here.*" Immediately, the warm, flat pad of his tongue was on me, and a soft cry slipped past my lips. Every nerve ending in my body seemed to shoot straight to my core, coiling and burning with need.

Finlay hummed against me, causing my back to arch slightly. "Not quite loud enough," he murmured, his voice husky, and before I knew it, he was swirling his tongue around my bud before sucking it into his mouth. My thighs pressed against the side of his head in response.

"Oh, gods," I moaned, as his tongue made a sweeping pass, thrusting inside of me. I gripped at the bedsheets but didn't find the traction I needed. I needed something to keep me grounded, lest I float away on this tide of bliss.

"More, little angel," he murmured, and slipped his fingers inside me while he sucked and flicked, creating a rhythm that increased in pace. I floated higher and higher until I reached an edge, and then — another expert flick, and I promptly fell straight off.

Before I knew it, I was loudly crying out a series of garbled words that included his name and a lot of "oh's" and "god's". It seemed to last longer than should be possible, but he rode it out as I rode his face, stealing each wave of pleasure as it arrived.

Eventually, I came back to the present moment, where I saw Finlay, still on his knees, with his hands on both of my thighs.

"I told you we could let all the citizens know you'd finally... come." He grinned triumphantly at me, and I groaned in response.

"You're lucky I'm too blissed out to mention how awful that joke was."

"And yet, somehow, you still did."

I snorted, but raised an expectant eyebrow at him. "Does this mean we're finished for the night?"

He winked. "Seeing as we have no plans yet tomorrow, I'd say we're just getting started."

Chapter Thirteen

Finlay strode into the meeting room with Kate at his side, taking note of the small audience the lords had brought with them. Whereas only Kipp was entering the room with Kate and him, there were several other Fae in the room with Aerrin and Thad. All were dressed impeccably, not a hair out of place or a speck of dirt on their clothing. They stood out of deference, murmuring, "Your Majesties." Their accents and clothing style told him they were from various surrounding lands and not, in fact, part of the brothers' immediate entourage. The sight of them — along with the knowing gleam in Aerrin's eye — had Finlay instantly on edge.

As they all sat, Finlay cleared his throat. "I was under the impression we were here to discuss marital matters."

"Ah, yes, my apologies, Your Majesty. On behalf of my *council*, we congratulate you on your engagement," Aerrin replied, leaning back in his chair and steepling his fingers.

Finlay paused, exchanging a look with Kate. They'd already been congratulated, and Sairas had its own council, with which to discuss manners with residents of each land. All laws — civil and criminal — were enforced by them. Was he to understand the brothers would disregard the royal council of Muiranvia in favor of holding their own here?

"Now that you're here," Thad drawled, "the council is dying to discuss things with you."

"If I had known such things were being discussed, I would have brought my cousin instead," Finlay put in drily, hoping the brothers would take the hint.

"We understand you're *quite* familiar with Darrya, yes?" Kate's question was polite but direct as she shot it at Aerrin, with an undercurrent of bite. It had the forwardness Finlay lacked, and he appreciated it.

Aerrin simply grinned, a snake raising its head to line itself up with its prey. "Indeed. However, the pressing matters to bring to you are not my own. They are matters of our people. Concerns that have thus far fallen on deaf ears when discussed with the late queen."

"May she rest in peace," came a soft echo, one that Finlay echoed automatically.

Shit.

Finlay wanted to discuss his cousin here, and discuss other royal decrees with his own council, but the brothers had knowingly put him in a position to reassess things the queen had already given voice to. If he refused, it would be an offense to these representatives of the lands, and proof that he would not bring a fresh perspective to his great-grandmother's issues — something he couldn't stomach. If he accepted, they would likely avoid the issue he'd set out to fix, and moreover… he faced the danger of being proven incompetent. Though Finlay knew all his training left him knowledgeable enough to hold a discussion on political matters, he was mere days into his own rule. He would prefer to rely heavily on the input of his own chosen council as he learned the ropes — one he knew carried boundless knowledge, empathy, and most importantly, his trust.

"Kuiper Slane, Your Majesty," a man with long, dark hair and equally dark eyes introduced himself. Finlay nodded at him, and the man continued. "There is mounting riffraff in the streets. Word is that Kaverí is disappointed that their demands for lower taxes have not been met. Businesses continue to hike the prices for their wares as a countermeasure, and yet wages remain the same. Living conditions are worsening."

"I appreciate you bringing this to my attention, Kuiper," Finlay began slowly, his wheels turning as he processed. "I'll be sure to re-assess the tax regulations and organize a visit to Kaverí at my soonest availability. I should like to see the living conditions for myself."

The man blinked at him in surprise, then nodded. Another man, stout and red-faced, stepped forward. "Norman Kerry, Your Majesty. We need more Faerie dust, and it must become more easily accessible. The people need to be connected."

"To my understanding, it is a limited resource, even among the royals. The expense for that would surely be outrageous," Kate pointed out, surprising Finlay with the unshakeable confidence in her tone. "We would need to raise the taxes to fund such endeavors, not lower them." Finlay felt his heart swell with pride at her instant grasp of the situation and utter fearlessness at voicing her opinion.

Though several councilmembers glanced at her with distaste, Aerrin and Thad regarded her with newfound curiosity.

"Is she... is she allowed to voice her opinions here?" Norman whispered, flicking his eyes to the brothers for confirmation.

"Yes. Irrefutably," Finlay snapped, leveling the man with a glare. He murmured an apology, and a soft snort escaped Kuiper, who gave Finlay a look of what seemed like appreciation. Another man cleared his throat.

"Niall Brennan, Your Majesty. If I may — the population of underprivileged citizens in Reviere is growing. Their wealth is declining, more and more are going without homes, and substance abuse is rife. How do you propose to combat this?"

Finlay opened his mouth, ready to volley a suggestion of raising taxes on such substances, but was cut off by another question.

Around and around they went, until Finlay was certain hours had passed and it felt like nothing had come of the meeting. Every concern raised felt like the opposite of another, wherein the solutions would surely cancel each other out. At some point, Kipp settled into a chair, writing down concerns to ensure they'd be addressed later. When the light outside began to dim and voices grew hoarse, Finlay began suspecting that the circles they spoke in were intentional. Even the council members seemed to be in on the ruse — though the purpose of that ruse, he couldn't be sure of.

Eventually, Aerrin yawned and stretched. "Well. We've been on this since lunch, and I presume we are well past dinner time. I suppose it may be time to retire the discussions for now."

The others murmured their assent, but internally, Finlay fumed. As the others bowed and removed themselves, he coughed pointedly. "Aerrin. Thaddeus."

The brothers paused, both sets of sapphire eyes swiveling toward him, and he continued. "Katherine and I would like to have a word with you. In private."

Aerrin and Thad exchanged glances, and Thad spoke. "It is late, and we still have preparations to make for Imbolc. Any conversations you'd like to have need not be rushed. Surely you'll want to get some dinner, perhaps see what our lovely city has to offer?"

For a moment, no one spoke. Kate's body stiffened, and she shot him a sidelong glance. Finlay had nearly forgotten about Imbolc — the Awakening Festival, which landed on the first of February. It was about a week away, now. He knew better than to tell them to push off preparations, as to do so would be seen as an affront to the goddess Brigid — a triple goddess they celebrated every spring as the symbol of new life. He shivered, his body rejecting the thought of another triple goddess, even one known for her benevolence and vitality. He chewed on the inside of his lip, thinking of a different approach. Clearly, they were putting off the meeting to discuss Darrya and her marriage with Aerrin. But why?

"Give us a specific time tomorrow, then, and we will make it a priority," Kate said. "Preferably early."

Thad glanced at Aerrin, who smirked, never taking his eyes off Kate. Finlay felt his internal fire flare, rising just below the surface of his skin. He was certain if someone touched him, they would burn. Before he could say anything untoward, however, Aerrin simply replied, "Eleven, then. Tomorrow morning. In this same room."

Kate nodded, and Finlay forcibly tampered down his flame, following her lead with a nod of his own. The brothers made to exit, but Thad turned around with one final farewell. "I hope you both enjoy your night."

Neither of them replied, and Finlay noted that while the words contained well wishes, his tone managed to sound exactly the opposite.

CHAPTER FOURTEEN

Wren smoothed her dress down and frowned at the restrictive sleeves. She wasn't sure how Darrya did it, keeping her strong sense of self while molding easily into royal decorum when needed. Wren could handle herself in conversations with royals — it was often required of her, when she took in or prepped royals' horses in the stable — but she never had to dress the part. Much to her brother's chagrin, she prided herself on her smart and practical wardrobe choices. If she found a comfortable woolen dress that covered her fully, but allowed unrestricted movement in her arms and legs, she would get it in three different colors and style it with her own earth magic. She'd had many a conversation with her brother about sprucing up her attire, mostly starting with him using words like "prudish" and "spinster" and ending with her reminding him that the only creatures who would see her bare skin were furry and four-legged.

Thinking back, she realized her side of the argument was a bit presumptuous. She imagined Cas and Kipp together, the way he would ruffle Kipp's fuzzy ears whenever the latter was in his wolf form, and smirked to herself. It was a wonder she didn't see the affection between the two decades ago; something that was just a bit... more than friendship, something that ran far deeper than any of Cas's myriad conquests throughout the ages. Wren didn't need that. She'd seen the emptiness in Cas any time a visitor left, a hollowness that was briefly filled, but would be empty once more by the following day. A warmth spread through Wren as she pictured him now, with Kipp. Her brother was still his witty, reckless self, but all signs of hollowness were gone. Now that — that was something Wren would hold out for.

She smiled again and glanced down, then raised an eyebrow at the way her modest chest was pushed up and in. The fabric tightly shaped her breasts to a height they'd never reached before. Two things to amend the next time she spoke with Cas, then, because there was something to be said for corsets. But seeing as her goal as a faux-lady-in-waiting was to not attract attention, this new attire was entirely disruptive.

She picked up the long skirts in her hands, trying her best to move silently as she navigated the palace halls. Finlay had given her a map of the palace, marked with educated guesses on locations where important paperwork could be found. She had slid into one room already — the one Finlay had marked as Aerrin's study — but after rifling quickly through every drawer, she'd realized they were only trade agreements. The room had a dark, uninviting feel to it, but it was sparkling. There wasn't a speck of dust to be found or a paper out of place, as though the room had recently been cleaned and cleared of anything potentially damning. Wren had a sinking suspicion that their presence here would make the brothers keep any paperwork on Darrya's marriage a little closer at hand; perhaps even in one of the brothers' personal bedchambers. And if that was the case... they were screwed.

She shook her head, dispelling the negative train of thought. Her footsteps stilled outside a large wooden door, the one Finlay had noted as Thad's study. She glanced around, assuring herself she was the only one awake at this early hour. The sun was just emerging above the horizon, and the only people awake were the early morning palace workers, likely prepping breakfast or royal wardrobes.

Think positive, Wren, she chastised herself. She'd trained with the best warriors, she'd helped Kate trap dark Faeries, she'd looked after a legendary war horse, and she'd even fought in the battle that ended Nemain's attempted tyranny. She could do a little snooping, and she would succeed. She blinked, refocusing on the task at hand.

Thad's office had a surprisingly warm atmosphere to it in comparison to Aerrin's, with a large window left open to allow the fresh, outdoor air to waft in. The walls were stacked high with books, and there was a large wooden desk in the middle of the room, littered with papers. The smell of spring was on the horizon, and Wren paused by the window to inhale deeply, closing her eyes and savoring the scent. On the surface, spring simply smelled like mud; melted snow giving way to large expanses of dirt. But under the surface, it held the scent of rainy afternoons, time spent gardening, the first whiff of snowdrops blooming.

Wren opened her eyes and scanned the room, her gaze drawing first to the papers on the desk. She pushed the chair to the side and ran her fingers over the papers. The first few on the top were half-hearted letters to people Wren had never heard of, stopped after the first sentence or two. His handwriting was small and precise, exactly how she imagined someone as tightly wound as a Byrne brother would be. Not a single ink smudge or erratically swooping line to be found. She pushed the letters to the side and stopped as the papers underneath were uncovered.

They weren't letters, but *drawings.* The first was an incredibly detailed, vivid drawing of a creature she had never seen before, but the intricate lines and shading made it appear real. It was hawklike, with broad wings spread wide, claws extended to reach its prey. It had horns rising from its head, and even the emotion in the creature's face was visceral, boasting a fierce, feral joy at its impending meal. She moved the drawing to the side to reveal another one, this one of a familiar creature, though still one that she'd only ever heard of in books. It was foxlike, with an adorable, mischievous face, half covered by one of its many fluffy tails. A kitsune — a trickster creature of lore. Why did Thaddeus keep drawings of mythical creatures? Had he drawn them himself? She ran a finger over the drawing thoughtfully, feeling the indentations with each stroke.

"Enjoying yourself?"

Wren jolted back from the desk, nearly tripping on her long skirts. Thaddeus stood in the doorway, his face neutral as he assessed her.

"You're Her Majesty's lady-in-waiting." Thaddeus tilted his head, piercing eyes narrowing. "Care to explain what you're doing in my study?" The last two words were spoken with carefully bottled fury, and Wren swallowed hard. His eyes tracked the movement at her throat and narrowed further. He knew she was panicking. Shit.

"I... I got lost." Her mind raced, thinking of the nearest room that would make sense for her to be in. "I was attempting to find the library, to find a few books Her Majesty requested."

"And you thought a small space with two bookshelves must be the best the Reviere palace could offer by way of literature," he deadpanned. His lips curled into a wry smile, but it didn't reach his eyes, which were still darkly narrowed.

Gods, he was toying with her, like a predator circling its terrified prey. She opened her mouth to answer, but Thaddeus held up a hand.

"Wait." He studied her. "I've seen you before. Before you came here as a lady-in-waiting."

Her heart hammered in her chest. "I'm sorry?"

"You're the stablehand in Sairas." He took a few steps closer, and Wren fought the urge to step back, to keep the protective space between the two of them. How did he remember her, a lowly stablehand? She remembered him, of course — always dressed in black, always requesting one of their largest and wildest mounts. And yet, every time, he also requested treats to feed them. He soon had them eating out of his hand, literally and figuratively. Almost as though... he cared for them.

Stop. She shook her head, reminding herself of what he and his brother had done to Darrya. She eyed him warily as he stopped at the desk, long fingers tapping on it as he gazed at her. His expression was carefully arranged in a look of mild curiosity. "How did you become Her Majesty's lady-in-waiting? A promotion many would dream of, I'm sure."

Wren took a deep breath to steady herself, cursing the tightness of the corset at this moment. Her chest strained against the material as she inhaled, as though her anxious energy was bound tightly against her body with it. She didn't miss the way Thaddeus's eyes flicked briefly down, then back up to her face. Her cheeks flamed, and she stuttered, "I — I still am. A stablehand, that is. Her Majesty saw the close bond I formed with her steed, and we formed one too, as a result. She trusts me with his life, and hers."

"That's right," Thaddeus mused. "Liath of Macha. The war-horse." He gave Wren a look that seemed borderline intrigued, and the attention made her flush hot once more. Then his gaze floated down to the desk, where his drawings were exposed. Surprise flickered across his face quickly before his lips pressed into a thin line, features stilling. Wren sucked in a breath, realizing instantly that the drawings weren't meant to be seen by other people. And Thaddeus didn't seem the type to show mercy to those who stumbled across his private things.

"These are really good," she said in a soft voice, hoping the compliment would divert any anger. "Did you draw that Kitsune, or did you have it commissioned by someone?"

He raised a brow. "You know what that is?"

"Of course," she replied, a small smile tugging at the corners of her lips. "I love learning about mythical creatures. Though I wasn't sure about this one, honestly." She pointed to the birdlike drawing, and Thaddeus hummed absentmindedly.

"That's a turul."

"A turul." Wren tested the word out, rolling the name across her tongue. "And what does legend state about this creature?"

Thaddeus shot an assessing look her way, "It's a protector. It's meant to guard pregnant women and fend off demons from them during childbirth. And then protect the infants."

"That's... amazing," Wren breathed, observing the drawing in a new light. She'd spent hours devouring legends, myths, and general knowledge on magical creatures, but that understanding only brought her so far. Many of those books also didn't have drawings, and those that did couldn't compare to the beauty of the ones in this office. "And you drew these?"

Thaddeus simply nodded, refusing to meet her gaze.

"What made you become interested in these creatures?" She wasn't sure why she asked, or why she wanted to know, precisely. But she saw the second she asked the question that she'd gone too far.

His posture stiffened, and he turned away from her and the drawings. He cleared his throat, roughly, and the sound felt like a dismissal. Still, she waited to see if he would answer the question, one that seemed harmless but had clearly struck a nerve.

Instead, he ran his hands through his dark hair, then pointed, his body only halfway turning back to her. "The library is down the hallway, take a left. First door on your right." When she didn't move, he added, firmly, "Best be going. Wouldn't want to keep Her Majesty waiting."

Wren's heart sank. Well. That was as clear of a dismissal as any. She picked up her skirts and attempted to keep her chin high as she strode past him, refusing to give him the satisfaction of glancing his way, even as the thought of catching his eye a mere hair's breadth from his face did something funny to her insides.

She pursed her lips as she exited the room, and strode to the end of the hall before pausing to catch her breath. Why had that interaction felt so terrifying, yet so exhilarating? Why did she want to go back and demand that he tell her more, and show her more? Why did his gaze on her affect her so? She shook her head, dismissing those thoughts. She should be more worried about what the others would say when they learned she'd been caught.

She bit her lip, leaned back against the wall, and tried to remind herself that, for all intents and purposes, what had transpired in Thad's study was a good thing. She had been caught, but let go. The curious questions it brought forth about him didn't matter — she was here to find out about Darrya. The only useful questions to ask Lachlan's sons were ones that pertained to Darrya. Drawings of creatures certainly didn't count.

Stop being silly, Wren. Finally, she took a deep but useless inhale, and turned in the opposite direction of the library to go find Cas. She would continue her search as soon as possible, but first — she needed to get out of this gods-damned corset.

Chapter Fifteen

Thad gazed down at his drawings, wondering at the odd cocktail of emotions the little stablehand had brought forth in him — fear, intrigue, attraction, and a strange sense of peace. He wasn't sure why he hadn't immediately kicked her out of his study. Clearly, she'd been snooping, and he suspected she was friends with more than just Kate. She was likely friends with Darrya as well, and hunting for the paperwork that Aerrin had leveraged to his advantage. Thad had to begrudgingly admire the lengths these friends would go to for each other.

What confused him far more, however, was how he'd confessed private things to her. It was nothing damning for the plot he and his brother had laid out, but those letters and drawings had still been personal for him. He supposed he could blame it on her captivating appearance: the way her chest had risen and fallen as she'd inhaled the fresh air by the window, unaware of his presence, those doe-like, chocolate-brown eyes, widening as she realized she'd been caught. The victorious rush he'd felt when his attention had brought a rosy flush to her neck and cheeks. It had been years since those kinds of feelings had stirred in him so prominently; not since—

He careened rapidly away from that line of thought. She was just his type, was all, he told himself. And, he had to admit, it had been interesting to speak with someone who understood mythical creatures. That had been unexpected. Most only had a passing fancy in the more common creatures, and their eyes glazed over the moment he ventured into more complex territory. And in a world where his brother planned nearly every step for the both of them, the unexpected had been unexpectedly... nice. Refreshing.

Gods damn it. He hated that he wanted to speak more with her.

He shook his head and stalked out of his office, being sure to lock the room behind him this time. He could have headed back to his chambers for breakfast and to relax the remainder of the day, but what he'd told Finlay and Kate had been somewhat truthful; they *did* have Imbolc preparations to make. And it was the first festival they were hosting without their father. His heart twinged once more at the thought, and he let his feet take him to the Grand room, attempting to think of anything else as he did so.

The festival was in just a few days' time, and as he entered the space, he saw the staff had already begun setting up the room. The overpowering scent of flowers assaulted his nose as staff packed bouquets full of early spring flowers — deep orange pansies and blue clusters of grape hyacinths, effectively signifying Reviere's main colors, as well as bright yellow wood poppies, a quintessential spring color. It didn't matter that it was still a bit early for most of the blooms; earth magic and a little extra love brought them forth as a hopeful sign that something beautiful was afoot in the ground, and all should beckon it forth with the celebration of Imbolc. A large, dark blue rug had been rolled out across the floor, and large banquet tables were being set up over it. Small, rounded windows near the ceiling let in pockets of sunshine, setting the crystal of the various chandeliers aglow with light that fractioned out across the space.

As the staff saw him enter, they ducked into bows and murmured their greetings. He approached the one barking orders, an older lady with curled, auburn hair, the beginnings of gray dusting their way through it. She commanded the room with her presence alone, and none of the staff dared defy her. Though she was technically the head of the female staff, she wore many hats, and did so with pleasure. She had made things run smoothly here for decades. She and Thad were technically, distantly related — a cousin of a second cousin, of some sort — and she had had a large hand in their upbringing.

He stopped in front of her. She eyed him reproachfully and chose not to bow, which only made him smirk inwardly. Stubborn old broad. "How are things, Edith?"

"Excellent, just excellent." She surveyed the room with a sharp eye, one that he remembered cringing away from as a young boy. Luckily, his brother had often been the object of her ire, so he had avoided the direct tongue-lashings. He suspected this was at least half the reason Aerrin had asked him to check on Imbolc proceedings instead of him.

"I heard we've been having some trouble with the organ. Everything fixed there?"

"Ach, yes." She waved a dismissive hand, still surveying the workers. "Just had to burn off the metallic hairs. All set now."

"Good, good," Thad mused, pretending he knew anything about such things. "And the straw to build the crosses? Is it prepared?"

"Boiled and ready to go." She paused, eyes snapping over to someone. "Arlynn! Ye'd better be leaving a spot for Brigid at the table, ye hear?!"

The staff member in question flushed and began rapidly reworking the table placement, leaving symbolic space for the stunning red-haired goddess, who was said to return in her maiden form during the celebration. Thad winced on Arlynn's behalf.

"And you have everything else you need? The candles, the water bowls, the brat Bhríde?"

Brigid's cloak — or rather, the representation of it — was a vital part, meant to be laid out the eve of Imbolc, before sunset, and brought back inside before sunrise. It was said to be imbued with healing powers that would remain for the rest of the year, until the next Imbolc, and it would be given to sick patients residing within the palace. Cloaks would be seen outside every doorstep that night, families desperate for a bit of extra luck to remain healthy for the year ahead.

"Do ye doubt me, little duke?" she scoffed, but then her eyes turned soft. "I am sorry this will be yer first Imbolc without him. But we will have a fine festival in his honor. I promise ye."

Thad's smirk faltered, that painful twinge returning. A memory of his father's joyful laugh flooded him, alongside a painful torrent of emotion. He rubbed at his chest, the anguish so strong it bordered on physicality. "Thank you, Edith. You are a dear." He paused. "I do have one more question, though. What's on the menu for the fire feast?"

"Ach, I'm dear nothing," she grumped, swatting at him. "But yer usual — spiced wine, potato soup, roasted carrots, bread and honey."

"Rice pudding with vanilla and cinnamon?" he asked hopefully, and his stomach rumbled, as though underscoring the question. Edith surprised him by laughing, the sound raspy, as though she was unused to making it. Even a few of the staff glanced over curiously, as though they'd never heard it before.

"Dinna be daft. I couldna forget yer favorite." She swatted his shoulder once more. "Now off with ye. I'll be sure yer meals get sent to yer chambers until Imbolc is over. Can't have ye wastin away on us, now."

Thad nodded and wandered off, his thoughts consumed by their conversation. They sidetracked him to the point that he forgot, at least briefly, about the doe-eyed girl and the way she saw his drawings like she'd seen straight into his soul.

"Do you have anything to report today, Kuiper?" Aerrin clasped his hands behind his back, looking expectantly at the leader of the Hounds.

It was still early morning, the sun barely beginning its ascent to the skies — not that they could see it from the room in the Den. They were nestled underground, where the passage of time couldn't affect them. And anything they said remained here, between the four of them. Thad glanced between Kuiper and Briar intently. He expected Kuiper to speak first, but it was Briar who lifted her chin and opened her mouth.

"We tracked them just outside of the palace, to the Brash Boar. They stayed for two drinks and returned back to the palace. Four of them, with four guards."

Thad nodded. "Good. I appreciate the observation. So, what is the plan?"

"The plan?" Briar choked out a disbelieving laugh. She shared a look with Kuiper. "There is no plan. Not if that will be their nightly ritual the whole time they're here. We need a little more help here."

Aerrin bristled, and Thad watched a dangerous glint spread over his eyes. "What are you implying, girl? Are you not up to this task?" He swiveled his gaze to Thad, who bristled defensively. "I thought you said they were the right ones for the job, brother."

"What she means," Kuiper cut in, "is that this gives us mere yards to intercept them, and in an incredibly public space. The proximity to the palace would never wash your hands of the deed. We need them pushed further into the city to successfully capture them, as well as help you effectively deny implication."

Aerrin considered this for a moment, then relaxed. "This does make sense. But how will we encourage them to venture further to the outskirts of Reviere? Simply recommend a sight to see?"

"They don't trust us," Thad reminded him gently. "We need someone else to put a bug in their ear. Perhaps a more detached staff member that can recommend an area of town, and pretend there is something lively happening there tonight?" His mind wandered back to the girl in his office, wondering if she would be joining them. He quickly shook off the thought.

Aerrin grunted. "Indeed. Leveraging an outside source would also help with today's plan. They won't need to see our faces."

Thad nodded, thinking it over. They were feigning a sickness today; a ghastly, twenty-four-hour bug that would have them glued to their chambers for the remainder of the day. It wasn't the most elegant excuse to avoid Finlay and Kate, but it was effective — no matter how many creative, scathing words the staff reported back directly from Finlay's mouth. It would also hopefully lead their group to levels of boredom that would force them to venture into the city.

"Will you be ready by tonight?" Aerrin asked, and Kuiper and Briar exchanged glances.

"We haven't had time to study their movements, their strengths and weaknesses in a group, or the way they fight…" Kuiper trailed off, obviously wanting to ask for more time but knowing it wouldn't be possible.

Aerrin's eyes narrowed, and Briar clocked the subtle change. "We will make it work," she announced, lifting her chin up. Her fingers went to her chakram, tracing over the weapon. "We have our abilities, our weapons, and the buair. We'll make it work."

Kuiper glanced at her, then back at Aerrin, nodding his agreement. Aerrin gave a curt nod back. "Good. We'll be back tomorrow morning to ensure it's done."

Aerrin spun on his heel without offering a dismissal, and Thad followed behind, his stomach flitting nervously at the prospect that by tomorrow morning, everything could change once again. They navigated the stairs of the Den in silence, but when they reached the door to exit back out onto the town, Thad reached forward to grab his brother's shoulder.

Aerrin turned, eyes questioning, and for a moment, Thad saw their dad — the twinkle of his blue eyes, the quirk to his mouth as he watched them practicing their magic, the way he guided them gently through their training. His stomach lurched, threatening to empty the contents of his breakfast.

Thad swallowed down his nausea. "I spoke with Edith."

"Oh? Everything going smoothly for Imbolc?"

"Yes and no." Thad paused, unsure how to continue. "Aerrin, she's planning for it to be a festival in dad's honor."

Aerrin remained silent, his face unreadable.

"Aerrin, there are going to be questions about him."

"And?" Aerrin's tone was taut, a string stretched to the point of snapping.

Thad let out a frustrated exhale. "We should talk about it. Talk about dad—"

"Why?" Aerrin demanded, cutting him off. "What's done is done. We have our story, and we have our next steps. There is nothing more to say."

"But—"

"Stop looking back, Thad. It's time you start looking forward. Or you'll get left behind." He swung the door open with an angry tug and paused to shoot Thad a final withering look. And though it startled Thad how much Aerrin looked like their father, this... this was never a look Lachlan had given him. Come to think of it, it had been a long time since Aerrin had shown an ounce of the warmth or compassion that their father had.

It was painful to think maybe there was nothing left of their dad at all.

Chapter Sixteen

Wren sat under the cover of an arched concrete pavilion, studying the slope of the ceiling as rain fell in torrents just outside of her reach. She'd never seen so much water before, with the constant rainfall filling endless canals weaving alongside each path, shadowed by buildings defying architectural sense as they sprouted from the edges of the bank. While she understood how some people found solace in being close to the water and around so many people, it personally made her uncomfortable. She enjoyed the vast forests and quiet nature that Sairas provided, especially given the way it fed into her earth magic.

While Sairas was technically the capital, it did not have many full-time occupants, with royals visiting only for special occasions. Usually, it was a slow-paced and quaint city, surrounded by lush trees whose ever-changing colors told multiple stories throughout the seasons. Here, there was only drab concrete in various shades of tan and gray, reaching high enough into the sky to obscure the stars' attempts at shining through every night. Whereas she could place nearly every face in Sairas, she was certain she had not seen a single face twice here. They became an endless blur of strangers — intriguing to watch, but each one stunningly distant.

She studied them now, mystified at the way the crowd moved through the early morning rain, either oblivious or uncaring about the droplets pelting their faces. Even the vendors on the plaza couldn't be deterred. They simply set up umbrellas or awnings and continued selling their various fabrics and foods, hollering out to the passersby. She had a feeling this weather occurred often, and if the vendors simply closed up shop for every rainstorm, they would struggle to make their rents. The passersby further confirmed her suspicions: they all seemed to hold a frenetic energy with a distinct edge of desperation.

Observing had always been her strongest suit — staying back in the shadows, learning what she could, never hasty in voicing an opinion. Cas had always had enough opinions for the both of them growing up, and it provided her with endless amusement to simply watch how his antics worked out. It also aided her as a stablehand; royals never wanted an opinion voiced, especially from someone who worked for them.

She'd only just begun to become comfortable in her own voice when she'd stumbled into her friendship with Kate and the others. Not only did she feel like her voice would be heard, it was genuinely sought out. She smiled as she recalled the several cozy nights they'd all spent together on the boat ride over, and her heart ached as she searched the obscure, rain-clouded faces for a familiar one. She hoped her friends were being safe, and that the conversations were going well.

Hold on.

Wren straightened, squinting out across the plaza. A small female face stood out that she recalled from yesterday. She remembered it distinctly, simply due to the age of the girl: *young.* Younger even than her nieces, perhaps seven?

And, like yesterday, she was all alone.

As she watched, the girl looked around carefully, as if looking for someone or something. The girl took a few steps closer to the building Wren sat under, to the point Wren could make out her features. Her rounded face was pale and cherubic, but pinched as she studied the ground for something. Curious. She wasn't looking for an adult, then. A pet, perhaps? Her short, chestnut hair hung in wet strands around her face, flinging from side to side as she searched, and her fingers twitched with an anxious tick. Wren felt her heart squeeze, and she sat up further, ready to go to the girl. She remembered the many times her nieces thought they'd lost their parents, and she'd consoled them back from the brink of tears. Perhaps this girl needed help finding her pet. And then her parents, since clearly she was spending too much time alone.

As she stood, however, the young girl's face visibly brightened, clearly having found what she was searching for. Wren followed her line of sight to — holy shit.

What was that?

A shadow moved next to a meat vendor, the size of a small dog. Wren squinted, but the more she tried to make out distinct features of the creature, the less it made sense. She thought she saw a tail, but in the next flash, it looked like a snake. It had a set of paws, but then — *hooves?* And four ears, or possibly, ears *and* horns? As she blinked rapidly, trying to make sense of it, the creature curled up, and she watched its ears flick back, studying the vendor and his stand. Finally, it rose onto its back haunches, waggling its butt as though ready to strike — but strike *what?*

Wren opened her mouth, ready to call out and warn the vendor, but words failed her as a pair of tiny wings shot out from the creature's back and it took flight, leaping past the vendor and directly toward a string of sausage links hanging off the back of the vendor's cart. It snapped a sausage in its distinctly catlike mouth, severing the links halfway down the string with ease. The creature glided down gracefully until it landed back on the ground, tucking its wings in and slinking back into the shadows, where it became nearly invisible.

The young girl met the creature in the shadows and bent over. Wren couldn't help but tense again, even though the girl clearly wasn't frightened by the creature. After a moment, the girl straightened and, in the next blink, the creature had disappeared entirely into the shadows, its tawny fur concealing it well in the murky weather of the day. When the girl turned, she was beaming with victory, and Wren couldn't help but grin at the sight.

Whatever had just happened had been well-coordinated, and quite obviously was not the first time it had taken place. But even as she bit back a laugh, she couldn't help but wonder — why was this young girl resorting to the help of what looked like a stray animal to get her meals? She took a step forward, ready to confront the girl and perhaps offer her some assistance.

"Hey!" The voice rang out across the plaza, clear as day even with the rainfall. The young girl froze, and Wren's eyes shot from her to the meat vendor. He held the remaining string of sausage links — now distinctly shorter — and was striding toward the young girl, shaking it angrily at her. "I *know* this was you! How many times am I going to have to do this before you learn your lesson?"

Wren didn't even think. Her feet moved of their own accord, leaving the dry safety of the pavilion to meet the growing crowd around the girl and the vendor.

"I— I—" The girl sputtered, her gaze flicking around the crowd nervously as though looking for someone to save her. *Ah, so she does have someone,* Wren thought. But whoever it was, they clearly weren't here. Wren suspected thieving might be commonplace in a large city such as this, as nobody so much as batted an eye when the vendor came to a halt in front of her and ripped the stolen meat from her hands.

"What the hell am I going to do with this? I can't sell it now!" The vendor's face grew red as his voice raised another decibel.

"I'll pay for it," Wren found herself saying, uncomfortably aware of how many faces swiveled to eye her curiously. Her neck prickled from the scrutiny as she stepped forward, removing her coin purse from her waist.

"Are you in charge of this young lady?" the vendor demanded, grabbing greedily for the coins as she outstretched her hand. Wren contemplated the question as she turned to face the young girl, handing her both halves of the sausage string. The young girl refused to take it, instead wringing her hands together while she rocked on her feet. Finally, she looked up. Her eyes were a dark navy that reminded Wren of the canals weaving through each street of Reviere. She smiled down at the girl, who glanced away nervously.

"For today, it seems I am."

"Hold up!" Wren called after the young girl, who was giving it her best shot to ditch Wren following their transaction with the vendor. They passed all sorts of buildings — taverns, housing, businesses — but the girl never seemed to lose her way as she navigated a myriad of streets and back alleys. At one point, Wren was fairly certain they'd made a full circle. It was honestly impressive, if a bit exasperating. "I have some questions for you."

The girl glanced behind her. She must have seen the firm look on Wren's face — similar to the one she used with her nieces when they were being bad — and decided Wren was being serious. She sighed and came to a stop. When she turned, she kicked at the dirt with her head down, and Wren had to bite back a smile at the pouty movement.

"I'm sorry I got you in trouble, miss," the girl said. "I can repay you. And I promise it won't happen again."

"It's okay," Wren replied, working to keep her voice gentle. "I don't want to be repaid. I just want to make sure you have something to eat."

The girl glanced up, surprised. Wren took it as a positive sign and continued. "Could you tell me your name?"

A slight pause. Then, "Lena."

"Hi, Lena." Wren smiled. "I'm Wren."

"That's a pretty name." Lena rocked on her feet. Clearly, she was feeling conflicted — like she wanted to keep talking, but also felt like she needed to be somewhere else. Wren again wondered what, or who, she was planning to get back to. She seemed starved of attention, though unsure what to do when she had it.

"I'm glad you think so. I like it, too. But Lena... I have to tell you a secret."

Lena's eyes widened. "What is it?"

Wren leaned in, making a show of looking around to be sure nobody was listening. Then, she lowered her voice to a whisper. "I saw what your little friend did."

Lena gasped, flushing, and Wren was quick to add, "Don't worry. I won't tell anyone. But... he was *super cute.* Is there... any chance I could meet him?"

She watched the hesitation play across Lena's face as the young girl grappled with the decision, and did her best to look innocent. Truly, Wren just wanted to know what she'd seen, and make sure the girl wasn't in any danger with the creature. Finally, Lena nodded and grabbed her hand. Wren willingly followed as Lena led her to an alleyway, distancing them from the plaza and its crowds.

After looking both ways down the alley, Lena let out a distinct, two-part whistle. Wren waited breathlessly for several long moments. Finally, just as she was sure nothing would appear and that she'd somehow seen the girl's imaginary creature, there was a rustling in the shadows. A high-pitched chirp emanated from a dark corner, under a wooden pallet.

"It's okay," Lena called out softly. "You can come out."

A slight shuffle, and then the creature emerged, its head poking out first before it appeared completely. Wren sucked in a gasp, taking in the animal's features — all of which she had seen correctly, even as they seemed to clash with one another. In general, the creature had the body of a lion cub, with front paws that seemed far too big for its tiny body and a fluffy, tawny lion face, eyes, and ears. Between its rounded ears sat two stubby gray horns, like that of a goat, and its hind legs indeed ended in cloven hooves. A pair of reddish-brown, leathery, dragon-like wings extended out from its shoulder blades, and where its tail was... *wasn't* a tail at all. It was a dark green snake, complete with a head and blinking, serpent eyes. It prowled forward slowly, crouched low, assessing Wren like the threat she was sure it saw her as. It eyed her with both the catlike eyes on its face and the eyes swishing on its snake tail.

A lion... a goat... a dragon... and a snake.

It's a chimera, she thought. *I didn't think they really existed, but... it has to be. It's a baby chimera.*

The creature wound its way through Lena's legs, curling its serpent tail around Lena's calf, and sniffed the air in Wren's direction with its lion's nose. Finally, it looked up at Lena with what Wren could only describe as complete adoration. Lena returned the look with a beam of her own.

"Who is he?" Wren breathed. Not what — she now knew what. But clearly, these two were bonded in a way that meant it had a name.

Lena looked up, directing a gap-toothed grin at Wren. "This is Angus."

CHAPTER SEVENTEEN

"Do they need to be following us?" Cas complained as they wandered through the streets of Reviere. Kipp and Kate followed close by, with Wren... well, Finlay didn't quite know where she'd gone off to, but if Cas wasn't worried, he wasn't, either. He hoped she'd found a good lead to follow under the ruse of Kate's lady-in-waiting. The bar scene the palace attendant had spoken of didn't seem like her style — though it had *certainly* piqued Cas's interest.

Finlay glanced in the direction Cas gestured, taking in the guards Larke had sent to Reviere with them as they loped silently in the shadows. He counted four of them — one for each of them, if he had to guess. Finlay felt better knowing they had coverage for everyone. If he reached out with his own magic, he could feel the soft presence of an air shield from one of the guards, encompassing them all.

"You know it was the only way Larke would want us to venture out in the city, and they answer to him. They know every exit here like the back of their hands. Besides," Finlay added, "they were here the entire trip over, outside the bar last night, and in the palace. Why does it bother you now?"

Cas shrugged, looking uneasy. "They weren't this... *close* before."

"Are you worried they'll be interrupting your private time later?" Kate goaded.

Cas scoffed. "Nothing could interrupt that. That's sacred time. Plus, I'm not opposed to a little voyeurism." He winked, even as Kipp growled in a clear warning that he, at least, was opposed. Finlay choked back a laugh. "It's just — we survived a war against the goddess of death. What could we possibly face that would be worse than that?"

Kipp let out an audible exhale, and Finlay shook his head as Kate covered her mouth. Cas spun around to look at them, eyes widening. "What?" he asked.

"Now you've done it." Finlay shook his head. "Now you've jinxed it."

"Oh, please. Kippers doesn't even believe in luck. He says everything is fate."

"Well, fates can be changed." Kipp raised a brow. "And now you've fucked with our fate. Why would you do that, Cas?"

Cas huffed and pulled his cloak in tighter around himself, but didn't argue. Kate let out a soft chuckle and looped her arm around his, dragging him forward as they walked. The sun was close to setting, casting a yellow-orange glow that hovered brightly at the tips of the concrete buildings. It didn't have the same wooded allure as Sairas, but each place had its own charm, and Finlay had learned quite some time ago that a place was only as beautiful as the people you experienced it with. They strolled along a small, paved path that aligned with the canal, and Finlay let the calm of the water and easy conversation lull him into a pleasant state of relaxation.

"Tell me something I don't know about you," Kate asked Kipp.

He paused for a long moment, and Kate tousled his hair as he considered. "Hmmm. How about we play two truths and a lie?"

"Ooooh, hold on," Cas cut in. "If we're playing two truths and a lie, we need drinks."

"Must you turn everything into a drinking game?" Kate laughed.

His reply was immediate. "Yes."

Finlay chuckled, and they began the search for a decent-looking tavern, following the streams of people leaving their shops for the night and doing the same. The more people that joined the pathways, the more Kate seemed to shrink away, looking to hide her face behind a curtain of hair and the shimmer of her clothing in the shadows. Word had already spread that they'd landed in Reviere, though the reasons remained, thankfully, unknown.

Finlay understood how she felt. He hated the fact that the murmurs and stares followed them like sparks following a flame, growing with similar speed as the people nudged one another, pointing and whispering. It was something he had actively avoided for decades, slipping away to the wilderness with a flask and a smoke. Only Kate had been able to drag him from such remedies. And even though an ocean separated their homes, in a town as large and well-connected as this, their appearances gave them away.

He pulled them to an abrupt stop in front of a store that was closing for the night, flipping the owner a coin to bribe him to stay open for another few moments. The owner instantly accepted, and they came out minutes later, all donning far less noticeable cloaks. Kate and Finlay put the hoods of the new cloaks up, and from there, they slid off to a side street, in the location they'd been directed by the shop owner to find a less busy tavern. As they walked, however, Finlay slowed, a feeling of unease settling over him.

Kipp noticed his hesitation first and slowed as well. His azure eyes flashed around them, assessing. "What is it?"

"I'm not sure," Finlay replied, scanning the area alongside Kipp. He noted the moving shadow of a guard, but something felt... empty. The hair on the back of his neck prickled, but it was interrupted by a whoop, followed by a laugh. That sweet, deep, genuine laugh ripped him from his observations and pulled him back to the present, and he faced Kate in time to grab the full, foam-capped ale she passed him.

"Let's hear it," she said. "Two truths and a lie."

"Mmmm..." He took the beer, considering. The area was crowded, with people smiling and engaging in loud, happy conversations. He relaxed slightly and thought over his answer. "I speak five languages, I despise anything flavored with cinnamon, and... I once ended up pantsless in Lachlan's bed."

"Finlay!" Kate hissed. "Should you be saying that in public? Here?" Alarm shone in her eyes, even as her mouth betrayed her amusement, twisting into a disbelieving grin. Cas howled in the background, leaning into Kipp to hold himself upright.

"Well, which is the lie?"

Kate passed a glass to Kipp and bit her lip thoughtfully. "I hope it's the pantsless one, but something tells me that's a truth."

Finlay nodded, grinning. "I only speak four languages. Fluently, at least."

"No fucking way." Kipp laughed so hard he dissolved into coughs, forcing him to take a long gulp of his beer. "Was Lachlan there?"

Finlay shrugged. "At some point, maybe. Or maybe he just let me have his room for the night. I never got the chance to ask him."

Everyone snickered and then quieted, presumably thinking, like Finlay, about the late duke. Finlay couldn't help but wonder if things would have been different, had he paid closer attention, forcing the Byrne brothers to join him in the battle against Nemain. It was hard for him to wrap his head around the fact that they were likely staying under the roof of the queen and the duke's murderers. They needed answers, and they needed them fast. He glanced down, noticing he was squeezing his glass so hard his knuckles blanched, and he switched the glass to his other hand with a weary exhale.

Kate paid the server and reached for a final glass of ale, but before she could take it, a young boy carrying empty glasses passed by — young and fair-haired, fourteen at most — and stumbled into the server. The glass shattered on the ground, the liquid splashing on the front of Kate's dress. Finlay straightened and the boy set down his glasses quickly, muttering his apologies as he rushed to find a rag.

"It's nothing," Kate assured him, removing her new cloak to dab at the stain. "Please. Don't worry yourself."

The tavern went silent, and Finlay raised his eyes to study the crowd. They were all staring at... Kate, no longer in her mundane attire. She now stood in her dress, shining with gilded inlays: personally oblivious, but to all the others, she was clearly someone royal, if not immediately recognizable.

"Boy!" A tall, burly man strode out from the back of the tavern. He wore an apron, but his clean-cut appearance and demeanor indicated he was likely the owner of the establishment. He draped a towel over his shoulder and gestured angrily between the young boy and Kate. "Did you do this? *To your future queen?*"

The boy paled, looking between the man and Kate. His mouth opened and closed, no words coming out, until finally, he dropped to his knees. "My deepest apologies, Your Majesty," he said, his voice high and trembling. He extended the rag to her without looking up. "Please forgive me."

"There is nothing to forgive," Kate insisted, and met the owner's gaze, a warning in her eyes that had nothing to do with the boy. "Truly. No harm done."

"Yes, there was." The owner glared down at the boy, still on his knees with his head bowed. "This will be coming out of your paycheck. Come with me."

He grabbed the boy's shirt, lifting him with ease — the boy couldn't have weighed more than eighty pounds. "Your Majesty," the man grunted, bowing slightly, and then continued dragging the boy to the back of the shop, where they disappeared. Kate stiffened and whirled to face Finlay, her intentions written clearly on her face.

"Kate..." Finlay warned, but he knew it was useless. She frowned at him and brushed by, stalking around the side of the tavern. He sighed and exchanged looks with Cas and Kipp, who nodded in unison, and they all trailed behind her.

"Leave him be!" Finlay heard as he rounded the corner of the tavern. Though Kate had shrunk away from the citizens' attention before, she stood tall and commanding now. The burly man held a leather strap in one hand and the boy's arm in the other. The boy didn't even struggle; rather, he cowered, expelling soft whimpers as he folded in on himself. Finlay could see where the boy's skin was already turning an angry red. He gritted his teeth, silently applauding Kate's intuition, and glanced back at the owner.

The man tilted his head, squinting at Kate as if to question if she really were royalty. While Sairas was a peaceful place where such beatings were forbidden, Reviere had a known 'don't ask, don't tell' policy for how disobedient servants were treated.

Well, fuck that, Finlay thought. It was time to enact change.

He strode up behind her, shouldering his own cloak off as he went. "Listen to her. You will be leaving the boy alone," he commanded, and the man's eyes widened as he realized who Finlay was.

"And," he added before the man could bow and remove himself, "I will be checking back. If I find that harm has come to the boy once we leave, I will personally see to it that this tavern comes under new management, immediately. Do you understand?"

Finally, the man released the young boy, who scrambled back a few steps. He grumbled an affirmative answer and bowed stiffly, giving the boy a final glare before returning inside. The door slammed shut, and the boy instantly collapsed.

Kate ran to him, skimming her hands over his arm and brushing his hair back from his face. She was careful not to touch the fresh wounds, but there were plenty of older marks marring his skin as well. "Are you okay?" she asked, her voice cracking.

"Don't touch him." The voice was female, her tone low and commanding. Everyone spun to where a figure approached from the shadows. When the woman appeared, she had long, red hair and a hard expression. Her eyes flashed across each of their faces, seemingly marking them before fixating on the young boy.

"I have a friend here, he's a healer... he can help." Kate gestured to Cas, who took a step forward, but froze when the woman whipped a hand up.

"*I said,* don't touch him." The woman approached, crouching over the boy. Finlay heard a murmured name, something like Brooks, and the boy nodded, muttering something in reply.

Kate rose, looking back to where the woman had appeared from, and her posture stiffened. Finlay followed her line of sight. At first, he didn't see what she did in the shadows, but then... yes, there was something. He squinted, and then a slow chill crept over him as the figure took shape: one of their own guards, sprawled out across the ground, his body twisted and misshapen in death.

"Finlay," Kate began softly.

Finlay grabbed her hand, halting her. "I see it."

Kipp and Cas froze as well, sensing the tension in the air, and realization dawned on Finlay. He'd only seen one guard earlier — the one that lay in front of them now. And the air shield that had been hovering over them was gone. He wasn't sure how long it had been, or how long this woman had been tailing them, clearly picking off their defenses. "The other guards are dead, too."

The woman in question straightened, and Finlay's fire magic flared to life. Out of the corner of his eye, he saw sparks dance across Kate's palms, vibrant white-gold against the now dark skies. The woman shoved the young boy behind her but made no move to approach their group. Instead, she raised a finger to her lips.

Finlay hesitated but didn't douse his flames. Instead, he barked, "Explain yourself."

She moved slowly to hold her hands above her head. When she spoke, it was nearly a whisper. "I understand how this looks, but listen carefully. You have targets on your back. It's my job to take you, dead or alive."

Finlay's fire burned brighter, and Kipp let out a snarl from somewhere behind them. The woman didn't flinch, though; she merely shook her head.

"Just this once, I'm leaving you be. For him." She nodded back at the boy, never taking her eyes off them. "But he's coming, and your magic won't help you when he does. If you know what's good for you, you'll run. *Now.*"

Chapter Eighteen

The sun was fading under the meridian, casting a warm glow on the town as Thad wound through the city. He'd taken measures to conceal himself in nondescript clothing, and for the most part, the wardrobe sufficed. He was aware of the lone small figure that followed him on silent feet, but said nothing, only kept one eye on it as it moved with him.

He needed this — the long pause before the big moment. He'd discussed the plans at length with Kuiper, and now he needed to take the next few hours to gather his thoughts, lay the plan back out, go over it time and again in his head. It helped him to see every possible path a plan would take, every possible outcome. And he preferred to go to the highest point of the city to review it.

Most assumed the palace was the highest point, but he knew differently. He remained silent as he snuck into the Reviere cathedral, mind heavy with his own thoughts. The stone walls stretched high above him, the stained glass casting warm colors across the wooden pews, depicting the mightiest gods and goddesses of centuries past. He padded across the main floor quietly, but instead of banking right at the end of the pews to head for the spiral staircase, he paused. With a soft exhale, he turned on his heel, eyeing a pew four rows back.

"You can come out now," he said. The feet that had been shifting underneath the pew froze, and he waited patiently, saying nothing. Finally, he heard an audible sigh, and his lips curled with amusement as the figure emerged, no taller than the pew, shoulders hunched in defeat.

"How did you know I was following you?" The young female voice was as small as the figure herself, and Thad studied her intently as she navigated between the pews.

The moonlight cast an enchanting glow on her round face, changing colors while she crossed in front of the large expanse of stained glass. Her expression was pinched in frustration, eyes narrowed and nose crinkled, which only served to amuse Thad further, even as it sent a pang through his heart. The expression, paired with her curly hair made her look so much like her mother. Every year, she looked and acted more like her. Those dark sapphire eyes, though... those were all him.

Thad glanced away, taking a moment to compose himself as he answered her question. "I caught sight of you darting across a street, Lena. You disturbed an entire carriage."

She let out a muffled 'hmph' of irritation, then went silent. Thad let her have the moment to herself. She was unique in that way, wise beyond her eight years — instead of arguing, she was digesting the information that had given her away. Thad knew she was marking the error, replaying it in her mind so that she would never repeat it. He knew, because her mind was so much like his as well.

"You're getting quieter on your feet, though," he added, hoping the compliment would cheer her up. "Good work, bug." He strode toward the staircase and motioned for her to follow. She beamed, eyes lighting up, and hurried to catch him. The echo of their footfalls rang in the corridor as they made their way upstairs. There was an iron gate that barred the path up to the final portion of the cathedral, but Thad had broken the lock on the chain ages ago. He pushed it open, allowing Lena to scramble forward ahead of him.

Finally, they reached the top of the building, and they moved carefully to find a flat spot to seat themselves, Thad keeping a soft hold on the back of Lena's shirt as she settled into her spot, feet kicking over the ledge. He frowned disapprovingly, but sat beside her, keeping his air magic called up close at hand. As they looked out across the city, his concern slipped into a sense of serenity. They could see the whole expanse of the city, giving way to a dark expanse of ocean that disappeared with the line of the setting sun. The breeze of the wind hit their faces, slightly chilled and fresh as it bounced in from the ocean at a height the rest of the population would never experience. Thad realized that no sane person probably enjoyed this, but as he glanced sidelong at Lena, he realized they both did. They both lived for the wild, the unruly, the things that others called reckless, but they saw as freedom.

He drank in the sight of her; her eyes closed, a soft grin lighting her face as she inhaled the fresh air. It reminded him of Kate's lady-in-waiting from his office, and he smiled absently at the comparison. His days were so filled with dark moments that he had forgotten how it felt to be free as a child, enjoying the freedom like Lena did. His routine consisted of meetings with the Hounds, carefully plotted political moves with Aerrin, and most recently, the even darker, closed-door discussions regarding Kate and Finlay — not to mention their father—

Thad sighed, dismissing the thoughts. The sound caused Lena to open her eyes again and look at him. A wild, particularly cold breeze chose the moment to whip around Lena's chestnut hair, and she tucked a piece behind her ear, shivering. Thad flicked his hand and brought an air shield up around them, and she gave him a grateful smile. She, like him at her age, was struggling with her elemental powers, and did not yet have a signature magic. He wondered idly if it was going to be water, like his, or air, like her mother's.

"Is everything going well at Ciara's?" he asked.

Lena fiddled with the hem of her shirt. "Fine." Thad narrowed his eyes, and when she looked at him, he opened his mouth to pry further. Before he could, though, she changed the subject. "I showed Angus to someone today."

Thad's heart stuttered, the question he'd meant to ask flying from his mind. "You did *what?*"

"She was nice!" Lena argued, her eyes going wide. Thad gaped at her, realizing her face showed no hint of regret, only pure excitement. "I could tell she could keep a secret."

"Lena! You can't be doing that!" He felt his pulse hammering in his throat. "Angus is special, like all of the creatures I've shown you. He needs to be kept safe."

Lena crossed her arms, lips and eyes both tilting down. "Angus liked her," she pouted.

Thad groaned inwardly and took a moment to think. If someone did see Angus with Lena, that didn't necessarily mean they *understood* what they'd seen. And Thad was careful to ensure nobody could tie Lena to him, or vice versa. She was just a kid with a pet. An unusual pet, yes, but nothing that required further scrutiny... he hoped.

He ran a hand over his face, mind still racing. If someone discovered who she was, she could be used as leverage against him. She could be harmed in the name of someone looking for political gain. "Who was she?"

"I don't know. I've never seen her before." Lena shrugged and pulled a tiny trinket out of her pocket, clutching it tightly. "Her name was Wren."

"Wren." Thad chewed on the name, turning it over in his head. He didn't think he'd heard the name before, but he couldn't be sure. Perhaps after tonight's plans were executed, he could enlist Kuiper and Briar to track this person down. He needed to know if they would be trouble.

He studied Lena, who was now fully sulking at Thad's obvious disappointment. Her head was down, and she turned a tiny trinket over in her hands. He bit back further chastisement and instead motioned to the trinket. "What is that?"

"I found it the other day after the vendors left," she said, passing it over to him. "I have this... this feeling, that it brings me luck."

He examined it closely, noting that it was a small, carved wooden horse. It was whimsical, but he felt a pang of guilt at the fact that he rarely gave her gifts like this. She was wise beyond her years, yes, but she was still just a *child.* Instead, she'd had to find her own gifts in the plaza. He thought that, by placing her under Ciara's supervision, such simple things would be taken care of. He looked back out at the capital, absorbing the sounds and movements below them. It was a dark place, one he had to resign her to with barely any control. One he was a part of, with the Hounds, committing dark acts in the dead of night.

One where she had no mother left to take care of her.

He swallowed down his guilt and handed the toy back to her, flinching slightly as her soft, tiny hands plucked it from his own. "I'm glad you have it, bug. We could all use a little luck."

Hours had passed since sundown, and still, Thad hadn't heard from Kuiper. He paced his way across the gardens, listening for any sort of rustling that indicated movement, but all he heard were his light footfalls in the grass. Lena was back at Ciara's place, the latter nowhere in sight. Thad had left a short note, hoping it would persuade Ciara into being more present.

His nerves were frayed, and not simply from the task at hand —
though that was, admittedly, a large source of it. He'd never enlisted
the Hounds' help with such a large task, and one that required
so much discretion. Not to mention, it was only one of a series
of questionable decisions lately that left him sleepless at night, gut
roiling uneasily during the day. He couldn't be certain he was doing
the right thing, but the only person he had ever trusted to ask such
questions of — his brother — was consumed by how unequivocally
right he felt their path was. Such certainty should have set him at
ease, but with each passing day, Thad felt his faith being chipped
away like the stone that lined the canals of their city, slowly eroding
from the lapping waves.

His feet dragged him toward the stable of their own accord. As
he approached, he heard the sounds of hooves stomping and horses
nickering, and the knot in his stomach unwound ever so slightly. He
slipped inside and approached the first horse, a sweet roan whose
belly swelled with new life. Thad suspected she'd foal within the next
week, and his face softened at the prospect of a new little creature
out in the pasture, all spindly legs and a small tail, flipping wildly as
it worked to figure out how to run.

"Feeling comfortable, old girl?" He stroked his way down the
blaze that marked the front of her face, sending white hairs flying.
She pushed her face into his hand, greedy for more scratches, and he
smiled, rubbing her nose. "Any day now."

A small, strangled sound emanated down the stable aisle, and
Thad whirled, his fingertips instantly sparking with magic. Was it
Kuiper? Or had Finlay and Kate somehow avoided their fates and

realized who had orchestrated the attack? Something moved in the darkness, and his pulse quickened. He spread an air shield over himself, cursing silently. The stories he'd heard about their battle with Nemain were nothing he wanted to witness firsthand, hence the carefully laid trap and personal distance from the actual event itself.

The figure that came out of the shadows, however, was the last one he expected. She was shorter in stature, and lean, instantly eliminating Kuiper and Finlay as the suspect. It was when her eyes came into focus in the soft lamplight, however, that he realized who it was.

The stablehand, Kate's lady-in-waiting. The warm, chocolate brown of her eyes twinkled, and as her full face came into view, he realized she was *smirking* at him. Thad felt a small flush course through him at the realization he'd been caught in a vulnerable position.

"My apologies for startling you, but—" she paused, her smirk broadening. "Was that a smile? I do *vaguely* remember you having one, but I didn't know it still existed."

He blinked in surprise. Was she making fun of him? Her words were more emboldened than those from their encounter in his office just the other day — though, he supposed, now they were in familiar territory. He wanted to be irritated that she was poking fun at him, but as he took in her grin, all he wanted to do was rise to her level and smile back. Something about it was contagious.

"What do you mean, remember me having one?" he asked, a brow raised.

"You're not the only one who remembers our interactions in the stables." The words themselves could sound coy, flirtatious even, but that wasn't her way. Her tone was gentle, like a soft breeze. It was a simple fact. Still, he felt flattered. "You were always so kind to the horses. Sneaking them treats and extra pats."

"They are a favorite creature of mine," he admitted, glancing back at the mare he'd been stroking. He remembered the toy Lena held earlier and made a mental note to bring her out to the stables to meet the new foal when it arrived. She'd be thrilled.

"Which one is yours?" The question broke through his thoughts. "I don't believe you ever made the trip across the ocean with your own mount."

"Indeed." Thad was impressed by her attention to detail. He turned and motioned for her to follow. Again, he wasn't sure why he entertained her questions, but... they didn't feel probing. They were asked out of a quiet sort of curiosity, which he found himself excited to indulge. He strode down the row of stalls until he came to a stop in front of a large stallion. The horse blended into the darkness of the stall, as black as night, save for a single white star emblazoned on his forehead.

Thad greeted him with a quick, affectionate pat, then turned and motioned for her to approach. "This is Tara."

She approached, eyes glued to the stallion, and Thad took the moment to study her. She wore a pale blue tunic with ruffled sleeves, and light brown leather trousers. The clothes were less revealing than the dress she'd worn in his study, but they seemed to suit her better, complimenting her light olive skin and shining, ebony hair.

Her skin looked soft to the touch, and Thad's fingers twitched with the subconscious urge to know how she felt. He swallowed and shifted his gaze to look at her hair, which fell in lustrous, gentle waves down her back. He noticed that she had woven light blue petals into it, the same hue as the tunic she wore. She must have the gift of earth magic, but as he reached out with his magic, he realized she wasn't Aes Sídhe, so... a Dryad, perhaps?

She tickled Tara's chin, causing him to whuffle over her hands, searching for treats. She giggled, and Thad shifted in surprise as a strange feeling coursed through him. He cleared his throat. "May I ask what you're doing out here, instead of at the palace, waiting on Her Majesty?"

"Her Majesty is still out, experiencing the city life. When I receive word that she's arrived back, I will tend to her needs."

"You didn't feel inclined to join her?" Thad asked, relieved to know she was here, safe, in the stable.

She ran a hand down Tara's nose, then back up his face to scratch behind his ears. The stallion extended his neck and leaned into her hand. *Traitor,* Thad thought. *Putting out for anyone who will give him attention.* "Not exactly my speed," she said. "I spent the day exploring the plaza instead."

A sudden wave of alarm crashed over Thad at the mention of the plaza. It wasn't even remotely likely. The chances were slim, as there were hundreds of people who frequented the plaza every single day. But... here she was, someone new, someone who clearly had an affinity for animals. Could it be?

Slowly, he inquired, "May I ask your name?"

She looked up at him, her mouth curling into a sheepish grin. "I suppose I never gave it. My apologies." She sounded genuinely surprised, not an inkling of suspicion or malice in her tone. "My name is Wren."

Gods damn it all. *Of course it was her.*

Thad inhaled sharply, causing Tara to rear his head and Wren to step back in shock.

"Wren." He ran a hand over his face and let the breath out slowly, working to compose himself. "And did anything interesting happen at the plaza today?"

"As a matter of fact, I did. There was the strangest creature there, a chimera, and..." She trailed off to study him carefully, and his heart sank. He shouldn't have asked. Should have counted on the fact that this woman — Wren — was clearly in tune with others' emotions, and could read them like a book. Read *him* like a book, despite only having seen him a handful of times in her life. And her attention to detail was unparalleled.

"Is it yours?" she breathed, eyes wide. "But of course, it makes sense..."

Fuck.

"You can't say a word, Wren," he cut her off. Panic worked its way up his throat, threatening to constrict it. In two strides, he was in her space, grabbing her arms. She shrank back instantly, eyes wide with alarm. Thad loosened his grip, a wave of regret washing over him, but didn't let go. It occurred to him, distantly, that her skin *was* as soft as it looked. She didn't shrink from him any further, but she stood stock still, her expression wary. He opted for another direction and knelt on one knee, moving to grasp her hands instead. "Please," he begged. "Nobody knows she's mine."

"She?" Wren gaped. "I was talking about the chimera."

Double fuck.

"Lena is…" Wren trailed off, and Thad watched as the pieces came together in her mind. He felt chilled to his very core. Aside from Lena's late mother and Ciara, the only other person who knew about Lena was his brother. This information, in the hands of someone loyal to Kate and Finlay — who were, at this moment, possibly in the Hounds' hands… it threw everything off course. It was the worst conceivable position for him to be in.

"She's your daughter," Wren breathed.

Thad bit the inside of his cheek until it bled, but nodded, knowing it was inevitable to refute the claim he'd so obviously laid out for her. He expected follow-up questions, which he'd have to answer with as much tact and little information as possible.

Instead, to his surprise, her face contorted in fury. She wrenched her hands from his and turned away, bringing her palms to her face. He remained kneeling in the straw, too stunned to react.

"How could you?" she finally demanded, whirling on him.

His mouth dropped open. "Pardon?"

"You'd let a girl, who can't be more than seven—"

"Eight," Thad cut in, but Wren seemed to barely notice, still on her tirade.

"—wander the plaza by herself, using a wild creature to steal her meals for her?" she finished. She glared down at him, cheeks flushed with rage, and Thad found himself taken aback. This was so at odds with the gentle, cheerful person she had presented herself as thus far, but what she'd said…

"She was *alone?*" Thad shot up off the ground. The anger he'd seen on Wren's face seemed to bleed into him, spreading through his veins. His own daughter, by herself, hunting for a meal. Where had Ciara been? Is this why Lena had hesitated earlier tonight when he'd asked about her?

Wren nodded, folding her arms across her chest. "Alone, and hungry."

The icy fear he'd felt moments before burned away at this information. "That should never have happened," he said through gritted teeth. "She shouldn't have been there."

"Well, she was. Where were you?"

Thad frowned at the accusation in her tone. "I was busy earlier, but I saw her not two hours ago. She told me nothing of this." He scrubbed a hand over his face again, guilt and irritation coursing through him in tandem. "She was supposed to have someone watching her while I was away."

Wren seemed to notice the emotions warring within him, because her expression softened somewhat. "Oh. Well, sometimes children can be slippery." She added in a gentler tone, "My cousins were nightmares at that age."

"Indeed. She is incredibly smart. Arguably too smart for her own good."

Wren snorted, and Thad felt the strange need to justify the chimera's presence as well. "For the record, Angus is no danger to her at all. He's spent practically every minute of his life glued to her side."

The corner of her mouth quirked up, the makings of a smile trying to force their way out. "I could tell." She seemed to catch herself smiling and rearranged her face into a scowl, but it looked forced, as though she was now only putting it on for appearances. "But it still doesn't excuse everything else."

"No, it doesn't. I'll have a word with her... caretaker."

"You're not her caretaker? As her father?"

Thad winced at both terms, fired his way in rapid succession. The word *caretaker* sounded so blunt, devoid of emotion. And yet, *father* was a title too big and important for what he deserved. While it pained him to keep his distance from Lena, it was the best thing for her. "It's... dangerous, to have her attached to me," Thad ground out after a moment's hesitation. "If my enemies were to find out, they would use her against me in a heartbeat."

"I see." Wren gazed at him with something akin to pity, and Thad averted his gaze, that uncomfortable feeling of vulnerability washing over him again. He noticed one of the blue flowers in the straw, having fallen out of Wren's hair.

"Thaddeus..." she began.

He instantly corrected her, hating the sound of his full name, especially in her mouth. "Call me Thad."

"Thad... I see what you're saying. You're worried I'll tell Kate and Finlay, and that they'll use it against you." Thad held his breath, realizing just how close she must be to the two of them to say something so casually. It made this all so much worse. "But I promise. I won't breathe a word of her, to anyone."

"You must know they're here to organize the dissolution of Dar-rya's marriage to Aerrin, then," he began. Wren nodded. "So, you're telling me you really wouldn't use this information as leverage to do that?"

She leveled him with a fiery gaze. "I would never use someone's family against them. No matter the cost."

Thad clenched his jaw, considering if her words were genuine. "Family must mean a great deal to you, then."

"Family and friends are the most important things there are." Her tone was matter-of-fact. "Without them, what else do we have to live for?"

He nodded slowly, at a loss for what else to say in response to such a statement. "Thank you, Wren."

She gave him a small smile and reached out, covering his hand with hers. He tensed, unsure what to do with the touch, her hand soft and warm against his. "I promise, Thad."

With that, she turned and left the stable, and he felt the loss of her hand like an icy ghost. He remained still for several long minutes, turning over her words in his head. Finally, he knelt and picked up the flower she'd left behind, clutching it in his hands as he returned to his chambers.

Family and friends...

What else was there to live for, indeed?

CHAPTER NINETEEN

My lungs burned as I pumped my arms and legs, willing myself to move faster. We were running sideways as much as we were forward, pushing through the crowds, but being packed in with the crowd seemed the safer option than getting stuck in an empty alleyway. I kept glancing behind and around us, trying to locate the threat that the mysterious woman had warned us about, but it only made navigating the crowds more difficult. We had ventured so far into the city, I wasn't entirely sure we were taking the fastest route back to the palace, either.

"Where the fuck do we go?" Kipp shouted, echoing my sentiments. He could have easily outpaced us in his wolf form — and similarly, Cas could've used his wings to fly away — but it wasn't lost on me that they both stayed glued to our sides. We would not leave each other, and there was a grim warmth to that fact.

I scanned the surroundings once more and ran into someone, causing me to stumble. Before I could fall, someone caught me around the waist, their hands like embers against my clothing. I glanced up to see Finlay above me, his eyes lit with an intense urgency that reflected the heat I felt in his touch. The second I was upright again, he let go and pointed to the twisting spires in the distance. "Just keep moving toward them!"

We ducked and weaved through the throngs of bar crawlers, and I wasn't sure if it was the effort of navigating the crowd with a stomach sloshing with alcohol, or merely the panic rising in my stomach that made me nauseous. Kipp let out a sudden growl, and our eyes snapped to him, but his own piercing blue gaze was focused in the distance. "There," he gestured. "I see something."

We slowed, panting, and I made out the shape he'd noticed to our left. A figure, seemingly male and dressed in all black, moving like silk on a breeze. He slid down a building and made his way through the crowd. The hair on the back of my neck stood on end as I watched the figure dart through the crowd in our direction, unaffected by the flow of foot traffic. For all his athletic prowess, even Blaise had never moved with such lethal smoothness. This... this was someone who had made it their entire life's purpose to go unnoticed, having the most impact with the least amount of recognition.

This was someone trained to take life as though they were a ghost themself.

"We need to get out of here." Finlay's voice was soft but firm, and Kipp and Cas nodded as well, clearly having sensed the same. I wasn't sure what kind of magic this figure possessed, but if we could avoid the altercation, I had a feeling we'd be better off for it. As a unit, we moved away from the figure, drifting to the right as we moved toward the spires, which still seemed pitifully far away. Oh, gods, why had we ventured so far into the city?

It was a trap, I realized. We had been set up to be out tonight, and this... this was a purposeful hit. Even though we'd had no interactions with Aerrin or Thad about going to this part of town, instinctively, I knew they had orchestrated this. They'd been stringing us along since the moment they dangled Darrya's engagement to Aerrin in front of us, all with the goal of getting us *here*. Their hands were on this somehow, but just removed enough that nobody could accuse them of anything, should we be found dead in the streets of Reviere.

"Those fuckers," I gritted out. "When we get back—"

"Let's just focus on the 'getting back' part, little angel." Finlay's tone was breathy, less measured than normal, and that, above all else, truly began to scare me.

I glanced at him as we pushed past a throng of people, stumbling out into a blissfully clear opening. His expression was pinched, a deathlike pallor to his face. "You know something."

"If it's the group I think it is..." Finlay shook his head. "Let's just move faster."

The figure darted along our right, now, and we banked left, still attempting to keep track of the spires. Another street full of people passed, and then he appeared in front of us, only two streets removed, blocking our path forward. Our combined footsteps stilled, and then Finlay jerked his head right. "It's the only other way through."

An alleyway. Empty and dark, dark enough that I couldn't see the end. "Kipp?" I asked.

He peered in, his lupine eyes narrowing, then shook his head. "I can't see to the end. But Finlay's right." He glanced nervously at the figure, who stood in the middle of the crowd, people seeming to part around him like a stone in the river. "It's the only path around."

Finlay brought his fire forth, lighting a few steps ahead of us as we rushed in, looking for an exit. Which, blissfully, there was — just there, a few strides forward —

Another, smaller figure jumped down from the top of the building, barring our exit. It removed its cloak, and I realized with a start that it was the woman from the tavern. The one who had told us to run.

"I'm sorry," she murmured, eyes darting behind us. She removed a sharp disc from a loop at her side, twirling it once with her fingers. "You should have been faster."

I whirled to follow her gaze, and another figure appeared, blocking the path we had come down. It was the one who had donned all black in the crowd, and he removed its hood, revealing an intense man with jet-black hair. He lifted his gaze, scanning the four of us, his expression entirely devoid of emotion. I took a step back as I realized I'd met him before. Kuiper. He'd been in the meeting we'd had with Aerrin and Thad. It left no more question in my mind that the brothers were behind this — and that they had no intention of us leaving Reviere alive.

Finlay let out a forced exhale. "It's them. It's the Hounds."

Before I could question him, I felt his power tap mine and, with a jolt, I realized he was silently requesting we power-share. I let him in instantly, panicked at the thought that we needed to resort to such a thing when we outnumbered them four to two. Finlay lifted his hands, beginning to cast an air shield, and I raised my hands to follow.

"Kipp!" Cas cried from behind, and we whirled to see Kipp on his knees, hacking, Cas crumpling behind him. A fleeting, confused thought raced through me at the sight of Kipp, who hadn't shifted into his wolf form. Why hadn't—?

My vision went blurry, a bright silver shimmer engulfing it, and I gagged as dust filled my airways. My knees slammed into the ground, cracking against the stone as a terrible sensation filled me. It felt like my entire soul had been wrenched from me. It felt like — like —

A Banshee scream.

"No," I rasped out, and stumbled back to my feet to see if the others were okay. I blinked rapidly, clearing the tears. Clearly, they'd all been hit with the same wave that I had. Cas remained on the ground, recovering, and Finlay was staggering to his feet, rubbing at his chest. Kipp was on his feet again already and circling the woman, but he still wasn't in his wolf form. It *was* the same kind of magic, then; the magic that kept him from shifting and the rest of us from accessing our magic.

In one strange, unpredictable swoop, this fight had just been leveled.

I unsheathed my sword with a groan, attempting to get into my fighting stance. The agony of my magic being ripped from me bordered on physical, and it took a moment to shake the sluggish discomfort away. Kuiper had stalked forward, a thin metal chain swinging in his hand. I eyed it warily, wondering what he had planned with such a thing, but when he noticed the stance I'd taken, he slowed, pocketing the chain and unsheathing his own sword. I raised mine, heart sinking at his confident smile. Before I could strike, however, a flash of gold leapt forward and Finlay was there, meeting Kuiper's blade with his own.

I hesitated, realizing I didn't really know how Finlay fought, never having seen him directly in the battle against Nemain. I watched, waiting for an opening as the two circled each other, darting forward to strike and parry. Finlay's skills in battle were honestly impressive, his footwork impeccable. It made sense, I supposed — he would've had the best teachers growing up, and though he enjoyed partying, he was far from out of shape.

What struck me as interesting, however, was how Kuiper fought. He didn't use any magic. Was he not Aes Sídhe, then? Daoine Sídhe, perhaps? He swung in a wide arc with his sword, causing Finlay to flatten himself to the ground, and Finlay struck out with a foot, making Kuiper stumble, but not fall. As he righted himself, Finlay shot to his feet, and they began circling each other once more.

I took the precious lapse in activity to see how Kipp and Cas were faring, seeing them locked in a similar circling game. Kipp had taken the sword sheathed at Cas's side, seeing as his own fangs and claws were rendered useless. I bit the inside of my lip nervously as I saw the small dagger Cas held in his palm, the only weapon left to him. His skills were solely in healing wounds, not inflicting them.

The woman, on the other hand, had split her unique circular weapon in two, turning it into something similar to throwing stars, but with seriously vicious-looking blades. Kipp and Cas seemed hesitant to move in close as they eyed the weapon, but I realized with a start that the woman was hesitating as well. She shifted uneasily, her gaze flicking from them to Kuiper. Clearly, she didn't want to be a part of this, but something was holding her loyal to the other man and whatever deal they had made with the Byrne brothers. With another glance toward Finlay, I made the decision and moved into their circle, pushing the woman to make a move and hoping she would choose to run.

She glared at me, but turned, dropping into a lethal stance. *Shit... no running, then.*

Even though she fought, she did so cautiously, with more careful footwork than lunges and swipes. We circled each other time and again, both taking a few slow strikes to figure out each other's strengths and weaknesses.

Kipp watched and waited from the sidelines until she left an opening to focus on me. At that moment, he struck her side. His speed, at least, hadn't been diminished, but for all the sluggish swipes she'd taken at me, the woman proved to be fast as well. She avoided his strike at the last second, darting away to fling one of her weapons in Cas's direction. Kipp whirled with a cry, but Cas had already seen it, and dropped to the ground. The weapon hovered in the air past him, then turned, flying back his way. Cas rolled as the blade embedded into the ground a mere hair's breadth from him and retreated to Kipp's side. The blade shuddered in the earth, then flew back into the woman's hand.

Ah. So she, at least, had elemental powers, and had found a way to make her air magic offensive to suit her needs. *Fuck.*

We couldn't let her use her weapons for anything but close combat. Decision made, I lunged forward, meeting one of her blades. She moved to swipe with the other one, but I'd anticipated it and ducked my arm, snapping my elbow up at the exact moment her wrist crossed over it. Her hand flew up with the momentum of my strike, but she maintained her grip on the weapon, a low hiss leaving her mouth as she realized I was more of a match for her than she anticipated. She looked ready for another blow, but was forced to untangle herself from me as Kipp advanced, barely missing his stab at her ribs.

She sneered at him and backed up from us all, her gaze flicking to Cas, clearly weighing if we were all equally adept and if we could be outmatched. Kipp and I both shifted closer to Cas, ready to form a unified front. She considered us all for a long moment, and I felt the air shift as she formed a shield around herself.

"Kuiper!" she called out in a strangled voice as she retreated, looking back only once she had begun scaling the building she had jumped down from. "Fall back!"

"No!" The command came as a snarl, and as I turned, I saw Kuiper block Finlay's strike, his leg kicking out to catch Finlay in the chest in the same breath. Finlay flew back from the force of the blow, landing on his back with a groan. He doubled over, coughing and wheezing, and I watched with horror as Kuiper strode toward him, sword raised. I ceased breathing and stumbled forward, attempting to close the space between us in time to reach him, even as I knew the distance was too great.

Even as I saw the scene play out before me, cementing into my brain before it had even happened.

The blow would land. I wouldn't make it in time.

Something whizzed past me in the air, and Kuiper let out an agonized yelp, dropping the sword with a clatter. A dagger — Cas's dagger — was embedded in the back of his hand. He yanked it out, his teeth bared in a dangerous grimace, but I was already there, standing between him and Finlay, sword in hand.

I wasn't sure if it was the pure, protective rage that coursed through my veins, or if the potency of the dust had truly worn off, but I had the sudden feeling of waking up with a jolt. The familiar hum began in my veins, and before I knew it, my power had returned in full force. The hum became a sizzle, and then a roar as it pounded through my veins. I grinned, meeting Kuiper's eyes as I summoned every spark of lightning I could. I knew now what he saw in my gaze was a terrifying, smoldering gold, and I'd never been more grateful for it. For the first time, Kuiper looked uncertain. He dropped Cas's dagger and reached to his side, unearthing a leather pouch. My eyes narrowed at the realization that whatever lay in there was the source of our dampened magic, and I straightened, ready to lunge for the item.

Before I could, Finlay struck his stomach and sent him staggering backward. Kuiper grappled for purchase on Finlay's shoulders, but

Finlay twisted and pulled him over his back, sending him flying to the ground with a thud. In the next second, Kipp was there, a blade to Kuiper's neck. Kuiper squirmed, and I noticed with alarm that he still grasped the pouch in his hand.

"Finlay!" I cried out, pointing with my blade as I stalked forward. Finlay followed my gesture and grabbed for Kuiper's arm, twisting until we heard a pop. He let out an angry yell, and I took a sick sort of pleasure from the sound. Still, he didn't release the pouch. I reached him, noticing the way he clutched his other hand — the wounded one — close to his side. I bent down and tugged on his hand, splaying his fingers wide. Blood gushed freely, and he gritted his teeth.

"Care to tell us what's in your other hand?" I asked, but he turned his head away, saying nothing.

I straightened and turned away from him. "Fine. I guess we're doing this the hard way." With a sidelong glance back down at his wounded hand, I lifted my foot and stomped on it, *hard.* He let out a strangled hiss, but nothing more. I turned back around to face him, keeping my heel on his injured hand as I twisted, digging in deeper.

He groaned and twitched, finally giving Finlay the leeway he needed to wrestle the pouch from his hand. We all took a moment to stare at the object, wondering about the dangerous contents within.

Kuiper took the moment for a final attempt at retreat. He whipped his hand from under my heel, sending me stumbling, and kicked at Kipp's feet in the same move. The blade grazed his cheek but missed, and he made to stand, Finlay's grip the only thing holding him back. Finlay dropped the pouch and curled his hand into a fist, taking a swing directly at Kuiper's throat. Kuiper gagged and dropped for a moment, but it was a mere deflection. He quickly rose again with an uppercut, which hit Finlay's chin with a resounding crack. Finlay stumbled back in a daze. Before anyone else could move forward, Kuiper was gone, disappearing out of the alley and into the crowd like a leaf carried on a breeze.

"Finlay," I gasped, rushing to his side. "Are you okay?"

He rubbed his chin, wincing. "I'll live."

"Thanks to Cas," I breathed, turning to face Cas. "Where did you learn how to do that, Cas?"

Cas didn't answer. Instead, he stepped forward and lifted the leather pouch from the ground, gingerly grasping it with only the tips of his fingers. A few sparkling pieces of silver powder trailed from the opening of the bag, closely resembling Faerie dust. He lifted his gaze from the bag to us. "What the *fuck* is this?"

Chapter Twenty

We stumbled into the palace in a heap, sinking back against the stone wall as we caught our breath. I glanced over, my eyes scanning everyone in turn to ensure we'd all made it in one piece. Though Finlay's chin was an angry red, promising a hefty bruise to come, nobody appeared seriously injured. Everyone's chest was rising and falling rapidly, sweat glistening like morning dew across our faces, which were all a shade paler than normal. The palace guards eyed us carefully, but we ushered them away, mostly due to the fact we couldn't form the words at present, but also from an undercurrent of distrust. I had a feeling, however, that they had no clue how deep the betrayal from their leadership ran, and they would feel differently if they knew how many of Larke's guards currently lay dead in the streets of Reviere.

As the footsteps of the palace guards echoed down the hall, continuing their perimeter sweeps, I sank to the floor. "What... just happened?" I asked, burying my face in my hands.

Finlay sank down beside me and slid his hand over my shoulders. "Those were the Hounds."

"The Hounds?" Cas asked.

"They're a vigilante group of sorts, but with a fearsome reputation." Finlay's voice was grim, and when I looked up, his face was equally somber. "The law itself looks the other way, here, when the Hounds get involved. They're trained extensively in combat, and typically, they recruit those with nothing left to lose."

I thought back to the woman who'd been with Kuiper. She'd let us go earlier in the evening; she'd told us to run. And even when she caught us, she hadn't wanted to fight — that much had been clear. A small kernel of pity lodged itself in my gut, and I shifted uncomfortably, wondering what had led the woman to join the Hounds. If she liked staring death in the eyes far more often than anyone should.

"There's nothing more terrifying than someone who believes they have nothing left to lose, including their own life," Kipp murmured. Cas hummed his agreement and shifted, pressing his body into Kipp's. Kipp wrapped his arms around him and gazed down, face solemn as he took stock of Cas, ensuring he was still whole. Cas twisted in his embrace to do the same, and reached his hand up, fingers tracing over a scratch on Kipp's cheek. There was a flash of orange light, and the scratch on his cheek disappeared. Cas smiled, and my heart tugged at the small, loving gesture between the two of them, even as a wave of guilt washed over me at the realization that they had been dragged into this mess because of Finlay and me.

I let out a deep breath, my heart rate finally returning to normal. "That was insane."

Finlay's body shook against mine as he let out a soft chuckle, and I blinked in surprise. "That, little angel, was karma."

"What are you talking about?" Now it was my turn to twist in his embrace, staring up at him in astonishment. He smirked down at me, then turned his gaze on Kipp.

"Listen, Cas. You've got six inches and a good sense of humor. But we warned you that you'd jinxed the evening."

Cas gaped at him. *"Seven."*

"You see, when you say it like that, it makes you sound like a liar. But I'll give you a pass." Finlay winked at him, and Cas pressed back into Kipp's chest as he tossed his head back, shaking with laughter. Kipp narrowed his eyes at Finlay, but couldn't mask the amused grin as he pulled Cas in tighter.

"How can you all be so... relaxed about what just happened?" I demanded, and Finlay and Cas exchanged a look.

"Because if we don't, Katie-cat, we'll spiral." Cas's voice was soft, hitching up on the last word.

Finlay let out an audible sigh. "And trust me, we don't need that right now. We need to think with clear heads."

"So, we all know who gave the Hounds the order, right?" Kipp asked, and when we all nodded, added, "So... do we confront them?"

"As far as they know, we're being held hostage right now, or worse." I shuddered. "The question is, *why?* Why do this?"

"I think it's obvious that they baited us into coming here under the guise of Darrya's marriage. As far as this…" Finlay shrugged. "They just want to lead?"

Two guards chose that moment to walk by, and we all fell silent as they passed. Kipp stood, grasping Cas's hand, and gestured for us to follow. "It's too public here. We should head back to our rooms."

I hesitated, apprehension curling in my gut. Now that we knew without a doubt that the brothers had put a hit out on us, being under their roof was the last thing I wanted. "Is it safe to?"

"There's a reason they lured us out to the city, Katie-cat," Cas said. "If they want to lead, there can't be any question of foul play. For something like that to happen under their roof, especially as people arrive for the Imbolc celebrations, it would be detrimental. As far as I see it, this is the safest place in the city for us to be." He looked to Finlay for confirmation, and he nodded.

"Agreed. Though I don't want to stay here any longer than necessary, especially now. If we don't make any progress by Imbolc, we'd better leave with the crowds." Finlay went silent for a few paces. "I think Darrya would understand."

He sounded like he was saying it as much to assure himself as us, and I squeezed his hand in reassurance. "She'd rather we all return in one piece," I confirmed. "Something tells me Larke would be fine with breaking her marital vows with her if she asked, though." I winked, attempting to lighten his mood as he had just a few minutes earlier. "Repeatedly."

Finlay let out a soft snort and flagged down a passing servant. "Are the lords in their chambers?" he asked, and the poor Fae paled at the dark tone he'd used.

"I — I don't believe so, Your Majesty. They had some errands to run tonight. They should be back tomorrow afternoon." He folded his hands in front of him, awaiting further instruction. Finlay tilted his head in dismissal, and the servant scurried away, clearly happy to avoid the obvious tension bubbling in our group.

A low growl formed in Kipp's throat. "I suppose they'll find out any minute now that we're not where they'd planned."

"Nothing to be done about it now," Finlay replied. "Like we said, this is the safest place for us to be."

"But you'd better lie low tomorrow," I put in, giving Kipp and Cas both a pointed look. "This is our mess to tackle, not yours."

Kipp scoffed, clearly ready to argue, but Cas pulled the leather pouch from his pocket, weighing it in his free palm. "We can try to figure out this mystery in the meantime. Wren might have a better idea than us, or at least be able to do some research under the radar." Cas's expression was one of stark relief as he added, "Thankfully, it seems like she hasn't really been tied to our group yet."

I eyed the pouch carefully. "Whatever is in there, it's like someone was able to bottle a Banshee scream."

"Do you think—" Finlay stopped and swallowed. "Do you think Nemain was able to work with Aerrin and Thad to imbue her power into this?"

"Shit," I breathed, thinking back to the chain the dark-clad male figure had carried. It was similar to the chain I'd seen on Clíodhna, the goddess the queen had kept captive in the dungeon of the palace in Muiranvia. If the chain had the same enchantment on it that the queen's had, it wasn't a far stretch to think they'd used similar enchantments to imbue a similar magic into this powder. "You might be right."

Kipp let out a low whine, and Cas pocketed the item once more, treating it like it was on fire. He turned to face us, eyes wide with alarm. "If that's the case, it means…"

Kipp finished for him. "It means Nemain helped create a weapon that can dismantle the very soul of nearly every Fae."

As soon as the door closed to our room, I leaned against it, allowing the emotions from the night to consume me. I buried my face in my hands, attempting to slow my breathing, but closing my eyes did little to ebb the emotional flow. In fact, it made it worse — the images from the evening came rushing back, as clear as they'd been in the moment. The circular blade that had nearly struck Cas, and the blow that had been poised to land true on Finlay. Ready to end his life.

"Little angel—" Finlay began, but stopped as he saw me with my back braced against the door. I heard his footsteps as he approached, and then he was pulling my hands from my face, using his own to cup my chin. He tipped my face up to meet his gaze, and I locked eyes with him. "What is it?"

"Finlay... I almost lost you today." I exhaled, my voice trembling. "I *saw it*. I prepared for the fact that I was going to lose you."

He gave me a lopsided grin, but it didn't quite meet his eyes. They remained solemn and, to my dismay, almost *pitying*. "But you didn't."

I gaped at him. How could he be so cavalier about this? I pushed him back, and he allowed me to easily, giving me space as he eyed me warily. "You big idiot!" Tears swam in my vision, and I blinked them away furiously. "I had it handled. Why did you step in the way?"

The grin fell from his face. "I knew who he was, Kate." I jolted at the seriousness of his tone and the use of my real name. "And your magic was locked away, and—" he paused, running a hand through his hair. "I would sacrifice myself for you, time and again. You know that by now, right? There is no scenario where I would choose differently. In every one, I would throw myself in front of that blade. I would choose *you.*"

I opened my mouth, then shut it again, scowling at him. "And what if I choose you?" I retorted. "What makes you think I would just accept your sacrifice? What if I'm willing to sacrifice *myself* for *you?*"

He returned the scowl, stepping back into my space. His gaze bore down on me, eyes smoldering the same blue of the hottest fires. "You stubborn, beautiful woman," he gritted out, and pressed me into the door again with his hips, eliciting a gasp from me. "Then I guess we'd just argue ourselves into early graves together."

I tipped my head up, meeting his gaze defiantly. "And I bet you wouldn't have it any other way."

"I wouldn't," he growled, and snaked his hand around the back of my neck, tugging me into him as he crashed his lips to mine. I met him there instantly, giving into the fear and frustration and, above all, *passion* that simmered between us after all that had transpired earlier in the day. His hands wound around my waist and down my ass, gripping and lifting so that I was propped in the air, pressing his hard length into my core. I immediately wound my legs around him, pulling him tighter against me. I bit down on his bottom lip and delighted in his moan, letting him slip his tongue into my mouth as he gripped me tighter and ground himself into me.

Finlay broke the kiss and worked his way down my neck, allowing me a moment to breathe. I shivered at the feel of his warm breath on my throat, and as his tongue followed the same path, I finally gasped out, "Bed. *Now.*"

He obeyed instantly, swinging us around, and in a few steps, we collapsed onto the bed. He moved to hover over me, but I shook my head, giving him a light push to send him to the mattress. In one fluid movement, I was straddling him, and he shuddered as I slipped my hands under his shirt, running them along the smooth, warm planes of his skin. He lifted off the bed for me to remove his shirt, and when it was off, I reveled in the dips and counters of his muscles. There were a few angry, mottled marks from the fight, already purpling against his smooth skin. I took a moment to brush my lips against them, enjoying the sigh my soft kisses drew from him. Once I finished my path across his chest, I paused, simply taking a moment to absorb the full sight of him. He lay silently, gazing up at me with those piercing blue eyes, his golden hair falling in soft waves around his face. His already full lips were swollen from our kissing, and his chin was purpling by the minute. I bit my lip, wondering absently if we should have gone to a healer before heading back here. Did it still hurt him? Even with it, he was still so gorgeous he took my breath away.

He reached up and dragged a thumb across my lips, then gave a little tug to pull my bottom lip from my teeth. "What're you thinking?" he asked softly.

I shook my head. "Just that you're beautiful." I brushed a finger against his chin. "And that I'm hoping that you're okay."

He smiled, snagging my hand in his and kissing it. "Never been better, little angel. Truly." He pulled back and stilled, a question forming in his eyes.

"What is it?" I asked.

He hesitated before answering. "Do you trust me?"

My response was instant. "Absolutely."

He grinned, his expression turning mischievous as he grabbed for the ties of my dress. He tugged them loose and pulled the dress over my head in two deft movements, leaving me in nothing but my underwear. His eyes gleamed as his grip tightened on my hips, taking a moment to devour my naked appearance. I felt my nipples pebble under his ravenous gaze, and in the next second, I was being guided onto my side.

He pressed up against my back, his hard length at my hip, and I gasped as he nipped at my ear. His voice was husky with need as he whispered to me. "I've wanted to try this since the moment we met."

Before I could ask what he meant, I felt it.

The tapping of his power against mine.

"Oh," I breathed as I realized where he was going with this. A hot quiver of excitement built low in my belly in anticipation. When we first power-shared, I had nearly come from the pleasure of that alone. To join it with the actual act...

I let him in, and felt the hot exhale of his breath against me as our magic joined. My nerves tingled with pleasure at the now-familiar feel of his power dancing with mine. It rushed into my very core, and I sighed at the way it warmed me, imprinting me in the way only Finlay's magic could. I felt his muscles tense against my back as the electric hum of my magic entered his system as well, intertwining us.

Riding the instant high the power-sharing gave me, I rocked my hips back against Finlay, and felt his breath stutter. His hands feathered their way over my bare skin, flitting their way down to my underwear, where they dipped into the front. I leaned back into him and spread my legs, giving him full access. He groaned as he felt how wet I already was for him, and began to swirl his thumb against me, causing my core to nearly melt at the combined sensations now coursing through me.

"I need to feel you," I whimpered, reaching my hand back to trail down his stomach and into his pants. I gripped his length and heard him hiss.

"*Gods,* Kate. Fuck."

"I know," I groaned, understanding exactly what he meant. The sensations were nearly too much to handle, but I wasn't about to experience them alone. I pumped him a few times, relishing the velvet-on-steel feel of him. He let out a string of curses and jerked himself away from me. I blinked, confused at the loss of him, until he grabbed my legs, tugging me to the edge of the bed. I raised up onto my shoulders to see him, pants removed, fingers wrapped around the edge of my panties.

"I can't wait anymore." His gaze burned into me. "Say it, little angel. Say please."

"Please," I begged, lifting my hips for him. My panties were off in an instant, lost to a distant corner of the room, and he plunged into me.

I lost myself to the feeling of him melding into me. Body, mind, down to our very souls, we merged. Everything else disappeared, and it was just us, chasing a high like we'd never known. I could feel his desire and his pleasure in the heat of his magic, playing off my own, doubling every sensation. I curled my legs around him, lifting shamelessly to deepen each thrust. I knew, somehow, that he could feel when he hit the perfect spot, just as I could feel the buildup as he came close to his end. Why the hell had we waited so long to do this?

I vaguely recalled begging for it. Begging for him to pull me over the edge with him. I wanted to cry out as we shattered, falling apart with each other, but all sound had ceased as euphoria filled my very being instead of oxygen. It was all I could do to ride the aftershocks that radiated between our power-sharing bonds, as my body had lost all other control.

"So," Finlay rasped afterward, crawling up to my side. "We will be doing that again."

It was all I could do to huff out a laugh and murmur my assent. It took us both several long moments to relinquish our power sharing, reeling our magic back into ourselves. I felt strangely empty without the warmth of his fire magic dancing around my soul and found myself snuggling closer to him on instinct. He opened his arms to me, dragging me against his bare chest and kissing me atop my head as I burrowed closer.

I closed my eyes and breathed in the scent of him, the decision I hadn't dared voice out loud finally bubbling to the surface. I could blame the post-orgasm high, but I knew that wasn't it — it was a decision I had made hours before, back when I had been convinced I'd lost the person I'd grown to love.

"Whatever happens next, I know what I want," I whispered, turning to lay on my side. He was already there, cheek resting on his pillow, gaze fixed on me.

"And what's that, little angel?"

"I want you." At his confused expression, I elaborated further. "I love you, and I want you, and I want to see this through. I want to marry you, Finlay."

CHAPTER TWENTY-ONE

Normally, the sound of raised voices was enough to dissuade Wren from their vicinity. Before the contentment Kipp now brought Cas, she'd had many mornings, hidden in her own room, listening to disgruntled suitors storm out of his house upon learning that it was all there would be — one night, and nothing more. As someone who couldn't separate the emotional and the physical, it had always confused her, and it was enough to dampen her own urges to experience much of the same. If she despised conflict already as a bystander, she knew she wasn't cut out for it directly. She wouldn't have the same tact — or quite frankly, disregard — as her brother did if directly confronted.

But she had promised to be the palace ears for Kate and Finlay, and after Cas's revelation of what transpired last night, the rage simmering in her veins was enough to draw her recklessly close to Thad's study, where the voices sounded. She needed to confirm for herself that it was the Byrne brothers who had orchestrated the hit on her brother and her friends. Especially when one of the voices belonged to someone she had talked with yesterday, while Cas and the others were presumably being attacked, and he hadn't *appeared* to be someone in the middle of a murder for hire. He'd been soft and affectionate with the animals in the stable, and when they spoke of his daughter, he'd seemed alarmed at the mere thought of her being in trouble.

Someone who cared that much for others couldn't be evil.

Could they?

"Why the fuck are you defending them?" Aerrin's voice sounded as though he'd already screamed himself hoarse for the morning, but with the vocal cords he hadn't fried, he spit every word with hushed venom. "We gave them the task, and they failed. Now they're loose ends, and we're left to deal with the same problem, only now, they're on edge. They *know.*"

"It was four to two, and you know we needed her..." Thad's tone was so hushed, Wren could barely make out the words. She squeezed in closer to the side of the wall, just brushing the corner that turned into the hallway where the study door was, presumably, open. Wren briefly glanced at her surroundings, ensuring there were no passing staff members. She brushed the hair back behind her ear and leaned in. "...all proved incredibly capable without magic. Even their friends, and even with alcohol. You heard Kuiper."

"So we kill the Hounds and start over."

Wren's heart sank. The Hounds, the hit, everything... they *had* orchestrated it. Aerrin and Thad both. She felt her pulse quicken as she realized what this meant for them. Even in the palace, they were no longer safe. Maybe they never had been. This first hit had been an unfortunate miscalculation, but she couldn't count on the brothers to try to remain tactful. They had a target on their backs and, next time, the brothers would send a bigger army to dispatch them.

"You can't solve everything by leaving a trail of bodies, Aerrin," Thad said, his voice strained. "There will be questions, loyalties severed."

Yes, she prayed mentally. *Whatever it is you want, whatever you're planning, don't do it with bloodshed.*

"Who the fuck cares for loyalty? We're running out of time. They're likely moving to leave as we speak, and that makes our plan insurmountably difficult. You're being ridiculous if you want to save those Hounds just because you want the loyalty of the rest. Silly things like loyalty and mercy won't get you anywhere. I thought you knew this, but..." he trailed off into a weighted pause.

"Just come right out and say what it is you really want to, brother." Thad's words were tense.

"We both know what it is without me having to voice it, but so be it." Aerrin sounded irritated, his voice rising as he continued speaking. "You have lost sight of what's important here. Just as we're on the precipice of everything we've worked for, you're pulling away. I don't know where the cold feet and weak heart are coming from."

Wren frowned. If Thad was pulling away from Aerrin's plans, that, to her, was the exact opposite of a weak heart. It meant he was learning what *was* truly important. A flash of protectiveness coursed through her at Thad's expense.

"It's you, Aerrin!" Thad cried, and Wren jumped back slightly at the intensity of his outburst, curling tightly against the stone wall. "I know what we've been working for, and I knew we would need to do some unsavory things, but…"

"But what?" Aerrin's question was so soft Wren barely heard it.

"I didn't think you'd go so far as to kill our own father, Aerrin."

Wren clapped a hand over her mouth to hold back a gasp. There was another pause, so long and silent Wren began to believe that was the end of their conversation. She backed up, mind spiraling. Maybe they weren't as much of a team as she and everyone else had suspected? What did this mean; that Thad hadn't been a part of the plan to kill Lachlan? What else had he — or *hadn't* he — been willing to do?

A cold laugh cut through the air, stilling her backward movement. "It's always been about the power he kept us from, Thad. In what world would he not have been an obstacle to overcome?"

"He was our *father*. He loved us."

"Family doesn't do what he did to us!" Aerrin bellowed, and Wren curled her hands into fists at the viciousness of Aerrin's words, sweat instantly pricking her palms. "He was too weak to take what he could for us, to provide us with all the power he had access to. His love was his weakness."

A thump came then, followed quickly by glass shattering, the harsh sound echoing off the stone walls. Aerrin's words dripped with vitriol as he continued. "If we want to achieve everything we've worked for, you need to harden your heart. I thought we already resolved this once. Kings can have everything, except weakness. And love is a weakness. For his people, and even for his family. Listen carefully, Thad — a king is free to desire love, and even experience it from time to time, but it will never help him reign. Only hinder." Wren heard an exaggerated sigh. "And that bastard of yours is nothing but a hindrance."

There was a choked sound, but before Wren could decipher what it meant or who it came from, footsteps rang out. She scrambled backwards to the staircase and made it halfway up before the footsteps strode by, along with a glimpse of red hair that told her Aerrin had left the study. She breathed out a soft sigh of relief when they stormed down the passageway without so much as a falter in stride, leaving her undetected.

She waited, counting to twenty — and back down, for good measure — before descending the staircase once more, trying to look as casual as possible. When she reached the bottom step, however, she yelped at the tall figure waiting just off to the right. The sound seemed to amuse Thad, whose eyes crinkled slightly at the corners, though the rest of his expression remained resigned. Wren eyed him abrasively, waiting for him to speak. She wouldn't admit to her eavesdropping unless he voiced it first.

"Enjoy yourself there?" he asked.

Wren immediately dropped her gaze. *Damn.* No getting out of this one, then.

She opened her mouth to respond, but was stopped by the raise of his hand, which she followed to find a small lizard on the stone wall next to her. She blinked as she watched it climb atop his hand, surprised. It was vibrant in color, starting crimson at the head and fading to blue that reached the tip of its tail. It scurried across Thad's hand and up his arm, where it stopped at the crest of his shoulder and tilted its head at her. She returned a quizzical gaze of her own, then shifted the look to Thad. He let out a soft laugh.

"He's an old friend of mine," he explained. "He can change his colors, and so he often eavesdrops on my behalf. Today, however, it appears he caught a second eavesdropper."

Wren pursed her lips. "An Agama lizard," she noted, and watched as surprise flickered across his face. "From what I've read, they tend to thrive in balanced and harmonious environments. That—" She gestured back toward his office. "—didn't strike me as either."

"Yes. Well." Thad sighed. "She hasn't been very happy with me lately."

"I can only imagine why," Wren mused wryly, stopping her bold response a second too late. She flushed, but continued, the observation burning its way up her throat. "So you *were* behind the attack on my brother last night."

The accusation hung in the air for a long moment, and she held her breath, staring up at him. Good gods, he was tall, and *strong*. And probably armed, not only with a physical weapon, but magic passed down his lineage from the incredibly powerful god, Manannán.

Here she was, alone with him, and she had just outed herself as what Aerrin had described as a loose end. It would only take a second for Thad to dispatch her, if he chose. But... he hadn't wanted that, had he? Based only on how the conversation had flowed and a gut feeling, she felt certain she would be safe.

But gut feelings weren't assurances, she reminded herself, and as the silence stretched for another heartbeat, she took an uncertain step back. Thad's gaze flicked to the ground, marking the movement, and back up to her. He dipped his chin, expression unreadable. "I didn't realize you had come here with your brother."

"I did," she whispered. Her heart clenched at the thought of Cas, and what she had been so close to losing.

"So that is the family you spoke of the other night," he mused. "He's what you live for."

She tipped her chin up, feeling emboldened. "They all are."

Silence fell between them again, heavy and suffocating like a thick blanket. Thad gazed at her, his lips parted, and she slowly became aware that he wanted to answer but didn't know how. He couldn't deny what he had done, and so, he wasn't attempting to offer an apology. She wouldn't have accepted it as truth if he had, and he seemed to know that.

Finally, he dropped his gaze and let out a sigh. "Come," he said, turning on his heel and waving for her to follow. Confused, she hurried after him, back the way they had just come. She slipped into his office behind him, watching as he shuffled through his desk drawers, unearthing a key. He turned to his bookshelf, running his hands along the spines until he located a thick, red one, and pulled it from the shelf. She lifted her brows as he set it on the desk, shoving the key into a lock where the paper edges should be.

"I can't apologize for what happened. I know my part, and I suspect you do, too." He avoided her eyes as he pulled out a few papers and passed them her way. She clutched them tightly, but didn't look down; instead, she watched Thad intently. He leaned over his desk, hands curled around the edges so tightly they went white.

"I can't... control a lot of decisions in my life," he continued, finally meeting Wren's eyes. They were sapphire orbs full of anguish and vulnerability, as though the confession had taken its toll on him. Wren had the sudden desire to go and wrap her arms around him, but pressed the urge down. "But if I were to say someone must have been snooping in my office, that's not in my control."

He motioned to the papers in her hands, and she finally looked down, reading them for the first time. The wedding by proxy of Darrya Egan to Aerrin Byrne, signed by the late queen and duke, with Thad himself representing as the proxy.

These were the papers she'd been searching for this whole time — the papers that would set Darrya free from her sham marriage with Aerrin.

"It's our only copy," Thad added softly.

"This is... thank you," she breathed.

He gave her a pained look in response. "Please, don't thank me. I'm the reason you're in this position to begin with." He let out a shuddering breath. "Aerrin knows exactly which levers to pull any time I begin to question the path he's leading us down. He knows how to keep me in line."

Wren nodded, remembering how Aerrin had brought up his daughter before his abrupt exit earlier. "Does he threaten her?"

"He knows he doesn't need to go that far. I'll work with him on anything if he so much as mentions her." Thad sighed. "Even when it leads to things like this."

"I didn't realize you and your brother had so many... differences in opinion."

"Familial disputes take a new meaning with us. It's been a few hundred years of differences in the making."

The corner of Wren's lip curled into a half-smile as she acknowledged his half-hearted attempt to deflect. "I didn't expect you to disagree on something as large as your father. Especially if you knew I was listening."

Wren kept her voice soft, but still, Thad took a long moment before answering. "I figured you would only believe it if Aerrin admitted it himself."

"Why do you care?" she blurted out, surprised that he'd put so much thought into this. "Wouldn't it be better to leave us all intimidated, thinking you didn't care about any loss of life?"

Thad offered her a grim smile. "I suppose I don't want to be known as entirely heartless. Despite his best intentions, Aerrin couldn't quite beat all the empathy out of me. And neither could life."

Wren hummed thoughtfully at his response. It was true — though the Fae had far longer lifespans than humans, it wasn't always a blessing. With every passing year, she understood a bit more when her elders cautioned how longevity could chip away at life's true meaning, making it easier to focus solely on the most intense emotions. Oftentimes, those could be a burning hatred or resentment for someone or, worst of all, the loss of most emotion at all.

"That's also not the legacy I want to leave for my daughter," he added quietly.

When she looked back up at him, she saw the sheen in his eyes. It was a grim determination, and for some reason, it made her believe everything she'd heard: his admission, his brother's plans, and his own for the future. And for the first time, she saw her opening.

Perhaps she could fix this all without bloodshed. All it would take was the one weakness Aerrin had pointed out: love. Specifically, Thad's love for his child. She just had to convince him, through his daughter, to end this madness with his brother.

She held his gaze steadily as she replied. "If you want that kind of world for your daughter, then you'd better figure out how to fix your brother's mess. Something tells me they can't coexist like this for long."

A muscle in his jaw clenched as he listened, but then he nodded. "Somehow, I think you may be right."

CHAPTER TWENTY-TWO

That following morning, everything in our room had been gathered and put away, ready for our departure. We had just finished closing our final bags when a knock came at the door. Finlay and I glanced at each other, and his hand went to the sword sheathed at his waist. The temperature of the room rose a few degrees as he stalked to the door and motioned for me to take up a place behind it. I did as he motioned, summoning sparks that played recklessly at the tips of my fingers.

It would be rash of Aerrin and Thad to plan an attack on us directly in our chambers, but not out of the realm of possibility. Clearly, they had wanted to distance themselves from our fate, but who was to say they hadn't changed their minds, deciding it could look like a simple breach of security? I inhaled and nodded to Finlay, but as he unsheathed his sword, the knock came again, followed by a soft voice. "It's me."

I blinked, then rushed to push Finlay aside and open the door. Wren stood on the other side, with a bag slung across her shoulders and Kipp and Cas behind her. I sagged against the doorframe in relief. "Thank gods. We were worried it was..." I trailed off, unwilling to say any more to the empty hallway. Instead, I moved aside. "Come in."

They did so, with Wren eyeing the bags we'd collected and placed on our bed. I peeked outside after they all came in, scanning the hallway to assure myself we were alone before I closed the door again. Even so, I leaned against the doorframe, putting myself between the people I loved — all gathered in this one room — and the dangers I knew lurked around every corner of this godsforsaken palace.

"What's this about, Wren?" Kipp asked, and our eyes swiveled to her. So, she'd been the one to summon us all together, and they were just as out of the loop as we were. I tilted my head at her expectantly, but she refused to meet my eyes as she fiddled with the end of her maroon dress. It was soft and simple, unlike the other dresses she'd donned this week as my lady-in-waiting, and cinched at the waist with ivy. The leaves fell in a simple but beautiful pattern at her hips.

"Yeah, you should know better than to interrupt Kippers this close to dinnertime," Cas said as he plopped on the bed. In contrast to Wren's orderly appearance, he wore only tight, dark leather pants and a disheveled, peach-colored shirt that billowed out to drape over his shoulder. Its untied laces did little to keep it in place. He adjusted the fallen sleeve, sniffed, and made a face. "It smells like sex in here."

I flushed and caught Finlay's eye, recalling our tryst from the evening prior and the conversation that followed. A warm, pleasant feeling curled in my stomach, and the look of pride and reverence on Finlay's face as he clearly recalled the same was almost too much to stand. My hand went to my necklace, and I toyed with the chain, averting my gaze to stave off the growing heat in my core. "Are you packed and ready to head out tomorrow?" I asked instead, desperate to change the subject.

"That's what this is about, actually." Wren smoothed her skirts out, then picked at one of the ivy leaves of her belt nervously. I exchanged a curious look with Cas, and even Kipp stood straighter. "I think we should stay," she began, then quickly amended, "Not for long. Another day or two. I have a lead on something, and I want to follow it through. But in the meantime, I wanted to make sure you had this."

She dragged her bag across her body and pulled papers from it, handing them to Finlay. He strode across the room and took them. After a cursory glance, his expression transformed into one of disbelief, and his head snapped up to stare at Wren.

"Are these —?"

She nodded. "Yes."

"How did you get them?"

Wren's face twisted as she considered what to say next, but her response was interrupted as Kipp leaned over Finlay to inspect the papers himself. "It's Darrya's marriage license!" he exclaimed.

Cas and I rushed forward to confirm, wrapping her in hugs and giving her congratulations as Finlay flipped through the papers, inspecting them with silent thoroughness. When we pulled back, Wren gave him a serious look.

"It's the only copy," she said quietly.

Finlay stared at her again for a long moment, then down at the papers as her words registered. In the next instant, they were aflame. The corner where his hand rested grew dark, the ashen color spreading as the flame ate up the side of the papers, curling them in on themselves. He switched the paper to his other hand and caught the gray, crumpled matter as it became palm-sized. My relief grew as the paper dwindled, knowing Darrya was finally safe from Aerrin's clutches.

Finally, it disintegrated in his hand, and he clutched the ashes in his palm, unbothered by the heat. Then he dropped the remains and hugged her. "Thank you, Wren." The emotion in his voice was impossible to miss, and I felt my chest expand with warmth.

"What else did you want to talk about, Wren?" Kipp asked.

"Yeah — if we got what we came for, why do you want to stay?" Cas asked, echoing the question rattling around in my head.

She gave him an exasperated look, even as she grabbed his hands. "Because there is more going on here, obviously. You almost died last night, Cas. They had a weapon we've never heard of and plans to either take or kill Kate and Finlay." She paused. "I think the marriage agreement with Darrya was just a ruse to get you here, I just don't know why."

"I agree," Finlay said. "They knew it was exactly what would get me here."

"But then we should rush home, shouldn't we? Clearly that's where we're safe," Kipp argued.

I remained quiet, letting the argument volley around me. Even though instinct told me we needed to run from this place, fast and far, an invisible string tugged at my insides. Why *had* they brought us here?

I thought back to the difference in how the Hound had fought me versus Finlay — as though he'd wanted me in chains, whereas he'd been ready for a death blow against Finlay. Why?

That single, three letter question burned in my chest, threatening to spill over until I blurted another one. "How, Wren?"

Whatever they heard in my tone, everyone hushed, turning to face me. I cleared my throat. "I want to get to the bottom of this just as much as you. Even if we go home, whatever this is is complex and deep enough that I... I really don't think we'll escape it there. I don't think this is the end of it." The truth of that statement made my voice waver. "I want to leave, but I do think it will take a few days for them to regroup. That gives us time, but not much. What's your plan?"

Wren shot me a grateful look, but it became conflicted as she answered. "To be honest, I didn't get that paperwork on my own. I had help."

"From who?" Kipp asked.

She wrung her hands and took a long moment before replying. "Thad."

"Thad?" Finlay and I echoed in surprise. One of the brothers who had orchestrated our attack on us? Who had signed the by proxy marriage license? Who had *killed his own father?* How did Wren have so much information, and so much confidence in someone who had crossed us at every turn?

Wren's brows knitted together, and she chewed on her bottom lip before responding. "It's difficult to explain, but I really think he's one of the good ones. Truly. His brother has been making all the decisions, and holding things over his head, and he's... conflicted." Her words came out strangled, as if she was still wrapping her own head around them. "If pushed properly, I really think I can persuade him off whatever path they're on. Or at least tell me what they're planning."

My mind whirred with this new information, and I watched as Cas studied her closely. His face turned dark. "And just how come you're on a first name basis with a Byrne brother?"

Her cheeks flushed — *interesting,* I thought — but she tipped her chin up. "A series of events. None of which I need to discuss with you. Some of us don't have your filthy mind."

Cas's eyes flashed, and he opened his mouth to reply, but Kipp beat him to it. "He killed his father, Wren."

"He didn't," she replied firmly. "I overheard them. Aerrin took responsibility for everything. Thad had no idea he'd planned to do anything to Lachlan."

I sucked in a breath, imagining for a moment what that would be like if my own family member orchestrated the death of my parents, unbeknownst to me. A wave of emotion coursed through me, one I never imagined I'd feel for either of those blue-eyed brothers — something akin to pity.

"Because there's no way he could have planned for you to over-hear," Cas drawled. The tone was sarcastic, but the concern underneath was clearly very real.

Wren paused, considering his words, but then pushed forward. "I don't think Aerrin would've openly admitted to his part if he thought anyone was listening. The things he said were... beyond private. Centuries of emotion in the making."

Kipp hummed at this, turning to me. I saw the same thoughts mirrored in his expression. This was an interesting turn of events, but a fortunate one. Wren was giving us insight into a relationship that had been firmly behind stone walls. Walls I'd thought were impenetrable, but somehow, she'd found a crack. And the Wren I first met almost a year ago was not the same one that stood before us today. She'd braved battles and snuck through palaces and here she was, ready to burst the cracks of this mystery wide open.

"Even if we can agree that Thad is second-guessing things with his brother, who's to say you could get the information from him?" Finlay cut in, using the same tone he commanded in political meetings. "Does he trust you, Wren?"

She worried at her lip again, contemplating, but when she answered her tone was firm. "I think so."

I blinked. Come to think of it, Wren had been rather absent the last few days. Though I hadn't thought much of it, considering we were all looking for evidence that would free Darrya from her marriage, I hadn't actually asked what she'd been up to. Clearly there was more at play here with Thad than I knew. Though I wanted to ask more, now wasn't the time. I filed my questions away for later.

Finlay gave a solemn nod at Wren's response. "Okay. We can take two days. Then we leave the day of Imbolc. Everyone will be too busy with their festivities to notice us leaving, anyways."

"No!" Cas cried out, whirling on Finlay. "Are you serious right now?"

"Wren seems confident. I trust her. And clearly, Thad does, too."

I nodded my approval, which was met with a barrage of additional complaints from Cas. I opened my mouth, ready to volley back a snappy retort, but Wren beat me to it. And her response had teeth.

"Cas, I swear to the gods, if you don't listen to me right now, I will pull out your *entire* garden at home and make sure you can never grow a thing on that land again."

He paused, stricken. "Even my penis plants?"

"*Especially* your penis plants." She sniffed. "And you know you always overwater those. Without my help, you'll never grow them again."

Well. I'd never seen this side of Wren, but I had to admit, I kind of loved it. Cas went silent, and Kipp let out a low whine. Finally, Cas crossed his arms, sending peach fabric billowing, and huffed. "Fine. But you will tell me *everything* that happens. Don't leave anything out. And if he does anything to you, I know about thirty different poisons that could work on him."

When I looked at Cas, I expected an expression as violent as his words, but his face was ashen with worry. I was sure it took something out of him, having to let his sister go on this potentially dangerous mission. I didn't blame Cas — though Wren had confidence in Thad, every interaction I'd had with him had been touchy at best, and near-death at the worst. There was only so much faith I could put in a gut feeling, even if it came from someone like Wren.

"Do you want me to go with?" I asked, attempting to bridge the gap between the two with a safer alternative, but she shook her head. Her mind was made up.

"He has lots of spies. And from what I've seen, you couldn't spot them even if you tried." A small smile played across her lips as she thought of something, though I couldn't for the life of me figure out what she was imagining. I exchanged one more look with Finlay, who merely shrugged and gave a small shake of his head. Whatever had transpired between her and Thad, clearly none of us knew the half of it.

CHAPTER TWENTY-THREE

T had stalked through the halls toward his study, thoughts rattling around in his mind like shards of glass, shattered and left abandoned on the floor. He couldn't seem to form a coherent thought — hadn't been able to, not since his argument with Aerrin and his talk with Wren.

He'd spent decades dedicating himself to this cause. More, even. He'd been plied with talks with Aerrin of how much would change, once they had their feet in the door, flush with the power their status bestowed upon them. Every instance of injustice could be rectified, every opinion they'd had squashed while they were young, now voiced and put into action. Thad had wanted that as much as he wanted to breathe. There was nothing else in the world, aside from the next step of his plans with Aerrin to obtain authority and implement change. He'd needed no one but his father and Aerrin, and most days, he only saw his brother. Though his father was still warm and accepting when they saw him, he grew more and more distant as they grew older. He came home infrequently and invited them to Daersill even less often.

Aerrin had been his only person.

Then, a moment of weakness, and the greatest gift he'd ever been given came tumbling into his life. It was only after he'd spent years with Lena — with her carefree, innocuous questions — that he'd begun questioning what he came home to: the violent fury and unending vitriol that seemed etched into every crevice of Aerrin's being.

What would he do when he had power?

It didn't seem to align with the Aerrin he'd once known; the one with grandiose ideas and a hopeful outlook for the future. That wasn't the case anymore. But he had to believe Aerrin when he urged that the ends justified the means. His brother had simply grown more desperate to finally see their plan through. The end was so close; everything they'd worked for, at his fingertips. Aerrin had simply lost himself to the cause momentarily. He'd come back to his senses, to the grand plans they'd spent days chattering about when they were younger. He had to.

Thad ran a hand down his face as he exhaled, and when he removed it, he saw a figure leaning against the door of his study.

Wren.

She straightened, and the dark, dusty rose dress she wore swirled gently around her ankles. A straight, corset-like portion covered her chest modestly, and soft straps wound over each shoulder. It wasn't a tight corset, though. It was loose enough that it didn't inhibit her motions. The whole thing was unique, as though she had taken the normal dress of the palace ladies and made it more carefree. It made sense; she wasn't a palace lady. She spent her days outside, hair flapping free in the wind as she cared for creatures. Thad hated that he noticed, that he imagined her that way, that he cared enough to know how it suited her. He couldn't afford to care about more people — not when that seemed to be what incensed his brother's rage the most.

He gritted his teeth. "What are you doing here?"

Wren blinked at his tone, but seemed to brush it off, as if it was nothing more than a passing breeze. "I wanted to see how you're doing, after yesterday. After the argument with your brother."

Thad waved his hand dismissively. "Aerrin is mercurial on his best days. It'll pass."

Wren gave him a look that said *I seriously doubt that*, but didn't comment on it. "What do you have planned for the day?

"Actually, I was going to go see —" he bit off the end of the sentence and looked around, realizing he hadn't checked to see if there was anyone else around. Wren's eyes widened with understanding.

"Oh," she breathed, and then her face lit up. "May I join you?"

He wanted so badly to say no. Putting them around each other more than they already had been could only lead to more complications, and he had plenty. He was already going to see her in part to avoid Aerrin, who would more than likely corral him at some point today to pivot their plans. But then, the image of Lena popped into his head, and the way she had beamed as she recounted meeting Wren and showing her Angus. She had so few friends in her life, and most were creatures Thad brought her to see or gave her as gifts. If it would bring Lena joy... "Okay."

Wren seemed surprised at his acquiescence, but recovered quickly. "When can we go?"

Thad huffed out a soft chuckle. "How does right now sound?"

"Right now sounds perfect." She grinned and gathered her skirts, ready to stride away with him. Thad shook his head, fascinated by her insistent optimism. But as she walked alongside him in comfortable silence, he wondered if such things were contagious. His chest already felt lighter, and his mind had cleared somewhat, just from her presence. If that's what she did to Lena, he thought, no wonder she'd had such fun with Wren. He supposed he would see for himself soon.

The second Thad laid eyes on his daughter for the first time, his entire world had shifted. Before that moment, he'd simply been treading water, following a current laid out for him without really knowing why. Then — looking into her eyes, feeling those small fingers wrap around one of his — it was as though he'd broken the surface, suddenly gasping for air, a new purpose settling deep into his bones. It had awoken something dormant in him, like a muscle he'd never noticed until an exercise suddenly brought it to his attention. His entire being was consumed by her.

Watching Lena with Wren now, his gut twisted with dread. Because he could feel it; that same sense was washing over him. The feeling of his world shifting on its axis.

From his position on a rock a few feet away, he had the perfect view of his daughter, bonding happily with the Dryad he barely knew. They had gone to the outskirts of Reviere to find a remote clearing away from prying eyes. Wren was sitting cross-legged in the grass with Lena, teaching her a game that involved chanting an upbeat tune to the beat of their palms smacking alternately between their legs and each other's hands. After a few examples, Lena caught on, smart as ever, and they were singing at a fast pace, grins spreading as they met each other's hands midair every few beats. Angus looked on, his round, feline eyes growing wider as he followed their movements closely. His scaled tail began twitching, keeping pace with their rhythm, and Thad smirked at the telltale sign that a pounce was soon to follow.

Finally, Angus couldn't bear it anymore and leapt between the two ladies, breaking their palms apart and collapsing in their laps. They allowed it to happen without much fuss, both laughing and descending on him with pats and scratches. His tongue lolled out, and he squirmed gleefully until his belly was exposed, giving optimal access for tummy rubs. The women obliged instantly, burying their fingers in his soft fur. Thad snorted, imagining what the chimera would look like in a few years when he attempted to do that at thrice his current size. He wasn't sure if the thought terrified or amused him.

Finally, Wren was able to guide him off their laps with a flick of her magic. She sent a flower blooming high a few feet away, wiggling suggestively at the tiny chimera. Angus rolled over and crouched once more, swiveling his backside in the air as he prepared for another pounce. Lena squealed in delight when he tackled the offending flower, and just as soon as his head popped up, Wren sent another one sprouting a few feet further. She repeated the process in a circle around them, and Angus was all too happy to follow each one.

When he finally collapsed, his breath coming out in happy little pants, Lena got to her feet and ran over to Thad. He opened his arms immediately to welcome her, but she skidded to a stop just short of him. Her eyes glowed with the unmistakable look of an idea that would certainly cause trouble. Thad tensed, lowering his arms.

"You should show her the Sanctuary," Lena urged, bobbing up onto her tiptoes in excitement. Wren swiveled her head from the girl to Thad, lifting a brow.

This was his biggest secret, something even Aerrin had no knowledge of. He'd carefully curated a protected space for creatures many had only read about in books, and in the wrong hands, it would be detrimental to the poor souls. They'd be sold to the highest bidder, regardless of the quality of life they'd be given. Lena was the only one who had ever set foot in the Sanctuary, aside from Thad himself.

A muscle in his jaw twitched as he contemplated, and with each passing second, Lena visibly deflated. Finally, Thad glanced away from her with a sigh, and then fixed his gaze on Wren. Angus had crawled over to her and resumed his collapsed state with his head sprawled across her lap, and she was absentmindedly scratching behind one of his horns. Something inside Thad unraveled at the sight.

"Fine," he acquiesced. "Perhaps tomorrow morning? Afterwards, I have duties for the upcoming Imbolc." He gave Wren a serious look. "But will you promise that everything you see there stays between us?" he asked.

When she nodded, he rose from his seat on the rock and strode for her. He eyed Angus in her lap and knelt beside her, opting not to disturb the chimera. But when he reached into his pocket and pulled out the knife, Wren lurched back in surprise. Her eyes narrowed, flitting between the blade and his hand, clearly piecing together his intention. Thad didn't blame her for her concerns. A Trinity Knot was an incredibly serious pact; something that usually transpired between a group that truly trusted one another fully. He hadn't given Wren any reason to trust him at all, much less to this extent.

He did his best to give her a reassuring smile as he reached out his hand. If she wanted to see the Sanctuary, unfortunately, this pact couldn't be avoided. Like Lena, the Sanctuary was something he wanted protected. It was another secret of his, carved out in the shadows, meant only to be shared with a sparing, trusted few. And now, between Lena's urging and something deep in his gut, something he wasn't ready to voice aloud... Wren was somehow one of them.

It took only a moment before she stretched out her hand in return, locking eyes with him as he reached for her. He clasped her hand in his gently, turning her palm to the sky. It was soft and warm, and he did his best to make the cut as quick and shallow as possible.

She sucked in a short breath when the blade skimmed across her palm. Blood welled in her palm as she gazed down at where their hands joined, but she didn't move. *Brave girl.*

"Whoa," Lena whispered, and Thad cast her a disapproving look. Part of him wanted to tell her to look away, that this was too violent, but... a more resigned part of him knew that she would likely see far more bloodshed in her lifetime. Better to introduce her with something as innocent as an enchantment.

"Okay?" he asked, returning his attention to Wren. She glanced up from the blood oozing in her palm, an unreadable expression on her face as she took in his question. She nodded.

After a moment, he dropped her hand, and the cold air rushed to meet his skin, wiping away any trace that he'd been holding it. He took a quick breath and drew a small slice of his own through his palm, reaching back out to grasp hers even more firmly. Blood dripped between their opened palms, and he stepped closer, never taking his eyes off hers. "Will you uphold this promise?"

Her response was immediate. "I will."

A white glow emanated from between their palms as Thad whispered the words, and as the glow disappeared, so did the blood seeping between their palms. He knew that once their hands separated, a small Trinity Knot would mark them both. But neither moved. Thad wasn't sure if it was the energy left from the promise that now bound them, or something else, but there was a comforting tingle that came from where their hands joined, traveling down each nerve ending. Wren gazed at Thad, her mouth opened slightly, but no sound came out. She ran her tongue over her lips, and his eyes narrowed at the sight. *Does she feel this, too?* Unable to help himself, he brushed his thumb over her knuckles, testing the theory.

Almost immediately, she tugged her hand back to her side, averting her gaze, and whatever had been building inside Thad plummeted.

He cleared his throat and turned away. "All right. Meet me back here tomorrow morning. We'll use Faerie dust to get there and back. It's the easiest way to travel quickly and with assurance nobody will follow us."

"Can I come?" Lena whined, but Thad shook his head.

"Not this time, bug. You know things can get... unpredictable. I don't want to have two people to keep safe." Lena crossed her arms and stuck her bottom lip out, but Thad ignored her tactfully, packing up the items they had come with.

"Wait," Wren said slowly. "Unpredictable? Safe? What do you mean?"

Thad tossed her a grin, deciding to shove his confusing emotions to the back recesses of his mind, and instead focus on the prospect of showing her what the Sanctuary had to offer. "I guess you'll just have to wait and see."

CHAPTER TWENTY-FOUR

Wren tucked herself in close to Thad as he withdrew a handful of Faerie dust, trying not to notice just how much solid muscle lay under his tunic as she slipped her hand around his upper arm. Or the way he pulled her in tighter. Or the way it made her want to sidle in closer as well.

It reminded her too much of yesterday.

His touch had been electric. Pleasant, in a heady way she'd never felt before, and suddenly she'd wanted *more* of his touch and.. she'd never been sucked into a moment quite like that. She'd purposely hid the Trinity Knot on her palm when she'd been with the others last night, knowing they would have disapproved. She couldn't answer any of their questions, because she didn't know why she hadn't put up more of a protest. Her mind couldn't make sense of all the emotions swirling around inside her. Darrya was out of harm's way, and as far as she knew, the others were safe as long as they stayed in the palace, but this — this was unpredictable, and dangerous. She was used to having problems that could be solved with rational logic and discussion. This, she couldn't discuss with Cas or Kate, and she couldn't rationalize it away. So she'd done the next best thing.

She'd removed herself from his touch, and pretended she'd felt nothing. But here she was, touching him again, and the feelings were back in full force. She closed her eyes and held her breath, attempting to chalk it up to the swirl brought on by Faerie dust.

When she opened her eyes again, they'd landed in a valley surrounded by green. Wren looked around, noting the moss-covered rocks and rolling, lush hills. Wherever they were, this land was untouched by the concrete masses they'd left behind in Reviere. Instead of the constant hum of shuffling feet and murmured discussions, all she heard was the wind whistling through the grass and the caw of a bird soaring happily above. It reminded her of Sairas, and her hands twitched happily at the surge of magic she felt from being so close to nature.

On impulse, she flicked her fingers. A vine broke through the grass between their feet, and a flower stem rose from beneath them. It grew higher, with leaves extending from the stem and finally, a petal that unfurled at the top, its stunning white color vibrant against the green.

"Do you just make a habit of causing things to sprout from the earth wherever you stand?" Thad stood beside her, an amused tone to his question. He brushed some Faerie dust off his jacket and eyed the flower carefully, as though it might extend to wrap around his neck.

"What's wrong with adding a little beauty to the world?" she asked, and Thad blinked at her, remaining silent. She flicked her hand once more, and the stem rose to her waist, where she plucked the flower and placed it in her hair.

He tilted his head and gave her a soft smile. "Nothing at all."

She smiled back, and they stood there for a moment, assessing one another. Wren's thighs clenched as he took a step closer, his gaze intent on her. Though she felt her heart thrumming in her chest, she hardly dared breathe as he closed in on her, large and solid and almost overbearing. He lifted a hand slowly to her face, hesitated, and then brushed a stray hair away from her cheek. She shivered, even as something molten swirled low in her core, the conflicting sensations surprising and overwhelming. Her lips parted, and his sapphire eyes shot to the movement.

A rustling broke the near-frozen moment, and something in his expression changed, turning almost pained. He glanced away. "We have company."

Wren turned and sucked in a breath. A massive, orange beak was in her line of sight, attached to a creature far taller than her. It cocked its head and observed her. Eyes wide, her gaze followed its beak to the point where it disappeared into a furl of white feathers, and to the intense, yellow eyes that shone brightly as they assessed her.

"Thad?" she asked, a tremble in her voice. The creature cocked its head in a rapid, birdlike movement, and two massive wings flashed out at its sides in a quick flap. Wren felt the prick of cold sweat bead the back of her neck, and she clenched her hands together, fingernails digging into her palms. *This is it,* she thought. *He's brought me here to kill me, and he made sure nobody would know where I was.*

Thad simply laughed, cementing the thought in Wren's head that she had truly entrusted her life to an insane person and, well, did that make her insane as well, for trusting him in the first place?

"This is Khepri," he said fondly. "He's an *axex* – a winged griffin."

The creature lifted a paw, shifting forward, and it took all of Wren's willpower not to flinch back. *I've been around thousands of massive stallions,* she reminded herself. *This is no different.*

Except it was — none of those horses had talons that dug inches deep into the ground every time they moved. Though the griffin had the head of an eagle, its entire body was a rich golden-red color, smooth and muscled like a lion. Wren was reminded of the frescoes that lined the hallway leading to Thad's chambers, with a similar winged creature chasing down riders on horseback as they attempted to escape with hordes of gold. "King of beasts, king of birds," she whispered.

Khepri inhaled audibly, and then let out a guttural, clicking noise, one that rumbled deep in his throat. Wren risked taking her eyes off him to stare at Thad. "What does that mean?"

"He's just taking you in." Thad chuckled. "They have excellent eyesight and sense of smell. He's using it to his advantage."

Wren couldn't help but think that such advantages were likely meant for hunting. She hoped she didn't smell like his next meal. "Is he... yours?" she asked breathlessly.

Thad shrugged, coming up to the two of them. He and Khepri stood level with one another, and he rested a hand on the griffin's wing affectionately. Khepri leaned into his touch. "He doesn't belong to anyone, really. But griffins are natural protectors of treasure, and every creature that lives here is a treasure. He decided to make it his home and protect them all."

"All of them? Are there other griffins, too?"

"Unfortunately, no. Khepri is quite old now, and his partner passed a while back." Thad was quiet for a long moment, but just when Wren thought he was done speaking, he spoke once more. "Griffins mate for life. When their partner dies, they live the rest of theirs without seeking another one."

"Oh." Wren looked at Khepri, who seemed to lower his head even further, as though he understood what they were discussing. Maybe he did. "That sounds... lonely."

"Perhaps." Thad pressed his lips into a thin line. "Would you like to see the others?"

It was an abrupt change in subject, but Wren was too curious to object. Thad spun on his heel and walked deeper into the expanse of rolling, lush hills. She scurried after, listening as he described each creature they passed. Most kept a distance, and she only caught brief glimpses of the kappa that lurked under the water, glaring mischievously at them, or the turul that flew high above. She had previously mistaken it for a regular bird, but as it dipped closer for a brief moment, she was reminded of the drawing in Thad's study.

Some of the creatures were approachable. The litter of kitsunes that leapt straight into her lap was certain to be imprinted in her memory for the rest of her life, as was the strange look on Thad's face when she couldn't stop giggling at the feel of several fluffy foxlike tails rubbing against her cheeks. Some creatures, however... were not. She learned this after extending a hand to a kelpie that gave her a curious look from where it floated in the water, only to have Thad snatch her by the waist, tugging her back just in time to avoid the flash of razorlike teeth.

That incident aside, Thad's demeanor grew relaxed as they navigated through the Sanctuary, returning to the more talkative, approachable version she normally saw with Lena. Wren even saw him smile so broadly once that she caught a glimpse of all his white — of course, perfect — teeth. She thought about pointing it out, but she figured it would make him stop, and selfishly, she wanted to see it more.

"I know why this is Lena's favorite place, Thad," she said earnestly as they sat on a log, watching the water tumble down a pile of rocks and continue its path toward the larger pond. Khepri wandered nearby, never quite letting them out of his line of sight, and she wondered if it was because he didn't trust her or because he was intrigued by her. She hoped it was the latter. "It's so great of you to show her all of this. Though I'm sure it was difficult to teach her not to touch certain creatures."

"Actually, she learned a lot quicker than you." Another quick smile. Only a few teeth this time, Wren noted absently. "But thank you. It would have been my dream as a kid as well." He paused and sighed. "It's just unfortunate that they're forced to find a home here, instead of their own true homes."

"About that," Wren said hesitantly. "How do you have all of these creatures? Where are they all from? Those I've heard of, I've only read about in lore. And others…" she shook her head. "I've never even heard of others at all."

"That would make sense," Thad said, "considering many technically belong in different realms."

Wren raised a quizzical brow. "As in, the human realm?"

"No. Other realms. There were multiple kingdoms here when the Tuatha Dé Danann split us from the human realm at the start of the sixth age."

Wren nodded, trying to grasp what Thad was telling her. "I always assumed that referred to the different lands, not different realms."

"That's what they would have us believe. All texts taught to the younger generations are… censored. For the last half a millennium, at least, they've taught unity and acceptance; a gentle understanding of the human realm as the only 'other' realm. And for a while, all the magical races *were* interconnected, even closer than we are with the human realm now. The separation from the humans was more predominant, as they were the ones we fought against directly. That split divided the magic and the non-magic. The magical ones lived in harmony for a while, and that's where we get the remaining wonderful creatures we see here. They were bought and traded amongst several magical facets."

It took Wren a minute to wrap her head around what Thad was insinuating, and when she did, she was left with more questions than answers. She eyed him, her lips parted with the beginnings of several of them. He looked at her patiently, as if encouraging her questions. So, she started with the most obvious. "If that's the case, why are all the magical realms no longer connected?"

"Well, it's tragically simple, really. Without a common enemy uniting the different magical folk, they slowly began to turn against one another, with minor disputes erupting into larger-than-life conflicts." His face grew contemplative, almost a bit... sad. As though the issues of generations past still upset him as though they were today's.

She hummed thoughtfully. "Well, that happens everywhere. The human realms are fighting endlessly."

"Well, even their most major wars are squashed within decades," Thad answered, dismissing them with a wave of his hand. "We're talking races with heightened emotions and boundless powers, not to mention semi-eternal lifespans with which to hold and worsen grudges."

Wren was caught off guard by his knowledge of the human realm. Even those who visited semi-regularly, like she and Cas, had only a general knowledge of the place and its folk. He seemed to know as much about both realms as Kipp, or perhaps more.

"The stories say that the fighting grew so bad, it nearly decimated all the kingdoms. Resources grew scarce; gods — both lesser and greater — were perishing, and the hatred became so profound that all the leaders knew one could not reign without destroying them all.

"So, the rulers of each kingdom came together and decided they couldn't continue like this. They chose to close themselves off from one another." Thad leaned forward, eyes glimmering with animation, and Wren gave him an encouraging smile. He still spoke with his typical serious tone, but the change in his expression told her he was genuinely excited to have someone to share this story with.

"They all knew what was needed to separate the realms, as well as how to open them up again. You've heard of an Ogham grove before, right?"

Wren nodded. Of course she had. Each child learned the different facets of the Ogham wheel growing up: The alphabet, which aided magical enchantments. The lunar calendar on the wheel, which dictated the seasons and celebrations. And the grove — the twenty trees which, when grown naturally together in a perfect circle, like the wheel itself, were said to be the perfect ground for any spiritual work. She'd always assumed it was the stuff of myths, something akin to haunted, sacred ground. Something never to be messed with, even with her own earth magic — not that it would have worked. The grove needed to be sourced and grown organically, without the touch of outside magic to corrupt it.

"You're saying an Ogham grove is the key to uniting the realms?" she asked, uncertain. If it was as simple as planting twenty different trees in a circle, why hadn't someone attempted this in the ages since the realms had been split? Surely she would've heard of this by now.

"Well, it's certainly part of it," Thad said, a faraway look in his eyes. "But not the only part. If the time came to reopen the realms, it would be possible for each to do so, and they meant to: in times of need, or if they believed peace would once again be possible. But the full knowledge of unifying the realms was precious — passed down to only one member of each of their lines as they aged."

"So... your family is the one here with the knowledge?" Wren asked breathlessly, and Thad nodded. "Why not Finlay's?"

"It was in his lineage, at one point. Who it was passed to, I'm not sure. His grandfather, or his great-grandfather, perhaps?" Thad shrugged. "But when Nemain came along and began targeting the royal family, the one who had the knowledge was murdered. Luckily, he'd taken notice of the targeted attacks, and had the wherewithal to mention it to my father as well, for safekeeping."

"And that's how you found out?" Wren asked.

Thad nodded. "Finlay's ancestor probably saw that the attacks had no end in sight. So, he entrusted the information to us several years ago, to ensure at least one family line would keep the knowledge intact."

Wren remained silent for a few long moments. This information was heavily guarded and carefully passed down through the centuries. Why was he even mentioning it to her?

As if reading her thoughts, he continued. "It's been an ambition of ours for the last decade. Think of all the power it would grant us to enact change? We've been meticulous with every part. Hell, we have the grove spacing down to the hair. But now, with everything that's happened — with who my brother has become, and who I have to protect... I'm not sure we're going down the right path anymore." He let out a soft laugh, but it was devoid of amusement. "Even saying the story out loud, I realize how wrong it sounds, trying to open the realms back up."

Physically, Wren froze. In her mind, however, everything went careening over an edge. It felt like she had been on a horseback ride, only for the horse to stop abruptly, sending her flying over its ears. She scrambled to make sense of his words. "I'm sorry?" she stammered. *"Open the realms back up?"*

She squinted at Thad, suddenly seeing him in a new light. At first, she'd thought he was just excited to share more lore with her, as an academic who inhaled stories as easily as breathing, like her. But this... had he not just told her how having the realms unified had led to senseless fighting and destruction? Why would he risk such a thing?

He stood frozen in front of her, his face gone bone white. "I... I didn't mean for that to come out the way it did?" His voice cracked at the end, pitching into a question.

"The way it did? What way did you mean?" Wren demanded. She still couldn't quite fathom that what he alluded to was possible, let alone that it was their end goal. Something this massive — this potentially destructive — in his hands, or moreover, those of his brother? She backed up a step, begging internally for him to backtrack. It was a joke, surely, or a misspoken part of the story.

"I didn't mean for it to come out at all," he admitted, and her gut plummeted. So, it was part of the plan... just not a plan he'd meant for her to hear.

"You've decided, after what you just told me, that opening the realms back up is the right decision? Why?" she cried out. "Because if you plan to tell me it's for peaceful reasons, I beg to differ. If it was, you'd be working with someone other than your brother."

The realms had been closed off for protection, and she could only imagine the careful navigation it would take to reopen them. One wrong step would likely cause the ages-old war to start anew. Wren shook her head and spun on her heels. She might have been opening up to the idea of Thad having good intentions, but Aerrin was an entirely different story. If Thad could even consider putting such precarious power in the hands of his brother, he was no better.

"Please, Wren, just wait a second —" Thad grabbed her arm, and she glared down at it.

"People like him are exactly the reason those realms should stay far away from us," she spat, and tugged her arm out of his grasp. She strode away, eyes scanning the lush green landscape ahead of her as her mind raced through everything she knew about Thad's brother. Aerrin was a cold-blooded murderer. He'd killed his own father without a second thought, and he'd held Darrya's future in his hands like a toy he couldn't wait to break. Hell, he'd threatened Thad's own daughter. How could Thad possibly believe he had anyone's best interests at heart, much less go along with this?

Thad cursed, loudly. She heard his footsteps begin following behind and lengthened her strides, trying to put any and all distance between them. A spot of reddish-gold caught her eye, and she swerved to follow it. She didn't know what she wanted to do, other than get the hell out of here. She'd sort out all the other things flying around in her head later.

Khepri raised his head as she approached, and she heard Thad call out behind her in warning, but disregarded him. She reached out her palm and the griffin eyed it curiously, then met her gaze. His intelligent, yellow eyes regarded her as she stepped into his space, coming to a halt, and her heart quickened as she willed him to understand her request. After a moment, Khepri shook his body, reminding her of a dog shaking water off its body after a bath, and extended his wings. She breathed a sigh of relief and reached a trembling palm to touch his feathered neck. He let out a soft rumble that she felt under his feathers and lowered the wing closest to her. She bit her lip, but took the plunge as she heard Thad's footsteps crunch to a halt behind her, climbing her way up onto Khepri's back. Once astride, she took a moment to orient herself, and then finally glanced at Thad.

He looked as though he'd just discovered a loved one was being held hostage, and she was the one holding the knife to their throat. He held his hands out on either side, palms facing up, pleading with her. But for what reason, she didn't know, and more importantly, she didn't know who he was attempting to protect. She had no idea who his loyalties were to — his daughter, his brother? Perhaps himself alone.

"Wren," Thad begged, and she was forced to look away from his beseeching gaze. She flicked her wrists, and with a flash of green, vines wound their way around the griffin's chest and underbelly, strapping her in. Another wound its way loosely around his shoulders, providing her with something to hold onto. She looped the vines around her palms, staring into Khepri's feathers. She sensed Thad's gaze like a physical brand, burning its way into her chest, but she forced herself to ignore it. Instead, she leaned forward, feeling the griffin shift beneath her. Her palm prickled, and she reminded herself of her promise — she had to be careful to keep the Sanctuary secret. She wasn't positive this would work, but something told her to try. The risk was worth warning her friends.

"Fly," she whispered, and with a snap of his wings, Khepri was airborne. She cried out as they ascended in the skies, but quickly dissolved into shrieks of joy as she realized her makeshift vine saddle would hold. After several powerful flaps, Khepri leveled out, wings straightening into a glide, and she gazed down breathlessly at the world below them. With a squint, she made out a small, black dot, which she presumed was Thad. The dot disappeared as quickly as she'd recognized it, and she sat back, her thoughts whipping as fast as the wind rushing through her unbound hair.

Somewhere in her racing mind, she realized that he would've had all the strength and magical power to subdue her. If he'd truly wanted to, he could have kept her from leaving — could have forced her to remain silent with threats and political schemes. But for whatever reason, even knowing that she would take this information to Kate and Finlay... he hadn't.

She sighed and leaned forward, burrowing her face into Khepri's feathers. Thad was a dangerously complicated man, with a new secret to uncover at each turn. But this secret was the only one she was concerned about for now, and she'd be damned if his keeping it endangered those she loved.

CHAPTER TWENTY-FIVE

Despite the fact Wren had taken Khepri, Thad knew he'd beat her back to the palace. He'd used his Faerie dust to bring him back and instantly called for Finlay and Kate to join him and his brother in a meeting. He sat in the room with the three Faeries, turning his palm over and eyeing the scar with curiosity. His Trinity Knot hadn't burned, signaling the fact that Wren had kept the griffin — and by extension, the Sanctuary — secret. He wondered if that was out of deference to the promise, the creatures, or Lena. Certainly, given her anger at him when she'd left, it wasn't out of any regard for him. He shifted uncomfortably at the memory of her final furious look at him, trying to tamp down the guilt.

Someone cleared their throat, and he glanced up to see Aerrin, seated and glaring daggers at him. Thad knew that if it weren't for the king and future queen in the room with them, his brother would likely be attempting to waterboard him with his magic — and not in the way they used to joke as children. Aerrin hadn't been that happy child in... fuck, when was the last time he'd even thought of the two of them as children? What was happening to him?

He shook his head, perplexed. Why was he even thinking of such things?

"Well, you have us here, Thaddeus," Finlay began coolly, his own eyes chips of ice. He and Kate sat a healthy distance away from the two of them, and he knew they were making no attempts to hide the flickers of magic in their palms, flashes of red and yellow as they shifted their hands. "Are you finally ready to discuss what we've truly come here for?"

Thad opened his mouth, but before he could speak, Aerrin cut in. "If you're referring to our trade routes, yes. We have plenty to discuss on that front."

Kate choked out a humorless laugh. "Aerrin, there is nobody else here. You can drop the act. Darrya never agreed to marry you, and by proxy marriage is an ancient practice. I doubt you'll find you're still in possession of a legally binding document. If you won't admit why you nearly had us killed the other day, what else is there to discuss?"

Aerrin's eyes snapped to Thad once more, the only sign of his distress, and Thad quickly glanced away. The scrambled plan, following their initial failed attempts, was to keep them here until Imbolc, the following day, and then drug them during the celebrations. Aerrin blamed Thad for the failed attempt that led to their knowledge of the plan, but now his brother would blame him for the loss of their last playing card — Aerrin's marriage to Darrya. While it *was* Thad's fault, this was a more pressing issue. What else would keep them here, if not that marriage?

"Like I said," Aerrin replied slowly, still eyeing Thad. "Trade routes. If we can come to an agreeable compromise, perhaps we can revisit whatever else it is you'd wish to talk about."

"Please," Finlay scoffed. "Whatever it is you're planning that involves my *entire* family and friends, I doubt it's comparable to trade route shifts."

Aerrin lifted a brow, finally swiveling his gaze to the king. "I don't know. Is it?"

Finlay shut his mouth, glaring at Aerrin. The young king couldn't argue, and Thad's heart squeezed at the realization of the lengths he would go to for his loved ones. He'd come all this way for his cousin, had his partner and friends put in harm's way, and he wouldn't back down now. Thad shot Aerrin a sidelong look, wondering absently if he would do the same.

Before they could continue, an urgent rap came at the door. Aerrin motioned to Thad to open it. With a sigh, Thad obliged, trying his best to ignore the twinge of annoyance at Aerrin's expectation that he would cater to his whims.

You do, a little voice chided in his mind.

He opened the door, telling the voice in his head to shut up.

The messenger that stood outside was warily eyeing the tall, broad, redheaded friend Kate and Finlay had brought with them. The messenger flashed Thad a grateful look as he slipped inside, and Thad couldn't blame the messenger for his unease. The friend was clearly an Urisk, and he exuded a protective energy that his fitness level promised he could follow through on. Creatures like him reminded Thad that not every Fae needed elemental magic to do damage.

Thad turned to see the messenger whisper rapidly in Aerrin's ear, and by the time he sat back down, the messenger had slipped out of the room as quickly as he'd come. Aerrin steepled his fingers and smiled, and Thad could tell he felt back in control of the situation because his demeanor shifted back to the sickly-sweet political façade he normally carried in public.

"It seems a member of your party has landed herself in a compromising position." Aerrin leaned back and stretched, looking like a sated panther.

Kate and Finlay leaned forward in unison, and Thad couldn't help his lurch forward either. *Her.* Aside from Kate, Wren was the only other lady that had arrived with their party. She must have come back, seeking Finlay and Kate, as he'd suspected.

But — he checked his palm quickly and noted that the Trinity Knot was still dormant — she must have dismounted from Kehpri some distance from Reviere, and found another way back to the palace. Had she demanded to see them once she knew Thad was with them? Had she spilled Thad's secrets to others? He felt his heart rate increase, but pressed his nails into his thigh beneath the table, forcing his expression to remain neutral. The brazen panic on Kate and Finlay's faces, however, spoke volumes.

"Wren? What have you done with her?" Kate spat out.

Aerrin waved his hand dismissively. "Ah, she's fine. She was causing quite a stir, though. Spewing some nonsense against us. We had to contain her, of course. Can't have such treasonous notions out in the open." He cast Kate and Finlay a sympathetic glance, but his tone grew harsher with each word. "I'm sure we will get it sorted soon enough, though. One night in holding should teach her the appropriate lesson. In fact, I'm sure we can have her released by the time of the party tomorrow night."

The words hung in the air, the silence that followed allowing them to linger. Kate and Finlay exchanged a long look, an unspoken conversation transpiring between them. If Thad had to guess, it bounced between their desire to be gone by tomorrow evening and the probability of them blasting Wren out of holding successfully. The temperature of the room had become stifling, and Thad wondered for a moment if they would really attempt an all-out fight right here, in the palace. His breath caught. Had Aerrin finally pushed them to the brink?

"If you do anything to her..." Finlay warned, flames dancing across his fingertips.

Aerrin cut him off. "We won't."

Though Aerrin's tone was surprisingly sincere, Thad felt the need to add, "We promise."

Both Kate and Finlay let out audible sighs, and they stood, striding past where Aerrin and Thad sat. Aerrin's eyes narrowed, marking the obvious insult, but Thad simply pushed back his chair and stood to follow. Aerrin might have made the decision to incarcerate her, but Thad was already thinking through ways to ensure it went no further.

Finlay strode to the door and opened it, nodding to their friend on the other side. Kate followed, but braced herself on the door frame and glanced back. "We'll see you at Imbolc." Thad dipped his head in acknowledgement, and she added, "I trust you'll take care of her."

The words were for both of them, but her eyes were locked solely on Thad. A sudden, heavy weight of responsibility settled on him, nearly suffocating him. Whatever he was experiencing with Wren, clearly, she knew about it. And in the moment that Kate had no control to help Wren, she was turning to him. *Shit.*

The two left the room, hand in hand, and Thad braced himself the moment the door clicked closed.

Sure enough, Aerrin rounded on him, seething. "What the *fuck* was all that?" he hissed.

"I'm sorry. Some information was compromised, and I had to be sure those two were rounded up before any news potentially got back to them."

"That girl, Wren, found out? How?" Aerrin shook his head. "Nevermind. I need you in the right headspace, Thad. We can't afford for things to go sideways now."

Thad lowered his gaze to the floor, feeling like a chastised child. "I understand."

His brother paused. "Is this about your daughter?"

"No." Thad's reply was immediate and truthful. Though his daughter played a part, she wasn't the one who had compromised the information. That — that was all him.

"Hmmm." Aerrin rubbed the back of his neck and frowned. "Either way, she is a distraction we don't need. Keep your distance, Thad. And go tell Kuiper he's got tonight to formulate a plan. In fact, we'll remove the regular palace guards outside of Wren's cell and place them there in case those two—" he gestured out the door where Kate and Finlay had just exited. "—decide to pull a jailbreak. The other day's blunder *cannot* be repeated, and I have a feeling once they have her, they'll all be organizing the next ship out of here."

Thad nodded, even as a lump formed in his throat as his chance to make amends diminished. He thought about the long, helpless look Finlay and Kate had shared, and the way they clutched each other's hands as they left the room, as if they knew their options were dwindling, too. He thought of Aerrin and what he would do if his last obstacle was removed. He thought of what Lena would say if she realized where Wren was right now.

His brother studied him intently. "Come on, Thad. Seriously, you should know better than anyone. This is just something you get used to."

Thad swallowed, but somehow, the lump had only worsened. His reply was quiet. "I have a feeling there are some things you never get used to. And I'm fine with this being one of them."

Aerrin's eyes narrowed. "Get the guards swapped. And just re- member what will happen if you don't. Remember what's at stake. *Who* is at stake." With a growl, he whipped around and stalked away. Thad took several moments, trying to settle his hammering heart and racing thoughts before willing himself to set Aerrin's plan into motion.

There was a reason Aerrin hadn't been specific about the place Wren now resided, and that reason was Finlay's unbridled rage. Sure, he could — and would — likely guess at it, but generally speaking, the dungeon hadn't housed criminals in ages. They had grown more civilized than that, keeping riffraff in new, heavily guarded buildings with far more light and far better air flow. But, seeing as this was an emergency, it's where Wren would call home for the night. The palace's neglected dungeon was just as much of a shithole as anyone could expect it to be. Though Aerrin had commandeered the area to test new use cases for the buair, Thad himself hadn't been down here since the days he and his brother had dared each other to see how long they could last in a cell.

Thad ran his hand across the dingy stone wall as he descended the stairs, wincing at the rough stone and sticky cobweb that met his skin. The light was too dim and the air too moist, making him feel as though his senses were restricted. Even small sounds were muffled, and the fact that both Kuiper and Briar, following behind him, were nearly soundless out of principle left him all the more disoriented. When they came to the bottom of the steps, Thad exchanged a few words with the existing guards, who left with little argument. He couldn't blame them — they probably felt that guarding a small, quiet lady in the pits of the palace was just as much a punishment for them as for her. He attempted to swallow his rising guilt and failed.

Speaking of... he hovered for a moment as the guards retreated up the stairs, wondering if he should join them or risk the trip past the walls of iron-clad cells. Finally, he gave in to the urge and turned on his heel, pacing to the end of the row.

She sat in the corner of the cell, her back facing him. His breath caught as he took her in. She was curled in on herself, looking smaller than usual, as though the posture would protect her from the evils of the outside world. The flowers woven into her hair had withered, barely clinging to her silky locks. She didn't fit in with the dark, dull stone surrounding her. She deserved to be out in the sunshine, thriving and grinning and causing beauty to blossom everywhere she went. Now, she'd been reduced to this, and there was nothing he could do about it.

She and Lena both deserved to hate him for this.

"Wren," he said, then swallowed. His mouth had gone bone dry. Her head rose, and she turned it slightly, just enough that he could make out the side profile of her lips and her nose. Still, she said nothing. "Are you okay?" he ventured.

Finally, she spoke, her voice a bit hoarse. "Are you here to let me out?"

He paused, unsure how to respond. He didn't have the keys; Aerrin did. Kuiper and Briar also stood between them and the freedom above, and though they answered to him, they also answered to Aerrin, and his brother's consequences would be far worse than Thad's if they disobeyed him.

All that aside, he knew he was on his last chance with his brother. One more misstep, and not only would he face Aerrin's fury, he suspected Lena would, too.

Eventually, his silence provided answer enough, and Wren let out an audible sigh. She shifted onto her feet, taking an unsteady first step as she approached him. He pressed in close to the cell, letting the bars hit his chest, the realization that she'd been curled on the ground this whole time filling him with a protective rage. As she approached, he wondered what she would do to him. He couldn't see her full face yet, but he imagined she was beyond enraged.

"I had no choice," he murmured as she came to a stop just on the other side of the bars. Her face looked weary, defeated. Thad stared into her chocolate brown eyes, unsure what all he should apologize for. The sham marriage? The attack on her brother? The upcoming plot with his brother? The incarceration? The list was endless.

She lifted a hand, and he braced for her to strike him. But instead, she completely blindsided him with a question. "To do what you've done... what dark places have you gone to in your mind?" She reached through the bars and touched a line that crinkled next to his eye, marking the feature where his troubles seemed to live. "Your very soul?"

The tender touch sent a jolt of white-hot electricity scoring down his entire body. He sucked in a breath, wondering when a simple touch had ever done so much to him. *So many dark places,* he wanted to reply. He wanted to lay himself bare before her, to see if it would fix any of the brokenness he felt inside to do so. He leaned in closer.

"I've made mistakes, too, you know," she breathed, and that — for some reason, that halted him. Whatever mistakes she'd made came nowhere close to the darkness inside him. His heart dropped at the realization that she could never understand that. She couldn't begin to understand how far he'd go to protect Lena. He'd leave an irreparable path of destruction to keep her safe. And he wouldn't look back.

So he pulled back, leaving her with his barest truth. "The only mistake you made was trusting me."

CHAPTER TWENTY-SIX

"The only mistake you made was trusting me."

The sentence reverberated in Wren's skull, and the silence of the dungeon only made the words burrow themselves deeper, repeating on a loop.

She'd been a fool. An absolute fool, thinking that someone with Thad's reputation could have been any different. She'd viewed him as someone torn between two paths, and she'd blindly hoped she could guide him down the right one. But she'd miscalculated. Decades of history and family blood were impossible to reconcile with — she was merely a stablehand he'd met a handful of times. Why had she thought she'd make any difference?

She rolled through these thoughts over and over again, dozing in and out as the time passed. Without a window, she had no idea whether it was morning or night, but she had to guess it was early morning. Every now and then, a dark-haired man or a red-haired woman would pace by, eyeing her but saying nothing. They brought food once, but she made no move to eat. The man frowned each time he passed her, as though she was an inconvenience, and she'd taken to glaring back in response. The woman, at least, seemed sympathetic. The last time she'd passed by, she'd nearly smiled at Wren. Wren wondered briefly if she'd be her way out — but no, the woman was never far from the dark-haired male.

At first, she'd hoped Finlay and Kate would have the power to break her out, or maybe Kipp and Cas. But as the hours passed, her heart sank. Had they all been captured by Aerrin and Thad? Or did they not even know where to look? Worse, she considered... what if they did know where to look, but she was the pawn in another trap? With each pass of her guards, she began wondering if that was actually what they wanted. Perhaps they were even the same people who had attacked them in the streets of Reviere. It had been a male and a female, if she remembered correctly. It made sense. An attack down here would be easy enough to keep under wraps, and they could dispose of bodies without a second glance. That's what the dungeons were originally made for, after all. She'd be the only witness, and not for long, if she had to guess. It was probable enough that she flipped her hopes around. *Leave me alone,* she sent out a silent plea to her friends and Cas. *Wait out whatever Thad and Aerrin have planned.*

Eventually, she heard muffled voices echoing through the stone corridor. She scrambled to the front of the cell, tilting her head to hear better, but she didn't recognize the voice. It just sounded like someone offering the guards some dinner, or perhaps breakfast? The voices went silent, and she heard a door close. With a sigh, she leaned against the iron bars of the cell, shifting uncomfortably. Whatever it was about this place, her magic remained dormant, as if she'd left it above ground with the rest of the world. It was like visiting the human realm; although, even there, she possessed wisps of her magic. Here, she hadn't even be able to summon a single sprout. She closed her eyes and attempted to sleep, hoping her dreams would be a far more comfortable place to pass the time.

"Wren?" A whispered voice broke through her slumber. Her eyes flashed open and she scrambled backward, craning her neck to see where the voice had come from. She was met with a mop of dark hair and a pair of deep, sapphire eyes, broken up by the bars separating them.

"Thad?" In her half-asleep state, she tried to reconcile her joy at seeing him and the information she had from their more recent interactions — namely, the one that had landed her here. She wiped her eyes, clearing the last traces of sleep, and studied him.

He wore an oversized jacket and stood at an awkward angle, as though he were hiding something underneath. There were dark circles under his eyes, and he looked around frantically, as though he was waiting for someone else to appear... or hoping they wouldn't. Was he here to silence her, once and for all? Where were the guards?

Where were her friends, her brother? She curled her hands into fists, attempting to stop the tremble she felt coming on.

"What's going on?" she asked, shoving to her feet. Thad reached into his jacket and pulled out a round, short-haired creature which looked like an oversized puppy. It thrashed in his arms, a blur of sandy beige, spotted fur. As its head came around, she realized the small beast was muzzled.

"What is that?" she questioned.

Thad wrapped an arm tightly around the flailing creature, placing his free hand over the muzzle. "Cover your ears."

"What?"

In a swift movement, he had the muzzle free, and the beast opened its mouth to reveal a horrifying set of dagger-like fangs, over an inch long and shaped like thick, curved needles. Wren's face went white. How could such a small face possibly have teeth that large? Her hands slid up to cover her ears.

It snapped at the air without abandon, and Thad positioned it so that it hovered in the air next to the padlock on her cell. The beast snarled and snaked its head forward, causing Wren to gasp and stumble back a few steps. There was a high-pitched snapping sound, the grating of metal, and the door swung in. Wren's mouth fell open as she took in the shreds of metal that now littered the floor, looking like they'd been bitten through as easily as a soft cheese.

She lowered her hands and shifted her gaze to Thad, but he was busy wrestling the creature back down to the ground, muzzle in one hand as he worked to fix it back over the beast's jowls. Her horror skyrocketed as the creature slipped away for a second, lunging for the door opening before Thad was able to tackle it once more. "What *is* that?"

"A crocotta," he ground out. The creature writhed in his arms, and he grunted as he worked to wrestle it to the ground, his muscles flexing with the effort.

She opened her mouth to ask more questions, but at that moment, a horrid shriek erupted from the creature. The shriek turned into a low howl, which then transformed into an even eerier sound. *Words.*

"Wren!" It screeched, and the voice it used... sounded like Cas. *"Help me, Wren!"*

The hair on her arms immediately rose, alarm bells going off. Her stomach plummeted as she recognized the voice as her brother's. "What did it do?" she asked, her voice rising. "What did it do to him, Thad?"

She stalked forward, disregarding the fact that the creature had torn the iron off her cell in two bites. If it had done anything to her brother, she'd find its weakness. And when she was done with it, she'd handle Thad next.

With a final yank, Thad tugged the muzzle onto the beast and moved it deftly out of her reach. It immediately went limp, as if all the fight had been drained from it. Her eyes snapped to Thad with a challenging stare, but to her surprise, he glared right back.

"I told you to cover your ears," he said.

"Why? So I wouldn't know what you'd done to my brother?" she bit back, arms crossing. With a sigh, Thad reached into his pocket and removed a handful of Faerie dust, which he scattered over the beast. A second later, it slipped away from his arms, disappearing to gods knew where.

Her eyebrows rose in alarm. "Why—?"

"That was a *crocotta,*" Thad interrupted, emphasizing the term. "Useful beast. Its teeth can pierce nearly anything. But also terrifying. It was not only muzzled because of the lethal bite, but because of its mimicry." He fixed her with a look. "It uses telepathy to weed out your most precious relationship, and uses their voice to lure you to it."

"I..." she trailed off. "So he's okay?"

Thad gave a curt nod. "Yes. Everyone is okay. Nobody knows I'm here. But that won't last long — we have to go. I'll get you back to your friends, and then you need to leave."

He stretched his hand out to her, and she eyed it, all the emotions and memories of the past few days flooding back to her. The back and forth of him, the way he sometimes acted like he wanted to change the world for his daughter and other times, like he would stand by Aerrin and burn the world alongside him without the bat of an eye.

She took a step back. "So nothing's changed?"

Confusion flashed across his face. "N — no?"

"You know the second I get back to Kate and Finlay, I'm telling them everything. And when I do, they're probably not going to leave this alone. What you have planned will shatter the realms."

He wiped a hand over his face, looking resigned. "Honestly? I hadn't thought that far ahead."

"You're a *coward,* Thad."

Wren spat the words out, and Thad reared back as though struck. For a moment, Wren hesitated. Who was she to speak in such a manner to *him?* He was a duke alongside his brother, a leader in his own right, one who had many powerful strings to pull. But, no — what she said was the truth, and she had seen what true leadership looked like. And those leaders believed that respect was earned, not freely given.

"After all this, you're still willing to put a decision like ripping the realms open in the hands of someone like your brother. You know what he's capable of, what he's likely to do, and you're still going ahead with it," she hissed. "I fought in a war with my friends to avoid seeing this realm torn apart. One that you conveniently missed out on, if you don't recall."

"I'm trying!" Thad exclaimed, and pinched the bridge of his nose. "Fuck, Wren, I'm trying. I'm so godsdamned tied up in this, I don't know. All I know is that when I'm with you, things make sense. You make me hopeful that I can come back from it all, that there's still something worth redeeming in me. You make my daughter happy, and you make me happy, and I just... I just..."

He broke off and strode forward, cupping her face in his hands. She sucked in a breath, but before she could do anything else, his lips were on hers — warm, soft, full, and achingly gentle. She let out a soft whimper.

He broke off, a look of alarm suddenly shining in his eyes. "Is this okay?"

Wren hesitated, the answers cartwheeling through her head. *Yes. No. Maybe? Yes. Definitely, yes.*

"Yes," she breathed.

He let out a low moan, barely audible on his exhale, and then his mouth was on hers again. It was still tender and exploratory, but now it also had urgency, and the promise of possession, and *gods* — she'd been kissed before, but never like this. Never had her mouth been explored with the expertise and raw hunger that she felt here. She sank into it, returning every move of his mouth carefully with her own, mirroring his actions. She felt him sigh into her, the curve of his mouth as he smiled, the way his large, warm palms ran down her frame to grip her waist.

She pressed further into him, feeling a need to get closer to him, to satiate the burning desire pooling in her core. Her mind grew hazy, dull. Where were they again? His lips traveled from her mouth down her jaw, trailing a path to her collarbone, and she gasped at the sensation of his warm mouth branding the tender skin of her nape. His hands tightened at her waist.

A sound came from above, breaking them apart with a jolt. Thad cleared his throat as Wren attempted to collect her scattered thoughts. "We need to go," he murmured.

Wren took a step back and shook her head, trying to clear it. Despite these new feelings, he was still the one who helped orchestrate the death of the queen and Lachlan. He'd done nothing to stop the attempt on her friends and Cas, and was doing nothing to stop his brother from opening the realms. "You... you told me not to trust you," she forced out, cursing the weakness in her voice.

Thad gave her a wry smile. "You listened. Good girl."

The way he said it, with his voice still husky from their kiss and low to avoid detection, made her stomach flip. But just as quickly, his demeanor changed from lazy and aroused to stoic. "You aren't wrong. I am a coward, but that all changed the moment you and my daughter were put in danger. This isn't just about me. I have an idea."

Wren gave him a guarded look, and his expression turned frantic. He extended his hand toward her, and she eyed it warily.

"Please," he rasped in a final plea. "If not for me. For Lena."

CHAPTER TWENTY-SEVEN

I rubbed my shoulders and sighed. Though we'd successfully navigated the dissolution of Darrya's marriage, we had given up something vital in allowing Aerrin to take Wren hostage. Though it was only for a night, I tossed and turned the entire time. Was Wren safe, wherever she was? Could we hold the brothers to their promise that they wouldn't hurt her? Perhaps we could trust Thad, but that didn't mean he had any say in what Aerrin did.

The only thing that had kept me from barging into the dungeons with Finlay was the knowledge that Wren herself would have gladly traded a night there for the information we needed — something even Cas had confirmed, though it looked like it physically hurt him to do so. And as Kipp had so dutifully pointed out, they were likely hoping we would do just that. The thought of my newfound magic being stuffed under wraps once more by that mysterious powder made me shiver at the mere prospect. No, we had to play along, for now.

The worst part was, however, that we had no idea what we would gain in return. Aerrin could still withhold the information, or worse, withhold Wren for another night, in which case I had no qualms about storming the entire palace in search of her. So, the tension that had been in my body before I fell asleep remained this morning, perhaps even tighter than before. Finlay hadn't spoken much, but he'd slipped out of bed at the first sign of light and was currently pacing the room, as if burning a path in the floor would burn off his anxious thoughts. We were in a game of chess, and we were moving the pieces blindly.

Fuck, I hated chess.

"Is this what it means to be a leader?" I asked. "Constantly making decisions that you can only pray have the least negative impact?"

Finlay halted his pacing and turned to me, his sigh echoing mine.

"Unfortunately, little angel. Rarely is there a decision that benefits everyone. You have to decide what is the most important." He gave me a tired, lopsided smile. "However, most leaders decide what is most important for them. By even considering the option that is best for the people, and not you, makes you leagues better than most."

I moved a few steps toward him and folded myself into his chest. His arms wound around me immediately, and I squeezed my eyes shut, allowing just a few seconds of solace in his embrace. "You do the same," I whispered. "But..."

Finlay stiffened and pulled back as I trailed off, studying me curiously. "What?"

"I don't know why, but I also feel like we were also just guided into the option that they actually wanted. I don't know what they would want with closed-door politics, open trade routes and hosting a massive Imbolc festival, other than reinvigorating their economy..." I bit my lip, contemplating. "It just seems like such a mundane arrangement. That's something Lachlan could have discussed with the queen. It's not right."

"I agree... but I don't know what else they have planned. I still think it's larger than us, but I don't think they're going to just stop with whatever their attack the other night would have accomplished. That's still key to this. Though I can't imagine what they have in mind with so many others gathering for the festival." Finlay grimaced. "I'm not sure I want to stick around anymore to find out."

I rubbed my arms, willing the chill that had washed over them away. "We need to get out of here as soon as we have Wren in hand."

Finlay nodded. "I'll write to Darrya to update her — you start packing."

He strode to the desk and pulled out a piece of paper and a quill. As he wrote, I began pulling together our clothes, my mind still racing. What had our entire song and dance with Aerrin and Thad accomplished in the days we'd been here? Had there been a point to our political arguments, or was it simply a ruse? Why had it seemed as though the Hounds had meant to hold me hostage, but not the rest of our group?

I shook my head, frustrated. If I'd had more time to study things like this, I'd understand. I was just a young woman who was barely old enough to share a drink with someone, let alone have whole festivals and trade routes to barter with lands. But at least we had Darrya back, I reminded myself. Darrya was free of that monster. And she would know what to do next.

A knock at the door had Finlay and me freezing in place. We eyed each other, and in a brief flash of flame, the letter he'd been writing disappeared — to Darrya or to ash, I wasn't sure. He rose and grabbed his jacket from where he'd thrown it, shrugging it back on in one smooth motion as he strode to the door. I followed closely behind, staying just in the line of sight to discover who was on the other side. I flexed my fingers, summoning magic into the tips.

Finlay paused with his hand on the doorknob, giving me one last questioning look. I nodded, and when he opened the door, I saw the two people I least expected to see: Wren and Thad.

The temperature rose instantly, Finlay's emotions of surprise and anger rushing through us as a physical response. Thad's eyes were lowered, but Wren met my gaze directly, and I blinked in surprise at what she conveyed. Her eyes were pleading, her lips pinched in a thin line as she waited for someone else to make the first move. So, I did.

I strode forward and wrapped her in an embrace. "Wren?" Her name, a question, an invitation; I wasn't sure which.

She cleared her throat, her expression slipping into nervousness. She exchanged a look with Thad, who gazed back, his look heated — with anger? Or was it something else entirely? "Listen," Wren began. "I think... I think you two will want to hear him out."

My apprehension turned to curiosity, and I turned to Finlay, waiting for his response. He glanced between the three of us once, then twice. I wondered if he clocked the same expression on Thad's face that I had. Finally, he pursed his lips and opened the door wider. "You'd better get in here."

We shuffled around awkwardly, making room for everyone. I sat on the bed on top of the clothes I'd begun to pack and patted the other side softly in an invitation to Wren. To my surprise, she stayed at Thad's side. I raised my eyebrows and glanced over to Finlay, whose surprised expression mirrored my own. It was brief, however, and then Finlay raised his chin and locked eyes with Thad. "You have five minutes."

Thad cleared his throat and tipped his head up in response. Whatever had humbled him in the doorway, he met Finlay's command with the impeccable posture his royal training had bestowed him as well. He crossed his hands in front of him and straightened, shoulders back and spine straight as he spoke. "I came to offer you and Queen Katherine a proposition."

Finlay raised a brow, and I couldn't help but note the use of my new title. "A proposition?" I echoed.

"Yes." Thad hesitated, eyes shooting to Wren, who had been looking at him intently the whole time. She gave a soft nod, and he continued. "I have a trade of my own to make. One that has nothing to do with the trade routes we discussed. I would like to offer vital information; information key to keeping you and Queen Katherine in power."

"I see." Finlay's tone was almost bored, as though he had no interest in the proposition. I was sure it was a power play, but it seemed to dishearten Thad. His mouth opened and his eyes widened almost imperceptibly, but it was the most emotion I had seen from either of Lachlan's sons, outside of their fake, broad smiles at the solstice. He looked... *panicked* by Finlay's disinterest.

If Finlay was as curious as me, he didn't show it. He didn't prompt for more information. I waited a breath, then two. *Dammit, Finlay.*

Unable to take it anymore, I blurted, "And what are you requesting in return?"

Thad turned his head to me and took a deep breath. "My... my daughter."

"Your daughter?" My head spun. "We don't have your daughter?"

It came out as a question, because I hadn't even realized he *had* a daughter. I took in his smooth face, long, dark hair and piercing sapphire eyes. He was handsome, but reserved, and still young in comparison to other Fae. That aside, children weren't all that common. How old could a daughter of his be? Surely, we didn't have her in our possession, and if we did, we wouldn't be keeping her under lock and key.

Shit – would we? My mind flitted to the image of Clíodhna, trapped in the dungeon, and hairs rose on my arms. I crossed them, dispelling the image and praying that she wasn't held captive against our knowledge.

His brows knitted together, and he shook his head. "No, I mean — I am requesting you take her. Take her back to Sairas with you, give her a position in your town. Something low-key. Keep her under your protection."

"Can't you keep her safe here?" Finlay asked, but while his voice had been harsh and devoid of interest previously, it was softer now. I understood, because I felt the same softness. After all, a child was innocent in all of this. If she had somehow been wrapped up in this, I already felt protective of her.

My heart went out to Thad as I considered the decisions he must have made, every single one taking her into consideration. *Not unlike my own father,* I realized with a jolt.

"No." Thad glanced to the ground, his face twisting into further anguish. "I — I don't trust my brother not to put her in harm's way, should I not heed his wishes."

The room went quiet as we considered his words and the offer. I bit the inside of my cheek as I considered him. He didn't hesitate to refer to me by my new title now, whereas with Aerrin, it wasn't even considered. He'd openly voiced that he didn't trust Aerrin. He'd rather entrust us with his own flesh and blood. It was sad, in a way, but it didn't surprise me in the slightest.

Every story, every interaction, every mention of Aerrin had only ever painted a terrible picture of him. Until recently, I'd thought that picture included Thad, but now? Whoever this Thad was, he was a completely different person.

The question was, which was the real one?

I eyed him carefully, thinking through every memory I had of him. He'd carried himself with the arrogance of a royal son, to be sure, but whereas Aerrin had instantly set off alarm bells in my head, Thad had more of a... calming presence when I'd been with him. Hell, I'd spent a whole day riding with him, and we'd had nothing but respectful conversation. All that aside, Wren had spent more time with him than all of us, and she trusted him. By extension, I trusted her without question. I glanced sidelong at her, and found her gazing at Thad.

But still. He'd been a part of the queen's death, and Lachlan's, two assassinations we still had no insight into. Even if he'd only been an accessory, he'd been there. And he'd had many chances since then to make it right; instead, he'd chosen to ploy us into coming here on a chase for Darrya's freedom. A chase that had very nearly become fatal for us — another thing we didn't have answers for.

"You have to understand," I began, "that this sounds ridiculous. How should we trust that you wouldn't give us false information to further your agenda with Aerrin?"

Thad tilted his head and offered me a thin smile. "Because you'd have my daughter. If I'm getting her out of here, just to put her back in harm's way by providing false information, what would be the point?"

I paused at that, but Finlay cut in. "Because you know we wouldn't hurt a child. She *is* just a child, yes?" At Thad's nod, he continued, his voice quiet but firm. "We wouldn't hurt her. We aren't those kinds of leaders."

Not like you. The unspoken words rang out in the air.

"It's *because* you're not those kind of leaders that I trust you with this," Thad insisted, but Finlay looked away. I felt the guilt in his movement, but the decision as well. And, though it tore my heart a bit to have it so much as cross my mind... honestly, I felt the same.

"I'm sorry, I just don't trust this. I can't trust you." I shook my head, trying to shake off the guilt that rushed in with the words.

"Trust *me*," Wren said suddenly, and everyone's heads whipped toward her. She continued. "Don't trust him. Trust me. I've met his daughter, and I've seen the way he is with her, and the way Aerrin speaks of her." She bit her lip, glancing at Thad, as if to apologize for airing his secrets. Thad dipped his chin in a single nod, urging her to continue. "I believe him. He wants his daughter safe, and that means being away from Aerrin. And he'll do whatever he needs to to keep her safe."

She glanced away from him and toward me. "Please, Kate. Trust me."

I held her gaze, taking in everything it expressed. I wanted to tell her that she was being too naive, that she was too trusting of people… but then again, that was everything I loved about her. And, I realized with surprise, that's what brought out the best in people. Sometimes you needed someone else to believe in the best in you to bring it out of you. She certainly did that with me. When I was in my darkest places — with grief or anger — she knew exactly what to say or do to bring me back to my true self.

It was true, I didn't trust Thad. But I did trust Wren. And I trusted that if anyone could bring out the good in him, it was her.

Slowly, I nodded. "Okay. I trust you." Wren beamed, and I turned to Finlay, who gave me a resigned smile of encouragement. Then, I pivoted to Thad. "What's your daughter's name, Thad?"

Thad let out an audible exhale, and his expression softened with the one word. "Lena."

My gaze slid to Finlay, who was studying Thad carefully. His expression turned contemplative as he eyed Thad, and he sighed. "Okay. We'll take her back with us."

Thad closed his eyes, relief flooding his features. Finally, he nodded. "I'll have a boat ready with her on it in an hour. Use that time to gather your things, and I'll draw a map with the best route out to avoid detection. In the meantime, I should be able to keep Aerrin preoccupied with the festivities."

Wren and I nodded in understanding, and Finlay grabbed the desk chair. He flipped it around and sat on it, leaning back lazily. "Now, it's your turn. What do we need to know?"

Thad rubbed a hand over his face, and Finlay smirked. Despite the rings under Finlay's eyes, they gleamed brightly with victory. I couldn't help but think, *checkmate.*

CHAPTER TWENTY-EIGHT

"**I** can't fucking believe this," Cas muttered into the mirror, fixing his hair.

"I know," I agreed emphatically. "They're planning to open up a gateway to all the realms. Realms that, for all we know, could still be filled with Fae that have unique powers and creatures we've never heard of, and centuries-old grudges to take out on us."

"Not *that,*" Cas said, and we shot him a look. "Well, okay, also that," he amended, "But I can't believe we're going to miss Imbolc here *and* in Sairas. This sucks!"

"Let's just be grateful we've been given an out," Kipp reminded him. "We've been set up at least twice now to be captured or killed, and Thad just gave us our get out of jail free pass."

"What's that mean?" Finlay asked, and Kipp and I exchanged a brief, affectionate smile, thinking fondly on the board game it referred to. The next second, however, my stomach twisted, recalling

Thad's words when he'd elaborated on the specifics of Aerrin's end goal.

They had wanted to kill Finlay and the others, but they'd wanted me alive, because apparently my lightning would expedite their plans. It had something to do with the power of lightning-struck oak, and the need to have it perfectly placed where they'd been planning to open the realms. The power of any lightning-struck tree was immense, but a lightning struck oak had magical properties beyond any other. How they had planned to make me comply, Thad wouldn't say. He'd simply averted his eyes and changed the subject.

I shook off the thought and sidled up to Finlay. "Just human realm stuff," I replied, nudging him. "I'll have to show you someday. It's a fun game."

"Would it be all bad?" Wren asked, stuffing clothes into her bag. "I mean, not that I want Aerrin to have the magical key to forgotten realms. He isn't fit to lead one realm, much less all of them."

I shuddered at her words, knowing that it wasn't a guess at his intentions anymore, but confirmed by Thad. Aerrin intended to immediately put the new realms under his heel, touting himself as a hero and savior of sorts for opening the portal and unifying the lands once more — even if it meant they were under his authoritarian, tyrannical rule.

Wren continued, oblivious to my unease. "But, if it were you, for example? I feel like you having knowledge between two realms only makes you a better leader. What if there is something we can learn from each of these realms, to better ourselves?"

I flushed at her compliment, still unused to flattery in regards to my leadership. I still considered myself far too young and inexperienced in the ways of this realm to effectively lead it. But in this regard, I had to admit she had a point. I tried to soak up everything I could from the knowledge and wisdom of those around me, and tried my best to combine my experience from both realms where possible to determine successes and avoid historical failures. If there was a way to do that here, it did make the situation sound less catastrophic and more... hopeful.

"It sounds ideal in theory," Finlay agreed. "But we don't even know if the other realms *want* to be connected again. And for every exciting thing we can imagine they've been doing over the past few centuries, we have to imagine the opposite could have happened as well."

"True," Kipp agreed. "It's not like we have everything figured out. Look at the war we just fought. There are still dark Fae out there licking their wounds, probably angry and wanting to retaliate. Not to mention the royal infighting, class discrepancies, and wealth inequalities, among other social issues." He held up a finger each time he rattled off an issue, and Finlay and I flinched at each one. He caught our look and gave a helpless shrug. "I'm just saying. We have our own shit to figure out without dragging others into it. I'm sure they do too."

Cas sighed. "What we need is someone like Darrya, but to connect the realms." Wren tilted her head at him, and he continued. "You know? Like a liaison. A middle-man, unbiased, who can converse with the people in each realm and help us determine who is receptive to opening the realms again."

I hummed in thought, an idea half-forming in my head. Finlay shot me a curious look, but I dismissed him with a wave of my hand. It was something worth discussing later, but right now there were more pressing issues. "It's not like Aerrin is having any negotiations, anyways."

Thad had told us his plan, and it was worse than we could have imagined. He planned on using their newest invention, *buair*, to subdue the leaders of the realms. If they didn't comply, they would be captured, and their realms conquered. He was planning to throw our entire realm into a war we hadn't asked for. And for that, it also meant he needed to rule this one... which was why although he planned on keeping me alive to open the realms, he had no use for me afterwards, and none at all for Finlay.

King was a title he needed to crown himself.

I shuddered and took Finlay's hand in mine, relishing the warmth and *aliveness* of it. He glanced at me briefly and, after studying my face for a moment, gave a soft squeeze in return. I closed my eyes and leaned into him, remembering our promises to one another.

"Ready?" Kipp asked, and I opened my eyes to see him cinch his bag tight and straighten. Wren nodded, and Cas shrugged his bag on his shoulder with a sigh. Once everyone gathered close, I pushed the door open. I expected to see someone guarding the door, but the halls were surprisingly empty.

"Everyone must be getting ready for Imbolc," Finlay mused. "Perfect day for an escape."

A short chuckle whooshed out of me, and I exited the room, slipping my hand back into Finlay's as we made our way through the maze of hallways, locating the side route Thad had specified. We walked just a touch faster than normal strolling pace, anxious to leave the palace but not looking to garner unwanted attention. There would be a narrowboat waiting to navigate through the canals back to a larger boat, already housing Lena as a stowaway, hidden somewhere off the main docks to avoid detection. If it was discovered we had left early, we'd hopefully be long since disembarked on a discombobulating course back that would be nearly impossible to follow.

Finlay jerked to a halt, dragging me to a stop with him. I was about to ask what was wrong when I followed his line of sight down the hallway, and I saw two figures moving. They were crouched low, and froze the second they noticed us as well.

Those aren't civilians, I realized, noting their lethal stances. In fact, if I had to judge based on their dark cloaks and the way they moved... I would guess they were the Hounds, back to finish what they'd started.

"Oh, fuck," I breathed, backing up a step.

"He sold us out!" Finlay spat, palms curling.

"I don't think so, Fin," Cas supplied, pointing. Down the corridor, barely visible, I discerned what looked like two original guards, crumpled as though they'd been knocked out cold. So someone *had* cleared the way for us, then; it was just that we'd been tracked down by our hunters first. How had they found us? Had they reached out with their powers, somehow tracking our magical signatures? Or had Thad second-guessed himself and sold us out at the last minute?

I shook the thoughts away, head reeling. No time to consider; we just needed to find another way out, fast. The figures began striding toward us in earnest, picking up pace. Finlay dropped my hand and held his up, a torrent of flame unleashing from them.

"Back here!" Kipp whispered, gesturing back the way we'd come and to the left. "I smell the kitchens."

"The kitchens?" Cas exclaimed. Regardless, we all turned to follow him without question, scrambling to reach the kitchens before the Hounds caught up. Finlay kept up the wall of flame behind us, and I prayed that the *buair* the two had brought with them would dissolve into ash before penetrating his shield.

"They won't kill us around others," Kipp supplied between breaths. "And I'm sure there's some way out where the garbage goes." Cas shuddered but said nothing more. Kipp shifted, taking on his wolf form.

We burst through the next set of doors, skidding to a halt when we realized we'd entered the Grand room. The overwhelming floral scent hit me as I took in the massive space, covered in yellow, orange, and blue flowers and endless rows of banquet tables. Chandeliers hung overhead like frozen teardrops. Though nobody had yet arrived to celebrate, servers were strolling up and down the endless rows of banquet tables, filling glasses with spiced wine in preparation. A door off the room probably led directly to the kitchens, but...

There, in the middle of the bright decor, stood Aerrin. For a moment, time slowed, and we stared at each other, taking the baffling sight in. But then the Hounds burst in behind us, shattering the moment. I glanced back and tensed, instantly summoning the lightning to my hands. My fingertips crackled and the hair on my body stood on end, the static becoming so thick I could taste it.

Aerrin scowled and held up a hand. "Now, now. What do you think you're doing?"

I glanced to him briefly, but decided to focus back on the Hounds. The red-haired girl lingered behind Kuiper, whose hand had gone to his pocket. If I saw him so much as pull a pouch out, I would fry him where he stood. "We're *leaving.*"

"That might be a bit difficult," Aerrin drawled, "seeing as the palace walls are warded against magical destruction, and your only other exits are now covered."

We all stood silently for a moment, assessing the situation. Not only were the Hounds blocking the halls, but now the other palace guards had filed in, curious about the commotion. I couldn't trust that they would defend us and forsake Aerrin, should it come to blows. Between their numbers and what I knew Kuiper held in his pouch, it was too risky. We wouldn't make it through without someone getting injured — or far worse.

I surveyed the room, my heart sinking. Aerrin was right; the palace was warded, likely just as heavily as Lachlan's castle had been during the solstice celebrations. But I remembered my awe at the magic that had been used during the festivities. It had made vines and berries blossom, fires stay lit, and... something else Darrya had told me.

I recalled the way the walls had shuddered, opening in a ritual that allowed the barest chink in the castle's armor, only during celebrations. I could only pray this palace had the same.

"Finlay," I murmured, so low only he could hear. "Where does the sunlight shine through from when the ceiling splits?"

Finlay took a moment to register my question, and then, moving only his eyes, focused his attention on a spot in the ceiling. I followed his bright blue gaze, and then leaned over to Wren. "Help me," I pleaded, and before she could respond, I doused my lightning and summoned all the earth magic I could.

For a moment, nothing happened. Panic clawed its way up my throat as I squinted, feeling with my magic for any sort of give in the palace ceiling. Come on, where was it?

Finally — *there*. I found it and tugged. The ceiling split with a momentous crack, giving into the pull without the grace the ceremony normally allowed, but there it was. The open sky, the sunlight pouring in, and most importantly, our way out.

For a moment, all my friends did was gape at the ceiling, attempting to see what I saw in the plan. I refocused my attention from the ceiling and gave Wren a look, putting my hands over the floor. In an instant, she knew what I was thinking and mirrored the stance. Together, we pulled at the floor, summoning mounds of soil and thick roots from the earth that climbed higher and higher, creating a natural staircase. Tables were shoved aside to make room for the columns of stone sprouting from the earth, glasses shattering as they hit the floor and spread wine like bloodstains. We worked quickly, but the agitated roar that came from across the room told me there wasn't much time.

"Go!" I yelled, and Kipp and Cas clambered up the steps we'd already built, putting distance between them and our hunters. Only Finlay remained beside myself and Wren, summoning his flame. Within seconds, he was painting the room with his flames. The straw meant for weaving acted as kindling, and soon, curtains and rugs caught fire, the flame roaring across the room like a possessed dragon. Through the dancing flames, I glimpsed Aerrin's face, contorted in fury.

We retreated onto the steps, and Finlay twisted his hands, bringing the flames in close, cutting off access to the base of the stone staircase. I saw the beginnings of steam making a path for us, no doubt Aerrin's attempt to cut a path through Finlay's flame. Still, Wren and I worked frantically, until the steps reached the rooftop, and Finlay kept his column of fire going, separating us from the base of the Grand room. Heat rippled from beneath us, causing dots of sweat to form on my brow. When we finally reached the top, I gritted my teeth and tugged at my magic with one final surge, sending our earthen creation crumbling. Though the whole event had taken perhaps two minutes, I prayed the two Hounds didn't have any strong earth magic to summon. Better yet, I hoped Finlay's show of power caused them to simply turn tail. The yells I'd heard ordering the guards to fall back were certainly promising.

"Come on," Cas said, unfurling his wings. "We need to get going."

We nodded and raced across the roof to the east side of the palace, where we knew the narrowboat was waiting. Cas lowered us down two at a time, the strength of his wings allowing a reprieve from what would have been a nasty fall. He grimaced at the weight but didn't complain, reminding me that though he could fly, his wings weren't necessarily made for carrying anyone. I was glad I hadn't even thought to ask him to lift us out of the Grand room — it probably wouldn't have worked, and we hadn't had the time for individual airlifts. He rubbed his shoulders as we sprinted for the canal, glancing behind us to ensure we hadn't been spotted.

We were greeted by a familiar face on the narrowboat.

"Maia!" I exclaimed. The Asrai blinked, surprised at my recollection of her face and name. She recovered quickly, however, and nodded, giving me a thin smile.

"Nice to see you again, Your Majesties." Kipp leapt into the boat, still in his lupine form, and she blinked in surprise as the boat lurched. He whined, and she cut a look to the palace. "I assume we need to make haste?"

Finlay gave a grim nod, which she returned, and then faced the back of the boat. With a few waves of her palms, the current shifted, sending us careening down the canal. Before long, however, she whipped her hands to the right, cutting a tight turn into a smaller canal. She repeated this two more times while we gripped the side of the narrowboat in tense silence, eyes peeled for any sign of pursuit.

Somehow, we made it to the larger boat undetected, and that was where Maia finally slowed her magic with a deep exhale, the only indication of her stress. "Your ride awaits," she said, motioning.

We climbed out of the narrowboat, making for the larger one, but I stopped, eyeing Maia. "Would you like to join us, Maia?"

She blinked in surprise and whipped her head around to look at her narrowboat, then back at our larger ship. A small crew — likely enlisted with Thad's discreet help — was already readying to set sail. The last thing I wanted was for her to be discovered aiding us in our escape, with her narrowboat tied to the location. She tugged nervously at a strand of her light blonde hair, twirling a charm, and I wondered if she was considering the same. Finally, she nodded. "Yes. Yes, please."

I grinned and motioned for her to follow. "Well, then come on."

As we clambered on board, a young girl broke out from the crew and ran toward us. "Wren!"

She skidded to a stop in front of Wren, who grinned and knelt beside her. The small girl broke out in an adorable, gap-toothed smile, and I knew without a doubt in that moment that everything Thad had said was true.

He'd gotten us out, on the promise that we would protect his daughter. And so, we would.

But we wouldn't stop there. I exchanged a grave look with Finlay and saw the same in his expression. No matter what, we'd have to stop Aerrin's plans as well. If we didn't, I knew, deep down, we'd all be damned — Thad and his daughter included.

Chapter Twenty-Nine

Wren flopped on the other side of the bed from Lena, sizing her up. Lena hiked her blanket up to her nose, looking slightly uncomfortable. Wren wasn't sure what it was from — being across the ocean from her father, being locked in an unfamiliar room in an unfamiliar palace, or a little bit of everything. She realized with a jolt that she was the only truly familiar face Lena had.

Well — she and Angus, who was currently rolling on the bed, a sock lolling out of his mouth as he grunted happily. At least he felt at home here in Muiranvia.

"If you need anything, I'm just down the hall. I'll show you before we go to bed. You can knock any time." Usually Wren would be headed back to Cas's place in Sairas by now, but Kate had fixed her up with her own room in the palace, telling her firmly that she was allowed for however long she wanted. She'd also added that it extended past however long Lena stayed, making a point that it would be a lot quieter than Cas's now that Kipp was officially moved in. Wren couldn't argue that, and the giant bed awaiting her made it easy to envision taking up long-term residency here. She could get used to this quasi-royal status.

Lena dropped her blankets, rolled over onto her stomach, and fixed Wren with a serious look. "Is my dad going to be okay?"

Wren found herself glancing away from the scrutiny. Her eyes looked so much like Thad's — that deep, sapphire blue, full of expression that asked more questions than they answered. "I hope so, Lena. He did this so that he can focus on doing what he needs to."

"And what does he need to do?"

Wren bit her lip. She'd already answered multiple questions on their trip home: why wasn't Thad joining them, what was his brother doing, *why* was his brother doing it? Those were all hard questions, but she'd at least had some sort of answer for them. The truth to this question was, she didn't know. She wasn't entirely sure what their next steps were, other than that they were dependent on what Thad did.

"He needs to do the right thing," she said finally.

"Will he, Wren?"

Wren sucked in a breath at the question, asked so innocently but so bluntly, and worked to keep her face neutral. She knew Lena would be studying it closely, taking in any hint from her expression. She desperately wanted to give Lena peace of mind, but even more than that, she didn't want to lie. Somehow, painting a false picture of

Lena's father seemed worse to Wren. So, she offered the most honest reply she could. "I... I certainly hope so."

Lena seemed to accept this, and turned to wrestle the sock out of Angus's mouth. He gave a squawk of protest, digging in his claws and hooves into the bedspread to pull it back. He flapped his wings for extra momentum and overcorrected, sending them both tumbling backwards into the pillows. Despite her current worries, Wren had to laugh. Lena and Angus popped up, and she swore both of them were grinning at her.

"Don't worry," Lena said. "I really think he'll do the right thing for you, Wren." The fact was stated with bravado only a child could boast.

"For me?" Wren furrowed a brow, and Lena nodded.

"Yeah. He talks about you a lot."

"Oh?"

Lena sat up straight on the bed and threw the sock for Angus, who glided off the bed after it. "He likes talking to you. He says you talk about the future like it's something to look forward to."

Wren crossed her legs, momentarily stunned. Finally, she managed, "Isn't it supposed to be?"

The bed shifted as Angus landed back on it with a soft thud, and Lena picked at a tuft of his hair. "I've never really thought about it."

"Well, you're young." Wren smiled. "I wouldn't expect you to. That's the kind of stuff adults think about. We like to make sure you have things to look forward to as you grow up."

"Did you?"

"Oh, yeah. Tons of stuff." Wren smiled as she thought back. "I was always excited to go to festivals with my family and friends. And to learn how to use my magic as it grew, and to visit the human realm."

Lena jumped on that, her eyes wide and glittering with excitement. "What's it like?"

"Oh, I've only been a few times. If you want to hear about that, you'll have to ask Kate. She grew up there."

Lena gasped, and Wren smiled. "And," she added, "I bet we could even get her to tell you about it over a visit to meet Gray."

The look on Lena's face reminded her that seemingly small wonders for her could be very big wonders indeed.

A soft rap came at her door the following night. She frowned and rose from the bed, wondering if it was Lena. She had just tucked her in for the night, after providing a story she used to tell her nieces when they had trouble falling asleep. Judging by the way Lena had been curled against Angus's small, furry frame — and the snores coming from one of them, though she honestly wasn't sure which one — she assumed they'd be fast asleep by now. Had Lena woken and forgotten where she was?

When she opened the door, however, it was Kate who stood on the other side, holding a cup of tea. Her hair was down and damp, and her face looked freshly washed. She wore a long, cream-colored robe, cinched at the waist. She offered the mug to Wren with a soft smile. "Can I come in?"

"Of course." Wren took the steaming cup with a smile and gestured behind her. Kate breezed in, her robe swishing against her ankles. Whatever it was, Wren relaxed slightly. Kate clearly didn't intend for them to go anywhere, meaning it couldn't be *that* concerning. The way Kate shuffled to a chair resting in the corner of the room and slid onto it, tucking her bare feet underneath herself, reaffirmed that.

Wren sat on the corner of her bed and sipped at the tea, eyeing Kate. Kate tilted her head and leaned against the armrest. "Do you think Lena had a good day?" she asked. Her bright, golden eyes shimmered with an earnest hope that reflected the question.

"I think so." Wren smiled as she turned the images from earlier that day over in her head. "You and Gray were both wonderful with her." As she'd promised, she'd led Lena to the stables that morning and sent for Kate. While they waited for her, Wren had introduced Lena to every horse in the stable. Lena had taken it very seriously, committing each horse's name to memory and ensuring there was no favoritism between them. Each one had received their very own carrot and pat.

Finally, when Kate arrived, she introduced Lena to Gray and offered to let her groom him. Wren knew Thad had to have brought Lena around horses before, because though Lena clearly wanted to squeal at the sight of Gray, she physically bit her lip to restrain herself, working hard not to startle him. Instead, Lena had rocked back and forth in excitement, her eyes wide as saucers, which remained that size the entire time she'd groomed him.

Because of his sheer size, she'd needed a stepping stool to reach the top of his back and the tips of his ears, even when he dipped his head patiently. She navigated around him, not missing a single spot on his shiny, slate-colored coat as Kate regaled her with tales from the human realm. Lena had soaked them up like a sponge, tongue-tied aside from a few gasps of amazement. By the time she'd asked every question she could think of, Gray was groomed within an inch of his life and Kate had announced she needed some fresh water. Lena had to be dragged away, but not before she had thanked Kate profusely and thrown her arms around Gray's thick, muscular neck one last time.

"I'm glad," Kate responded, and a flicker of nervousness crossed her expression. "I've never spent much time with kids."

"Well, you learned the best secret," Wren said. "Just put an animal in front of them, and they'll be occupied for hours."

Kate laughed. "I suppose that's true. Poor Gray."

"Honestly, I think he liked it. Being a retired war horse suits him well."

"It certainly does." Kate smirked, but the smile soon gave way to careful regard. "I can see this other side of Thad better now."

Wren frowned, confused. "How do you mean?"

"Because of Lena. If her mom wasn't in the picture, and her other caretaker basically abandoned her... everything she's grown up with has been an example from him." Kate paused for a long moment, and Wren could guess where her mind was drifting. For so long, she'd been raised by only one parent, too. "But despite her hardships, she's a great kid. Polite, curious, happy. She's been given all the right tools in life to succeed. I don't think that, if Thad was as much like Aerrin as I originally thought, she would have turned out this way."

Wren couldn't help but smile at her words, remembering the way Thad had played with Lena on the rolling hills just outside of Reviere. The way he'd been so patient with her, humoring her with all her games. The term of endearment he'd used for her — *bug*. "Yeah. He's a good dad."

Kate hummed thoughtfully. "This is about more than just helping us all out, isn't it?"

"What do you mean?" Wren choked out the question, realizing where this was going.

"I mean, you took his daughter to protect her, and you vouched for him when nobody else did. Hell, you even squared off with your own brother in his defense." Kate gave her a little wink. "You like him, don't you?"

"I..." Wren trailed off and felt her cheeks start to burn.

"Oh, shit." Kate let out a chuckle. "Something has already happened between you two, hasn't it?"

Wren clutched her mug tightly. "No! Well," she amended, cheeks flaming further, "just a kiss."

"I love it." Kate looked all too pleased by the revelation. "And that makes what I came here to tell you all the better."

"What's that?"

"I have a way for you to communicate with him while being positive Aerrin doesn't catch wind of it."

Wren's eyes widened. She hadn't been sure how they would make it work. Letters could easily be intercepted by Aerrin or those loyal to him. Not to mention, if Thad left for Muiranvia without Aerrin, it would raise far too much suspicion. They needed a way to communicate that left his brother none the wiser and didn't deviate from his normal daily routes.

"Do you remember when I released Clíodhna from the dungeon?" Kate asked.

Wren repressed a shudder. "Yes."

The beautiful woman had long ago fallen from her goddess status, her love taken advantage of. The late queen had kept her hostage in the palace dungeon, stripped of her magic as she attempted to figure out how to siphon the Bean Sídhe's powers for herself. Wren ran a hand over her arm as a shiver skated across her skin, remembering when she'd been trapped in a similar palace dungeon. Luckily, Kate had been able to free Clíodhna, allowing her to restore the magic that had been lost to her for the gods only knew how long.

"Well," Kate leaned forward, her eyes gleaming with excitement. "She once communicated with me in a dream. And so yesterday, I wondered to myself, would that be possible again? Could she do it with someone else? And furthermore, could she join two people in the same dreamscape?"

Wren's mouth fell open, realizing where this was headed. "And?"

"I attempted to summon her last night in my dreams to ask her myself. And it *worked*. She came to me, and told me it was possible!" Kate flashed her a triumphant smile. "So, prepare to enter that dreamscape tonight."

"Holy gods," Wren breathed, feeling her heart thrum with excitement. "How do I make sure I'm... receptive to entering the dreamscape?"

"Don't worry. I tried my best to think of her before I drifted off last night to summon her, but I don't think you'll need to. She knows whose minds to pull at tonight to enter her realm."

Wren blinked, considering what it would feel like. Would it be a tugging sensation? Suddenly she felt anxious. What if she didn't sleep deep enough to dream? Would they miss their chance?

Kate, seeming to to sense where her thoughts were going, motioned to the tea. "Drink up. Cas gave me a blend that should help you drift off. The longer you're asleep, the more likely you are to overlap with Thad's sleep schedule and give you both more time."

Wren let out a small sigh of relief. "Thank you."

Kate smiled and stood, as if making to leave the room. As she did, a terrifying thought flashed through Wren's mind. "Wait!" she exclaimed. When Kate lifted her brow, encouraging Wren to continue, she blurted, "You won't tell Cas, will you? About — about Thad and me?"

Kate let out a soft laugh. "Don't worry, neither of us want to see that happen. But behave yourself in that dreamscape." She paused, considering something. "Or don't. I wonder what all you can do in a dreamscape? Could be fun to find out."

"Kate!" Wren shrieked, and Kate held up her hands with a laugh.

"I'm going, I'm going!" She skipped out of the room, but popped her head in one last time to give Wren a final wink. "Sleep tight."

Chapter Thirty

Sleep felt impossible since Lena left Reviere. Thad was plagued by the fear of never setting eyes on her again. It took forever for him to fall asleep, and waking up was its own event entirely. Today in particular, rising from his sleep felt like emerging from underneath a pile of sand. He rubbed at his face groggily and peered around, alarm growing as he realized he wasn't in his own bed. He wasn't even in a bed at all. He was laying in a large expanse of lush grass, the green tendrils tickling at his bare skin.

As his senses slowly returned to him, he realized he could hear waves crashing against stone. He rolled over and pulled himself up to a sitting position, glancing up at the sound of birds singing. Three colorful birds circled above, and he gazed at them for a long moment, blinking away the fog of sleep. Did he recognize them? He didn't think so. Where was he?

"Finally," a soft voice mused from behind him.

"What the —?" He scrambled to his feet and grabbed at his sides. Realizing he wasn't armed and was, in fact, as shirtless as he'd been when he went to bed, he reached inside for his magic. It swelled in him but remained slippery in his grasp, fueled by his disoriented state. He took a few steps back, eyeing the woman in front of him. She was clad in a simple green dress, billowing in the breeze. Her hair was dark, a brilliant contrast to her porcelain skin.

"Relax, child," the woman crooned, her jade eyes twinkling. She was beautiful, but unfamiliar, and he knew just how lethal such a woman could be. He took a deep breath, willing his magic to settle and become useful.

"Thad?"

Now, that voice, he knew. His heart stuttered, and he dared a glance to his other side, refusing to fully turn away from the strange woman. "Wren?"

"Finally," she breathed, echoing what the other woman had said. "I was waiting for you." Her gaze dipped to his bare skin, and he felt an unbidden sensation course through him at her scrutiny for a brief moment. He thought over her words.

"Waiting for me?" he demanded. "Where *are* we?"

Wren stepped further into his line of sight, and he noticed she was wearing a simple shift. Clearly, he wasn't the only one who had woken up dressed in exactly what he'd worn to bed. Her shift was a pale cream color and nearly shapeless, except where it perched across her chest, held together with a simple string of lace. If he looked close enough, he was certain it was transparent enough to see every piece of her bare skin.

"Clíodhna brought us to her dreamscape."

He tore his gaze away to address the woman on his other side. Her name was familiar, though he couldn't quite place why. "This is your dreamscape?"

"Yes. It is. It is the safest place to have a conversation. No one need know what transpires here." Her gaze became somewhat steely, and when she continued, her tone had hardened. "You're lucky Kate and this young lady vouched for you. I am aware what was done to me went beyond the queen herself."

With those words, her name clicked into place. *Clíodhna.*

She was the goddess the late queen had spent decades testing on — perhaps longer, even he didn't know — in an attempt to weaponize her power to remove magic from Fae systems. He wasn't even sure if her testing on this goddess had led to the breakthroughs they'd made. Nemain had been the true driving force behind those. For all he knew, Clíodhna's capture and subsequent torture had been all for naught.

That realization, paired with her presence here before him, practically took him to his knees. He averted his gaze. "If you know what we've done, why would you help me?" he murmured.

"As I said. I've put my trust in Kate, who has put her trust in Wren." Clíodhna paused. "And she has put her trust in you."

The words were meant to comfort him, to provide explanation, but they were like an arrow to his chest. He remembered his words to Wren, how he'd said trusting him was a mistake. And to his knowledge, she'd believed him. Another in a long list of bridges he'd burnt.

The way she looked at him now was hopeful, if a bit guarded. Was this her way of stating that she trusted him regardless? Or did she only trust Lena, and want to do right by her? Maybe he couldn't earn her trust now, but this could be a path toward it — despite the fact that another example of why he couldn't be trusted stood in front of them now.

"I—" He turned to face Clíodhna, attempting some sort of apology. But to his shock, she had disappeared.

"She wanted to give us some time alone," Wren said, eyeing the spot where the goddess had disappeared. "We'll be here until we wake up or choose to leave."

He ran a hand over his face in an attempt to recalibrate his emotions and felt her assessing gaze on him. "I feel like all I've done lately is apologize," he admitted.

"Maybe that's because you have a lot to apologize for," she stated simply.

Well, she wasn't wrong. "I do."

"But that's good," she added. "It means you're making amends. You're righting wrongs."

Thad let out a breath. "I'm certainly trying."

Wren extended her hand to him, and he took it cautiously. Again, he was struck by how soft and gentle her touch was, and he focused on that point of connection as she led him across the grass, until briny ocean air hit his cheeks. He peered down at the large expanse of dark waves, which crashed against the tall stretch of cliff.

"How is Lena?" he asked, unable to keep the question in any longer.

Wren smiled. "She's amazing. She spent all day learning each and every name of the horses in our stable."

"That sounds like her." Thad smiled, allowing warmth to spread alongside the pang of guilt, both taking residence at his core. He wanted to be the one to give that to her. But, he conceded, he had given it to her — just not in the way he would've liked. He'd given it to her by giving her up. *Only for a short while,* he reminded himself. *Only until I can get us all out of this mess.*

"Do you have any information we can use?" Wren asked. She turned to face him, and he watched as her gaze slipped back down to his bare skin, tensing subconsciously at her attention. He remained silent while she perused him like one would examine a piece of art, but his restraint finally snapped when she twisted her hands in the hem of her shift, lifting it to expose several additional inches of soft, smooth skin.

"See something you like?" he drawled, and her eyes finally snapped back up to his. She flushed, and he drank in the sight. She dropped the hem of her shift, and he wondered what those hands would feel like on his bare skin.

"I — I was asking if you had any information," she stammered.

He smiled, basking in the openness of her emotions, written plain as day across her face. She was loyal, fierce, and honest, and seeing her flustered gave him a sense of victory, because he knew everything she felt was the truth. "As much as I wish I could give you more, I don't have any," he said. "All I know is he's still researching a workaround to make lightning strike the oak tree as soon as possible. And he's sent someone to Talamu in case it happens naturally."

Talamu, an island south of both Muiranvia and Brytham, was where they were making the attempt at opening the portal between realms. Everything grew in abundance there, trees included, and since the land was mostly devoted to yielding crops of all sorts, it was sparsely populated. Though it rained often, lightning striking exactly where they wished — even if they added a makeshift lightning rod — didn't guarantee anything happening for quite some time. And with Kate being nigh unreachable now that she knew Aerrin was after her, Aerrin's plans had been halted for the foreseeable future. All that being said, Aerrin was in a truly awful mood.

Wren hummed as she considered his words. "Maybe we should just go there," she mused. "We can wait for him to arrive."

"No." Thad shook his head. "He has spies in Sairas, and he'll know if you all leave. He'll plan to sabotage the palace, and that will all be before he goes on the offensive at Talamu."

"Oh." She looked crestfallen.

"I think it's best for us to wait this out." Thad shrugged. "Who knows? Maybe his whole plan will crumble without us having to lift a finger."

She gave him a sidelong glance, one that held an undercurrent of disapproval. "And what would you do then?"

What *would* he do, then? A month ago, the future he'd envisioned had been the one Aerrin laid out for him. He had been content to let Aerrin call the shots, pull the strings, and look the other way when the journey to get there had involved questionable actions. He'd had Lena to pull him back, to remind him when things had perhaps gone too far, but he'd paid the price for loving her. Aerrin knew exactly where his weakness was, and it was wrapped up in the entire small existence that he called his daughter.

But now... now, he had her out of Aerrin's reach. Aerrin hadn't even noticed Lena's absence, having been too wrapped up in Kate and Finlay's escape. Lena had spent the day happily exploring a stable. She was safe, content, and had a wonderful future ahead of her. One he had no worries would be fulfilling for her.

And Wren had made that possible.

Thad stepped up to her, closing the small space between them, and whispered, "I'd spend my time with you."

Her eyes grew wide at his words, lips parting in surprise. His eyes narrowed in on the movement, and he lifted a hand, running his fingers through a piece of her silken hair.

"Me?" she breathed. "Why me?"

He dropped his hand from her hair, brushing his knuckles against her soft cheek. She closed her eyes and his chest tightened, relishing the way she reacted to his touch. "Have you ever fallen for someone, body and soul?" He leaned in closer. "Without so much as sharing an intimate touch?"

Her eyes opened, but remained hooded with clear lust. "Is... what we did the other night not intimate?" she asked.

"Oh, sweetheart." His voice dropped an octave. "Not even close."

She blushed furiously, the rosy hue radiating from her chest straight up to the apples of her cheeks. The sight of her, flushed by desire, made him lose his last piece of control. He needed those lips against his again, to bask in the way they fit together, to prove the promise of everything else they were capable of together.

He wrapped his hand around her waist and tugged her flush against him, barely containing a groan as their bodies collided, the thin fabric of her shift the only thing separating her breasts from his bare chest. He lowered his face to hers and, just like last time, the moment their lips connected, there was a sense that washed over him, a sense that felt like he'd been wandering aimlessly and just now found his way home.

She melted into him, turning soft and compliant in a way that drove him mad. He ran his hands through her hair once more, tilting her head up to gain better access to her mouth. He ran his tongue across her lips, requesting more, and when she sighed into his mouth, the simple sound awakened something primal in him. He let out a soft moan and slipped his tongue into her mouth, exploring there as he ran his other hand down her throat, skirting over the top of her shift, teasing at the neckline.

She shuddered against his touch and he pulled her tighter against him, grinding his hips against her body. When she put her hands on his bare chest — tentatively, lighter than a butterfly's wings — he released her mouth and leaned his forehead against hers, exhaling deeply. "That's it," he encouraged, his voice husky with need. "Good girl. Keep going."

Invigorated by his words, she splayed her fingers out and skated them across his chest. He pressed into her hands, enjoying the simple feel of being explored by her. Instead of returning to her mouth, he pressed his lips down her jaw, the curve of her neck, and then her collarbone. By the time he reached her chest, he watched the rise and fall of it, her breathing having turned heavy. His hands hovered over the lace of her shift, and he raised his eyes to hers.

"May I?" he asked, and watched as she bit her lip, then nodded.

With a few deft movements, he had the lace undone, and ever so slowly, he peeled the front of the thin fabric back, revealing her beautiful, palm-sized breasts underneath, peaked in pleasure. He bit back a groan at the sight. Gods, it was like she was made for him. He couldn't waste any more time.

Taking one in his hand, he brushed a thumb over her nipple, reveling in the soft cry it elicited from her. Needing more, he lowered his head and took the other in his mouth. He heard her let out a garbled curse and smiled, running his tongue over the peak once, then twice as she bucked softly into him. He would truly enjoy worshiping every piece of her.

Before he could wring any further noises out of her, however, her hands fluttered down to the waistband of his pants. He pulled back, studying her. Her expression was feverish, gaze intent on the goal in front of her. Her hand dipped under his waistband and he let out a guttural moan and snatched her wrist before it could travel lower. "Gods," he muttered. "Wren."

Her wide, chocolate-brown eyes finally rose to meet his. "Did I do something wrong?" she asked.

All traces of heated temptation rushed from his body, replaced by what could only be described as shame. He hadn't meant to make her feel as though she'd done something he hadn't wanted, because fuck, he wanted it. He wanted that and more. He wanted to hear just how loudly she would cry out from the right touch, to see just how low that blush could run across her heated, sweaty skin. And then he wanted to taste every single piece of it, reveling in just how soft and sweet he knew she would taste.

"No," he said, shaking his head. "Not even close. You have no idea how right this feels."

Her brow furrowed. "Then why...?"

"Because, sweetheart. This isn't real." His voice was grave, and he traced his hand across the swell of her breasts once more, enjoying the final shiver she gave him. "If we go any further, I want to feel it. *Really* feel it. And I want you to, too."

He could tell she was wavering, driven by lust and logic both warring in her expression. Finally, logic seemed to give in, and she pulled the strings of her shift back together. He bit back a smile at what could only be described as an adorable pout when she nodded at him.

"You're right," she conceded. "We'll finish this when we're together again. In real life."

"You'd better count on it, sweetheart. Next time," he promised, shoving back the nagging voice in his head that said, *And what if there isn't a next time?*

CHAPTER THIRTY-ONE

Finlay fidgeted and glanced out the window for the countless time during this meeting. The sun reached inside with long, bright fingers, teasing him with its warmth. He'd missed Sairas. The nature that rose up from all around to greet him was a stark contrast to the concrete jungle of Reviere, and today was a perfect example of its beauty. The grass was turning a radiant green and there wasn't a cloud in the sky. It was the perfect day to venture outside and feel the warm spring weather on his skin. He let his mind wander to the idea of riding out into the forest with Kate, watching her ride with unabashed joy written across her face, hair whipping wildly around her face. He imagined what it would be like to disappear for a while, where nobody could find them and there were no responsibilities on their plates, no hard decisions to make. Only the two of them.

"Finlay?" His cousin's voice pulled him from his wandering imagination.

He blinked, catching her eye. She sat next to Larke down the long, rectangular table. The two sat with their chairs pressed close together, as though the few inches of distance between them were still too much to bear. Darrya's fingers grazed the edge of the table, hesitating near Larke's. She caught his eye for a fleeting moment before dropping her gaze, a faint blush coloring her cheeks. It warmed Finlay's soul to see his cousin so content and cherished, and he couldn't think of anyone better for her than Larke. She deserved every ounce of happiness this relationship brought.

Finlay cleared his throat. "Yes?"

"Anything to add to what Kate's explained, regarding the situation with Aerrin Byrne?" she asked, steepling her fingers on the table. She looked at him expectantly, but he didn't want to admit how his mind had wandered in front of the entire royal council. *His* royal council, a blend of those who had been employed by the late queen and new members he and Kate had appointed. All that aside, he trusted that Kate, sitting next to him, had provided a thorough explanation.

"Not on my end," he replied smoothly. "But I'm happy to answer any clarifying questions."

Immediately, Rindal, one of the queen's old advisors, leaned forward. "Why don't we simply storm Reviere and take him on charges for magical misconduct? Let alone attempted kidnapping?"

"He's been extremely careful to cover his tracks," Kate said. "We won't have any evidence linking him to the actual deeds. It would be our sources against his. That would just lead to a stalemate and bad blood, not to mention more underhanded acts."

Finlay was grateful for the way she tactfully avoided Thad in the conversation, referring only to Aerrin and their sources. They hadn't mentioned Thad to the royal council in one way or another, wanting to leave him out of the equation. If they asked, Finlay and the rest planned to simply state that he wasn't a part of any of it, as far as they knew. Thad was to be treated as a wild card for the time being.

Though Wren seemed to trust him without question, Finlay wasn't sure what he would choose, should it come down to Aerrin's future directly. To put aside decades of family bonds... he didn't trust that it was a simple thing for Thad to do, but he hoped Thad would do right by his daughter.

"Just do what he did to you," Whit, another advisor, huffed. "Use third parties to take him out. Deny responsibility. He made this bed; he can lie in it."

"There are already too many civilian rifts," Patrick put in gently. "To take out the newly named duke for no reason would cause alarm, distrust, and animosity. We don't need to divide the lands further."

"So we tell them what he's planning," Whit argued.

Patrick shook his head. "Personally, until we have more information, I think that will just stoke fear en masse. We just asked all the lands to join us in one war. Can you imagine the response if we tell them there is a possibility of being thrust against their will into another war, especially against an unknown enemy? Chaos will ensue. We will lose their attention and our control to their panic. They'll start infighting and hoarding resources before the real fight can even be confirmed."

Kate shot Patrick a grateful look, clearly approving of his contribution, and he returned her look warmly. This was his first sit-in as part of the royal council, but he carried himself with a calm confidence that made him appear as though he'd always belonged. Finlay was grateful to have someone with his years of experience here, and as someone who had been a part of both realms, his advice was invaluable for this particular conversation.

"All that aside, he will have accounted for a retaliation by now," Larke said. "It will be nigh impossible to reach him. He'll have others run his errands, taste testers for everything that enters his mouth, and guards on watch day and night."

Sufficiently rebuked, Whit wilted in his seat, lips set in a thin line. Finlay waited a beat for any other questions or comments, and when none came, he leaned forward.

"Carisa." Finlay addressed the newest member of his council directly. The young Fae straightened, a look of surprise flickering across her face momentarily. "I would like to hear your thoughts on the situation. Please, hold nothing back."

He had discussed leadership tactics at length with Kate during their time on the ship, reveling in the easy way their ideas sprang back and forth, building on one another. This was one of the tactics they agreed upon — allowing the youngest, least experienced members in meetings to speak first. Too often, Finlay had sat in on meetings where only two or three voices were ever heard, and they were often the most seasoned members. The others either didn't get a chance to speak or felt it wasn't their place. Finlay felt it was important that future generations of the council found their voice, developed their skills, and offered the new perspective their age lended to situations.

When he'd mentioned this to Kate, she'd also voiced her displeasure about the way younger advisors were snubbed. "It's important to have fresh thoughts and ideas in meetings," she'd said. "And oftentimes," she'd added, "those that speak the least listen the best. Those are opinions that should, under no circumstances, go unheard."

So, he made it a point to start with Carisa today and work up from there. He was excited to hear what she had to say, but she still looked stunned that she had even been addressed by name. She blinked rapidly, as though organizing her thoughts.

"Go on," Kate insisted, flashing her an encouraging smile.

"Um," she began, then swallowed. "I think... the biggest question we should address is whether or not we want to open a portal to the other realms. That would dictate what should happen next."

"Interesting," Finlay murmured. "How do you mean?"

She flushed, astounded that she'd been directly addressed thrice now. "Well," she stammered. "If we don't want to open the realms, it would make sense to go to Talamu and destroy the grove before Aerrin can act."

"That still doesn't solve the problem of removing Aerrin," Rindal said.

Finlay expected Carisa to shrink back, but was impressed when she responded, her voice more confident, "No, but it takes away his motivation. It would be easier to deal with him if that's gone."

"And less urgent," Darrya mused. "It would buy us much needed time to recalibrate."

"And if we did want to open the realms?" Kate prodded, and all heads swiveled back to Carisa.

"Then we still go to Talamu," she said and twisted a ring on her hand, the only sign that she was still slightly nervous to be put on the spot. "And you do exactly what Aerrin hoped you would do. But on your terms."

The room was quiet for a moment as everyone seemed to play this out in their minds. Finlay's pulse ramped as he considered what the future would look like if that scenario came to pass. He barely felt capable of his role as a leader of the current realm. Would others look to him for leadership across multiple realms, if the portals opened? He flicked his gaze to Kate, but her expression was shuttered and unreadable as she processed alongside him.

Finally, Patrick spoke. "That could work."

"What?" Whit cried out. "You want to open—"

"Think about it," Patrick cut in. "We could warn the other leaders about Aerrin and his invention. Perhaps they have something similar. Perhaps they even know how to counteract it. If we came as allies first, it could benefit us. We have no idea what the merging of realms could do to improve the state of things."

"Or it could be the exact opposite," Rindal countered. "They could be barbaric. They could be violent and want to conquer us, the same way Aerrin wanted them. This is a terrible idea. We could be inviting war to our doorstep. We know *nothing* about them!"

"You're right," Carisa said, paling. "Oh my god, you're right. I'm sorry, it was a terrible idea."

"It absolutely wasn't a terrible idea," Finlay stated firmly. He wasn't about to let the new council stomp on one another like this, and this first meeting was the place to put his foot down. "We're here for exactly this — all ideas are welcome. So thank you, Carisa."

"But he's right," Whit said. "We have no idea how such a meeting would turn out, even if *we* came to it with good intentions."

"Not necessarily," Kate mused, and Finlay glanced at her. She was biting her lip, and her soft, halting tone told him she was lost in thought, her mind racing through several possible outcomes. He rested a hand on his cheek, waiting to see what her brilliant mind came up with. Finally, she turned, speaking to the group at large, but with her eyes on him.

"It might be possible to see the outcome," she said. "Or a few different possible outcomes. But either way, I think we could explore what the citizens' responses would be to having the portal between realms opened. That could dictate a go-forward plan."

Ensley. She didn't have to say the name for Finlay to know the card up her sleeve. The Valkyrie's brand of magic wasn't a perfect science — there were always things that could change in the moment. If one question was asked, perhaps they'd answer one way, but another might have a completely different outcome. Life hinged precariously on the little things, something that became all the more apparent when Ensley's powers were used.

"That's all fine and dandy, but what if their civilians don't feel the same? What if they lie to you, and they see that we have something they want?" Whit rattled off the questions without so much as a breath in between. "What's to stop them from changing their attitudes down the road?"

Finlay wasn't necessarily a fan of Whit's doomsday attitude, but he had to admit, the issues he voiced *were* valid. "All great questions," he said. "Questions we will take one at a time. I think we have a go-forward plan. Kate and I will see if we can gain some insight into how a meeting would go, and we will meet with Larke to discuss the logistics of reaching Talamu with enough force. It sounds like, either way, we have another trip overseas in front of us."

Everyone shifted in their seats, and there was a bit of disgruntled murmuring at the abrupt dismissal. Finlay disregarded it, though — he had heard all he wanted to, and he could guess what the late queen's advisors would have said, had they been given more speaking time. He wasn't in the mood for any of it, especially considering some of the terrible advice he'd heard them dole out to his great-grandmother. He thought Carisa's go-forward plan was solid, and based on how his friends and family had responded, they felt the same. He was confident in their next steps. He was ecstatic about how this first meeting had gone with the council's newer members.

In fact... he felt something brush against his leg, climbing its way up the top of his thigh. It was Kate's foot, the shoe discarded somewhere under the table. He cleared his throat, attempting to ignore the movement as the others gathered their things, rising from the table. He avoided her gaze, but couldn't avoid the way her touch felt, causing him to tense. He gritted his teeth and nodded as Patrick slipped out of the room. Clearly, though, the rest were moving too slowly for Kate's taste. Her foot found its way between his legs and, after a moment, *squeezed.*

His eyes snapped to hers, and he bit back a groan of approval at the heat he saw in her gaze. "Everyone, out, now," he barked. "I need to speak with my fiancée. *Alone.*"

He held as still as possible as the others exited, tactfully avoiding the smirk tossed his way by his cousin. As the door closed, however, Kate's mischievous smile broke the last of his restraint, and he tugged her into his lap. *Fuck the forest,* he thought, dismissing his earlier daydreams as he brought his lips to hers. *Wherever she is, I'm happy.*

Chapter Thirty-Two

It was harder than I'd anticipated to go back and visit Ensley. The last time I'd been here, I discovered the truth about Blaise's prophecy. The grief from that — compounded by the realization of his sacrifice — was still fresh enough that I felt the pain physically as we approached. I rubbed at my chest absently, as if that would fix the ache buried deep under my skin. My other hand squeezed, and I glanced up to see Finlay, gazing down at me. His mouth was curved upward, seeking to comfort me, but the crinkle at the sides of his eyes betrayed his concern. He knew the pain and anger my last visit here had inflicted. He'd been the only other one to know about Blaise's sacrifice, and it had been a point of contention for us. I attempted a smile and squeezed his hand in return, just as much to reassure him as myself.

As soon as we pushed the dark curtain aside, calling out Ensley's name to announce our arrival, I knew she'd been expecting us. She sat behind the table she practiced at, both fists resting under her chin as she surveyed us. Though her walls were littered with fascinating trinkets, she alone drew an enchanting presence. Large, tawny wings stretched out behind her, strong and feathered like a hawk's. Her flawless, toned brown skin was adorned with gilded jewelry, and her face was sharp and inquisitive.

"Greetings, my king and queen," she called out, her tone formal, yet slightly amused. "I've been expecting you."

I exchanged a look with Finlay, taking in his startled expression. As a divine agent, I knew her precognition was unparalleled, but it still managed to surprise Finlay that she could know such things without so much as making physical contact. She motioned for us to sit, and we slid into the seats across the table from her.

"Does that mean you've already got answers for us?" Finlay asked, shooting her one of his best smirks.

She returned it, her deep brown eyes twinkling. "I may be good, but not that good. I can only sense when it will impact me — for example, when it is going to take time away from my day."

"Our apologies for interrupting your schedule," Finlay returned smoothly. "I can assure you, we'll do our best to make it worth your while."

"If it helps, we're here to ensure I uphold my promise to you," I put in, "to avoid asking you to join any more wars."

The corners of her mouth turned up and she let out a soft laugh, the sound itself nearly ethereal. "I am glad to hear that," she said, "but it's certainly not going to be easy. I sense that your request will have something to do with opening the portals."

Finlay jolted, again in surprise. I bit back a smile, remembering when Ensley's powers used to startle me as well. "How did you know that?" he asked. "I wasn't aware it was even a possibility until a few days ago."

"Neither was I," she admitted. "But I always knew there had been different realms, as my sisters and I are from another one. And I sensed an outcome, not one day ago, that would impact us."

I blinked, taking in the information. I had always wondered if Ensley's powers, being so different from the others in this realm, meant she'd descended from a different being. There weren't many of her kind, despite being so powerful. Would there be more if we opened this portal? Could she help guide the conversations? Was this something she wanted? I shifted in my seat, biting back the barrage of questions swirling in my mind.

"What kind of impact?" Finlay asked, his tone hesitant.

Ensley pursed her lips. "Hard to say. A series of paths crossed my vision in rapid succession, each with different outcomes. What I can say is the worst of them did not involve you. You being here already assures me those are the least likely outcomes."

I breathed a sigh of relief. "Did the worst ones... involve Aerrin Byrne?"

Ensley considered this. "He is the son that looks like his father, yes?"

Finlay nodded, and she continued. "Yes. His involvement brought rage, destruction, mistrust... not only between realms, but between our own people, and his own family." She shuddered, as though reliving it. I pursed my lips, considering her last words.

His own family... I wanted to ask about Thad, but shook it off. There were more pressing questions. "Can you tell us if opening the portal will be the best option?" I asked instead.

She offered us her palms, which we both took willingly. I closed my eyes but knew what I would see if I opened them. Her own gaze would turn a grayish-white, swirling and shiny like marbles. I heard a shuddering exhale as she worked through whatever visions came through the connection.

"It's... it is possible," she began. "There is a path that would lead to a bright future for everyone. It's not the straightforward path you're on right now, though."

I stiffened, my hand instantly becoming sweaty. *This* was the straightforward path? This path already felt like a winding, precarious bridge. One with no guardrails and pouring rain. I couldn't imagine what other route would be available. Before I could inquire, however, she continued.

"Let me see if there is more I can provide you with..." She paused. "Yes. In order to convince the citizens of the other realms, you'll need to come prepared. Know about their customs, their desires. Barter with their leaders."

"But how can we possibly know that?" I heard Finlay ask next to me, his voice cracking in exasperation. "We don't even know their names. What powers they possess."

I frowned, understanding how he felt. We didn't have any books on the other realms, and no stories passed down from generations aside from what we'd heard from Thad. We were wholly unprepared.

"I am not sure," she rasped, and I could hear the strain in her voice as she dove deeper into the vision, exploring for answers. "There must be a way, but... it is unclear. It's likely there is magic involved that I cannot see with my powers."

My brows rose at this new piece of information. I knew magic similar to hers had blocked my past from her before, but to not access a future path? What kind of magic was involved that she couldn't see? Did it involve the new dust Aerrin had created, or something even more powerful?

"And if we don't open the portal?" I ventured, my mind flitting to the other fork in our road.

She was silent for a moment as she considered this. "If you can keep Aerrin's hand out of things, this will cause the least disruption. Things, for the most part, will stay the same."

I felt Finlay shift next to me, physically slumping in what I assumed was relief.

"That doesn't mean there won't still be problems for us to face," I murmured, thinking of the issues we'd discussed in Reviere that concerned our current citizens. While the issues that had been raised were, at the time, deflections, they were very real problems that deserved our attention. Ones that for the most part didn't have easy answers.

"No, it doesn't." Ensley dropped our hands, and I felt the cold air of the room rush up to meet my damp palm. I opened my eyes, and met her gaze, a warm brown once more. "But I say this as someone with both real insight and a general gut feeling. Our realm is in good hands with the two of you."

She beamed at us, and something about the expression reassured me, filling a space where kernels of self-doubt had previously been settling and festering. I offered a small smile in return. Finlay dipped his head, murmuring his thanks, and then fished out a handful of coins, extending them to her. She waved him off, looking offended at the mere notion of payment.

"Thank you, Ensley," I finally managed. She nodded at me, understanding I meant far more than the simple favor of her palm reading. We exited the building, my mind turning over our options.

The safest bet, it seemed, would be to take Aerrin out of the equation and remove the option of opening the portal. Either way, we were preparing to set sail tomorrow morning for Talamu. Our sources confirmed that Aerrin was still at his palace, so we hoped we would beat him to the land.

Because we expected him to have reinforcements stationed there, however, we were taking two ships — one that would set sail later today, with Larke and a small force of troops, hoping to pull any of Aerrin's men away from the grove. This would leave us, on the second ship, an opening to approach the grove from another angle, with fewer forces and less resistance. Darrya, as the wonderfully stubborn being she was, had insisted on coming along with Larke, though he'd privately informed us that he planned to keep her on the ship once they hit land. I smirked to myself. I would love to be a fly on the wall for that conversation.

"Do you want to go see Kipp and Cas while we're in town?" Finlay asked, interrupting my thoughts. We were on the path headed back to the palace, but Finlay had stopped just short of leaving

Sairas. A warm spring breeze blew past, ruffling his golden hair away from his face as he gave me an expectant look.

"Possibly…" I trailed off, my mind still on our options. "What do you think Ensley meant when she said there was magic involved in the path that would work for us to open the portal?"

Finlay frowned, considering, and I took a moment to survey him. The frown lines looked more permanent, his blue eyes darker, and his hair stood at more chaotic angles than its usual casual disarray. My chest tightened. He looked so serious these days, taking every burden personally on his shoulders. I knew he blamed himself for not seeing the signs sooner that Aerrin had been planning to put this all into motion ages ago. I hoped desperately that we could resolve this all with minimal impact, and he could return back to his more carefree, relaxed self.

"I'm not sure. Some enchanted item to commune with other realms, maybe? Or another powerful Valkyrie with that ability?" he finally ventured. "Either way, it sounds like a long shot. The safest route seems to be to just take the portal option out of the equation entirely."

"I think so, too," I murmured, my mind snagging on something. But — wait. Was it possible?

Didn't we owe it to ourselves to try, to see if we could make the realms a collectively better place to be? If there was a chance?

"Little angel?" Finlay prodded. "Do you want to go see Kipp and Cas?"

I shook my head. "Not quite yet. I have a detour in mind."

"Where to?" He raised a questioning brow.

"Any chance you have some Faerie dust on you?" I grinned. "I think we need to make one more trip to the Otherworld."

CHAPTER THIRTY-THREE

Wren stared off into the high seas, listening to the half-inebriated state of her friends behind her. They had started another disjointed rendition of a familiar song, one most kids learned during their schooling. It talked about the Tuatha Dé Danann, and how they first arrived on land in a cloud of mist. Kate had no idea what the words were and, much to everyone's delight, couldn't carry a tune to save her life. It had turned the night into a mix of loving mockery and recitation of all their favorite childhood songs — the difference being, of course, that now there were strong cocktails involved.

The song finished, complete with a distinct crack in Kate's singsong-y voice, which had the others dissolving into chuckles. "What? Did I say the words wrong?" she cried out, earning another chorus of laughter.

"Not at all, Katie-cat," came Cas's voice, rife with his familiar taunting lilt. "We're just happy to find the one thing that you're not good at."

"Oh, go pound sand, Cas," Kate volleyed back.

Wren smiled and turned her attention from the large expanse of water to the sight of her favorite people on the deck. They were all there: her brother, Kipp, Kate, Finlay, Darrya, and Larke. At the last minute, Patrick had offered to lead the first set of troops to Talamu in tandem with Larke's second-in-command, insisting that Larke should join Kate and the rest of their group. Kate had resisted at first, but as Wren herself knew, it was hard to argue when your father was trying to look out for your well-being. That kind of love was a trump card.

She let out a soft sigh, wondering how Lena was doing. They'd left Thad's daughter behind at the palace, as that was the safest option, but Wren's heart squeezed as she realized how alone Lena must feel. She'd had to leave her father behind, and now Wren had left her behind. She only hoped the guards would take Lena to the stables frequently, as she'd explicitly requested.

Wren went to the others and sat down, accepting the drink that Darrya passed her way. She took a small sip, smiling as she surveyed her friends. Larke was the only sober one of the group, but Wren also didn't want to drink too much. Not only did she want to be on guard, should anything happen, but she wasn't sure what would happen if she went to sleep with too much in her system. Would she not dream, then? She hadn't heard from Thad the last two nights and, she realized, she desperately wanted him to visit again. Not only to let him know that they were on their way to Talamu, but because she wanted to see him again. Perhaps kiss him again, or convince him of more. She rubbed away the goosebumps that rose on her skin as she remembered the way they'd ended things last time, a warm desire gathering in her core at the memory.

"All right, no more songs," Kate complained. "What else can we do to pass the time?"

Finlay reached into his pocket and pulled out purple and gold dice, tossing them in the air. "We could always play dice?" he offered, and was met with loud, half-drunk cries of approval. Wren took another sip of her drink and locked eyes with Larke, who shot her an amused look that said, *brace yourself.*

By the time she teetered back to her bed, she was more than a little tipsy and definitely ready to dive into a deep slumber. She nestled her head into her pillow, and the last thought that crossed her mind as she drifted off was if she would see Thad on the other side.

"Wren? Wren!"

She woke to the sound of her name being called out and a strange, jostling sensation. She opened her eyes to find herself staring directly into a pair of deep sapphire ones. They narrowed, assessing her, and she realized who they belonged to.

"Thad?"

His expression transformed from one of careful scrutiny to relief. "Yeah, sweetheart."

Wren pulled herself into a seated position. "Are we back in the dreamscape?"

"We are." Thad nodded and lowered himself to sit beside her. He tossed her a tentative smile. "But I've been here for a while. I wasn't sure if you would come. And when you did, you didn't wake right away. Is everything okay?"

"Erm, yes." Wren rubbed at her eyes. "We just did a little drinking last night. That's probably why it took a minute to wake me here."

Thad let out a soft laugh, but then his face went serious. "I'm glad I was able to catch you tonight. Something is up. Aerrin left two days ago without telling me. I'm fairly certain he's on his way to Talamu, but I don't know why. You'll have to let the others know."

Wren's heart rate picked up at the prospect that they would run into Aerrin, but she did her best to remind herself that they had accounted for this possibility. Their first ship should get there soon and act as a distraction, which meant they could proceed as planned.

"Good news, then," she said. "We left this morning for Talamu as well."

Thad's eyes widened. "And Lena?"

"Safe, at the palace," Wren assured him. "We left her with a caretaker and several guards."

Thad's shoulders slumped and he left out a soft exhale, but another thought occurred to Wren. "Why didn't Aerrin tell you he was leaving?" she asked. "Does he suspect you're working with us?"

"I don't see how. I think he just was tired of my incompetence." Thad flashed her a halfhearted smile and shrugged. "Honestly, it's fine by me if that's the way he feels."

Wren bit her lip, hoping that was the case. "I wish you could join us."

Thad straightened. "I actually might be able to. You left this morning, you said?"

When Wren nodded, he continued. "You'll have to go around Dahín anyways. The grove is on the eastern side of Talamu. Using my water magic, I *should* be able to meet you by the coast tomorrow."

Her heart rate picked up again, this time in anticipation. By this time tomorrow, she might be with Thad again, really be able to see him, speak with him, *touch* him. "You would do that?" she asked.

The corner of Thad's mouth quirked up. "Absolutely. I started this, and especially now that Aerrin's gone rogue, I need to see it through to the end."

He studied her for a moment and raised his hand, tucking a strand of her hair behind her ear. His hand lingered by her ear. "And even if that weren't the case, I'd do it for you."

"For me?" she breathed.

He flatted his palm, cupping her cheek, and she leaned into the warm touch. "You have no idea what I'd do for you," he replied. "I'm still learning myself. And I haven't found a limit yet, sweetheart."

The next day, Wren found herself in the same spot above deck, squinting at the fast-approaching shoreline of Dahín. It was difficult to make out. Unlike the tall, solid buildings that greeted them from miles away as they'd approached Reviere, there was no real sign of life. There weren't any hills or trees sprouting up from the shallow marshland to guide them, either. Only their shipmaster's prowess told them they were on the right course.

"Do you think he's here yet?" asked a voice, and she glanced over to see Kate coming to a halt beside her. She gazed out into the expanse of water, eyes narrowing in search.

"I hope so," Wren answered honestly. "We can't just leave him stranded out here."

"We won't," Kate assured her, sidling in to nudge her shoulder against Wren's. They refocused their attention on the shoreline and basked in the silence for a long moment together, broken up only by the consistent lapping of waves against the side of the ship. It was, thankfully, a clear and sunny day, giving them the visibility they needed and ensuring the trip was a smooth one. Once they found Thad, it would be easy enough to bring him on board.

Kate leaned over the rail, peering into the distance. "Wait. Do you see that?"

She pointed, and Wren followed the gesture to a flock of white birds, collectively rising from a spot further east in the marshlands. Their short, shrill squawks echoed across the flat land and water, meeting Wren's ears as they cursed whatever had taken their spot. They rose like a cloud, gathering tightly in the air before they moved west as a unit in search of a new resting place.

"Something must have disturbed them," Wren realized.

"Or *someone.*" Kate flashed Wren a smile. "I'll go tell the crew to head that way. You keep watch."

She strode away and Wren kept her eyes glued to the spot they'd pointed out. As they drew closer, the sounds of wildlife grew louder.

Thad approached on a small boat, barely large enough to fit four people. For a moment, Wren's heart spasmed — how could he be so reckless, trying to cross this water in such a small thing? — until she remembered the easy way he manipulated water. If anyone was safe out here, it was him. Indeed, as he approached, she saw the casual way he flicked his hand, guiding the current to reach the ship without so much as raising an oar to aid him.

Once he'd been hauled aboard, Wren hung back, suddenly shy, but it didn't matter. He'd immediately been surrounded by the rest of the group first. Kipp and Cas greeted him cautiously, but pleasantly enough, and Finlay and Kate both gave him a warm welcome. The only two who hung back were Larke and Darrya. Darrya's expression was reserved, but Larke's was steely, sharp as the blade that hung at his waist. The soldier's hand hovered over the hilt, like he was undecided on if he should draw the weapon.

When the others in the group parted, giving Thad a direct line to those two, he hesitated, and Wren took a minute to inspect him. He looked haggard, as though he'd been having trouble sleeping. He'd shown up without any more than a small satchel, and his clothing was plain — dark leather pants and a simple, cream-colored shirt, unlaced at the chest. His dark hair was windblown and damp from the spray of seawater. He clearly hadn't shaved for a few days, with a shadow across his jaw that threatened to turn into the beginnings of a full beard. His eyes, accentuated with dark rings underneath, jumped back and forth between Darrya and Larke. Instead of going to either of them, however, he dropped to one knee. He hung his head.

"Darrya. I know what my brother has done to you," he rasped. "And what I have *not* done to change it is just as bad. I come begging for forgiveness that I haven't earned, in the hopes that I can spend the rest of my days on the right path. I can't change the past, but I am striving to change the future for the better."

Out of the corner of her eye, she saw Finlay nudge Cas. "Why didn't we get that apology?" he muttered, just loud enough for Wren to hear, but was cut off by a swift elbow to the gut from Kate. Kate didn't so much as take her eyes off the scene in front of them, but when Finlay doubled over and coughed, a slow smile spread across her face. Wren covered her mouth with a hand to smother a grin of her own.

Darrya exchanged a look with Larke, her eyes asking an unspoken question. His face remained impassive, a barrier that Wren couldn't even begin to decipher. But whatever was exchanged in that moment was monumental. Larke dipped his head, just slightly, and Darrya reached a hand to his face, brushing his cheek in the barest of touches. She then turned and approached Thad.

Thad remained kneeling, not even so much as glancing up in her direction. It was the ultimate sign of deference — with his title, officially, he was only required to kneel to Kate or Finlay, and only if explicitly requested. Aerrin would never be caught dead kneeling to anyone, and probably would defy even the king and queen. But here Thad was, willingly kneeling to Darrya. If Wren had had so much as a lingering breath of doubt, she knew now how much he meant his change of heart. Something had changed in the moment he'd chosen to rescue her from the dungeon, and he wasn't turning back.

Darrya put a hand on his shoulder and finally, he looked up, the dark blue of his eyes contrasting sharply with how bloodshot they were. As soon as his gaze met hers, she smiled, all the warmth and radiance that Wren knew and loved about her.

"You're not him, Thad," she said. "And you never have been. I decided long ago not to judge someone on the misdeeds of their family. The only mistake you made was putting your faith in someone who didn't have anything to offer you in return."

Thad's mouth opened and closed, but he said nothing. Darrya bent over and, in a small movement, pulled him to his feet. She rested a hand on each of his arms, like a mother imparting wisdom on her child. "Blood or not, you deserve to be treated with love and respect. You've got us, and we've got you. You've already proven that you're one of us, Thad. Welcome to the family."

With that, she pulled him into an embrace. At first, his eyes squeezed shut, his face twisting in what looked like pain. But after a long moment, his arms wrapped around her and tightened. He let out a long, shuddering exhale, and Wren heard two muffled words, words that seemed like the beginning of something significant.

"Thank you."

CHAPTER THIRTY-FOUR

Thad should have been exhausted. He couldn't remember the last time he'd had a good night's sleep, and the physical and magical exertion of traveling to meet the ship had drained him. But the little dance he'd done with Wren today — exchanging looks, brushing hands, exchanging superficial pleasantries — had him wound up in a way that wouldn't unravel itself until he did something about it. Finally, after tossing and turning in his bed for at least half an hour, he rose and dressed, knowing where his feet would take him before he even left his cabin. The night air was refreshingly cool, and the sounds of waves lapping against the side of the ship relaxed him as he strode to his destination.

Wren answered the door mere seconds after he knocked, and he grinned as he looked down at her, knowing she had been waiting for him. She wore only a shift, the same one from the dreamscape, and as his eyes traveled down her chest, a flush rose on her cheeks, as if she knew exactly where his mind had wandered to.

"Hi," she said, almost shyly.

He lifted his eyes back to hers and gave her a heated smile. "Hi."

"Do you…" she swallowed. "Do you want to come in?"

He nodded. "I couldn't sleep."

"Neither could I."

He strode into the room and removed his coat and shoes, his gaze never leaving hers. She watched him intently, backing up until her legs hit the side of the bed and forced her to sit on the edge of the mattress. When he approached, he felt like a predator, sizing up its prey, and he had to remind himself to take it slow. He'd had partners in the past where they'd devoured each other like flames on dry kindling, rapidly and over quickly.

He didn't want that with Wren. He had to treat her properly, and part of him worried his harsher side would scare her away. He wanted to savor her slowly and carefully, like a fine spirit. When he came to the side of the bed and she reached for him, however, he nearly forgot all decorum.

She pulled him gently to her, and his mouth melded against hers. The way her lips felt on his was like coming home. She sighed into him like she felt the same, and he pushed her back on the bed, lowering her body slowly. He crawled over her body as he kissed her, pressing her into the mattress with his hips. His tongue explored her mouth for a long moment before he broke off, trailing kisses down her neck and chest, eliciting soft moans from her.

"More?" he asked.

She let out a breathy exhale. "More."

With that, he shifted off of her, turning her so that they lay sideways in bed, her back against his front. He trailed a hand over her breasts, still covered in the thin fabric of her shift, but doing nothing to hide her hard peaks of desire. She writhed under his touch and sighed his name. The way she said it sounded like a prayer, like nothing Thad had ever heard before. Gods, she was so open with everything. Her fears, her hate, her love, her *lust*. He craved it. Needed to wring more of it out of her.

He slid his hand down her thigh and back up, resting a palm between her legs. Fuck, there was nothing under her shift. Not a damn thing.

"I need to feel you," he whispered, voice already hoarse from want. "May I?"

"Please," she whispered back, and that was all the invitation he needed. He dropped a finger lower and, finding her drenched with desire, groaned and added a second. She let out a soft cry that shot straight to his groin, and she tilted her legs, spreading them to give him more access. He shifted, sliding behind her so that his body was flush against hers, and her breathing hitched as she felt the hard evidence of his want against her hip. To his surprise, she pressed back against it, rocking into him in a taunting motion. *So that's the game she wants to play, is it?* he thought, but let out a soft chuckle.

"Not yet," he husked. "Just you."

With that, he swirled his thumb against her, the easy, circular motion making her head fall back against his chest and confirming his choice. It made him near-delirious, watching her body begin to tremble and her cries grow more desperate as he continued his circular pace, and he plunged two fingers inside her to the same rhythm. He'd been with plenty of others — gods knew Lena was the result of one such occasion — but never quite like this, and never with someone like Wren. When he curled his fingers inside her, hitting that sensitive spot, the way she squeezed him and cried out his name made him curse gruffly in response. He barely had the wherewithal to cover her mouth with his free hand.

"Careful, sweetheart," he murmured. "While I fucking love that sound from you, we don't need any uninvited guests here."

She squirmed against his hold, but as he stroked her, bringing her back up to the edge, her attention was diverted. Her back arched as he worked to bring her back up to the breaking point, relishing in the feel of her walls squeezing his fingers and her hot breath panting into his hand.

He brought his lips to her ear. "Come for me," he urged, and groaned as she bit down on his palm, stifling her cry of release as she came undone. His cock jerked at the sensation, and he grinned to himself, realizing his sweet girl had some bite to her as well. He'd do his best to make that side come out to play more often. He waited until he'd wrung the last throes of pleasure from her, and then shifted his hand to run up and down the length of her thigh, simply enjoying the feel of her body against his.

They remained that way for a long moment, letting their combined ragged breathing return to normal. Finally, Wren turned to face him. There was a softness to her gaze, paired with incredulity and a bit of uncertainty. He wondered if she had ever lost control and let go like that with anyone before. If she'd lose control with him again, and again. He certainly hoped so.

"What are you thinking, sweetheart?" he asked. This was a new expression from her, one of several he planned to commit to memory.

"I think…" she swallowed, and he eyed the flush that remained on her cheeks and chest, slow to leave her beautifully soft skin. "I think I need some water."

He smiled and nodded, lifting his arm to let her rise from the bed. She straightened her shift and pulled a coat over it. She shot him a shy smile before padding out of the room, and he laughed to himself. Was she… embarrassed? She shouldn't be, but gods, he could get addicted to this, the soft, sweet manner in which Wren carried herself at all times.

He waited patiently for her to return, listening to the sounds of the ship. Boards creaked, waves lapped at the side of the vessel, and he heard footsteps and murmured voices above. Every now and then, he heard a raised voice and a scuffle, which quieted after a moment. It was well past sundown, so he wondered what all the commotion was. Perhaps they were nearing the shore of Talamu — but no, that should still be hours away. Maybe he and Wren weren't the only ones having trouble sleeping. Or perhaps this crew just enjoyed their drink a bit too much.

After several minutes without Wren's return, he grew worried. Had he done something wrong? Had he taken things too fast? Had she changed her mind about them, about him? *Shit.*

He threw his coat and boots back on and opened the cabin door, ready to hunt her down. He'd apologize, assure her they could take it as slow as she needed. But as soon as he climbed the steps to the top deck, he was met with the sight he least expected.

"Brother," Aerrin said.

Thad froze, eyeing him. His brother was *here*, on this boat, showing not so much as an ounce of surprise at seeing Thad on board. In fact, Aerrin's expression was terrifyingly blank. Though Thad couldn't see Wren — he couldn't decide if that worried or relieved him — they were far from alone. Aerrin's soldiers gathered behind him, weapons glinting menacingly in the moonlight. "I wondered when I'd see you again."

Thad didn't respond, but internally, his mind was racing. Aerrin had left him in Reviere. What reason would he have to suspect that Thad would follow him here?

Unless...

His brother let out a sigh and continued. "I had suspicions you were switching sides. Too much had gone wrong and too much information got in the wrong hands. You were the only common denominator. I can't say I'm surprised. You've always had far more weaknesses than me."

Finally, Aerrin grinned, his face transforming from expressionless to pure malice. Thad's stomach plummeted at the change. "But those weaknesses are also what made you *so* easy to control. There's a reason I always kept tabs on what's most precious to you. And guess what? It turns out, it paid off even better than expected. I got two for the price of one!"

Aerrin signaled to a soldier behind him, who disappeared behind a stack of barrels and other crated supplies. Thad dared a glance around, realizing that the small force of troops that had been milling around earlier on the ship were absent. That signature royal purple was nowhere to be seen. Instead, he was now surrounded by Aerrin's guard, decorated in the orange and blue of Brytham. What had happened to everyone? How had Aerrin seized control of this ship?

A second later, the soldier reappeared, dragging two figures out with him. Both were bound and hooded. The soldier lifted the first hood, revealing Wren. Her lip was split, with dried blood trailing down her chin, and her eye was puffy, already turning a bluish-purple. She was gagged, but she struggled against the restraint regardless, writhing and causing the soldier to growl in annoyance. Thad stepped forward at the sight.

"Wren," he breathed, and when the second hood came off, his voice cracked on the word. *"Bug."*

Somehow, Lena was here. She was bound and gagged, too, and her eyes shimmered with panic. She looked untouched, but Thad seethed regardless at the sight of her in the hands of someone capable of unimaginable violence. How had they gotten his daughter? Had she ever truly been safe?

He took another step forward, but Aerrin held out a hand and tsked. "You can have this one back. She's been a pain in our ass."

Aerrin grabbed Wren from the soldier and shoved her toward Thad. He caught her as she stumbled forward, then glared over her shoulder at his brother, who gave him a flippant wave.

"But... I think we'll keep this one as collateral. Say goodbye to your daddy, Lena."

With that, Aerrin pulled her backward and a wave of soldiers descended.

CHAPTER THIRTY-FIVE

"Dad!" Lena screamed, tumbling out of sight as Aerrin dragged her below deck by the throat. A fury Thad had never felt before consumed him, and he saw red as he dashed forward, drawing his sword. Two soldiers stepped forward to block him, and he parried, disarming the first easily and turning to the second, even as more approached. There had to be over two dozen, likely more as they kept flooding the main deck. Thad brushed the second soldier's sword aside and kicked him to the ground, turning to face the others. He summoned his magic, ready to pull each and every soldier off of this gods-damned boat to get to his daughter.

Before he could, however, a wave of dust hit him square in the face and he staggered back, squeezing his eyes shut as a wave of agony crashed over him. The hilt of a sword hit him in the back of the head, and he dropped to one knee with a groan, disoriented. Through the stinging pain, he thought he heard Wren cry out.

"Leave him to me," someone commanded. Thad glanced up through blurred vision to see that Aerrin had reappeared above deck. There was a hard expression on his face as he observed Thad, on his knees and hacking, and Thad finally registered what he'd been hit with. Buair.

"Against me, brother?" he cried out, feeling his magic wane. Aerrin knelt beside him, winding rope over his wrists with angry tugs. The draining feeling intensified, and Thad realized with a start that Aerrin had really done it — he'd managed to infuse the buair into other substances. This went past the tests in their dungeons or the late queen's rare, enchanted chains. He shivered as he realized what this meant: chains, charms, ropes that could keep all the most powerful Fae at bay. Aerrin had *commercialized* this weapon.

"You're playing the part of a god, Aerrin," he warned, straining against the ropes. "This isn't the way it's meant to be."

"You chose your side," his brother replied with a growl. "Now you get to watch as the right one wins."

He yanked Thad over to a post, trussing him up against it. He gagged him and strode off, reappearing moments later with Wren, who was still bound and sporting her injured eye, which had swelled to a new level. He tied her to the same post and paused for another moment at Thad's side. The commotion of their exchange had summoned others from their beds, so more troops were funneling onto the deck, meeting Aerrin's soldiers. Past the yelling, boots slamming against the boards, and sharp ringing of swords clashing, Thad heard his brother's voice.

"I only hope you live long enough to see me murder everyone you were weak enough to love," he whispered, and then strode off, leaving Thad to watch the way things played out.

Thad squeezed his eyes shut, listening helplessly to the commotion around him. The loss of his magic left him throbbing with emptiness, as though part of his soul had been cleaved from him. It paled, however, in comparison to the pain of knowing Lena was somewhere out there without him to protect her. He groaned against his gag and collapsed into the post.

After a moment, he felt something brush his hand, and he jolted. Soft fingers wound their way through his, and he realized it was Wren. She squeezed his hand gently, and after a pause, he squeezed back. With her hand in his, he summoned the courage to look up and take in the battle being waged without him.

A dark cloud had cut through the sky across the moonlight, plunging them into near darkness. Thad squinted and made out Larke, using one hand to whip water through the air. The other held his sword, readily fending off the remaining soldiers that managed to make it past his magic. Thad had to admire the commander's skill in battle; he was certain none in the Brytham army could hold a candle to him. Behind Larke stood Kate and Finlay, back-to-back, fighting with everything they had. Kate shot bolts of lightning from her palms, while Finlay followed with flame. Thad noted that none of the soldiers' swords or magic even came close to them, and he wondered who was wielding the air shield — whoever it was, it was impressive work.

Magic sprung up across the ship in gusts and vines, flames and waves. Where magic failed, swords collided, flashes of purple and blue darting and weaving their way across the deck. A barrel came flying at Thad's head with magically enhanced speed, and he ducked. The barrel crashed into the floorboards, leaving a sizable hole. Thad peered through it and saw the blur of a reddish-brown wolf, followed closely by a flash of Pixie wings that he recognized as Wren's brother's. His heart lifted. *Find Lena,* he prayed.

"You," someone snarled, jerking his attention back to the main deck. A Brytham soldier he vaguely recognized stalked toward him, sword raised. "You're the traitor brother."

Thad's pulse sped up, and he ripped his hand from Wren's, bucking against the ropes. The soldier grinned, picking up his stride — until he hesitated, his steps stuttering unnaturally. He gasped and collapsed, an arrow tactfully placed through his neck. Thad froze, his eyes following the arrow's trajectory to find Darrya. She was grim-faced, hair whipping in wet strings around her shoulders as she swiveled from her high position. She didn't even glance at Thad; she had already reloaded her bow, aiming for another soldier in their vicinity. He wasn't sure if it was because she had truly forgiven him earlier that night, or because of her fondness for Wren, but either way, he sent her a mental thanks.

An enraged roar dragged his gaze back to Larke, who was doubled over in agony. Dust settled around the commander, and Aerrin was stalking away, a dark, satisfied smile on his face. Though several Brytham soldiers leaped forward, hoping to capitalize on the commander's weakness, they were pushed back by a sea of purple and a collection of arrows. Aerrin continued forward, his sights clearly set on Kate and Finlay. The two took notice and braced to meet him, but Thad's eyes flicked to movement behind them, and he struggled against his restraints once more. *No.*

Kuiper stalked behind them, dressed in his standard black and stealthy as a panther, dust in hand. An arrow whizzed past his head, narrowly missing, and his face jerked up to glare at Darrya. Thad looked as well, just in time to see Darrya duck and throw her bow out in front of her to brace against the strike of a blade. The bow snapped in half, and Darrya dropped it, throwing her hands out to push the soldier back with a hefty gust of air. *Ah* — so she had been using her air magic to shield the king and future queen.

But... if she'd been shielding them, and was now directing the magic elsewhere, that meant —

Thad glanced back at Finlay and Kate, alarmed. They flared their power, focused on his brother and oblivious to Kuiper behind them. A quick exchange of looks between Kuiper and Aerrin, and the dust was launched, carried on a wind straight into Finlay and Kate. Both collapsed in a fit of agony, clutching at their middles and bracing against each other. Kuiper grinned and brandished a sword, readying himself for what would most assuredly be a killing blow. Finlay rolled over to shield Kate, and Thad tensed.

He heard an angry bellow and in the next second, Larke launched himself at Kuiper, sending them both tumbling to the corner of the ship and crashing against the rail. Thad watched Kuiper's weapon go skidding in the opposite direction. With no weapons and Kuiper's magic being healing, Thad knew they were on surprisingly even fighting ground. They rolled to a standing position, and Larke bared his teeth as the two began a lethal dance with only their bare hands.

Across the ship, Kate and Finlay had begun the fight for their own lives with Aerrin. They were quickly joined by soldiers from each side, though Brytham's soldiers had begun to outnumber the small force the king and future queen had brought along. Finlay fought with all the tact of a professionally trained soldier and the passion of a man with his life on the line, his sword stained crimson. Kate fought... well, there was no way about it; she fought dirty, alternating between clean strokes with the sword and small cuts with a dagger.

Eventually, they were disarmed, the sheer numbers working against them. Still, they resorted to fists and feet, inflicting as many wounds as possible until both had been grabbed by a Bytham soldier. Thad sagged back against the post in defeat, glancing away from what seemed inevitable.

He surveyed the carnage, looking for other familiar faces until movement from the deck floor caught his attention. Larke rose and strode forward from where he left Kuiper's lifeless body, grabbing a sword from the ground as he went. He began cutting a path through soldiers to where Kate and Finlay had been, though Thad couldn't see them now through the wall of blue.

"Stop."

Aerrin's voice rang out, and as quickly as the fighting had begun, it stopped. Though Thad had not been a part of it all with the rest of them, his own chest was heaving. Everyone stood frozen in a face-off, but a quick once-over of the scene made it clear Aerrin and his men had the obvious advantage. Lena was still locked somewhere below, and Kate and Finlay were tied to one another with a buair-infused rope. Both were soaking wet and smeared with blood; even now, bright crimson blood dripped from Finlay's forehead onto the deck in large droplets.

Larke stood tall, facing the hijackers with his sword still in hand, but it trembled visibly. His men that remained were slow to stagger onto their feet behind him, some groaning, others crying softly. Darrya stood amongst them, and she clutched her broken bow, panting heavily, face contorted in panic and fury. The dark clouds had picked up speed, sweeping through the skies as though attempting to escape the chaos in the ocean as well.

Thad exchanged a glance with Wren, and a pang thrummed deep in his chest at her defeated expression. How had it come to this? His mind raced as he considered his options, but he couldn't see an avenue out that didn't involve decimating everyone aboard this ship — including Lena and Wren. If only he had more time; perhaps they could escape their ties, their magic would return, and they could use their elements to get safely to shore... but no. Even then, land was too far away. He was drained, not only from the dust but from his journey earlier that night. They would exhaust themselves before they could make it.

He could pretend to switch sides once more, but... Aerrin was no fool. He would make him pay, and he would start with Lena. Thad gripped the frayed rope tightly, desperation threatening to drown him before the ocean did. A drop of water hit his cheek, and he blinked, wondering for a moment if it was rain or if he'd started to cry without noticing.

Suddenly, a low rumble echoed across the ocean surface. It sounded like the earth slowly splitting apart, despite the fact they were surrounded by water on all sides. Soldiers began to stumble back, staring around the ship and out beyond. The noise cut harshly through the air, puncturing the quiet that had fallen over them all. There was a brief lapse, sending the ship back into silence, and Thad held his breath.

Then it was back, the rolling grumble louder and deeper now, reverberating against his very ribs. Every hair on his body stood on end. It was an animal, surely. Its call was far louder than Angus's growl, louder even than Khepri's.

What is that?

Everyone glanced up and around, trying to place the noise, including Thad. Only one person's eyes weren't narrowed in confusion, he noted: Kate. Hers were hyper-focused on Aerrin, as though the look could kill, and shining like molten gold. The water began to ripple, and her lips parted in a sinister grin. A flash of lightning lit the dim sky, followed shortly by a low boom of thunder. Thad lifted a brow in surprise as he noted a slight spark dance in her palms. She'd essentially been double-dosed with buair. How was that possible?

"What is this?" Aerrin demanded, swiveling to face her. He paled as he took in her glowing eyes and crackling palms. "How are you doing this?"

The boat began to sway, causing the soldiers to stumble and murmur in panic. Kate choked out a mirthless laugh.

"Oh, Aerrin. You can take my magic, but you still can't harness it. Only those formed from the harshest conditions can weather the storm."

Another bright flash of lightning sizzled through the sky, another clap of thunder, and then something burst forth from the ocean. Water sprayed down across the deck as the figure rose high, blending in with the dark navy of the atmosphere. Its long, scaled body swiveled as it ascended out of the water, and Thad sucked in a breath as its head tilted down, assessing the ship from where it had risen high in the sky. The vast sea itself seemed to bow in reverence to the creature.

A beithir.

It was unmistakable, breathtaking, and terrifying. Two spiraled horns extended down its back, and its eyes — *its eyes.* They gleamed the same bright gold that Kate's did. When lightning struck next, a web of white-gold light danced its way down the creature's scales, as if it were a living, breathing conduit of the chaos happening in the clouds. It opened its mouth, large fangs glinting against the lightning, and let out an even more ferocious growl than the ones prior. The sound blended with the thunder that echoed through the skies, drowned out only by a low, gravelly voice that resounded through his head.

And we are the storm.

CHAPTER THIRTY-SIX

The power coursing through me was unlike any I'd felt before. Despite the way the buair had stolen my magic, the storm had quickly replaced the emptiness, filling my soul until it overflowed. Even I couldn't say which came first — the storm or Grom. Either way, I was immensely grateful for both. The crackling static from the lightning danced across my skin, making my hair stand on end, but left me unscathed.

I watched the way it spilled over Grom's scales and took in the faces of the soldiers around me, including Aerrin. He stared at the scene before him, paling as Grom unleashed another shuddering roar. I couldn't help but let loose a second maniacal laugh. "What's wrong?" I asked.

When Aerrin turned to face me, I flicked my fingers, sending a white-hot lash of power across the rope that bound both Finlay and me. The fried remains fell to the floor with a thud. I rubbed my wrists, straightened, and strode for Grom, who curled his head toward me affectionately.

I rested a hand on his large, scaled nose, power hurtling from the point of contact through my veins. Grom let out a soft rumble, one that reached only my ears. I knew without confirmation that my eyes were blazing gold, and so, I turned to stare directly at Aerrin. "Finally found something you're afraid of?"

Aerrin took a step back, but shook his head. "Attack!" he bellowed, and even I had to admit, the loyalty — or perhaps fear — that he instilled in his troops was remarkable. Each blue-clad soldier on deck rushed forward, sword and magic brandished.

Finlay raced across my line of sight, picking up a sword from the deck and raising it to meet a soldier head-on without breaking stride. An arrow whizzed past my ear, narrowly missing Grom's eye. Though it rebounded easily off his scales, he jerked his head back with a hiss. I rounded on the attacker, summoning the lightning and casting it in a well-aimed line toward the archer. He was temporarily engulfed in light, and by the time it cleared, he had collapsed. The ease with which I inflicted such damage with my magic might have startled me under other circumstances, but I was past caring. Aerrin would stop at nothing to achieve his goal, and I could be his downfall. I would not fail.

The boards creaked and the ship shifted as Grom rested his front feet on the deck, each talon a dagger in its own right. His lips curled in a menacing snarl and his eyes flashed. Lightning peeled down from the skies, hitting three, four soldiers in its wake. Sharp cracks rang in my ears as wood splintered anywhere lightning struck the ship. Wafts of burning wood and flesh stung my nose, making me gag.

Any soldier in Grom's vicinity that was not hit by the lightning met their demise from a wayward claw or tooth. Any cry that emanated from them was blissfully short-lived, but followed by a crunch that I didn't linger too long on. Instead, I sidled back up to Finlay, who was holding his own with a sword, but remained without his magic. We quickly settled into a rhythm, with me striking down any Brytham soldiers that came at us from a distance with their own magic, and him handling any that ventured close with steel.

The rain came down in earnest now, the winds whipping it sideways, and I blinked rapidly to clear my vision. Though I wasn't sure how long we'd battled, the number of Brytham soldiers had dwindled to single digits. My eyes skirted over those who remained motionless on the main deck of the ship, fatally wounded by blade, magic, or monster, and I attempted to compartmentalize the lives lost in Aerrin's name.

Though I searched, I didn't see any sign of Aerrin. His soldiers, having sensed the changing tides of the battle, were diving overboard. They'd rather risk the wrath of the churning sea than the monster that had come from beneath to face them.

Grom arched his neck, surveying the remaining soldiers on the ship. He let loose another rolling growl. *Should I kill them?*

Before I could shake my head, the horrified cries from the soldiers told me he'd sent off the message to them as well.

"No, please!" one cried out. "We surrender!"

"Yes, yes," another joined in, dropping their sword to the deck with a clatter. "We surrender! Please, spare us!"

One by one, each dropped their weapons to the ground and threw their hands in the air, claiming surrender. After a brief pause, Larke began calling out orders, guiding the remainder of his own crew to gather their weapons and restrain them, to which they put up no fight. In fact, a few thanked our soldiers profusely, casting nervous glances back at Grom. When I looked back over at Grom, I swore I saw a glint of serpentlike amusement in his eyes.

"Did anyone see where Aerrin went?" I called, the answer coming in the form of silent head shakes. I'd been combing each crevice of the ship to account for everyone. A good chunk of our already small portion of soldiers were either lost or unaccounted for, the realization of which lived in the harsh set of Larke's jaw as he surveyed the damage. Luckily, Darrya was fine, and remained glued to his side as he swept through the ship with both Finlay and me.

Cas was busy helping heal those who remained, dealing with the most serious injuries first. At my urging, that included both Muiranvian and Brytham soldiers. They'd given their allegiance, and while it wasn't exactly settling that they would switch sides so easily, we needed to reciprocate this new bond. That aside, *anyone* with injuries deserved tending to. Cas caught my eye as we passed by, giving me a smile of approval.

Finally, we entered the quarters where Lena and Kipp resided. In order to avoid having her see any more than she already had, Kipp had guided her to a cabin the moment she'd been left unguarded. She still clung to his fluffy, cinnamon fur, even though her father and Wren had joined her immediately after we'd untied them. Thad had his arm around her back, seeming even less inclined to move from his position than she was — or Kipp, for that matter, who looked half asleep from the ear scratches he was currently receiving. I made a mental note to tease him about that later.

"Did any of you see where Aerrin went?" I asked. Kipp simply blinked in answer, and Wren shook her head. But Thad's expression darkened.

"I did," he spat. "The second he had his troops attack you and the beithir, he took advantage of the distraction and stole off the ship in the boat I arrived in. He's a... " he paused, his gaze sidling to his daughter. "Coward," he finished.

Finlay ran a hand over his face, clearly holding back a barrage of curses similar to the ones running through my mind. "So he's on his way to Talamu regardless."

"I'd guess so," Thad said. "And with his magic, he can get there quickly from here."

Wren cast him a helpless look. "And with his head start, we prob-ably can't catch him in time, can we?"

Thad hung his head, remaining quiet, and that was answer enough. Except... I tilted my head, wondering if Grom was still nearby. Could he hear my thoughts from here, if I cast them loudly enough?

Grom?

"Are you okay, Lena?" Darrya asked, crouching to where she sat on the bed with Kipp. Lena nodded and buried her head further into Kipp's fur. "Don't worry. You can stay here as long as you like."

Darrya scratched Kipp's other ear, earning a narrowed glare from him. "Oh, stop," she chided. "You know you like it."

Lena giggled in response, the sound like a salve for the soul. Thad leaned over to kiss her forehead, and Finlay slid his hand into mine. "We can't take her there," he murmured in my ear. "She shouldn't be anywhere near this."

"I know," I replied, and in my head, asked louder. *Grom?*

Finally, an answer came, slightly amused. *Yes?*

I let out a sigh. *Are you still nearby?*

A rumble came from outside in response, and I snorted. *You don't have to be so dramatic. The soldiers are still terrified of you.*

As they should be.

Even though he couldn't see me, I rolled my eyes. *Could I ask a final favor of you?*

What is it, child of Cú Chulainn?

Could you carry some of us to Talamu? We need to be there as soon as possible.

A pause. Then, *Yes. Though I can only carry a few.*

My knees nearly buckled in relief. *Thank you.*

"Grom can take us," I said aloud. "But only a few. We can try to beat Aerrin there and take the other ship back. Those on this ship can head back to Muiranvia now."

"I want to go, but I should stay here," Larke said, looking torn. "With all the Brytham soldiers aboard, I need to maintain order."

"I'll stay and help," Darrya offered. Larke shot her a grateful smile.

"I can't," Thad said, shaking his head. "Now that Lena's here, I…"

"Say less," I assured him. Wherever his daughter was, he would be, especially after the events of today. I couldn't fault him for that.

My gaze went to Wren, who looked between me and Thad, uncertain. Clearly, she wanted to stay with Thad and Lena and, besides, she was still not the strongest fighter. Then I glanced at Kipp, who thumped his tail, but remained trapped beneath Lena. Best to leave him here, then, and with Cas, who was still needed for healing.

Finally, I turned to Finlay. "I think it's just you and me for this one," I said, summoning as much courage as I could. I shot him my bravest smile and thought back to our first adventure together. I'd barely known him, then, and had just learned how to use the first bits of my magic. Still, he'd joined me without question, and it had been the first proof that we worked well together. As long as I had him, I knew I could face whatever lay ahead of us. "Ready for one last adventure?"

He squeezed my hand and returned the grin with a broad one of his own. "I'm always ready for a new adventure with you, little angel."

CHAPTER THIRTY-SEVEN

The trip to Talamu was one I wasn't likely to forget in this lifetime, or any other. Even though Gray was fast — faster than any horse had a right to be — riding atop Grom was like harnessing the wind itself. I clutched his scales, my knuckles going white from effort as we sped across the sea. Salty seawater sprayed my face, and the waves lapped at the soles of my boots, reminding me I was one jolted movement away from plummeting into their cold, murky depths. Though I wanted to turn and check on Finlay a few feet back, I didn't dare turn around. I only hoped he had a better grip on Grom's back than I did.

By the time we reached land once more, my hair and clothes had completely dried off in the wind, and there wasn't a storm cloud in sight. The sun was carving away the morning chill, and the sounds of birds chirping told me we weren't the only ones awake on this island.

Grom clambered halfway onto the shore, front claws digging deeply into the sand, and lowered himself to the ground. Finlay and I slid off onto the beach, and I leaned into Grom. It wasn't lost on me that the first time I'd met him, I'd been terrified — and now here I was, feeling a sense of kinship with him.

"Thank you," I whispered.

An answering rumble came from his chest, deep and affectionate.

"I haven't forgotten my promise to you, Grom," I added. "I will help you find your family. And I know Thad will, too. We just need to deal with his brother once and for all."

He inclined his head. *Thank you, child.*

He slid back into the water, his nose dipping under last, and I marveled at the way such a large creature could disappear with only a ripple disrupting the surface of the ocean. A part of me felt like it went with him as my magic normalized, no longer spurred on by the storm or his nearness. I wondered if his family had the same magic we did, and if any other Fae out there had my magic, too. It wasn't unheard of for other creatures to share the same elemental magic as Fae; there were plenty that harnessed earth and water magic. But Grom had remained hidden for ages until we'd gone in search of the talismans, and I hadn't heard of any other creatures with our magic. Were he and I the last of our kind? A mystery for another day, I supposed.

Finlay's hand slid into mine, pulling me from my thoughts. "Let's finish this," he said, and guided me toward the vast expanse of emerald green that awaited us further inland.

We picked our way through the terrain, heading in what we hoped was the proper direction based on Thad's earlier information. The trees grew thicker and more plentiful as we wound deeper into the forest. The air was sticky and humid, and the ground was flush with thick moss, growing in abundance from the constant water source of little streams and brooks. Twigs snapped underfoot with each step we took, and I had to keep my eyes glued to the ground to avoid roots that threatened to wind around my ankle and tug me down.

As I worked to navigate the complex footing, I felt a pleasant awareness growing in my veins. Somehow, as we walked, I felt more alive. It was like a shot of caffeine to the bloodstream, flowing from the tips of my fingers, only heightening as we wandered further into the forest.

"Shit," Finlay grunted, pushing aside the leaf of a shrub that was nearly the same height as him. It swiveled back instantly, and he spat as it slapped him across his mouth.

I huffed out a laugh. "You can feel it, though, can't you? The magic?"

Finlay tilted his head, as though considering, then nodded. I wiggled my fingers, urging the magic of this biome to fill me even further. Though earth magic wasn't my strongest anymore, I could still sense the vast ecosystem above — and especially, below — us: the shallow root system that wove each tree together like its own village. It carried a sense of belonging in its roots, a powerful network of magic that had me buzzing from tip to toe. If I had questioned it before, there wasn't a doubt left in my mind now. This was definitely the place for the Ogham grove.

Finally, a break came in the dense foliage, shedding light that the canopy had previously barred. "There," I gasped, and pointed. A well-defined path cut across our current route, with what looked like fresh footsteps indented into the soil.

"He's already here," Finlay said. "Hurry."

We scrambled forward, using our arms like shields against the undergrowth that barred our path. Sweat coursed down my back and gathered on my face, but I didn't take so much as a moment to wipe it away. *He's already here.*

In my gut, I knew Finlay was right. I just wasn't sure if that meant we were out of time or not.

We stumbled into an opening, and it took both my eyes and my soul several long moments to catch up. Aerrin was indeed there, surprisingly alone, leaning against a tree. His hair was plastered against his forehead in obvious exertion, indicating that he hadn't had much time to rest before we had found him, but his bright blue eyes gleamed triumphantly.

"When I discovered my army had followed a force to the other side of the island, I figured it couldn't have been yours." He grinned, even as his chest heaved. "Despite your monster's arrival, I left you with plenty to keep you preoccupied. I should've expected you'd leave them to clean up the pieces."

"Just like you did, when you left your troops to die?" Finlay countered, to which Aerrin simply waved a dismissive hand.

I attempted to focus on their exchange, but the tingling sensation in my body was nearly impossible to ignore, like countless pins and needles delivering energy to my bloodstream. It wasn't unpleasant, though — it was simply *overwhelming*. If the other trees of the forest offered a brief, sweet breath of fresh oxygen, this grove carried an entire life force in its being. I could inhale deeply for hours and still not be satisfied. The forest was full of individual musicians, but this grove was the conductor of the orchestra; it generated a stunning, life-generating symphony that left me enraptured.

It was like the Ogham wheel I'd once studied with my father, brought off the aged parchment into real life. The inner wheel was drawn carefully into the center of the soil, like an ancient clock lying upon the ground. The center boasted the powerful numerical sequence I recalled from the pages of text: 1,1,3,5,8,13.

From there, it spiraled to the outer wheels — the lunar calendar, the representation of each solstice and equinox, the ancient name for each tree, and finally, the full grove of Ogham trees themselves. Instead of simply being written in the soil, however, each tree rose physically from the exact point in the wheel where they should be, reaching for the sky like a new dimension on a coexisting fabric. All twenty were depicted in the order my father had recited to me. Birch, rowan, alder, willow... evenly spaced in a perfect circle around the wheel. Each tree had their respective Ogham letter carved into the bark. I nervously noted the vertical slash with two dashes through one side, denoting the oak tree. Finlay tilted his head, and I realized he had noticed the same thing.

Aerrin pushed off the tree and gestured around him. "Beautiful, isn't it?" he called out. "You can feel it, can't you? The grove holding all the different spiritual realms together. It used to be that any time we encountered a grove, the earth magic would whisper to us, show us visions, and guide our path. Hell, seers and mystics used to traipse between veils like they were running errands. These days, however, it's far more difficult." He sighed and rubbed his hands together, as though wistful. My gaze shifted to Finlay, and I raised a brow. *Is he serious right now?*

Finlay shook his head and called his fire. A surge of heat hit me as steady, solid flames rolled over him in moments. I unsheathed my sword, readying myself to proceed with our plan. Burn the grove, then eliminate Aerrin. I would avoid calling my magic unless absolutely necessary, in case I inadvertently hit the oak tree.

Aerrin looked entirely unaffected at Finlay's display of power, and I swore his smile widened as I took a step closer to him.

I stilled. Something wasn't right. He should have called his own magic, or pulled out the buair, or at least unsheathed a sword. What was he playing at? I flicked my gaze around the grove, stomach churning as I attempted to place what was wrong with the moment.

A droning hiss filled my ears, and Aerrin tapped his chin, feigning innocence. "Oh, did I not mention? Using any power outside of the lightning is forbidden in the grove. It makes the *Genius loci* very upset."

Movement caught my eye as he spoke, and I whirled, watching as a figure dispatched itself from one of the trees. What had seemed like part of the tree trunk now broke off, unwinding its scaled body to drop to the ground. It was a snake of sorts, but larger than any I'd ever seen.

I stumbled back into Finlay as it slithered toward us, its tongue flicking out, eyes fixated on us. Finlay immediately doused his flames, but it was no use. The massive snake kept coming, trailing over the marks of the Ogham wheel without so much as disturbing a speck of dirt. It was easily seven or eight feet long, thicker than my arm, and yet it moved as though it wasn't a physical part of this world.

"What is this thing?" I cried out, clutching my sword tighter.

"It's the guardian spirit of this grove," Aerrin said smugly. He stepped in closer to us. "And it knows you want to burn it to the ground."

I tucked in against Finlay's side and leveled my sword on the creature, now mere feet away. "Don't," he muttered. "It's a spirit. It can't be killed. If you fight against it, it will come for you, too."

"But I can't just let it take you!" I argued, pointedly ignoring the shake of his head. When the snake lunged, I braced to cut through it with the sword, but my footing fell away. No — I saw the flash of Aerrin's hair in my peripheral, and realized with a start that I'd been *shoved* away.

Before I could right myself, hands wound around me, pinning my arms to my side. I was roughly turned to face the scene in front of me as the massive snake wound its way over Finlay's body, time and again. A scream worked its way up my throat, but I couldn't seem to force it past my lips. I could only watch, helpless.

"You know, this worked out better than I had planned." Aerrin's voice was low in my ear. He sounded gleeful, and I felt a white-hot rage seep through me, even as I bit back the urge to vomit at the sight of the snake, pressing itself tighter around Finlay. "I had hoped you'd bring someone — perhaps my brother — to do the dirty work. But here we are, with the one you love most. Time's a-ticking. Now it's not just what I want, but what the grove wants."

"What will it do to him?" I whirled on Aerrin.

He simply shrugged and jerked his chin at Finlay. "It will take him. As a sacrifice."

I turned once more to watch, helpless. Finlay struggled, but I could see the loops tightening around his middle, the way his breathing began to slow as he worked to keep what little oxygen remained. His eyes grew wide, and his complexion began to take on a purplish hue.

I shook my head and squeezed my own eyes shut. "How do I make it stop?" I pleaded.

"The grove demands a sacrifice, now that the sanctity within has been desecrated. But…" Aerrin trailed off, as though considering, and it took everything in me not to slice him open on the spot. I clenched my hands so tightly I felt blood well up in my palms, nails digging deep enough to draw blood. But I waited, praying for him to give me a sign, a possible way out of this.

Finally, he continued. "Sacrifices need not be physical. They can be imbued in your magic… magic you'd have to use to open the portal, of course."

He grinned, and I felt a spasm of terror in my gut. This was what he'd wanted from the beginning. He hadn't brought any secondary option to open the portal. He'd been counting on me all along — counting on me to bring a loved one, someone that he could use to force my hand. And he'd done it.

"What kind of sacrifice, then?" Even though I hadn't screamed, my voice felt raw, resigned.

Aerrin hummed. "Something personal. Memories, or stories. Something close to your heart, like fallen heroes, loved ones. Things like that, if you have them."

I remembered something my father said as we'd discussed the magic in the old Ogham book, so long ago now. *"Trees have always been considered sacred, kiddo,"* he'd said. *"They've been a place to share concerns, stories, memories, lore. They're a repository for everything we've ever loved and lost."*

"So I offer up a story for them, imbued with my magic, and it might accept that as a trade?" I swiveled, catching Finlay's eye as I said it out loud, asking for permission in the words themselves. "And it would open the portal?"

Aerrin nodded, but I had eyes only for Finlay. He'd stopped struggling, and that terrified me more than anything. But I couldn't do this without him. I would do it for him in an instant, but only if he said so. If this would change our world, *his* world, I needed him to say it. I needed him to agree.

Please say it, I begged silently, pleading with my eyes. *I can't lose you, too.*

Finlay closed his eyes. He was silent for a long moment. But eventually, he choked out his answer. "Do it, little angel."

Chapter Thirty-Eight

Finlay watched as Kate's eyes shuttered closed. After a moment, her hands illuminated, the spark dancing from fingertip to fingertip, and Aerrin broke out in a triumphant grin beside her.

Through the weaving branches of the trees, he saw the light above dimming, clouds pulling in from every side to cast the grove into a shade of dim gray. The snake pressed in tighter, the warm, smooth scales sliding against his skin. He blinked rapidly, unsure if the black dots swarming his vision were from the pain or from his halted blood flow. He suspected the latter, as most of the pain had subsided to numbness.

As Kate drew on the magic, he tasted the distinct, copper-like tang of ether on his tongue which he'd come to associate with the summoning of her lightning. The snake stilled, seeming to sense what was coming as well, and he sent a silent thanks to Kate. He still couldn't get more than a shallow, seeking breath, but he had a suspicion that his ribs were close to cracking, and he hovered on the edge of consciousness.

Kate's lips pursed, and he wondered what the sacrifice was costing her. What memory was she reliving? What story was she offering to the grove? That of Lachlan, who guided her to her destiny, only to be sacrificed by his jealous sons? That of Blaise, who gave her strength and taught her to defend herself, knowing she'd be capable of forging forward once he was gone? Or that of her mother, who raised her and died at the hands of a goddess, never knowing the truth about her husband or daughter?

Maybe none of those were the stories of others. They were, in fact, small parts of a story simply her own. She was so brave. Far braver than he was. If he had to give the grove a story, it would be hers, just so he could show the spirits what an incredible being they had the honor to behold. She had sacrificed so much already, and here she was, sacrificing once more for him.

There was a flash, and light streaked across the sky, zigzagging in a pattern reminiscent of branches. The lines crashed together in the center, only to spark back out again, thin fingers of light reaching through the storm clouds. The flashes brightened, then dulled, and then a clap of thunder announced their arrival above. Still, it didn't strike home in the grove.

"Come on," he heard Aerrin urge. Finlay gritted his teeth. He hadn't known a fury like this could exist. He'd always despised Aerrin for what he'd done to Darrya, but in the last few weeks, that anger had simmered, and brewed itself into a poisonous fury that burned through every vein in his body. Aerrin had tried to destroy everything that Finlay loved, including his kingdom. And here he was, getting exactly what he wanted. He bit the inside of his cheek until it bled. It was too late to stop it now. Kate had already begun.

The clouds above began a dance of light, one turning orange, then white, then going dark once again as the lightning began in another. The rumbling thunder grew, turning louder until, with a sizzling crack, everything around him went white.

For a moment, Finlay lost every sense except one. He squeezed his eyes shut against the blinding, supersonic strike, and his hearing went hollow from the boom that followed. Though Kate had used lightning next to him not even the day prior, he was certain it had never been a shock wave as large as this. He felt the moment the spirit released him from its clutches, however, dropping him to the ground like a stone. He clutched his sides, lungs heaving as he sucked at precious mouthfuls of air. His ribs complained at the sudden push, but he barely noticed as he worked to get his breathing back under control.

He coughed, then blinked, his vision spotty but normalizing quickly. There was smoke and light, and he was certain other things were now happening in the grove, but he had eyes for only one person.

Kate.

Her eyes and hands still glowed a golden white, though she was now lowering them to her sides. She muttered something, as though speaking with someone — someone beyond the veil, perhaps? Whatever she'd done was clearly working, but she still seemed to be in a trance-like state. He pushed to his feet and stumbled forward, intent on reaching her and shaking her from the reverie. As he did, however, movement in his peripheral vision caught his attention.

It was Aerrin, holding a handful of dust in one hand and a dagger in the other. His face was set in grim determination, the beginnings of a triumphant smile spreading across his face, as he headed for Kate. Realization washed over Finlay and he tried to cry out, but the pressure still releasing from his lungs prevented words. It all made sense; the second the portal was fully opened, Kate ceased to be a key, only a threat. Aerrin intended to kill Kate while she was still vulnerable from opening the portal.

Finlay didn't think. He simply reacted.

In one swift movement, he lunged forward, ducking to pick up the sword Kate had abandoned when Aerrin had grabbed her. As he pushed up, he drove the sword home — straight into Aerrin's back and through his chest.

A garbled cry emanated from Aerrin, but Finlay didn't move. He refused to second-guess his actions. Instead, he willed every ounce of the rage he'd kept pent up inside to disintegrate as Aerrin collapsed to the ground, to let the poison bleed out of him alongside the reason for it all. *Let this be the end of it,* he thought, and tugged the sword free. He didn't have a scrap of remorse to give the fallen Byrne brother.

He straightened and sheathed the sword just as Kate began to sway. He stumbled forward, clutching her shoulders to keep her upright. "Kate?" he asked worriedly. He brushed her hair back from her face, watching as the gold flickered in her hands and eyes before fading entirely.

She blinked up at him a few times in confusion. "Did it work?" she mumbled.

"I'm not sure," he replied, studying her. "Are you okay?"

She nodded, and he took a moment to make sure she could stand on her own before releasing her. Then, for the first time, he turned around, taking in the impact of her magic on the grove. Each line that had been carefully drawn in the soil now pulsed with a soft, yellow-white glow, extending all the way to the trees. The symbols carved into the trees shone as well.

"I think it worked," Kate whispered, and he turned to see her staring at the oak tree. The lightning strike had slashed a perfect spiral down the length of the trunk, carving back the thick layer of bark and exposing the soft wood beneath. The symbol for the oak tree was, surprisingly, left untouched by the strike, and its glow pulsed brighter than the others. As they watched, that light spread until it worked its way into the new scar that wound around the trunk.

The gash illuminated the tree to a near-blinding point, then flooded the grove with a light so daunting that Finlay shielded his eyes with a hand. It was unrelenting and all-consuming; there was nowhere in the grove that the light didn't touch with its radiance. All Finlay could do was squeeze his eyes shut and wait. When the light finally cleared, several figures stood in front of them, and Finlay sucked in a breath.

The portal between realms had been successfully opened.

Finlay clutched Kate's hand tightly, using it as a lifeline between the two of them. This was it — the moment that, according to Ensley, could either be the moment that propelled them into a prosperous, wonderfully blended new era, or be the spark of destruction for them all.

"No pressure," Kate muttered under her breath, as if reading his mind. He coughed out a soft laugh, thankful for the break in tension. Though Finlay sensed that the portal remained open, the blinding light had blinked out, leaving only the lightning-struck tree behind the cluster of strangers that stood before them now.

The group comprised several elegant-looking Fae, all varying in stature, skin tone, gender, and wardrobe. Several wore long, flowing gossamer robes, while some wore almost nothing at all. Many were dripping with gems, faces painted in colorful powders or plain, un-blemished skin, though still others wore scars like armor, more akin to warriors than dignitaries.

The way they carried themselves, however, with chins high and shoulders thrown back, left no question that they were the leaders of the other realms. It was an intimidating group of at least two dozen, though from the way some stood, with their hands clasped together or with arms wound around waists, there were several couples in attendance. Finlay wondered what magic — and, more importantly, what morals — lay under the surface.

There was a general sense of bewilderment as they all assessed the situation and each other. At least a third of them disappeared in a blink, while several others looked on uneasily. Finlay didn't blame them. He didn't know what precisely had happened in the other realms when Kate opened the portal. Whatever magical pull the leaders felt had likely given them the option to heed the summons, and curiosity had led them here. He hoped they hadn't somehow been forced here against their will, with a magic akin to Faerie dust. That *definitely* would not help their case.

Kate inched closer to Finlay, and he cleared his throat, attempting to find the kindest expression in the group to focus his attention on. Kate had done her part; now, it was his turn. When he spoke, he did so in the oldest Fae language he'd learned in his studies. He prayed it was a unifying language.

"My name is Finlay Egan, and this is my betrothed, Katherine Doyle. As king and queen, we want to officially welcome you to our realm." He paused and scanned the group for reactions. A few looked irritated, but others seemed curious now. It seemed that the choice of language worked. He swallowed and continued. "We understand you may be confused. Please know, it was not our intention to open this, ah, portal."

He stumbled over the word, unsure if it was the proper equivalent. It seemed to work, however. The group began to shuffle, some exchanging looks with their partners. Hushed discussion broke out amongst them, until finally, one man came forward. He was tall and broad, with long, whitish-blonde hair and pale, pinkish skin. He had a slight gut that spilled out over his trousers, tucked into a deep blue, woolen tunic, but the way he stood told Finlay he could crush bones with his bare hands. He came to a stop at the front of the crowd and stroked his graying beard. His stern, pale eyes darted back and forth between Finlay and Kate before landing behind them.

He motioned with a jerk of his chin. "You killed him?" he asked.

Finlay paled, realizing what the others had likely seen upon their arrival. Aerrin's corpse still lay behind him. Finlay didn't glance back, partially to avoid looking uneasy and partially to avoid the scene himself. He didn't need to look to know what he'd find. Instead, he simply nodded. "If it were up to him, he would have brought you here to kill you."

Nervous chatter broke out in earnest at his blunt response, and he bit the inside of his cheek. *Fuck.* Kate shot him a wide-eyed look. But the burly gentleman simply came forward another step, peering curiously over Finlay. He didn't dare move. He barely breathed.

The man's gaze slid back to him. "You stabbed him in the back?"

Finlay opened his mouth, then closed it. Finally, he dipped his chin. It was the cowardly way to kill someone, he knew it as well as anyone. "Yes."

He braced for the impending accusation, the lack of trust that would ensue. The sound that came out of the man, however, surprised him. He *guffawed,* the sound deep and genuine. "Poor bastard! Literally stabbed in the back. What a way to go. Gods, though, he must have deserved it."

Kate choked out a laugh, one of her genuine, surprised ones that ended in a snort. She clapped a hand over her face and shot an alarmed look at Finlay. He shot her a warm grin, one that broadened as the bearded man laughed even harder at her response.

"I'm sorry, I—" She swallowed another laugh, and started again, in English. "I have no idea what you were saying, but he just *laughed* at the sight. Aerrin must be rolling in his grave."

"You speak English?" Another voice called out from the crowd, surprised. Finlay and Kate both glanced up, startled, in time to see two men come forward.

"Yes," Kate called out, and surveyed the remaining crowd. A few more had disappeared at the sight of Aerrin — not that he could blame them — but at least a dozen still remained. The man that had spoken stepped forward, followed closely by another male. They were roughly the same height as the first man, but lean and muscled, their skin a warm brown and their eyes dark and searching. One had long, dark hair, while the other kept his cropped short, but both wore crowns garnished with beautiful, gilded jewels. Clearly, whichever realm they led, they were regarded as equals.

"What are your names?" Kate asked, her tone soft and soothing.

The two men exchanged a look. The one with longer hair smoothed his light, pleated robe and spoke. "I am Amon," he said, then gestured to his partner. "This is Ramses."

The bearded man cleared his throat, clearly understanding the conversation and not wanting to be left out. He extended a hand and spoke in heavily accented English. "I am Harald."

Finlay took his hand and shook it. Unsurprisingly, it was a strong handshake, and he felt the bones in his knuckles grind against one another. He grimaced but played it off into a toothy smile. After a moment, another from the group stepped forward, this time a smaller, graceful female, donned in silken robes. When she spoke, it left no room to dispute her sole authority of her realm. "I am Hua."

One by one, the introductions continued, alternating between old Fae and English, and Finlay exchanged a long look with Kate. She met his gaze and nodded. This was it. This was the moment they had prepared for, should all else fail. The names kept coming, all familiar, all with backstories they had learned on their latest trip to the Otherworld — a trip that had been a long shot, but had paid off in this moment. Each name was another victory, solidifying the future that had seemed so far-fetched, only days ago.

And so, they responded, Finlay in old Fae, echoed by Kate in English. "It's a pleasure to meet you all. We have plenty to discuss."

Chapter Thirty-Nine

The grove proved to be a perfect meeting spot, not only for the ease of travel that it allowed to others, but for the safety it allowed, in that magic could not be used. Trust, naturally, could not be earned overnight, but the fact that magic couldn't be leveraged — paired with a designated spot to lay down other weapons — went a long way to instill confidence between leadership.

Trusting everyone not to kill each other, however, proved a far cry from trusting one another in political conversation. The first few conversations were superficial, guarded, and mostly unproductive — what types of land were in each realm, the climates, the infrastructure. I listened, remaining relatively silent, until the fourth gathering had gone in the same circle as our first. Exasperated, I finally pulled Finlay aside and demanded he be the first to open up. If we couldn't offer honesty, how could we expect it from the others? We had started this, after all, and we needed to lead by example, showing it was safe to navigate more sensitive topics. Besides, we had the advantage of knowing the others far better than they suspected.

Ensley had been right. We'd most certainly made it this far without any hiccups due to our careful study of the others' realms. My hunch had, blissfully, been correct. I'd taken Finlay with me to the Otherworld, where I had questioned Arawn at length. As the god of death, he had access to every being that passed through, regardless of realm. He had the knowledge we needed, as well as a natural barrier to Ensley's magic, being one of the highest gods himself.

From there, it became a study of each realm's leader, their beliefs, laws, customs, arts, languages. Arawn could tell us who to trust and who was ruled by someone their people deemed as greedy, bloodthirsty, or selfish. Though some of the knowledge had blended together — there was only so much I could retain in the limited time we'd been given — there were names that stuck, for better or worse. Everyone that sat in these meetings now had been given the stamp of approval by their own people.

"From everything we know, we can trust them to do right by their citizens. If we offer the same, I know we can be allies," I'd urged, a final attempt to convince Finlay to take the lead in opening up.

He'd begrudgingly agreed, and in the next meeting, he stayed true to his word. He admitted to the troubles we'd experienced, the way we had opened the portal, the issues we were trying to overcome. I was pleasantly surprised with the patient curiosity that came from the majority of the group. They were open to an allyship. The ones who didn't want to play nice, it seemed, had mostly disappeared before Harald had even approached us.

It also helped that many of the leaders who answered the call knew far more than Finlay or I about the history of the portal. It gave us more control over how the portal was opened, and with which realms. One of the first steps was to determine *who* was receptive to the idea of travel between realms, the goal being to form a camaraderie and learn from and support one another.

We sent a summons once more, and though some declined, we received positive responses from some who had been scared off the first time. We honored the wishes on a case-by-case basis. It was understandable — some places were still healing on their own or had a history that made them distrustful. Hell, we had gone back and forth on the idea as well. Who was to say what would have happened, had Finlay been allowed to burn the grove to ash?

That being said, each conversation made me more grateful that we hadn't. As we had more discussions, others opened up in turn. Amon and Ramses brought food to our next meeting, some of the most delicious, spiced meats I'd ever tasted. In turn, I made them something from my mom's recipe books — an apple turnover, topped with ice cream — and watched as they nodded appreciatively, finishing every last bite. I learned that Hua's realm had many of the same socioeconomic issues ours had, which evolved into a conversation on potential avenues to address the struggles, and lasted well after the sun set. Finlay and I had collapsed into bed that night, exhausted but pleased beyond words at the passionate dialogue from the day.

Eventually, Ensley came to visit, which led to a surprisingly emotional conversation with Harald. In order to give them privacy, I snuck away with another leader, Bimpe, and requested she teach me some new fighting techniques. The one-off session led to me getting my ass sufficiently handed to me, and after laughing at me for a solid minute, she promised to continue teaching me after each gathering.

When the weeks turned into months, and we all felt confidence in our relationships with one another, the topic we'd all been skirting was finally broached: would we allow our citizens to travel between realms? Would they be safe? Could we count on the other leaders to protect them as their own?

Everyone went quiet as they contemplated. "We can promise one another peace and camaraderie, but who is to say our citizens will do the same?" Ramses said.

"Are you saying you can't control your citizens?" Harald shot back, raising a brow.

"He's not saying that," Amon put in, "but you can't account for everyone's response to this."

"Indeed. What would you have us do to avoid that?" Hua asked. "Keep them sequestered in our palaces, never exploring our lands, our customs?"

"What? As opposed to painting a target on their backs?"

"Are you saying there *would* be a target on their backs?"

Around and around they went, firing off thinly veiled accusations. I could see the work we'd been doing, the walls that had been falling down, slamming right back into place. My breath caught in my chest, and I shot a panicked look at Finlay. *We can't let this happen. We can't let the realms tear each other apart, before we've even begun rebuilding.*

"Stop, stop!" I cried out, waiting until everyone was quiet.

"We have fought for our lands. We have all loved, and we have all lost. Regardless, we have opened the realms to one another after centuries, and here we are, all from different backgrounds, but with common desires for the future we see. Not just for ourselves, but for our citizens. We've chosen, week after week, to learn from one another, because we see that in each other, and we see what everyone can contribute to building a better future. *Together.* We are the voices for our realms for a reason, and we owe it to them to give them their best chance."

I paused, letting Finlay translate where needed, and took in their expressions. A few shifted uncomfortably in their seats, but most watched me intently. Some even looked ashamed.

"It will not be easy. The gods know, this conversation proves it will not be. We have our differences, and we have our concerns, and they're all valid. It'll take time, planning, and education. What won't help is this." I gestured between us all. "This *fighting* with one another. That is exactly what broke us apart in the first place. But I've seen the passion you all put into the challenges your lands face. I know you want this better future for them, and I know we can learn to trust one another. I have faith in us all. Do you all agree? Can we do this, together?"

The grove went silent, leaving only the chirping of birds to fill the space as everyone absorbed my words. As the moment stretched out, my heart plummeted. Perhaps this was the moment where our precarious truce between realms broke. I closed my eyes, giving an inward sigh. Maybe this wasn't so bad. Maybe they'd all allow the truce to carry over long enough to seal the portal between realms peacefully —

"I agree."

My eyes shot open, meeting Amon's. He smiled at me warmly. "If anyone can work through these challenges with us, I believe it is you. I have faith in you, Katherine."

"I agree," Ramses put in, and I grinned at him, feeling the sting of emotion behind my eyes.

"I agree."

The unified decision wound around the circle, with not a single leader voicing disagreement. Finally, the verdict landed on Finlay, sitting next to me. He shot me a smile, his expression overflowing with pride and love. "Naturally, I agree."

He steepled his fingers and leaned forward. "So," he said, his gaze holding mine, the question meant for me. "Where do we begin?"

EPILOGUE

KATE

After such a momentous occasion, and all the effort that went into the uproarious change, I had to actively remind myself that for most citizens, things wouldn't change overnight. For the next few months, things remained relatively... unchanged. It was as though everyone was holding their breath, sizing up one another to see who would take the first big step. But between the responsibilities of leadership we'd previously left unattended, as well as the new, careful negotiations between realms, the months bled together like watercolor on paper. One moment, I felt as though nothing had changed, then it was as though I blinked and the development started to show.

Finlay and I made a point from the beginning to visit every realm in turn, doing our best to disappear into the communities and embracing the differences we witnessed — for better and worse. With the help of brilliant minds from across the realms, we were able to bring in some stunning technical advancements that aided everyday life. We didn't push in our discussions with leadership, but we offered perspectives where we'd found solutions to political situations that plagued the others, and I felt a surge of pride every time I watched a contemplative gleam take over someone's expression at our words.

Even the others immersed themselves with gusto. Every time we spoke with Cas, he prattled on about new healing techniques and diagnoses he wished he could go back in time to redo, as well as some of the herbal remedies he'd been able to pass on to other Fae interested in more natural remedies. Wren joined in on the excitement of new plant discoveries, which expanded her earth magic in turn, and Larke launched himself into relationship building with each realm's armies — a task that made me nervous on his behalf, but one that filled his expression with awe every time he returned.

Thad had been more than happy to sift through Aerrin's paperwork, intent on finding Grom's family members. When he'd successfully reunited them, he shifted his focus to returning many creatures to their own respective realms, but it seemed as though every time he did so, he was rewarded with another as a thank you. His Sanctuary grew in size rather than dwindling, and he opened it — cautiously — to the public, with the help of many new workers. He hired them to ensure the safety of the creatures within, but Wren liked to remind him that the people who visited needed just as much protection. His response was always the same: "If Lena could learn to respect these beasts at three, the adults who come now have no excuse."

I'd wandered through a few times myself, and for the amount of wayward fingers I saw reaching for creatures with fangs the size of daggers, I knew the employees earned their pay. Lena was smarter than most.

Darrya had made it her personal mission to chart lineage that had been cut off at the same time the realms had been closed off, making an extensive documentation system for those who cared to learn if they shared an ancestral god, albeit under a different name. She loved the idea of connecting families. For all her research the past few months, however, she hadn't discovered anyone with powers like mine — not standalone, and not from Lugh's lineage, or under other potential names, like Jupiter or Iuppiter. Perhaps that was another reason why the realms hadn't been reopened until now. I had the only key, and I had unlocked it without express permission from the others.

It could have been a big mistake. It *did* make me nervous, especially at the beginning. But the seeds of change slowly took hold, and one by one, blossomed. People were allowed to come and go, but they weren't pressured one way or another. There were a lot of celebrations that overlapped between realms, and I watched with joy as curiosity in the communities grew, especially during these times. New traditions were introduced, and ours were shared in turn, with some of my personal favorites being the new sports and games that made their way across realms (Ramses, it turned out, was incredible at wrestling, and it was beyond entertaining to watch others try to best him).

I'd even seen some laughter, flirtation, and — after some imbibing — trysts in dark corners. It was likely only a matter of time before traditions between realms were merged in the same households, and the thought warmed my heart, even as I chuckled at the thought of the stories that would be told about how some began.

It wasn't perfect — I wasn't sure it ever would be — but it was a work in progress, and it helped immensely to have the guidance of other leaders. I enjoyed the work more than I could've ever imagined, though every time I voiced this to Finlay, he simply gave me his "I told you so" look. His unwavering faith made me all the more excited to jump into the throes of change, even when the days ran long, and it seemed we were taking two steps back. Still, I rallied, with him by my side.

Today, however, was not a day for work. Despite that, my body was wracked with nerves as though I had the eyes of several leaders on me. I took a deep, steadying breath and reminded myself that everything had been taken care of today. Darrya, Wren, and Cas had made sure of that — with occasional, begrudging help from their partners.

I had only one job: to put one foot in front of the other. And even that, I had help with.

I looped my arm around my father's and nodded. "Ready."

He beamed down at me and gave my arm a reassuring pat. Then, he frowned. "Wait... there's something missing."

"What?" I blinked, alarmed. I started turning, examining myself, but he put a hand on my shoulder to stop me.

"You need a necklace," he said.

I shot him an exasperated look. "It's a bit late to go pick one out, dad."

"No need for that." His face softened, and he reached into his pocket. When he pulled the necklace out, his hand was trembling slightly. It was a delicate, silver Claddagh necklace that shone when it hit the light. Something about it seemed vaguely familiar.

"Dad..." I frowned. "What is this?"

"This was the very first necklace I ever gave your mother." His voice was thick with emotion as he spoke. "I... I took it when I left. I needed a memory to keep close."

My throat became tight as I realized where I recognized the necklace from. My mom had always worn it when I was younger. I'd often played with it when I was young, marveling at the intricate detail of the two hands, joined by a heart and topped with a crown.

"She thought she lost it," I whispered.

My dad sniffed, his eyes downcast as he handed it to me. "It's never been truly lost. It's just been waiting to become yours."

"Dad..." I trailed off, staring at the piece of jewelry that was so small and yet, so significant. I swallowed. "Will you put it on for me?"

He nodded, and I turned, gathering my hair in a hand so that he could drape the chain around my neck. As it rested against my skin, I closed my eyes and grasped the necklace with my free hand, pulling the image of her into focus.

I hope you're here with me now, mom. I love you so, so much.

"Now am I ready?" I asked, blinking back the sting of tears and attempting to get my emotions back in check.

"You're perfect, kiddo." He cleared his throat and came back to my side, offering his arm. I took it, and he took a deep breath. "Okay. Let's do this."

As we entered the secluded portion of the forest, a stillness washed over us. It was as though even the creatures of the forest were waiting in hushed anticipation for what came next. I blew out a low breath and felt a nervous smile spread across my face as I glimpsed the carefully carved stone path, made just for this moment. Flowers blossomed alongside them, and garlands hung from the trees, marking the spot in a beautiful canopy of flora.

There were only a handful of people that waited for us, out here in the outskirts of Sairas, anxious to witness this ceremony. A few of the leaders I'd become closest to from the other realms, ready to acknowledge this moment. Members of my inner circle from the palace. All my dearest friends and my father.

And of course... Finlay.

My best friend, my partner, my king. And today, he would officially become mine — by law, by marriage. And I would become his.

I glanced down at the skirts of my dress as I stepped onto the stone path, praying I wouldn't trip. The dress I wore was the perfect blend of royal modesty and seductive beauty. It covered all of my scars and marks but accentuated the curves at my waist and neckline. It was an off-white color, cinched at the waist and laced up the back, allowing it to flow out at my hips and leave my legs free for movement. Intricate, Celtic designs wove in and out of the cream fabric, standing out in brilliant gold. They traced a pattern up over my hips and across the décolletage, peaking at the shoulders before running back down the billowy fabric of the arms.

A dainty, golden crown sat atop my carefully curled hair. Darrya and Wren had fussed over it all morning, until I shooed them out to give me some breathing space, leaving me with warnings not to do anything to mess up the curls.

I had run my fingers through it just once, hoping to ease the curls into more natural waves, and I was sure I'd see a look of amusement on their faces as I came up the aisle.

When I did, however, I had no idea what their reactions were, even though they stood up at the front, waiting. I had no idea who sat where in the crowd as I walked alongside them. I only had eyes for Finlay.

He had looked radiant in his ensembles for the solstice, and somber for the Last Honors Ceremonies. But neither of those events had been for us. In none of those had he dressed for *me*. There was something about the fact that he had picked every piece of his wardrobe specifically for this moment that tugged on my heart. His hair was tamed, combed to perfection, leaving his devastatingly handsome facial features on full display. He wore sleek black pants and a black undershirt, with a black and gold vest and a full, white long overcoat. It was embroidered in gold, matching my dress, as though even our outfits were uniting us as one. He wore a crown as well, even more understated than mine, placed as though it was an afterthought.

His eyes locked on mine, and I swore neither of us breathed as I strode down the aisle toward him. A muscle in his jaw worked, and I watched his throat bob as he swallowed. Unconsciously, I picked up the pace, eager to reach him and have his hands on me, and mine on him. His lips parted as I drew close, but he seemed to rein himself in, clasping his hands together in front of him as he waited.

My dad stopped us, and with a quick hug and squeeze, he stepped off to the side. I continued the two steps up to Finlay, vaguely aware of the table that held three candles and a stone in front of us. The officiant stood next to it. My eyes flicked to him, and I nodded a greeting. He was the royal artist who had marked me — and consequently, re-marked me — with my Shield Knot. He dipped his head in return, and my gaze slid back to Finlay.

"You look beautiful," he whispered. His pale blue eyes swam with emotion. "Absolutely, breathtakingly beautiful."

Heat rose to my cheeks as I basked in his compliment. "So do you," I whispered back.

The officiant grinned, allowing us the brief moment, then began his speech. His words slid over me, not registering as I chose instead to absorb all of my loved ones that stood in silent support with us. My gaze swept over their smiling faces, their dapper wardrobes. Kipp, Cas, Larke, Darrya, Wren, Thad.

The officiant paused, and I blinked, trying to catch up to where we were in the ceremony. Luckily, my father stepped forward, reminding me of the unity candles. He brushed his middle and pointer finger against his thumb, bringing a small spark forward to light the candle on my side. As he did, he leaned in, and I caught his eyes shimmering with unshed tears, now aglow in the candlelight. "Your mother would be so proud."

I blinked away tears of my own as I smiled back at him. "I love you, dad."

"I love you too, Katie. Always."

He moved back, and Darrya stepped forward, lighting Finlay's candle as representation for their family. She pulled him into a tight embrace before pulling away and sent me an air kiss as she retreated. I returned it, my heart squeezing at all the love that surrounded us.

Together, Finlay and I lit the middle candle with the wicks of our individual ones, uniting our families symbolically as one.

When we stepped back, the officiant handed us the stone in front of the candles. It was carved with three interconnected arcs in what I had come to know as the Trinity Knot. Once Finlay and I both grasped it, the officiant dropped his hands from it and cleared his throat. "The Triquetra is the simplest of all the marks. Though our lives are complex, this is meant to represent the easy decision you've made in loving one another. This unending knot represents a binding promise and cannot be untied; likewise, we cannot separate that which your love has brought together today."

"You may now state your vows." He bobbed his head at us, and we locked eyes over the stone, reciting the vows we had memorized as one.

"I will not command you, for you are a free person.
I cannot possess you, for you belong to yourself.
I give that to you which is mine to give — my honor, respect, and my
truest love, without reservation.

I shall be a shield for your back and you for mine, to protect you from
harm and comfort you in times of distress.
I will grow with you, as my partner in life, in both mind and spirit.
I pledge to you my living and my dying, each equally in your care.
This is my wedding vow to you. This is the marriage of equals."

As we finished, our officiant asked us in turn to confirm we took each other in marriage. The moment Finlay said "I do," a light emanated from the stone. As I repeated the same, I felt a warm, tingling sensation in my palm. I knew when I removed the stone, an enchantment would have transferred the mark into my palm as a physical reminder of our vows. To further mark the moment, we exchanged rings — his, a simple, thick silver band engraved with the Triquetra mark and flames, and mine, a beautiful, looping ring that looked as though it was made of tree branches dipped in silver. Instead of an opulent diamond or rare gem, I'd had a relatively simple request for the stone inset: sardonyx. Finlay grinned as he slid it on my finger, then raised my hand to his lips to kiss it. The tender gesture made my breath catch.

"Well, it seems we are getting ahead of ourselves," the officiant interjected, causing a chorus of chuckles around us. "But you may now kiss."

Before I knew it, I was being dropped into a romantic dip, and Finlay's soft lips were pressed against mine. It started tender, then slowly grew more passionate with the promise of what was to come. My heart picked up speed as his tongue swept across the seam of my lips, and hoots and hollers registered dimly in the back of my mind as

I opened my mouth to allow him access. I felt his grin against my lips as he swept his tongue into my mouth, allowing us a heated moment before he pulled me back upright. I didn't miss the fire still left in his gaze as he pulled back from me, a bit reluctantly. I was certain he saw the same in my expression.

The officiant announced us as husband and wife and, heart pounding, I turned with Finlay, his hand interlaced with mine. We strode down the aisle to the music of cheers, whoops, and whistles, and my grin grew bigger with each step. Finally, we reached the outskirts of the little ceremony space, where two horses stood. Lena held them both, her tiny frame dwarfed by Gray. If it had been any other horse, I would have worried about her being whisked away, but Gray knew better. He stood absolutely still, but dipped his head to greet me as I approached.

"Hey, old boy," I murmured, tickling under his chin. Someone had draped parchment over his rear, with the word "JUST" written across it. If I had to guess, Finlay's horse had "MARRIED" on his. I laughed as I pulled it off, wondering who in our group would mock the human realm tradition. Kipp, most likely.

I swung up on Gray's back, struggling only slightly with the large skirts. He either didn't notice or didn't care as I took my time adjusting them around him. "Off to the honeymoon cottage, then, husband?" I asked, grinning as the new term danced deliciously off my tongue. *Husband.*

"Absolutely, *wife.*" Finlay swung up on his horse and grinned at me. I shivered pleasantly at the sound of the term coming from his mouth. "Are you sure you don't want a quick detour, though?"

I shot him a confused look. "To where?"

"To where I first met you." His eyes gleamed with mischief.

"Where you first — oh," I trailed off in realization, then shot him a glare. "Do you *really* want me to get this dress wet?"

"It's either getting wet or it's getting ripped off of you. The former sounds safest."

"Well, you know..." I gathered Gray's reins into my hands. His ears swiveled and he tensed, picking up on my excitement. "If you want to rip it off me, you'll have to catch me."

I dug my heels into his sides, and he took off like a shot, his hoofsteps quickly overshadowing the sound of Finlay's complaints. I enjoyed the feel of my skirts billowing in the wind for a long moment before I slowed Gray's pace to a level lope, allowing Finlay to catch up. Then, I tipped my head back to enjoy the wind in my face and the Fae at my side.

When I looked over at him, he beamed back at me, the neat, combed-back look of his golden locks completely ruined by the breeze. It made him look wilder, less restrained and more carefree, and my heart thrummed joyfully at the visual. He nodded forward, indicating the challenge he wished to issue. His grin turned into a teasing smirk, and he winked at me.

Oh, it's on.

I grinned back and dropped my reins, giving Gray the freedom to surge forward with more speed. Finlay let out a whoop and followed suit. With that, we raced off — into the wild and into the future that, for once, felt full of promise.

More From Jayme Hunt

This is the final book in the *Marked* trilogy, but if you're looking for more romance, sass, and fun characters, stay tuned for the newest works from the author, planned for 2025. Please follow @author-jaymehunt for more updates!

Acknowledgements

One thing I love about getting older is how everyone really starts to embrace the weirdness that is life. When we're young, we try so hard to fit in. We shove ourselves into too-tight t-shirts with the brand emblazoned on the front, douse ourselves in the perfume we choked on whilst buying the aforementioned shirt, listen to the same three artists, slap on makeup and pluck our eyebrows pencil-thin (or was that last one just me?).

But as we get older, we realize life is too short not to dive into the things we truly love. We throw out the branded t-shirts and swap the fads for our real favorite hobbies. Maybe that's fringe bands, collecting dolls, crocheting, making sourdough bread, or learning to fly a plane. The older we get, the more excited we are to share those things with one another. And the best part? Everyone finally accepts it and loves it, because it's a piece of you. And wow, am I ever grateful for finding the bookish community that really embraces my weird (and encourages it... sometimes to a detriment; I mean, there's a reason my TBR is 100+ books!).

To my hockey teammates and coworkers who have listened to me drone on endlessly about my reading and writing — thank you for lending me your ears and your positivity.

To my steadfast bookish supporters, Lindsay and Diana — thank you for always cheering me on, even when you are reading the dumpster fire first drafts. Your cheerleading keeps me motivated on the worst days.

To my brother, who may or may not ever read these books (let's be honest, you probably shouldn't), but is always ready to hype me up and meet my weirdness with his own wonderful brand of weird. Thanks for reminding me not to take life too seriously.

And to every one of you readers, who realized you're never too old to enjoy a good fairytale: keep embracing the weird.

About the Author

Jayme Hunt studied marketing and data analytics in college, and continues working a full-time job in the marketing field. In early 2022, she rediscovered her love of reading and writing, and has rarely put down a book since. *Marked by Fate* is her debut novel, followed by *Marked by Gods* and the epic conclusion, *Marked by the Crown*. She resides in Colorado with her husband and two dogs, who often make cameos in her social media posts.

@authorjaymehunt
www.authorjaymehunt.com

www.ingramcontent.com/pod-product-compliance
Lightning Source LLC
Chambersburg PA
CBHW031837310726
48972CB00005B/1313